Shenkin

by Davey Davies

Clink Street

Published by Clink Street Publishing 2022

Copyright © 2022

First edition.

ISBN:
978-1-915229-02-1 - paperback
978-1-915229-03-8 - ebook

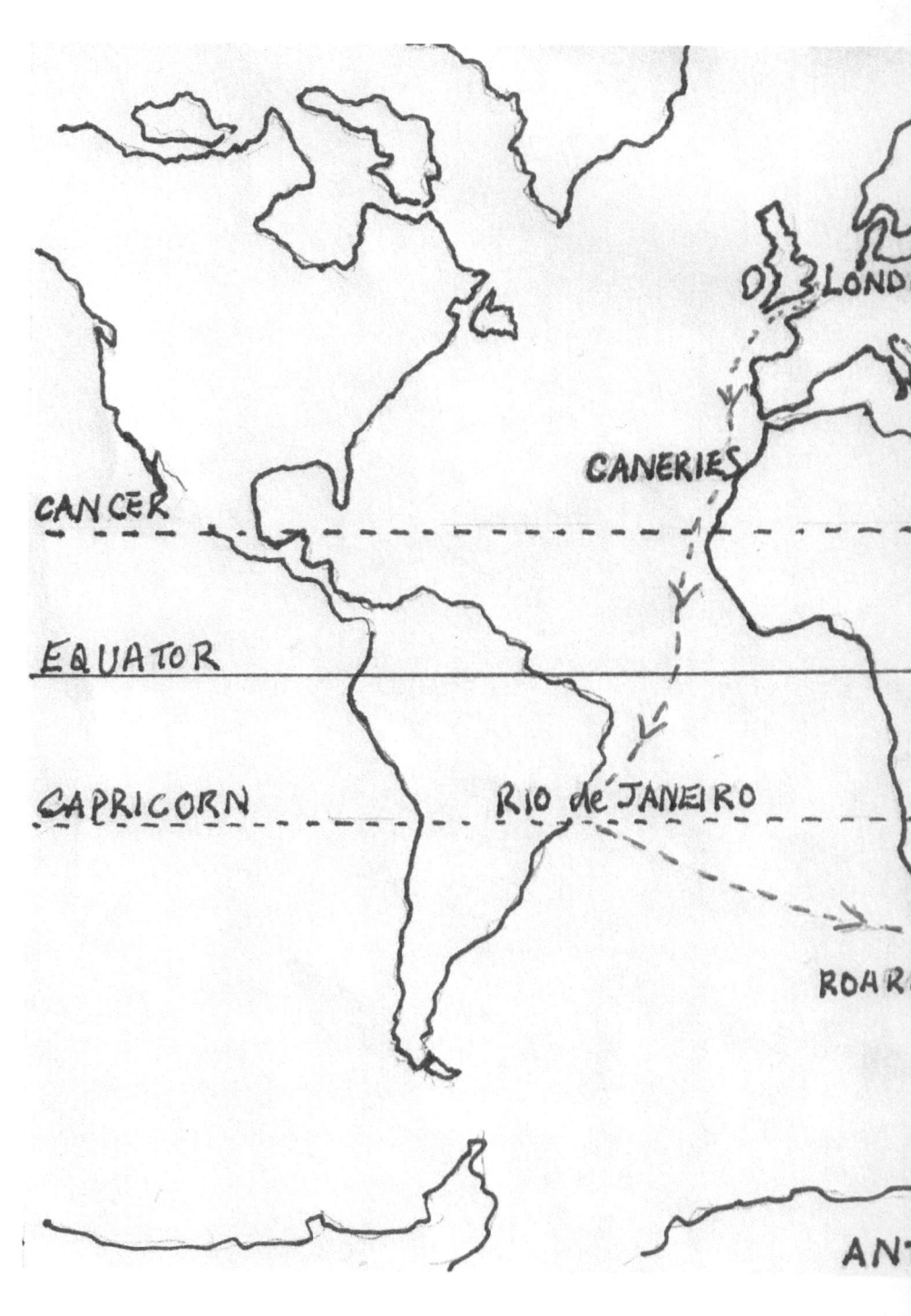

VOYAGE OF THE RUNNYMEDE
1832

CAPE TOWN

FORTIES

SYDNEY

...TICA

Acknowledgments.

The Merthyr Rising - Gwyn A. Williams.

The Convict Ships - Charles Bateson.

The Fatal Shore. - Robert Hughes.

Blood & Guts. - Roy Porter.

Pack Of Thieves. - Hamish Maxwell-Stewart & Susan Hood

Publishers Authoright for all their guidance and patience with special thanks to their CEO Gareth Howard.

My grateful thanks to my good friend John William Foster for his unfailing assistance in guiding me through the Digital Age.

To family and friends for their continued support and encouragement over the long period of writing this book.

To Jack, Matthew and Allanah Davies
the next generation of Australians.

He alone deserves liberty and life
who daily must win them anew.

GOETHE.

CHAPTER 1

North Atlantic Ocean – Winter of 1832

It can't end here thought Shenkin, but the knife in Kettlewell's hand said differently; even in the poor light of a cold winters morning the blade gleamed long, sharp edged, deadly. Kettlewell expertly tossed the knife from hand to hand, a twisted smile on his face. Shenkin moved back, one step, two steps. Dear god he thought I'm going to bloody die unless I do something quickly. The knife slashed inwards then upwards forcing Shenkin to move back across the tilting deck. Smirking, Kettlewell moved closer; the knife came flashing forward again, Shenkin lunged at Kettlewell's knife hand but missed as the swaying deck of the ship sent him off balance. He felt the knife blade sink deep into his left side, feeling desperately behind him his hand grasped what felt like the top of a heavy stick. He swung it up from behind him and brought it down hard onto Kettlewell's skull. He was gratified to feel gristle and bone collapse under the blow. The last thing Shenkin heard was Collins calling out his name, as he dropped to his knees and collapsed onto the rolling deck of the ship.

To the sound of the wind and the pounding sea Shenkin came to his senses. The knife wound in his side rejoiced at his consciousness, sending waves of pain flooding through his body. While the ship pitched and rolled, he tried to stand but was sent reeling across the cabin. Tight leg irons bit into his ankles and tripped him up just short of the bulkhead. The sudden stop jarred his whole body, causing the wound in his side to open again. He tried anxiously to stem the flow of blood, as voices and the rattle of keys announced the arrival of visitors.

'Sweet mother of God haven't I told you to stay laying down?' said Tarn, pushing roughly past the armed guard as he spoke.

Dr Michael Patrick Tarn was short, thickset, with a barrel-chest that threatened to burst open his black salt-stained coat. He was blunt, abrasive, blasphemous, and Shenkin was fortunate he was the Surgeon-Superintendent on the *Runnymede*, a three-masted, ship-rigged convict ship of 594 tons. She was built in Calcutta in 1802 of the finest teak, classed in the Underwriters' Green Book simply as Ship. She was still seaworthy but evil smelling, poorly ventilated, and badly in need of recaulking. Consequently, below the waterline sea water seeped through the seams, so that everyone and everything was damp and cold.

Nevertheless, Tarn set about his duties to keep his patient alive, while the weather continued its brutal assault on the ship. Earlier that day the bleak January morning had frozen the image of London's Woolwich Docks onto the eyes of the men aboard the ship. A pale watery-eyed sun had watched them sail down the Thames. Then out into the English Channel, a maelstrom of freezing wind and roaring waves. By Dover the weather was at gale force, where a north-easterly wind blew them down the English coast. After almost three days of hard sailing, they finally passed the Eddystone Rocks lying ghostly and threatening just eight miles off Rame Head on the starboard bow. The lighthouse stood aloof on top of the reef, it gave a one-eyed blink of goodbye to the *Runnymede*. Then they were into the full embrace of the North Atlantic where rolling seas carried the ship across the shallows of the continental shelf.

The crew moved slowly in response to mist-muffled orders, shouted into the numbing cold; they were tired, short tempered and cursing. Their laboured breath hung in the air, a latticework of frozen breath. The rigging glistened in a spray of silvery frost as the wind howled at the floating prison of human cargo.

In the hold between decks, converted to take the criminals of the British Empire as far from her shores as possible, 119 convicts were shackled in a union of suffering. They were wet to the skin, and blue of face, having had to stand on the open deck as the crew busied themselves with the ship. Their guards, muskets at the ready, had finally taken them down to the between deck. All the while the ship was pitching about like a cork in the tumultuous waves. The guards cursed as they issued some dry broad arrow marked clothes. These came in two sizes small and large, with nothing in between. The convicts tried to swap the clothes among themselves for the best fit they could find. Some with clothes half on, others with the arms of their tops tangled up they were pushed, shoved and cursed at towards a covered hut. There, blacksmiths began inspecting their leg irons, painful repairs were made. The more dangerous among them, their clothes marked with a red cross, were now doubled ironed, had it not been for the knife fight, as a political dissenter this would have included Shenkin. Painful shouts went out as metal trapped the skin pinching it tight between the metal. At long last they were marched back down to the dark damp between decks below the forecastle. Rows of iron grilled cells lined each side waiting with open mouths to devour their human cargo. First they were seated at long rough wooden tables. In front of them lay bread and cheese on tin plates, all of which were too hard for men or weevils to eat. Not that they had any appetite to eat; over the past hours most had been seasick, the deck was awash with sea water and vomit. Two of the convicts were already dead, but still sat upright in their collective bondage. Water rations lay ice bound in frost-decorated tin mugs. Bedding soaked by freezing cascading water from the upper decks hung over the bunks stiff with ice and dead frozen lice. Armed marines stood grim-faced at the foot of the companion ladders to the upper decks. These initial long hours of the voyage already seemed like a lifetime of pain and misery, if there was a worse place on God's earth, then only he knew where.

In the sick bay Surgeon-Superintendent Dr Tarn continued to treat his first patient of the voyage.

'Sweet Jesus! Another bloody voyage, with stinking convicts, and bad bloody weather,' said Tarn, muttering to himself. 'Why in hell's name do I do it?'

Behind him Corporal Burke stood impassive at the cabin door. The keys in his large hand swinging to the roll of the ship. From time to time a scar just below Burke's right eye, placed there by a French Grenadier Sergeant in the battle for Toulouse, caused his eyelid to twitch involuntarily. In fact, most of the guards of the *Runnymede* were serving British soldiers hardened by years of fighting the French. No longer required by their country to fight the career men and dregs from the war were being despatched to her colonies throughout the Empire. To save the War Office money, sergeants, experienced men, and raw recruits were often sent out on convict ships. Guarding in many cases their former comrades in arms. Many of which had taken to crime, stealing, rowdiness, destroying civic property, and killing for money or pride, no different from their days in Wellington's army really. The Duke had called them "the scum of the earth" – they did their best to live up to the description. Now that they had won the battles and done most of the dying they had been discarded or redeployed. Their government felt that coming back from the war in rags with no money or jobs, was quite unforgivable. Begging on the streets of London was a constant reminder of a war best buried on the battlefields of France and Spain. In short, their country wanted rid of them together with all the rest of its criminal and political malcontents. Over a decade after Waterloo the government was still sweeping them under the dirty carpets of the British Empire's penal colonies. So their former brothers-in-arms the guards of the good ship *Runnymede* spent the first long days settling them into their new surroundings. Iron fetters needed to be checked against men's legs for size and movement. At least that was the terms laid down in the government contract, in truth both skin and bones would soon be reduced to the correct shape and size by the tight iron bands.

While Captain Josiah Moxey dealt with easing the ship through the gale, the crew moved smartly to shouted orders for dealing with the weather, battening down the hatches, penning and straw bedding the livestock, and to a myriad of other things that were needed to secure the ship for a long voyage. Late on the third day all the crew were assembled on the well deck of the ship to bury the dead, as fast as possible. Two had died of hard labour and hunger after their time on the prison hulks at Woolwich, the third had been killed in a knife fight. The bodies lay shrouded in burlap, heavy weights were tied to the feet of each man to ensure a fast sinking. Each corpse lay on a mess table which was balanced on the ship's top rail. While at the other end of the table two crew men stood ready to lift and slide each corpse into the turbulent ocean.

Josiah Benjamin Moxey, Master of the *Runnymede* opened his Book of Common Prayer. Then hard of face and tone of voice he shouted into the icy wind, first their names then their convict numbers. 'We therefore commit their bodies to the deep to be turned into corruption.' As he spoke, he fought to stay upright against the force of the body bending blasts of wind. 'Looking for the resurrection of the body when the sea shall give up her dead and the life of the world to come through our Lord Jesus Christ who at his coming…' The wind caught the pages of the payer book and almost tore it from his hands. Recovering himself he continued, missing a few lines as he did; nobody cared they just wanted it over with. 'According to the mighty working, whereby he is able to subdue all things to himself. Amen.' A brief pause, then with a nod from the captain the burial parties upended the mess tables and over the side they went. Two had been soldiers in the war against the French but no Union Jack marked their exit from this world to the next. The third had been a thief who had preyed all his life on his fellow man. No difference now, all equally shrouded in dirty burlap sheets. One of the shrouds had become torn at the side and a blue white limp hand poked through the coarse hemp material, as if to wave farewell to his fellow convicts. Not even their entry into the water was heard above the roaring wind. Slamming the prayer book shut the captain turned on his heel and shouted. 'Hats on! Every man to his duties, Mr Lawson if you please.'

'Sir,' shouted First Mate Lawson, turning to the Bosun. 'Mr Travis make all secure.'

'Ay, ay, sir,' said Bosun William Travis, a small compact man full of efficient energy, who in spite of the cold had his arms bared. The short powerful arms were festooned with anchors and buxom women who danced on his muscles as he moved across the deck. 'Lash those deck boats tighter to their blocks. You two there, aloft I want that loose staysail tightened,' said Travis, pointing up at the foremast. One of the crew had one leg shorter than the other but went up the rigging as nimble has a monkey.

Not seventy hours had passed since leaving port and they were burying them faster then they could feed them.

Doctor Tarn returned to the sick bay to tend his wounded convict. His hands so numbed by the cold that they fumbled with the instruments in his bag. Although he had wedged himself into bulkhead corner, he cursed as he swayed in time to the lift and fall of the ship. He tore the blood-soaked bandages off Shenkin's side so fast it caused Shenkin to wince with pain. Leaning forward Tarn sniffed the wound then stood back bumping into Burke behind him.

'For Christ sake! Give me room man,' said Tarn, his nerves and temper at breaking point, and this was only the beginning of a voyage that would last more than a hundred days.

'Yes sir! Sorry sir,' shouted Burke above the roar of the sea.

'How can a man work on this bloody floating, rotting, bastard, stinking ship of hell?!' said Tarn, red in the face with anger. As the ship pitched it sent his instruments flying across the tilting deck.

'Bloody hell and damnation!' cried Tarn, as he watched the tools of his trade dance nimbly across the wooden deck.

'It's because there's a hell of a following sea running sir,' said Burke, steadying his back against the door.

Tarn glared at the man. 'Don't! Don't bloody tell me what this swine of a ship is doing, it's not my first bloody voyage.'

'No sir,' said Burke looking down at his feet.

'Do something useful man get the bleeding shackles off his legs,' growled Tarn, as he bent to pick up his instruments.

'Sir' said the guard propping his India Pattern musket against the door. The musket slid to the deck as the ship dipped into another trough.

'Leave it man! Leave the bloody thing,' said Tarn, as Burke struggled with numb salt-soaked fingers to pick up his musket. The gun, manufactured by Henry Nock of London, was Burke's pride and joy, lovingly called Brown Bess. He looked with concern as the musket continued its sliding across the tilting deck.

'Sir,' said Burke bending to his task. After some moments of struggling with the leg irons that stubbornly refused to release, Burke gave up.

'He'll need to stand up sir.'

'Damn! Damn! Damn! said Tarn. 'Get on with it then or we'll be here all bloody night.'

Burke lifted Shenkin roughly to his feet. Causing Shenkin to wince again with pain. Burke pulled hard at the lock-pin his scarred eyelid twitching in time to his grunts and pulls. Finally, the shackle pin came out sending Burke across the cabin with the pin held tight in his raw right hand.

At last Daniel Shenkin stood before them, he was an impressive figure. Twenty-four years of age, dishevelled, bloodstained, unkempt, but the look on his face was one of fierce defiance. The face spoke of hardship and pain, it also looked much older than his young age. He was tall, for a Welshman that is, five foot eleven inches. Jet black hair fell over his muscular shoulders, most of the hair was tied back into a ponytail, with what had once been a colourful scarf. The hair framed a face that would have been described as handsome were it not for a thin scar, which ran down the left side of his face just above his cheekbone to the corner of his mouth. No stubble grew over the jagged scar, which had a strange blue tinge to it. Pulling himself up straight Shenkin shot a piecing look at Burke causing the guard to hesitate.

Tarn was also looking at Shenkin and saw the ruthlessness in those eyes as the man before them flexed his shoulders. Many a man had sensed the untamed animal power of this man. It had made them think twice about getting too close to him and many a woman who wanted too and did.

Now that his feet were free, Shenkin tried to find a more a comfortable position on the rolling deck. But keeping his balance was too much for him and he fell heavily against Burke.

'Get him on the bunk, for Christ sake!' said Tarn, as he continued to gather up his instruments.

Shenkin sighed as he lay back on the bunk although cold his body ran with the sweat of pain, but he would not give them the satisfaction of showing it.

'You are a lucky man that the blade did not puncture the lung. We must now hope, indeed pray, that there is no blood poisoning,' Tarn said, soothingly as if his voice had become part of the treatment. The corporal was taken aback by the doctor's change of disposition, so much so that he felt bold enough to offer an opinion.

'Kettlewell was a nasty piece of work sir, kept picking on young Collins he did back on the hulks until the Welshman here stood up to him,' said Burke. Like the late but little lamented Kettlewell, Corporal William Burke was a London cockney himself who had left London's East End at only twelve years old to join the army, by thirteen he was beating the drum into battle.

'So I understand Burke,' said Tarn.

'They called him Cutter Kettlewell around Limehouse sir, on account of him using that knife of his to slit the purses of the passing gentry. Relieving them of the weight of their coinage, so to speak. A smile played at the corner of Burke's mouth as he spoke.

Tarn shook his head in dismay. He was never sure who the villains were, the convicts, the seamen, or the bloody guards. All were the dregs of a nation still reeling from a long and costly war.

'Well my fighting Welshman you've put paid to Cutter Kettlewell that belaying pin crushed his skull like an eggshell, he's cut his last purse,' said Tarn.

Shenkin just looked defiantly at the doctor, but said nothing.

Tarn was lost in thought for a moment then added. 'Mind the sailmaker sewed him up all neat and tidy in a burlap shroud. Just to make sure he was dead the last thread of the needle went through his noise. He kissed the waves off Ushant together with two other of your fellow convicts. Went over the side to the cursing of the crew, who had to stand in the freezing cold while the captain read out the burial service. But by god it was a neat piece of stitching that closed those hemp shrouds, couldn't have done them better myself.'

After a moment he looked down at Shenkin. 'I'll wager you'll face trial for the killing of Kettlewell if, god willing, we get to Australia,' continued Tarn. 'I looked up your charge sheet Shenkin I must say it's an impressive list – treason, inciting a riot, causing injury to soldiers of the Crown, damaging private property.' He paused. 'That last one alone would have got you here, the ruling classes don't like their property being damaged.'

17

Shenkin looked up and spoke for the first time the voice firm deep. 'Not a riot, but a rising of the ordinary workingman for justice, for the right to determine his own future,' Shenkin said before falling back onto the bunk exhausted, his face glistening with sweat.

Shenkin's words were sharp reminders to Tarn of another time and place.

Tarn was from a land-owning Irish family, a proud stubborn people who felt it was their right to rule the land. Their eldest son told his father of the political meetings he had been attending in London on the Reform Bill to give the vote to ordinary workingmen. That their own tenants should have better wages, a vote on decisions effecting their working conditions, annual general elections, equal rights. That following the French and American Revolutions change was in the air throughout Europe. That Ireland was more guilty than anywhere else in Europe. Its absent aristocracy together with tax driven landowners, coupled with a weak executive, it would not be long before the people of Ireland would revolt indeed, should revolt.

The fracture between father and son was complete. A row broke over Michael Patrick Tarn like a tidal wave. His father demanded, now that his medical studies were over, he return to the family estate and assume his full responsibilities. Michael Patrick refused, disinheritance filled the air. Tarn returned to London and his more enlightened political friends. After an unsuccessful private practice, more to do with his Irish background then his skill as a doctor, he bought a commission in the army and was in Portugal by his twenty-eighth birthday. In the Peninsular campaign his surgeon's skills were put to good use. None questioned his Catholicism or politics as arms and legs needed to be cut off.

Moments passed as Tarn reflected, he slowly took out a silver snuff box, he stared for a moment at the family coat of arms engraved on the top. Then with a sigh he tapped the box lifted the lid pinched some snuff and inhaled it deeply while he continued to be lost in thought as the wind and sea roared around the ship. Burke shifted awkwardly in the long drawn-out silence, as he moved his feet the movement caused the keys to rattle in his large chapped hands. The movement broke the spell, Tarn looked up. 'I understand Welshman,' he said., putting the box back into his waistcoat pocket.

'You understand nothing, your class never do.' Shenkin spat out the words like broken glass, bitterness laced his tone his face angry, rebellious. 'Your bloody class are more concerned with profits than men.' Bitterness edged every word.

Tarn gave a knowing smile. 'Rest now and we will speak again when you are better able to converse.' As he spoke he continued to swab the wound in prophylactic vinegar that took Shenkin's breath away.

'It's an ugly wound that's ripe for mortification,' said Tarn. 'I've packed the wound with raw sugar to fight any infection. But if it does putrefy, you'll have a raging fever. If so, then may your God go with you Shenkin for I can't.'

Shenkin looked up at him questionably.

'It's in your chest man! I can't cut that off to stop the mortification, can I?' Then speaking quietly. 'Sure it may not come to that for I've seen worse.'

Shenkin, sensed for the first time that this man, in spite of his swearing and shouting, actually cared. Then after a moment Shenkin said almost resentfully, 'Thank you doctor.'

Tarn nodded. 'I'll see you tomorrow to look for any possible poisoning. You'll stay in the hospital for the next few days.' After a pause he said, 'I'll try to bring you back to good health Shenkin.' Then with a shrug of his shoulders he added, 'So they can hang you in Sydney or Van Diemen's Land'

Shenkin said nothing the defiant look now back firmly on his face.

Tarn turned to the guard. 'Leave the shackles off, Burke.' The guard hesitated. 'The doors locked man and in his condition he isn't going anywhere.'

Burke shifted uncomfortable. 'Can't do it sir. Captain's orders sir, man in chains, is man in chains sir.'

'Do it then if you must I'll speak to the captain over supper tonight. That's if we don't bloody sink before then.'

The ship continued to make difficult progress but Tarn noted the deck did seem steadier. 'I swear she's coming around Burke we may cross the Bay of Biscay yet by gad!'

'Yes sir,' said Burke, fumbling with the leg iron lock and key. Then lifting the lantern he began towards the cabin door. Tarn stopped to look back at Shenkin, causing Burke to bump into him. Tarn looked at the guard and sighed. 'I'll do what I can, Shenkin.' The clank of the chain, the slam of the cabin door and the turn of the key became one as Tarn's hand gripped his way along the passageway. Then up the companionway into the fresh air.

From the upper deck Tarn could see that the sea was less turbulent, the ship steadier. Looking up to the quarterdeck Tarn saw the captain standing beside the helmsman swaying slightly but in full command. Tarn could swear Josiah Moxey actually had a grim smile upon his weather-beaten face. Turning to the rail Tarn was pleased to see that although they were standing well off the coast they were now beginning to cross the long wide Bay of Biscay which lay astern off the port bow. It would take them the next few days to get across the Bay but they were safely on their way. 'Steady as she goes,' said Tarn to no one but the screaming wind.

CHAPTER 2

Shenkin stared into the chill damp darkness of the cabin. Only a bulkhead away he could hear the muffled voices of his fellow convicts, the bellowing of the guards, and the continual clank of doors and the rattle of chains.

The ship seemed calmer but his head still spun. Having clamped the shackles back in place the guard had locked the door, taking the only light with him. The darkness enveloped Shenkin like flying black flour, he felt as if he was choking on the blackness. He heard the sound of his own heartbeats fill the cabin. He recognised it for what it was, gut-wrenching fear. He had known it before, in the blackness of the coal pits where as a child of only six years old his father had taken him down into the bowels of the earth for the first time.

***

He remembered it so well, so very, very well. His mind drifted into a feverish dream, he was back home in the town of Merthyr Tydfil in South Wales. 'He is too young Idris,' his mother said, holding him close to her a hand upon his tousled-haired head. She had been protesting for weeks, but in the end had sadly, tearfully, let him go but not before making sure he had a clean shirt, a pair of cut down trousers, some thin pieces of bread covered in fat dripping, and a small bottle of cold milky sweet tea. She watched tearfully as father and son walked up the cobbled road of their miner's cottage on Quarry Row, Daniel stumbling forward his small legs running to keep up with his fathers' long strides. From the defiantly white-washed cottages in their black-stained valley, came other miners. They would risk their lives again this day against the hard unforgiving earth for a handful of coins. Times were difficult, families needed every penny they could earn, his mother knew that only too well, but standing in the low-framed open doorway, a shawl wrapped tight around her to keep out the winter wind, she wept.

The cage that lowered them into the dark bowels of the earth seemed to young Daniel to go down forever. It came at last to a shuddering stop in a cloud of coaldust, a miner beside Daniel spat onto the ground. The gob of spit and tobacco made a small pool in the dust, it stank of rotten vegetables. Pushed roughly forward by the press of men around him Daniel almost fell over on the coal wet slimy ground he grabbed quickly at his father's hand. He was pleased to feel the squeeze of reassurance his father gave him. But his father did not look down at him instead he pulled him along the dark twisting wet tunnels until finally they came to a door of sorts. His father, a candle strapped to his skullcap, cast a giant shadow around them.

'You will sit here Daniel and open the vent doors when you hear the drams carrying the coal coming,' said his father, his rich voice booming in the confined space. 'At the end of the shift I will come and fetch you.'

'Yes Da.'

'You're a trapper now, do you understand?' said his father. Not waiting for a reply he went on, 'When the dram passes through make sure you close them quickly mind. That's what trappers do see, they keep the air current going around the workings,' said his father, sitting the young Daniel on a lump of coal that made a makeshift seat. Above the trouser polished coal seat someone had written in Welsh.

'Duw yn y nefoedd helpu ni I gyd.' Under it was the English, 'God in Heaven help us all.'

'Are you listening Daniel?'

Daniel tore his eyes away from the writing.

'Yes, Da.' Then in a small voice he said, 'Can I have a candle Da?'

'No!' said his father, then added in a softer tone. 'They are too expensive see, but your eyes will get used to the dark Daniel. You must raise above the fear my son in that way it will make a man of you,' said Idris Shenkin, squeezing his young son's shoulder. 'We all feel fear at sometime in our life Daniel, but you must learn to control it, to use it to your advantage. In so doing it will build your character strong,' said his father, then added, 'and whatever you do don't leave food about or the rats will be all over you.' Daniel gave a shiver. 'Now! Are we going to be brave, for I must get to my work area?'

He wanted to scream out, please, please don't leave me, but instead he looked hard at his father. Then as tears rolled down his cheeks, leaving two clean lines on his coaldust covered face he said simply.

'Yes Da.'

'Good boy.' With that his father turned and walked away into the darkness. The faint candle light formed a silhouette of the broad shoulders that had carried him on Sunday mornings up to the top of Dowlais mountain so many times, and with a shock he knew it would never happen again. Then his father was gone into the blackness and coaldust filled the roadway of the drams.

He was alone, the blackness, his own heartbeats, with only the scratching rats for company. He took a deep breath. The rats scurried around him searching out the smell of the food that came from his Tommy Box. Quickly and for the tenth time Shenkin again made sure that the lid was firmly closed. That first day, he remembered, he never ate, he was too afraid to open his food box. He swore he'd overcome the terror of this black hole, these feasting rats, these dark long tunnels of loneliness.

For eighteen hours a day Shenkin would sit listening for the welcome rattle of drams of coal, for someone to say a few words to. All for a wage of six pennies a shift that with great pride he handed to his mother at the end of each week, a child's offering in a dirty coal-stained, torn and bloody hand. His mother's tears fell on those hands for the first few weeks then he became a man and she would not show him her hurt.

To this very day he hated confined spaces. But he soon learnt his hard trade, he became used to the vast blackness of where he worked, he even gave the rats names. The hours, days, and finally the years passed. Shenkin saw in his mind's eye again the different jobs that took him to the blunt cruel coal face. Crawling on his hands and knees, a heavy basket of coal on his young back, he'd strain and heave his way along the dark wet tunnels. Then Dai Thomas the under-foreman spoke to his father. 'Strong, that boy of yours Idris we'll promote him to hurrier,' he said, adding 'same hours, but nine pence a day.' Shenkin remembered how proud he felt when his father told him. He stood upright and thrilled as the girdle and hook was strapped around his thin waist for the first time. It led to a chain attached to a dram of coal, then on his hands and knees he would pull it to the bottom of the shaft. Proud dear God! proud to be nothing more than an animal crawling on all fours. Tethered to a metal dram to make profit for men already rich from the sweat and deaths of others. *Shenkin twisted on his salt damp bunk of pain, angry at the memory of it.* At eighteen he finally joined his father working at the coal face. At first he hammered timber props into the roof to stop the roof collapsing on the men below has they cut the coal from the seams. Some seams were over six feet in width, others just two or three feet. Men standing or lying flat on their stomachs, to rip the coal out with picks. Mother earth moving and shifting as men raped her for her black gold. Falls of rock and coal soon scarred his young arms and back. Then the day came when he stood shoulder to shoulder with his father at the coal face. Swinging a pick while stripped to the waist, his muscles now fully developed, they rippled in the dim light cast by the lanterns. He was a sight to behold just under six foot tall, slim of waist, a powerful chest and a winning smile. Long jet-black hair, dark brown flashing eyes and handsome features set off a striking picture. A young god naked to the waist, glistening with sweat and covered in a fine dusting of coal. *Even now in this cold sea cabin, his vanity smiled through his fever and pain.* How he revelled in his strength. He could cut coal faster than any man, drink jugs of ale quicker, brawl better, and make love sweeter. Women were attracted to him, they were drawn to his pure sexual presence, Daniel always took full advantage of it.

His father, a former bareknuckle fighter, had been training him for a few years in the noble art of prize fighting. By nineteen he had already won a number of local fights with good purse money. By twenty-one his father told him, 'You are ready to challenge the Cardiff champion Daniel, mark you it will be the hardest yet, the biggest purse and with plenty of side bets, but we must be careful. Cardiff men were at your last fight, and they'll advise their man of your strength and punching power, also of your youth. But the size of the purse will lure them into a fight. Their man is older, bigger and with a good record behind him,' said his father. 'We can't risk anything, plan careful see, that's what we'll do.'

Many hours of training followed day after day Shenkin lifted bags of coal, run ten miles a day, pickled his fists in vinegar and brine to harden the skin until they were almost yellow. Then finally the date day and hour was set. A few weeks later, late in the evening both father and son stole out of the house not to let his mother know what they were up to. Slowly they climbed up the mountain behind Quarry Row, at the top men were already gathering. Shenkin changed in the corner of an open windswept field. Then with an old dressing gown over his shoulders he entered a circle of whitewashed stones at a place they called the Lilywhites. Tar-soaked torches blazed around the scene of the contest. The area was surrounded by wind-blown trees bent to the will of nature, on a flat area marked out with limewashed stones that were as white as lilies. The stones stood like silent sentinels, waiting for the bare-knuckle fighters to enter the arena. Lookouts were in place at each corner of the wide flat field that looked down into the valley. Prize fighting was illegal, these men would warn of any constables coming to stop the fight. Some off-duty constables were already placing bets along with a crowd that had grown to about four to five hundred men. The air was full of the roar of excitement, men jostled each other for a better view, or argued who would be the winner, a few fights broke out in the crowd as the contestants moved to their corners. Each side had put up a purse of £10, his father had spent the last two weeks raising the money. Daniel had never seen so much money at one time. He felt the heavy weight of responsibility that the money had placed upon him. He looked around the dense crowd of men some were calling his name, some jeering. Taking a deep breath, he turned his attention to the man he was about to fight. The Cardiff champion was a big bear of a man. The odds were four to one against Shenkin. Finally, the two men stepped into the ring to deafening applause and cheering. Then a hush fell over the crowd and the odds began to go down on Shenkin as he dropped off the tattered old dressing gown, for the first time the crowd took in his sheer physical presence. Each man stood in their corners flexing their muscles moving arms and legs while their helpers fussed around them. In his corner Shenkin had his father with Willy Stitch as his cut man. Both corners were busy with last minute instructions, alcohol rubs, smears of axle grease over the eyebrows. His father looked at the length of his son's hair and heaved a sigh.

'Why the hell you have your hair that length I don't know,' he said. 'I keep telling you to have it shorn, but no, you will not listen. This man will grab it and pull your head down. You shave your face but not your head,' he said, then after a moment. 'You are too bloody vain, that's your trouble.'

'Yes Da.,' Shenkin said, with a smile. 'Stop fretting.'

'You look like a bloody girl. Well, it's too damn late now isn't it Willy?' Willy Stitch smiled and just nodded his head.

'Alright Da don't go on about it,' said Shenkin, the smile still not leaving his handsome face.

'Another thing if you are cut up bad don't come home for a few days, stay with Willy, if your mother sees you all black and blue she'll play hell with me.'

'That's what I needed to hear Da.'

'Win or lose he's going to catch you a few times isn't he, just don't make it too easy for him, that's what I'm saying, we've got to time this right boy.'

'Yes, yes, yes, Da,' said Shenkin, exasperated now. 'We have been over and over it haven't we?' Then he placed his hand on his father's shoulder. 'It'll be fine Da, don't worry.'

'Alright then, and remember to keep your left up high.'

'Dear God, Idris you've taught him well and he's the best I've seen since you were fighting, so let him get on with it,' said Willy, shaking his head. Shenkin smiled at these two men whom he loved and trusted, he vowed to himself that he'd make them proud of him this night.

Idris sighed again. He wished he was fighting, but his son was good, he knew that, that right upper cut he hated to admit was better than his. He also had an instinctive animal sense of the kill. So he put his mouth to his son's ear. 'How strong are you my son?'

'Very strong.'

'How strong? You are not in chapel now, so tell me.'

'I'll rip the bastard's head off his shoulders.'

'That's a good chapel boy.' They both laughed, Idris tapped his son on the back sending Shenkin dancing up to the square yard mark in the centre of the ring of stones, both men were greeted with a roar from the crowd. At the mark Shenkin took his first long up-close look at Mitch Harris. The Cardiff Chopper was built like a casting shed, the flickering light from the torches highlighted his broken nose, cauliflower ears, and eyebrows that were criss-crossed with old scars. His head was shaved to the skin, exposing a scar that ran over the top of his skull. Ten years older than Shenkin with over a hundred fights behind him. Harris was confident, a contemptible sneer played across his fight scared face, as he looked at the smaller younger man. Shenkin took a deep breath and shifted his feet on the mark. Willy had tied back his hair with a piece of cloth while his father muttered all the while. Shenkin had just one mark on his face it was just above his right eye placed there by a hot cinder when he was taking some food to his father in the ironworks. Harris took note of it, he'd open it if he could. The umpire then explained the fight would be conducted under Broughton Rules.

Standing in the middle beside the two fighters he shouted out the rules.

'Rule one, each round will end when a fighter was knocked down or out of the roped area. Rule two, the fight will end when one fighter was unable to rise from a knock down or return to the scratch mark within sixty seconds. Rule three, no set number of rounds. Rule four, no rest periods, Rule five, the fight will end on a knockout, capitulation, or by constable's intervention. Rule six while adhering to these rules, everything else is allowed to secure a win. Do you both understand?'

He waited for each man to nod. Each did.

The umpire was a Monmouth man of good repute, a former bare-knuckle fighter himself who would make sure the rules were observed. Both fighters were stripped to the waist. They wore three-quarter length breeches held up with brown wide sashes. The sashes were examined for salt or sand. Both men opened their fists palms up for any hidden iron bits. The fists were pickled a yellow brown from being soaked in vinegar and brine, some of Harris's knuckles were pushed back into his hand due to so much punching. Finally, satisfied that all was correct the umpire stepped back. Then called each man back to the mark, dropped his arm and the fight was underway. They circled around, sizing each other up. Harris, older, taller, battle-marked and confident against the much younger man. He leaned in close to Shenkin. 'What are you fucking doing here kid you should in bed at this time,' said Harris. Shenkin just gave a slight smile. A straight right flew out from Harris that caught Shenkin high on the side of the head. The blow stopped him moving forward for a moment. Then he returned the blow, hard enough to cause a red mark to appear on Harris's left cheek. A roar went up from the crowd, coins flashed in the light of the tar flames, as bets were placed or increased. Backer Johnson the bookie wrote furiously in his little black betting book. Backer also had the purse money swinging in leather pouches tied around his neck. Another roar went up as Harris hit Shenkin twice with lefts and rights aimed at the scar above Shenkin's eye. Shenkin lifted his fists up higher to protect it.

Harris pulled Shenkin's head down and whispered into his ear. 'I'm going to close that fucking eye kid, you'll never see right with it again.' This time Shenkin stopped his talking with a right cross that put Harris's face into a twisted mass. Blood shot onto one of the limewashed stones. The power of the punch surprised Harris and he shook his head. Men screamed their exhilaration and called for the ale and tobacco sellers. Shenkin blocked a number of wild blows with his forearms. Then he countered with a straight right into Harris's face. Harris's head snapped back once, twice, then a left hook sent him to his knees. The first round was over. Harris's lip was split, his left eye slightly swollen, but he quickly got to his feet. The seconds brought them up to the mark to start the next round. Harris grabbed for Shenkin's throat and began to strangle him. Shenkin chopped down with the edge of his hands into Harris's sides, driving the wind out of him. Harris staggered back, his arms dropped, Shenkin drove his head into Harris's face. The crowd roared as Shenkin then hit out with a combination of blows. Idris Shenkin shouted out. 'Steady lad just push him back, time it right, keep him at arm's length.'

Shenkin nodded and danced backwards. Harris shook his head, recovered his balance and charged into Shenkin chopping at his throat. Shenkin coughed and dropped to one knee spluttering. End of the second round, they had been fighting for nearly an hour. Both men carried marks about the body and face. Harris still looked the stronger but was moving slower now. They came up to the line again and squared up to each other. Shenkin had a vivid red welt across his throat but still moved lightly on his feet. The crowd urged their man on while bets exchanged hands, has Backer Johnson called out new odds.

'Go on hit him Harris go for the eye.'

'Use your uppercut Shenkin, hit the ugly bastard.'

'Split his face open Mitch.'

For another five rounds they hit each other with every blow within the rules and few that were not, but neither man would stay down or give way. Then Harris caught Shenkin with a right-cross that landed on the already swollen eyebrow. The scar split open and Shenkin went down. Harris's supporters roared their delight. The odds increased again against Shenkin. Willy Stitch pulled the open skin back together neatly placing a few stitches into the split from a needle stolen from his wife's sewing box. When done, he smeared axle grease over the eyebrow.

Looking at Shenkin he said. 'You're as good as new boyo, but keep your left up higher to protect it, there's a puffiness under the eye as well.' said Willy.

'If it closes up Willy, slit it open.' Shenkin said, his breath fast but easy.

'We are almost there now, Daniel, just hold on.' his father called out.

Up to the mark they came again. The crowd screaming, blood sweat and snot covered much of the once white boulders that made up the fighting space. The torches cast red tinged flickering shadows over the two fighters as they grunted and swung punch after punch. It was a scene out of Dante's *Inferno* as light and shadow spread over their glistening bodies. For the next two hours they battered each other to the ground, but again neither stayed down nor gave ground. After each round their seconds threw buckets of water over their man.

'For God's sake Willy you'll bloody drown me before I can toe the line.'

Willy looked at Idris Shenkin. 'Well?'

'Let's wait a few more rounds. Is the eye alright?'

'Yes it's holding out. The ice took some of the swelling down,' said Willy, tying the cloth again around Shenkin's hair as he had done throughout the fight.

Both men came out again. Harris looking to have the greater stamina. Backer called out, 'I'm giving "Odds On favourite" for Harris with Shenkin two to one against.' Friends and supporters of Shenkin took up the bets, the rest were pleased with the odds they already had with Harris to win. Then a bet for £5 went on Shenkin, a number of gambling addicts followed suit with good size bets.

By round 13 both men carried cuts above their now puffy eyes, the red welts round their bodies shone livid in the night light. Then Shenkin's hair was flying loose, for the first time the cloth had unravelled and lay at his feet. Harris rushed forward grabbed the hair pulling Shenkin's head down onto a raising knee. Shenkin went down. Backer shouted I'm giving three to one against Shenkin.

'Didn't I tell him Willy, didn't I, the length of his bloody hair?' said Idris Shenkin, muttering swear words. Shenkin got to his feet, his father and Willy rushed to his side. 'Well?' said Idris Shenkin.

'He's alright, bit dazed but strong as a bloody ox,' said Willy.

'I'm alright,' said Shenkin

Idris nodded to someone in the crowd. Another big bet went on Shenkin at the new odds. Backer Johnson waited for any more, but then became very nervous. 'No more bets, book is closed,' he shouted.

Idris spoke into his son's ear. 'All the monies on Daniel so let's go home,' he said, as he tied back the hair.

Shenkin came up to the mark for the 23rd. A smile played on the bloody face of Harris. Through split swollen lips he spat blood into Shenkin's face. 'You are finished boy, the eye first then I'll fucking cripple you for life.' It was the last thing Harris probably remembered. Shenkin straightened up and began punching blows up the length of Harris's body. A left, then a right, a left again. Starting at the stomach a tattoo of vicious blows moved up Harris's body ending with a brutal right cross to Harris's chin. Shenkin danced back just far enough to let Harris's body come down. When Harris's head was level with Shenkin's waist he chopped down with a fierce right. Harris was out before he hit the damp earth.

A hush settled over the crowd. Shenkin stepped over Harris's still body. 'Twenty pounds in my hand now Backer,' said Shenkin. 'Any side bets my father will collect.'

Backer Johnson was standing perfectly still he too was in a state of disbelief his eyes fixed on Harris's unconscious, spreadeagled body.

Shenkin pulled him around and looked him in the eyes. 'Unless you have a problem with that?'

Backer recovered. 'No problem Shenkin,' he said, as he untied the pouches of money from around his neck. Then Backer gave a small smile, after all most of the money was on Harris.

Shenkin turned on the narrow bunk at the remembrance of the fight. He now lay in a bath of sweat. His eyes came open, but they only registered the grim reality of the swaying motion of the Runnymede *as she ploughed her way into warmer blue waters, and God knows what else. Chains still rattled from the other side of the timber bulkhead. Orders barked from guards increased the noise of the chains. Someone cried out for water. Shenkin's throat was dry too from fever and the warmer air. I must survive thought Shenkin I must, damn it I will. Not this sentence to a penal colony, not this ship, nor this knife wound will stop me I will survive.* Then he passed out.

***

But it would get a lot hotter yet in the confines of their stinking floating prison. The air was heady with the stale stench of closely packed bodies. Regan O'Hara had called for the hatches to be opened but the guards made no move. In full uniform they too were sweating profusely continually dipping drinking mugs into the casks of green scum covered lukewarm water.

CHAPTER 3

'From distant climes, o'er wide spread seas we come,
Though not with beat of drum.
True patriots all; for be it understood,
We left our country for our country's good '... Convict's Poem

Making no impression on the guards to open the hatches for air, Regan O'Hara lay back on his berth. The chains making a deafening sound around him, as convicts moved and shifted in their cells to the barked orders of the guards.

'Thank god Kettlewell is no longer with us Regan,' said Collins, with a sigh. 'I'll sleep tonight,' he said.

'A nasty bastard that one, so he was,' agreed O'Hara. 'But Shenkin will soon be back with us lad. Then we'll get things in order.' At least I bloody hope so, thought O'Hara to himself.

Not for the first time did he look around him to take in the layout of the convicts holding area. Men were close packed, the air becoming more and more foul, a stench filled the air that now pervaded every corner of the hold. How O'Hara missed the cold of only a week ago.

Collins broke his thoughts. 'The water is coming through Regan,' he said, running his hand over the leaking seams. Trickles of seawater and condensation run down the timber frame spilling over the bunk bedding. Everything was damp their skin constantly wet and burning from the salt sea water.

'Now if we only had soap, we could have a bath.' O'Hara said, making Collins smile. Then Regan added. 'But whatever you do don't drink it, for the salt will make you more thirsty.'

'No I won't Regan, I promise.'

O'Hara turned back to the prison area. In the centre of the gangway about midway along stood a black stove, from the top of it a smokestack ran up through the decks. Long irons were lent against the side of the stove. At the top of these irons was a shape in the figure of a broad arrow. Sweet Mother of Jesus, their branding irons thought O'Hara, letting out a slight shudder.

'What is it Regan?'

'Just the old damp getting to me lad,' said Regan, not wanting to alarm the youngster.

The cells run the length of the between decks on both sides of the ship forming fifteen cells a side. Each bunk being six feet long by one foot and a half wide. They would live, sleep, or die in this overcrowded space. Each man was shackled on both legs the chains running down through iron eyelets that were driven into the front timber frames of the bunks. The front of the cells had iron barred doors running the length of the hold, that amounted to cages. There were a series of hatches between the centre beams to let in light and air, these were also strongly grated and shut. They gave little air and almost no light. Military guards stood each side of the companionways to the upper decks, which had iron grill gates at the top that were also barred and locked. One hundred and twenty men confined in the hold of a ship thirty-one feet in breadth by ninety feet in length with a height of about six feet between beams and just five and a half feet below the beams. At six foot four inches Regan O'Hara had a serious problem with this construction. To add to his discomfort his leg hurt like hell, the closing of the iron manacle had pinched the skin between the metal, causing him pain with every movement he made.

O'Hara's eyes ran over the other convicts again. They made a Dublin pub on a Saturday night look like a church gathering. Criminals of all kinds, thieves, pickpockets, murderers, rapists and political dissidents. O'Hara wondered which the state worried about most. After sentencing the courts had marked their documents. Sentence – Penal Colony for a period confirmed by the court then stamped – Transported FOR THEIR COUNTRY'S GOOD. The documents stated the convict's name, crime, term (in years), and the penal colony.

That piece of paper would hound them for the rest of their lives. Their cell was down to just himself and young Collins. They had elected Shenkin the mess captain, responsible for cleanliness and good order in the cell. Kettlewell had been opposed to this on the grounds that he had been in the prison hulk at Woolwich Warren for three months before Shenkin and O'Hara had arrived by rattler from Cardiff gaol. But like his father Shenkin was a natural leader, so the hulk officials had recommended him to the Surgeon-Superintendent whose responsibility it was to make these appointments. Doctor Michael Patrick Tarn had acted on that recommendation. Tarn wanted just one thing, a well-disciplined cargo of convicts, and with a strong mess captain in each cell they hoped order would be maintained. Disruptive behaviour would cost the mess captain his meals for three days, thus weeding out trouble makers from within. Good order would be rewarded with extra meat for the mess captain and extra bread for all in the cell. O'Hara searched the hard faces of the men around him, he doubted the positive effect these rules would have on such men. But at least the demise of Kettlewell was a good start.

'Yes lad, the loss of Kettlewell is a great gain at least for this cell, but he had friends among the convicts and the guards, so we must be careful,' O'Hara said, a apprehensive note in his voice. Glancing at Collins he quickly added. 'We'll be fine, so we will.' But he remembered how it was on the hulk. Tempers had run high among the men awaiting transportation, and since it was from London that most of them came from; they all knew or had heard of Kettlewell. The first time he had met Kettlewell was still very vivid in his mind. Ebenezer Kettlewell was a ferret of a man his eyes were close together and never seemed to blink as if he was afraid he may miss something. Thin and tall he seemed a collection of bones thrown into a bag of rags that was drawn too tightly together. Unkempt mousy-coloured hair sprouted in disarray on a head that came to a blunted point. The head sat upon shoulders that sloped to never-ending dangling arms – one arm was peppered with the marks of an old shotgun wound, his broken fingernails were encrusted with the grime of London. The hands were never still, they were forever moving and twitching about his body searching for something to steal. He told them he had taught his fingers all the tricks of his trade from stealing bread when he was five years old, to silk nose wipes and purses at the mature age of eleven. Then came his first prison sentence in Newgate Prison where he met the well-known of his profession, which included some that were now on the *Runnymede*. His schooling was made complete when he graduated from Newgate with honours. He was soon stealing to order which were requested by London's fences, in fact many of London's gentry owned their art collections to Kettlewell. So favours were granted from time to time. A better cell at Newgate Prison, a more comfortable berth on one of the floating prison hulks. At thirty years of age Kettlewell had had his final sentence commuted to transportation instead of dancing to the tune of the Newgate hangman. They were told a valuable painting had made a grateful judge find a lesser offence below the forty-shilling mark thus saving Kettlewell the Newgate jig. A ship owner was found, for a consideration, who would take care of Kettlewell along with his acquired goods.

On the hulk he had picked on Collins continually, before Shenkin and O'Hara had arrived, blaming him for every discomfort Kettlewell had to endure. When on the day they were due to board the *Runnymede*, he punched the lad in the face for not bringing water quick enough. Shenkin stepped in splitting Kettlewell's eye open and breaking his nose. He'd vowed to get even, boasting to the other convicts that Shenkin would soon find a shiv scraping his ribs. Thank the Sweet Mary he was now feeding the fish thought O'Hara. But where were his stolen goods now, and who were Kettlewell's associates wondered O'Hara.

Collins pulled at O'Hara's shirt. 'Do you think Shenkin's alive Regan?'

O'Hara forced a smile to his broad Irish face. 'Don't you worry your man will take some killing.' He fell silent as he too began to think of Shenkin, he resolved to speak to one of the guards if he got the chance.

O'Hara looked around at the cells again, before turning back to Collins. 'Well it could be worse for didn't I share a bed with my brother back home in Ireland. And here we are now with four bunks between us, why sure it's luxury.'

'Will we be here long Regan?'

'As long as it takes and not a minute longer, I'll wager.'

Collins stared around him. 'We may have the extra beds, but we can't move around can we?'

"No," said O'Hara, glancing down his legs dangling over the end of the bunk. The shackles on their legs were clamped with pins which had indents to take the keys that locked the pins firmly in place. Not for the first time he thought to himself that they would need to unshackle them in the morning to move them out of the hold. At least he hoped to God they would. Deterrence through fear, their minds were also manacled he thought. Sweet Mary in heaven how long indeed.

Collins was looking about him with panic in his eyes. 'Do we really stay here for as long as it takes Regan? If so then I ...I ...' his shaking voice trailed off.

O'Hara still had a forced smile etched on his face. 'Sure we'll be on the upper deck in the morning passing the time of day with the captain.'

'Do you think so Regan?

'If not, the captain then the two guards we can see at the bottom of the ladder there. Sure they both look happy friendly lads, don't you think?'

The guards in question stood unsmiling and hard faced as the Jack lanterns swung their light back and forth across their harsh features. Their musket's seventeen-inch bayonets flashed in the swing of the lanterns, the last thing they looked was friendly.

In spite of his fear the boy began to laugh while trying to hold back his sobbing.

'See you are laughing already, and we will soon have Shenkin back with us.'
Then came their first all-embracing introduction to Sergeant Thomas Ketch.

Ketch came heavy-footed down the passageway between the cells. Hearing
Collins laugh he said. 'Who thinks it's all a great bloody game? Quick to
laugh are we, well you'll be sorry you ever saw light of day when I'm through
with you. You'll curse your mother, if you ever had one, for bringing you into
this world. You belong to me now, every miserable bastard here, don't you
make the mistake of forgetting it. What! no laughter anymore? Why I heard
you were the most dangerous scum London had. Well you came to the right
place, by the time we get to Australia those of you who are still alive will wish
you had died along the way. Three of you are already dead and over the side.
From what I understand the convict named Shenkin will soon join them, for
he's bleeding his ungrateful life away in the sick bay. Anyone want to hold
his hand? No! then from now on you'll eat, shit and piss when I say so, and
not before. Do you understand?' He paused, then added in a shout, 'Well do
you?' Some of the more hardened convicts, the world of crime writ large upon
their faces just sneered, a few of the more timid earnestly nodded their heads.

Ketch looked at the hard faces in front of him then smiled a sickly smile.
It was a smile that came limping to his one eye. 'Good, I like to break men,
that's why we have the rack, the cat o' nine tails, and the branding irons. Also
I have my lead cosh, please give me a chance to use them all,' he said swinging
the cosh from side to side. The ship took a broadside, men fell dangling out of
their bunks their chains pulling tight around their flesh. Ketch braced himself
against the timber table that was bolted to the deck in the middle of the hold.
Chains rattled as men tried to twist their bodies straight again. Ketch smiled.
'Nasty business – the chains rip the skin something awful they do, but your
hard aren't you? In fact, since you are so tough we'll skip water rations tonight.
Do you hear Corporal Burke no water?'

'Yes sir, no water tonight sir.' replied Burke.

All eyes were on Ketch now as he stood waiting for any other sign of
defiance. He was a large sadistic ugly looking man with a mouthful of uneven
black broken teeth, he had a patch over one eye that added to his mean
miserable face. He had a habit of pulling down his uniform jacket over his
beer gut, but it always failed to cover it. A Light Infantry Sergeant in the
52nd Regiment of Foot, Ketch had seen action at Ciudad Rodrigo, Badajoz
and Salamanca, where he was wounded for a second time. Then across the

Pyrenees and down into France. He was a man brutalised by a London slum upbringing and the Napoleonic Wars. He thought little of men's suffering or pain, and even less of their deaths. He had lost the eye at the siege of Badajoz in 1812 and was looking to get even ever since.

Shouting over at Burke he said, 'When we was fighting old Boney, these bastards were light-fingered or worse still, plotting against the crown,' he said looking at O'Hara as he spoke. 'We should have had them at Waterloo they would have served their country better by acting as cannon fodder for the Frogs, and so saving the lives of decent infantrymen.'

Turning to the convict whose shackles he had just checked. 'Do you see this you piece of shit,' Ketch said, lifting his eyepatch to reveal the dark empty socket. 'Lost it fighting for my country I did while you were stealing from elderly ladies on the Old Kent Road.' The man started to say something but Ketch stopped him. 'Don't give me your bloody lies or I'll have your backbone opened with the cat.' With that Ketch hit the man across the head with the heavy lead cosh. The man fell back on his bunk blood pouring down the side of his face. Then looking around at the cells Ketch shouted. 'Anyone else want to laugh, sneer or say a few words.' Corporal Burke gazed at Ketch with disgust. He had also been at the battle of Badajoz and knew the truth. Ketch a young corporal at the time, had urged his men through a gap in the Santa Maria breach. He had then hidden behind the protection of a low wall as his men passed. The wall was blown to pieces by cannon fire and in an effort to get away Ketch had turned towards his own advancing infantry and was hit by musket fire. At the time the good eye noted the man and musket responsible. Scrambling through the breech the infantryman never reached the other side of the breach, a .71 musket ball in the back of his head blew his brains into what was left of the wall, courtesy of Ketch. When he came to in the hospital his eye was gone, but he had been made a sergeant, mainly because he was the only corporal left in his company.

'They should have hung them all, every Welsh, Scottish, and Irish scum in the land,' Ketch said, hate etched deep into every word, as the ship continued to roll violently his hands gripped the table tighter. Men retched, the vomit flowing under the cell doors. Many called out for water, the stench of excrement pervaded the confined space, while the never-ending sound of the chains clanged to the sway of the ship.

'Yes I'd hang ever last one of them.' continued Ketch still steadying himself against the table his knuckles white with pressure. 'All in a fucking row from the bow to the stern.'

Burke looked up. 'We'd have been in a hell of a spot if they had Sarge when I was with the West Middlesex every other man seemed to be Irish. If they all hadn't been at Waterloo, I wager we'd be speaking French by now,' said Burke, no smile on his face now as he warmed to his memories.

'I remember a little Welshman just before our charge at Waterloo, went straight for the Frenchies he did, all on his bleeding own. Shorter he was mind as cannon fire sliced off his legs.' Ketch glared but there was no stopping Burke now.

'And then there was the Inniskilling Dragoons, the Union Brigade they called them because they had English, Scottish, Welsh and Irish in it from different heavy cavalries, the Royals and Scots Greys led by General Ponsonby. A right bloody mess they made of a massive assault by French infantry and cavalry. Of the 400 who charged 193 died including the General. And what about the Grenadier Guards, they...' Ketch cut him short.

'Shut your bleeding mouth, who the hell asked you?' Ketch said, his face infused with anger. 'All that dying and these bastards are laughing. I'll give them something to find funny I will.' Ketch struck another man full in the face with his cosh. A gash opened on the man's cheek blood spilling down onto the iron shackles of his legs. The man tried to put his hands to his face but the manacles would not allow it. He lay screaming until Ketch silenced him with another blow that rendered him unconscious his bowels emptied involuntary as he lay in a pool of blood piss and excrement.

For the first time the hold became silent only the chains broke the stillness.

Defiantly O'Hara turned to Collins and whispered, 'When they are trying to make your life hell, it upsets them when they think you are cheerful, so it does.'

But the smile had left Collins' face, sheer panic was back. Ketch was working his way down the line of cells on their side. 'Damn!' said O'Hara under his breath. He'd wanted a word with Burke who he'd seen taking Shenkin to the sick bay, but the man was on the other side. O'Hara tried to catch his eye but the guard was stooped over one of the convicts tightening a leg iron.

Ketch was only one cell away now. 'No, you can't have any water Watson, or should I say number 71011,' looking down at the list in his hand. 'And when you speak to me you snivelling piece of shit you address me as Sergeant.' With that Ketch's hand came up, he swung the cosh first to the right, then left, it travelled fast and hard across the man's face. Watson screamed and fell back in a tangle of chains and flying blood.

By now even the most hardened of the convicts were realising that they were totally at the mercy of this man and the confined space that they were chained in. It afforded no room to avoid whatever punishment he felt inclined to meet out to them. The smell of fear began to add to the pervading reek of the hold.

Burke called out 'For God sake Sarg! It'll be lights out soon and still the rest to do.' Burke hoped this would distract Ketch from his continually taunting.

'You trying to tell me my duty, my son,' Ketch said, pulling at the stiff leather stock around his neck then pulling down his tunic, which slowly travelled back up his stomach. 'Watch yourself Corporal or I'll have you cleaning out these cells come morning. There'll be a nice lot of shit and vomit by then,' said Ketch, with what passed as a smile.

'Sir,' said Burke and stooped again to his work. Shouting out. 'Leg irons secure on Walker. I mean 71116 sir.'

Clang! Another cell door slammed shut. So on down each side of the hold as guards and crew grunted and cursed each stubborn pin or lock. Added to this chorus of metal on metal was the verbal abuse that Ketch goaded each man he came to. As Ketch came up to their cell Collins shrank back into the corner of the berth causing the irons to bite into his ankles. He gave out a small whimper, he bit his bottom lip to stop the sound. But Ketch was in the cell and pulled at the lad's chain. 'What's this lad? Not afraid of me are you. I only hold your life in my hands I do, but that's all. There's nowhere to hide from me, I can do what I like to you see, and no one would know, no one would give a shit about what happened to you.' An uncontrollable yell of terror went up from Collins. Regan O'Hara tried to move forward to stop Ketch, who was swinging his cosh in front of the lad's face.

Ketch turned. 'Yes! You Irish bastard try it, just try it and you'll be joining your mate Shenkin,' Ketch said, the cosh at the ready the two guards standing behind him their muskets pointing, flintlocks, cocked hands steady, ready to fire.

Ketch smiled his sadistic smile and turned again to Collins.

'You're a friend too of that Welsh bastard Shenkin, he defended you against Kettlewell didn't he?'

'Yes,' said Collins.

'Yes, what?' snarled Ketch, pulling on the chain.

Collins screamed. 'Yes Ser... Sergeant,' Collins said, between sobs the blood trickling down his ankle.

'And no Kettlewell to sing you to sleep either. Kettlewell was a mate of mine see so you aren't or you Irishman, you'll both be lucky to get off this ship alive. One dark night I'll have you both and that Welshman too if he survives,' said Ketch, giving the leg chain a final vicious pull. Collins bit deep into his lip, causing blood to run down his chin, but he didn't make a sound.

'Right! Ketch said turning sharply, 'let's get these lanterns alight.' As the lights came on outside each cell they swung to the deep roll of the ship, causing shadows to grow then shrink on the wet stinking beams, bulkheads and bodies of the convicts. Hell surrounded not by fire, but by an ocean of water with only one way to leave it, a roughly stitched burlap shroud. The semi-darkness brought out the rats, scratching and sniffing the air for food. They ran around the deck, jumped onto the bunks of the chained men, the ones the men could reach managed to brush them off, the others feasted where they would. The sweat of fear increased as the night drew out like a knife. The human instinct to fight or flight was no longer an option for them. They were held secure with heavy chains in this dark damp tomb. Their battered bodies were covered with bruises, sores and blood and were offered up to the lice and rats.

Ketch shouted. 'Let's have you crew and guards back to quarters, sharp now. We'll leave them to their rat-infested hold.'

'Guards check your sentry duties before turning in.'

A chorus of 'Sir' responded to the order.

'Corporal Burke, lock each top grating fore and aft.'

'Sir.'

Ketch made his way to the companion ladder.

Burke was last to leave, O'Hara called out to him. Burke turned.

'How is Shenkin?'

'The surgeon changed the dressing when I came on watch, but it looks bad Irishman. I'll look in on him after I've locked up,' Burke said, kicking one of the rats out of the way as he moved to the aft companionway, keys swinging in his hands, but he stopped and turned back. 'Watch yourself Paddy, Ketch was a friend of Kettlewell something was going on between them. I don't know what, but some dodgy scheme or other. Ketch is as bent as a used nail, and just as trustworthy. He's a dangerous bastard, you'll be lucky to reach Australia alive.' Then added, 'I'll go down to the sick bay to see how he is and get word to you. But careful does it see,' said Burke tapping the side of his noise

'Thanks Burke,' said O'Hara.

Burke raised his hand in farewell and moved to the companionway ladder, pushing the guards in front of him.

Apart from the convicts who were vomiting their hearts up the place had gone quiet again, only the roar of the sea and the squealing of the rodents drowned out Collins's continued sobs.

O'Hara looked over at Collins who was sitting as small as he could make himself in the cramped corner of the cell.

'Do you think he'll live O'Hara?' said Collins, between sobs.

'Shenkin I bloody hope so, we been through a lot Daniel Shenkin and me.' Melancholy and pride coloured his words as he covered up Collins' bleeding ankles.

Shaking his head O'Hara said. 'How old are you Collins and what in the Holy Mother of Jesus are you doing here?'

'I'm twelve or thirteen, not sure, stole a jug of milk from the big house I did,' said Collins, guiltily.

'Sweet Mary in Heaven,' said O'Hara under his breath while he eased his burning leg around the caught skin. 'Heard say you are from Tolpuddle lad is that right?'

'Yes, Dorset way,' replied Collins.

'Bloody funny name for a place' said O'Hara, still fiddling with the leg iron.

'Good farming land, but trouble with labourers. That's how come I'm here see.'

'How's that?' said O'Hara.

'The court lumped us all together like, said I was one of the troublemakers. The magistrate said we had taken some sort of oath against the crown, so must be transported.' Bewilderment spreading across Collins young face.

After a moment he looked across to O'Hara. 'More trials going on when I left, some farm labourers holding public meetings they are.'

The lad's sobs were slower now. 'We was taken to Poole prison first, then all the way to Portsmouth.'

'And why there?' asked O'Hara

'Prison hulks laying off shore, cut down old warships made into prisons. Rotting on the tides they are, green scum hanging down their sides like the long velvet curtains I once saw in the big house. The hulks were filled with convicts waiting for transportation. We were made to work in the docks loading and unloading ships. Any heavy labour that was needed we'd be rowed over from the hulks to do it. The lash was used all the time Regan across backs already weak and feeble,' said the boy, not looking at O'Hara but out into space, as if gazing upon the horrors afresh.

'We was there for a time, Jim and me.'

O'Hara stopped moving the leg iron and lifted his great head. 'Jim?'

'Jim had been with me since the trial see,' Collins said, reflectively.

'Where is he now?'

'Dead, died on the hulk night before we left for London.'

O'Hara lent forward. 'What happened?'

'He had the bunk above me, see? I woke up that morning to what I thought was water or piss dripping on me. But it seemed hot and sticky like. I looked down on my sacking, it was covered in blood,' Collins said, the faraway look still in his eyes. 'I jumped up and peered into Jim's bunk. Someone had cut his throat to steal his food,' said Collins, wild-eyed now. 'Jim was cold and stiff, but strange as it may seem, he looked more at peace then I'd ever seen him when he was alive.'

Before O'Hara could say anything, Collins went on. The words coming fast, as if Collins needed to get rid of them.

'Jim was younger than me, ten I think, a pickpocket from Portsmouth. He was caught stealing a handkerchief. He'd already served two three-month sentences for picking pockets and vagrancy. The court decided both they and Portsmouth had had enough of Jim Bickle, so they sentenced him to transportation for seven years. He'd been homeless for most of his life, but do you know what he said to me Regan?'

'What lad?'

'That since being on the hulk it was the first time in his life he'd ever had regular meals and a warm place to sleep.'

Regan O'Hara nodded his head remembering the many famines of his beloved Ireland.

A long silence followed as the ship rolled and pitched, O'Hara thought Collins had finished.

'Then our own clothes were took, and these give us,' he said pulling at the coarse convict shirt imprinted with the broad black arrows of the government mark.

This caused O'Hara's mind to go back to the branding irons shaped like arrows, god knows how the lad would deal with that he thought.

Now the words seemed to rush out of Collins. O'Hara settled his broad back against the rough damp timbers of their cell.

'The food was bad Regan and I had a 14 lb iron ball fixed to my right ankle.' He stared over at O'Hara who looked puzzled. 'I didn't have any money see, to pay the guard's bribe for "easement of irons" they calls it.' A shiver went through Collins frail body. A scream went out from a man in the next cell somewhere in the dark he was shouting, 'Get off me you black bastard, please pull him off me I can't reach please pull him off me he's biting into my leg.' The rat let out a squeal as someone in the cell kicked out a it.

Collins sobbed. 'Dear god I can't take this Regan, we are just chained here waiting to be gnawed. We'll be eaten alive,' he said, his voice shrill with terror.

'Calm down lad we'll soon have Shenkin back with us. He'll find a way through this, you see if he don't.'

Regan O'Hara's eyes went down to the lad's legs where ulcers had formed around Collins lower right leg. The new wider shackles had cut into the ulcerations. This meant that Collins was continually having to lift the bottom edge of the manacle to prevent it cutting deeper into to the open wound. Collins' hand went down again and came up covered in blood. 'The rats will smell the blood, what will I do Regan?' Regan fed the chain through the hanging hoop that allowed a man to just about sit upright. Then he stretched over to Collins's bunk. Tearing a piece of sacking from under the side of the bunk mattress he wrapped it around the lad's ankle, between the iron fetter and the wound then put the thin blanket back over it. Tears welled up in Collins eyes.

'Thank you, Regan.'

'Well! What happened after Jim died?'

'Mother came to Portsmouth and brought a parcel of food. Bread, carrots, and a small jug of cider. They took them from me Regan, the other convicts, right in front of my mother. Weeping she was but they just laughed, including the guard who dragged her away while she tried to say her goodbyes to me. Later that day I was made to eat the others food, cheese and biscuits. The cheese full of maggots, the bread green with mould, but I was forced to eat it all,' Collins said, tears rolling down his cheeks uncontrollably, but still not a sound passed his bleeding lips.

'Shut your ugly trap Collins or I'll finish what Kettlewell started.' Cried out a cockney voice further down the line.

'Leave the child alone hasn't he suffered enough, he shouldn't even be here at his age.' This from a convict called Nisbit who had run a group of children pickpockets in the notorious Whitechapel area of London's East end.

'Fancy him do you Nisbit? We've heard about your little darlings.'

Chains clanked as Nisbit sprung up the leg irons wrapping themselves around his legs. 'Close your gob,' called Nisbit.

'You going to do it then?' came the reply.

'Shut up both of you, does anyone have water,' shouted another voice.

So it went on and on amidst the retching, peeing, and rats squealing, until one of the sentries at the top of the companionway shouted down. 'Quiet, or I'll call Ketch back from his supper, then god help you all.'

They had witnessed Ketch's on the spot punishment so fell silent.

Many had already been violently sick, and though there was a tin bucket between the bunks, most had urinated in their beds or worse. The foul smells caused the guards at the upper deck to tie cloths around their noses and mouths. The ship ploughed on through heavy seas pitching the deck upwards then down again, on and on into the night. Most of them by now were bruised all over from the violent movements of the ship, their skins torn the saltwater burning deep into the wounds. The ones asleep were indeed fortunate, but few of the 119 convicts managed this, the rest waited in the darkness for the cold dawn.

CHAPTER 4

Burke unlocked the sick bay cabin door. He found Shenkin laying in a pool of sweat and blood. He was breathing in fitful gasps calling out in mumbled words that Burke could not understand. He put his hand on Shenkin's arm. 'Alright mate I'll get the surgeon,' Burke said. Not that Shenkin heard him or was aware that anyone was in the cabin. Hurrying quickly to the above deck Burke made his way to the doctor's cabin and knocked.

'Enter!' Tarn said, looking up at Burke. 'Well! What is it now man?'

'Beg pardon sir it's the convict in sick bay. He's in a bit of a state like,' said Burke, stumbling over his words.

'Is he alive?'

'Yes sir, just.'

'You surprise me Burke, you really do. The man must have a strong constitution by all that's holy he should be dead.' After a moment Tarn turned to the cabin door. 'Well come on then let's see him.'

Sea spray met them as the cabin door swung open, it came off the burly figure of Captain Moxey. He was a bear of a man, his face weather-beaten and leathery, it told of a life spent voyaging the great oceans of the world. He was not a man to be trifled with, during this long journey to 'a place beyond the seas' his word would be law. A harsh law that could break men's bodies and spirits. They said Moxey's ships, for he owned or part owned three ships in the service of transporting convicts, was not the way to embark on a self-fulling future. Many wished, crew, convicts and soldiers alike, for the dubious comforts of the harsh prison hulks of the Thames rather than Moxey's severe discipline.

The three men swayed violently to the rolling ship; once they had recovered their balance Josiah Moxey stared into Tarn's face. 'Bloody foul weather Tarn, but I've got her steadier now,' he said, saltwater flying off his wet weather jacket and landing neatly on both Tarn and Burke.

Burke saluting had stepped sharply out of the captain's way. 'Beg pardon sir,'

Moxey didn't give the soldier a second look, as he continued to address Tarn. 'You'll join me for supper Tarn, devilled kidneys, what say you?'

Tarn nodded. 'It would be my pleasure sir. But first I must see to my patient, apparently the man's still alive. Mind I did give him hope, he seems to have acted upon it.'

'Right supper it is then, regardless of if he's dead or alive. But do bear in mind doctor we are paid on the head count.'

Tarn nodded his head 'Then let's hope he does us the courtesy of staying alive,' said Tarn, sarcastically.

Moxey ignored the remark for neither man saw eye to eye on a number of matters.

'Obliged to you.' This in response to Tarn opening the door to the captain's cabin. The aroma of the cooking wafted into the passageway. It urged the surgeon on to the sick bay.

Having made their way forward, then down to the between decks they entered Shenkin's own private hell.

'Off with the irons man. Let's get him over on his back before he breaks a bloody leg as well.'

'Right sir,' said Burke moving quickly to the task.

Holding the lantern as steady as the roll of the ship would allow Tarn removed the bandages and swabs. Leaning over the wound he smelt, then did the same with the swabs. 'Putrefied,' Tarn said, stating the obvious for the cabin reeked of it.

Burke nodded he had smelt that sickly smell many times before, mixed with the acrid rotten egg smell of gunpowder. On the battlefields of Campo Major, San Sebastian and Badajoz where it hung in the air like a curtain of death. Then across the Pyrenees back into France and the battlefields of Toulouse. Finally, on a wet Sunday evening on the 18th June 1815 after the carnage of Waterloo, it had risen from the dead and dying like rancid mist.

'No sir, no doubting that smell. Infantry man at Waterloo I was, just eighteen at the time, but I can still smell it on me. Begging your pardon sir.'

'Pass me that green bottle corporal, the one in the corner of my bag and be damn careful with it.'

'Sir.' Burke found the bottle then handling it as if it was hot grapeshot, he held it unsteadily in his hand.

'Shall I pour it over the wound sir?' Burke said, uncorking the bottle.

'Dear God no!' Tarn frowned. 'It's for me.' The heady smell of brandy mixed with the putrid air as Tarn drunk deep. He let out a small sigh as the raw brandy hit the back of his throat.

'Right Burke! Hold his legs,' Tarn said, leaning across Shenkin's waist. He poured the remainder of the brandy over a short thin scalpel blade, then bent over the wound. He cut down in one steady brisk slash. A cry passed Shenkin's lips then silence. The wound burst open like an overripe melon splattering Tarn in a putrid yellow puss.

Tarn looked down at his hands and coat. 'What a bloody profession!'

Wiping his hands in a piece of linen he began cleaning out the wound. Selecting a fine needle, he expertly sutured the open wound leaving a small opening for the wound to weep. 'Good,' said Tarn, tying off the thread. 'Right Burke pass me that fresh linen.'

'Sir.'

Wrapping the linen around Shenkin's chest he cut back the cloth and tied the bandage in place. Standing up, Tarn looked down at his patient who had remained unconscious. 'It's now up to faith and the power of healing, or not as the case maybe. If the fever breaks he'll live, if not we will be holding another burial service. The next few days or weeks will tell, for he's certainly putting up a hell of a fight,' said Tarn, looking down at his patient again. 'Jesuit's bark that's what I need Burke.' Burke looked blank. 'Quinine man!' said Tarn. 'But my supplies do not run to such expensive medication. So it's up to him and his God now, for I've done all I can.'

Burke none the wiser but a few shades paler, after the surgeon's stabbings said nothing.

The ship's bell rang out four times indicating the end of the first dog watch. 'Supper I think before the captain and the paying passengers eat all them lovely kidneys,' said Tarn. At the very thought of kidneys Burke almost threw up, but swallowed hard as he fitted the leg irons back onto Shenkin. Still unconscious, Shenkin inhabited a world of his own one that was filled with flowing faces. His father beckoning him, his brother laughing. His sister was laying the table in front of a blazing fire. The old black kettle sung on the heat of the coal. But above all he saw his mother's face smiling at him. She was as clean and as neat as a new pin. He moved to touch her, but she melted into a dark space, Shenkin drifted in after her.

The Master of the *Runnymede* looked up at the knock on the cabin door and Tarn's entrance. 'Well! Alive or dead, how fair's your convict?' Not waiting for an answer Moxey went on. 'Not put you off your supper I trust. Pour yourself some madeira man and join us,' Moxey said, beckoning to the steward to serve Tarn.

'Thank you sir,' said Tarn, lifting the flat-based decanter, he poured himself a liberal amount of wine.

'Uncle you are unfeeling, Yes, you really are,' said Elizabeth Jane Moxey in response to the captain's surprised expression. 'The man acted with courage and honour in protecting the young convict from that ruffian. Who would, I am sure, have killed the lad had he not intervened. And was I not also in danger for I stood no more the a few feet away?' Elizabeth Jane said, visibly shuddering at the memory of it.

'Ah! And have I not told you, you must not stray from the quarterdeck madam?'

His niece shook her head in dismay. While they spoke, Tarn was observing his fellow table guests. Top of the table sat Captain Josiah Benjamin Moxey bristling with his sense of command. To his right his niece Elizabeth Jane, fair of hair and complexion and with a smile to soften any man's heart. Eighteen years old, full lips formed that smile and a full figure completed a heart-stopping beauty. Not for the first time did Tarn's breath come a little faster at the sight of her. To her right Mr and Mrs Alfred Scrimshaw, a clerk in the employ of Captain Moxey who was to take up a position as chief clerk in one of Moxey's Sydney 'bayside' concerns. Stooped, as befitted his profession, narrow of chest, lean of face, and with a beak of a nose that reminded Tarn of a vulture he had once seen scavenging among the dead after the battle of Toulouse. Tarn poured himself another drink, Moxey looked over, but said nothing. Mary Scrimshaw was marginally better in that she had more hair on her head, but apart from that they were a matched pair. To Moxey's left sat Lieutenant Charles Hugo Feltsham, Commander of the Guard. A position secured for him by his uncle Percival. He was young of age, round of face and trying to look older with the help of thin pale whiskers, but failing badly. The Lieutenant's eyes were glued onto Elizabeth Jane opposite him, Tarn didn't blame him.

Finally, Lord Percival Hugo Feltsham and Lady Edith Jane Feltsham née Wetherspoon. Full of the worst traits of the aristocracy, his lordship occupied the chair at the other top-end of the table. Feltsham a nobleman by an accident of birth, landed gentry by his ancestor's sacrifice of their archers on the battlefields of medieval France, and elevated to power by a grateful king. The present Lord Feltsham was secure and aloof, in an inherited baronetcy that dated back to Norman times. His wife sat to his right, she came to him dowdy but with a large dowry. Her father was a rich successful purveyor and manufacturer of Wetherspoon's soap in Manchester, who rued the day he moved into the rarefied air of nobility. He found no honest tradesmen there, only the immutable need to shore up the finances of the house of Feltsham. Lord Feltsham's debts, the only accomplishment he could really claim credit for, were the result of his losses on the gambling tables of London. The debts at the time of their marriage were reputed to be in excess of the family estates in Norfolk. But as Feltsham told his dear mother at the time. 'They maybe trade mater, but I'll make her a Lady and her dowry will clear some of our more pressing debts.'

A fine upstanding bunch of travelling companions, so they are thought Tarn. Apart from young Elizabeth Jane may the good lord protect me from them all. Tarn instinctively crossed himself as the thought passed his mind.

Elizabeth Jane was still talking as Tarn took his seat between Lt. Feltsham and Lady Feltsham. Moxey noted another full glass in the doctor's hand. He would admonish him later.

'Do you not agree Mr Scrimshaw, that he was the hero, not the villain of the piece?' Elizabeth Jane said, her eyes alight with cheerfulness.

Scrimshaw hmm'ed and glanced at the master of the ship who glared back at him. Scrimshaw's future depended on the captain's good will and he was not about to jeopardise that. He mumbled again but really said nothing. However, there was no doubt in his own mind that the convict Shenkin, for he had indeed seen the brawl, acted in a manner that Alfred, if he had the courage, would have done. But finally came out with. 'I fear I saw very little of the fracas Miss Elizabeth,' Scrimshaw said, in his high thin, simpering voice.

'Do not look at me to justify the scoundrel young lady. The lower classes should be kept in their place,' said Feltsham turning to his mousy wife. More madeira my dear?' She shook her head, a head that was already a little dizzy.

Exasperated Elizabeth Jane turned to Tarn, who was halfway through his fourth glass, 'Doctor Tarn I implore you sir, surely you will support me in this.'

'Alas, I was not on deck at the time I'm afraid,' Tarn said, raising his hand to stop the captain's niece from protesting further. 'But I am reliably informed that the convict known as Shenkin was indeed protecting one of the young convicts and himself from the villain known as Kettlewell. I understand the fellow had vowed to do harm to them both at the first opportunity. I raise my glass to him. One down, a troublemaker at that, but two spared, as the ship's Surgeon-Superintendent I see a definite benefit,' Tarn said, smiling in the captain's direction.

Captain Moxey moved his considerable weight in his chair, his face red with anger and made to stand to rebuke Tarn. But Elizabeth Moxey smiled in triumph. 'Uncle please sit down, this is all my doing. I pray the man lives to a great age and makes for himself some kind of future in Australia.'

'If he lives madam,' said Moxey, raising his voice. 'I'll see to it that he hangs, and you'll oblige me Tarn by seeing me in my cabin at the start of the forenoon watch tomorrow.' The outburst caused a chill to settle over the supper table, like a sheet of frozen ice. Tarn inclined his head at the captain, lifted his glass in acknowledgement and drained it.

***

Shenkin was now deeper into a black delirium. He twisted and turned on the narrow bunk in time to the turmoil of the sea. A ship full of unwanted men tossed about by nature and an unjust world. Their country had swept them under the carpet of the sea, they would never again be heard above the roar of the oceans. Shenkin was a mass of pain, he could find no peace physically or mentally; he drifted about in the recesses of his mind. I must hold on to my thoughts I must think, think, remember... he would survive he would...

He was home again in their small cottage on Quarry Row, the family were gathered around the kitchen table. From the turn of the century Shenkin's father, and many others, had been deeply involved in the struggle to give the working people of Wales a voice. Religious revivalism and the continued industrial revolution of the last century had caused unrest and uncertainty. Now in the early part of the 19th century ironworkers and coalminers were seeing their wages cut and cut again. Many wages were in truck payments, company token coins, that could only be spent in company shops, The goods in these shops were at inflated prices. The Shenkin family, better off than most because four wages came into the household, lived in the mining parish of Merthyr Tydfil in South Wales. Boasting a population of 27,000, most of whom worked either in the four large iron works or the coalmines. Therefore, they were dependent upon the goodwill of the ironmasters and coal owners for the food on their tables, cloths on their backs and their future. But with no vote they were but pawns on a vast industrial chessboard. Then with the introduction of the first ever Reform Bill in London they saw at last their chance to have a voice. Thousands rallied to the cause, in the vanguard of this cause was the Shenkin family. The green lush landscape around them had been reduced to no more than tips of ironslag and mountains of small coal. Its working people living in squalor, poverty, dying of malnutrition, cholera or the unsafe surroundings of their workplace. The town had become the centre of the iron industry expansion. The land ripped apart for her minerals, men burnt by hot cinders or coughing their lungs up to rid themselves of coaldust. Their once beautiful pastoral countryside gone forever.

'We must have reform now,' Idris Shenkin said, his voice raising on the word now. 'Self-assertion, that is our greatest need.' Head of the family Idris Shenkin was an organic intellectual, self-taught in reading and writing he had absorbed the political pamphlets from London on the French and American revolutions. He learnt that it was Richard Price, a Welshman, who had influenced the Founding Fathers of the United States. Holding the view that all men are created equal.

'The Jacobins were right my sons, civil liberty and equal rights for all,' he would quote to them from the Welsh revolutionary pamphlet 'Seren Tan Gwmwl' – ' The Star Behind the Cloud'. Each night after their days work they would read first from the bible, then the political writings, in equal measure.

His sons Daniel the eldest and Owain the youngest would read out loud and with verve.

'In the 20s we were campaigning for our rights, not wondering if it was going to rain. Read it again with more feeling.'

'But that was nine years ago Da and the troops from Brecon soon put a stop to it,' Daniel said, his finger on the line so as not to lose his place. 'I know you are right, but this time we must be better organised. We...' His father cut him short.

'Not now Daniel we will speak later, this talk is upsetting your mother.'

Megan Shenkin was a tall woman, strong of face and character. She was a beauty when their father had married her and even now, after all the hardships and difficult times, she was still a striking woman. Her hair was now flecked with grey but the rest still as black as a raven's wing. Her daughter Rachel sat at her side, Megan's self when young.

'Don't listen Mam, you know what these men are like. They only think of two things and politics is the second one,' Rachel said. The beauty of her face marred by the cinders and heat of the iron foundry. Her hands covered in burn marks from handling the hot rails. She was to marry Hugh Williams, a puddler up at the Cyfarthfa Works which was owned by the Crawshay family. Their works had orders for supplying rails all over the world including the East India Co. As a result, the company were making huge profits and had no intention of their workmen reducing those profits. Hugh worked the

'Long Turn' at the Crawshay Iron foundry starting at six o'clock on Sunday morning and did not finish until twenty-four hours later. Living with his mother, Hugh hoped to save enough money to marry Rachel the next spring and rent their own home.

'That's enough of that my girl. Those women you work with up at the ironworks, most of them are from Chinatown area, they are a bad lot my girl,' said their mother.

Rachel sighed. 'Alright mam but if Hugh is persuaded to join them, and loses his job, I'll never forgive any of them.'

Megan turned to Idris. 'I know you are right, but no work last time you went on strike, leaving us with no money in the house, and no food on the table. Who washed cloths and scrubbed the floors of Penydarren House to keep us from staving, answer me that?'

'I know cariad, I know, but it will be different this time you'll see.'

'Yes this time they'll hang you all including my sons. Is that what you want?'

'No of course not Megan.'

Their mother was in full flow now. 'As if mountain fighting for money isn't bad enough now you are getting Daniel into things that could get him hung. At least Owain is too young.'

At the sound of his name Owain looked up. 'I am going to the rally though aren't I Da, you promised.'

'Dear God! what's this, and Owain only eight years old. Isn't it enough that he's already down the pit working sixteen hours a day for six pennies a shift.'

A sigh passed Idris Shenkin's lips, he lifted his hands to calm his wife. 'Now, now Megan I didn't promise him, but if he is old enough to work then he must know what the men intend to change. It's what we are fighting for, his future.'

'Damn you and your politics! I draw the line when it comes to my son's lives.'

Their father was startled by their mother's language. 'Megan!'

'It's my house and I clean it. I'll swear if I want to.'

'Yes Megan,' said Idris Shenkin. 'But this time we'll demand our democratic rights, you see if we don't.'

'This time they will either hang you leaders or transport you and it's you who'll see if they don't.' Megan said, tears in her eyes now, which she hated, a woman thing she knew, but she felt it looked like weakness and that always made her angry.

Wiping her hand over her eyes she said. 'What do your reformers in London know about bringing up a family. They should try living here not scribbling on pieces of paper. Parlour politicians that's what they are useless and dangerous the lot of them.'

Their father looked hard at their mother. 'I will not have anything said against men of reform. Not in this house, or anywhere in my hearing, they are all bloody working-class martyrs.

'And I won't have any swearing in this house. Their mother said. 'Clean floors it is and I'll have the air just as clean.'

'But you just…' Megan cut him short. Tears rolling down her cheeks.

'My floors, my air see.' For heartbeats there was a heavy silence, only breathing moved the air. Then after a moment she put her hand tenderly on Idris's arm. 'I know cariad how you feel, but remember Tom Shrops, died in your arms he had a bayonet buried deep in his belly from a Brecon soldier. Not again Idris, please, not again.'

The family fell quiet again, the wind-up clock that their father had won for beating the Swansea middleweight champion thirty years before, the only sound in the house.

Idris Shenkin lifted his proud head. 'Yes, I watched Tom Shrops die. His life sighed through my arms like a flutter of wind and he was gone. Heavier in death he was mind then he'd ever been in life,' Idris said, with a sigh.

'He'd clip my ears and kick my arse.' Tut tut from their mother at this. 'Sorry love but that's what he'd do. Until I got it right see, then a slap on the back as the iron began to run. It's heat as hot as Satan's breath. We'd coax a ball of molten iron out of the furnace, flowing all red and orange in colour. Beautiful it is like a roll of silk cloth from Jones the Draper. A life of its own that metal has, licking and caressing the side of the mould with its hot tongue. Then filling it hungrily to overflowing. Spilling and splashing up, up into the air. Burning everything in its way, men and matter,' said their father, whose face bore the marks of many a kiss from the hot cinders.

Thomas Wilks was from Shropshire a small wiry man, all energy and opinion. The English ironmasters had brought men into South Wales from all over England and Europe with skills at working the ironstone in the new process for the manufacture of rails. Tom Shrops was one of the best, but also full of resolve to gain more rights for the workingman.

'Let him not die in vain then. Let us finish what he started,' said Daniel, in a firm strong voice. 'I for one will not go on as we are, forever at the mercy of the iron and coal owners. More and more workers coming in from outside and all prepared to work for less wages than us. We have no say in it, but we feel it in our pockets and our pride. If we could only all join together Merthyr men and the outsiders then we'd all be better off.'

Their father nodded his head. 'Yes, you are right Daniel we must do something to improve our lot. Tom would say one day we'll make cannonballs not to fight Napoleon, but for ourselves to fire at the oppressors in our own country,' said Idris, his eyes ablaze.

'We may be here to teach you illiterate Welsh how to turn iron ore into rails for the rest of the world to use, he'd say, but we'll also teach you how to melt men together to form a strong union of voices. Choirs of workingmen singing for their rights. I've heard you Welsh sing, powerful voices raised to heaven, but this time we'll do it for ourselves.'

'That's what democracy is about, see cariad?' Idris said, turning to their mother.

'And that's revolution Idris Shenkin,' said Megan.

Daniel threw his hands in the air and raised his voice 'Mam you don't understand we are slowly dying under the boots of these men. I will not, can not, accept it, whatever the outcome. I am too young to give up my life for their profits.' Daniel was shouting now. 'No ironmaster or coal owner will own my life, not while I have breath to breathe. I'll see them in hell first,' said Daniel, at the top of his voice

His father slammed his fist down hard on the kitchen table. The table bowed, as if to break in two. The blow rattled the dog ornaments on the mantlepiece above the fire, waking them from their china sleep. They all watched them sway then slowly settle. He lowered his voice to a whisper. 'That's enough, do not raise your voice at your mother,'

'Sorry Mam but we only have one life, and if I have to fight this on my own I will,' said Daniel.

'You are too bull-headed, we must plan carefully.' his father said, while trying to calm his voice and mind. 'You'll not be on your own the men's feelings are running high and this rally will settle it.'

'And wait another ten years I suppose,' said Daniel, anger still in his words. 'We must act now. You are on the working group Da let me speak at the rally, will you support me?'

Idris Shenkin looked at his wife then his son. 'Yes,' he said.

'So its up to Waun Hill is it Dada,' said young Owain, his young face alight with excitement.

His father did not answer but looked at their mother. 'The time is getting late,' he said, taking a timepiece out of his waistcoat pocket. The timepiece; another boxing trophy, won for beating the Neath champion Tommy Morris in eighteen blood-soaked rounds. It was their father's pride and joy. Pressing the tit on the side of the piece. the dust cover sprung open the inscription read;

Idris Shenkin
Bare- knuckle Champion 1801
A fighter of courage, and valour.

He remembered he'd had to looked up the word valour the first time he'd read it. The word always gave him great pleasure. Giving a sigh, after reading the words, he turned to Daniel. 'Now read with some fire in your belly, show me how you'll speak on the top of Waun Hill.'

'Yes, Da,' said Daniel, unglueing his finger from the page and clearing his throat.

'Men proposes, but God disposes,' said Megan, having the final word, as usual.

Then she poured the tea that was now stone cold.

CHAPTER 5

The soldier straightened his back as the Surgeon-Superintendent came up to the sick berth. 'How is he?' said Tarn.

'A lot of moaning and groaning sir, with a few shouts in the night. Also the Corporal told me to tell you one of the sailors took ill during the morning watch sir. Sergeant Ketch thinks its rotten grog or the pox.'

'Does he, I'll see the man later. Unlock the door let me see my patient.'

'Sir.'

On entered Tarn found Shenkin laying on his back soaked in sweat, his head moving from side to side.

'Well! Still alive then, but only just,' said Tarn, in mild surprise. 'I give you credit Welshman you are putting up a hell of a fight. Let's see that wound.'

Shenkin lay oblivious to everything but his tortured fevered thoughts.

Tarn called the soldier to hold Shenkin still. Then he removed the blood-soaked bandages. The gash was raw where he had slit open flesh, but the puss was less, and the weeping clear, the smell better which was a good sign. The doctor applied more prophylactic vinegar to the wound and bound it up with a fresh dressing.

The guard let the arms and legs go. Shenkin in his delirium thrust his right arm forward his fist in a tight ball. The blow only just missed the guard.

'Jesus! wouldn't want to be on the end of one of those blows sir.'

'No indeed,' said Tarn.

'If he lives the Sergeant will take the fight out of him sir,' the solider said, a sneer spreading across his face as he spoke.

'If he lives, which is a big if at the moment,' said Tarn, 'I'll have to see the captain about removing these leg irons. The man's delirious he'll do harm to himself if they are left on. Right! this sick crew member I'll take a look at him.' Then turning to the guard. 'You can lock up now.'

'Yes sir.'

With Tarn gone the guard looked down at Shenkin, a hard sadistic look on his face. The chain joining the leg shackles still in his hands, he dropped the heavy links across the bandaged wound. Shenkin screamed. The guard smiled slammed the cabin door shut, clicking the lock into place.

As the pain slowly subsided Shenkin turned on the bunk.

I'll not die, I'll not, no roof fall could kill me nor will this floating prison...

***

He was back in the bowels of Waun Wyllt's Number 2 pit. The miners were working a new seam where Shenkin together with a small team of men were driving pit props into place to secure the roof. It was always a dangerous job for the roof was forever moving causing cracks to appear along the road way.

'Are you fighting this weekend Shenkin?' said Tommy Morgan at his side, sweat running down his coaldust-covered face.

Shenkin stopped for a moment from swinging the big sledgehammer he was using to drive in the wedges under the tops of the timber props.

'No Tommy but training mind for the fight against the Cardiff Champ. My da won't let me off that and me with a date tonight.'

'Time you married instead of chasing women around the mountainside,' said Tommy who was married with three children and another on the way.

Shenkin looked at him. Poor Tommy thought Shenkin up to his neck in children and debt.

'One day perhaps, but not just yet.'

Tommy eyed the roof as Shenkin drove in another wedge a powder of coaldust sprinkled down on them like black wedding confetti.

'It's been moving all day the bloody earth doesn't like us taking the black gold from it see; so it's angry. We need to get these bloody props up fast before it all comes down,' said Tommy, spitting dust from his mouth.

Shenkin smiled Tommy was a born worry guts. Then above all the noise of picks and shovels a sound like the crack of a whip caused them both to look up. A latticework of small cracks spread across the roof.

Tommy swallowed hard letting out a small sigh. 'Bloody hell it's moving.'

Shenkin slowly and gently put the sledgehammer down. For heartbeats they said nothing, only their breathing disturbed the hanging coaldust in the air. All along the galleries flicking candles danced in the darkness as men stood still. Picks stopped hacking the seams, wide faced shovels stopped scraping the floors, the drams silent on their worn iron rails.

The sound of boots along the roadway determined the silence it was Phil the Flame, once the fireman up at the old No1 Pit, now an Overman in charge of the section Shenkin was working. Phil Clark to give him his correct name, was determined to become an Under Manager at Waun Wyllt. As supervisor it was his job to make sure the men were working the seams, that the coal was continuing in a steady flow to pit bottom and hence to the surface.

'Are you all in bloody church or waiting for the pubs to open?'

'It's the roof Mr. Clark been moving all day it has,' said Will Parker.

'Well, it's not moving now is it?'

'No Mr. Clark.'

Exasperated Clark raised his voice so that all could hear him. 'So get bloody on with it, this shift is already below its tonnage. Me it is who will have to answer to the pit manager.'

The noise of metal striking earth and rock began to ring out once more as the men resumed their work.

Shenkin gave a look of resignation to Tommy Morgan as he lifted his sledge. Tommy pushed a prop into place. It was then that a deep groan came from above them looking up Shenkin saw a wave of roof move along towards them. As if in slow motion he saw the roof cascade down, a waterfall of earth, rock and coal. Dust clouds filled the air as pit props exploding into splinters, men screamed as they were swallowed up and buried alive under the avalanche. Shenkin tried to keep on his feet as the rock, coal, wire fixings and timber logs all began to spin around him. The side of his face burned with an intense pain. Men in front of him seemed to become part of the swirling mass. Clouds of coaldust swallowed everything up like a black mist as men choked and died in the debris-filled air. Tommy Morgan pulled Shenkin into a corner as another run of roof collapsed. Time became nothing as Shenkin fought for breath. He felt as if his lungs were going to burst as all the air was being sucked out of him. Bloody hell I'm going to die he thought. I won't I can't, I will live I will, he told himself, as Tommy's hands pushed him further into the corner. A man in front of Shenkin was slammed into the opposite wall. One of the timber pit props followed him, both man and prop became one as they smashed into the wall of rock. The man's face dissolved into a mask of rock, coal, timber and wire. He just hung there as if someone had put a picture on the wall, a picture of revulsion blood and coaldust. Then as quick as it began it stopped. Shenkin had his hands over his mouth, his eyes now tight shut. The silence, after so much noise, almost hurt his ears it was a deathly ominous silence. For what seemed like time without end they just clung to each other like two small children caught in a nightmare they couldn't wake up from. Their heartbeats seem to become one in the terror of the moment Shenkin felt Tommy's breath on his face it was coming in jerky stops and starts. Then finally with the last of the coaldust settling, a tomblike quiet fell around them time and silence becoming one in their coffin of blackness. This frozen tomb like time went on and on, both men not wanting to let go of each other. Had it all happened thought Shenkin in seconds or hours or days he had no way of knowing perhaps they were already dead, now part of the earth they had raped for her coal. If so then it is truly a just and fitting end…

**

In the salt-drenched bunk of his fevered dreams, he heard remembered voices.

'Is anyone there?' Waldo Evans shouted again, has he had done for the last three hours.

'Is there anyone…?'

'Over here Waldo quick as you can.'

'Shenkin dear God is that you, boyo?' Waldo said.

Turning around he called out. 'I've got them, they are somewhere behind this bloody lot,' Waldo said, facing a wall of rock, coal and buckled pit props bodies picks and shovels.

'Bring up more men, picks, shovels hurry now, and send a message to the surface to let his father know. Wait, is anyone with you Shenkin?'

'Yes, Tommy Morgan hurt bad he is he's breathing strange like.'

'*For God's sake hurry,*' *shouted Shenkin , into the darkness of the convict ship's salty sick bay.*

At the shout the guard outside stirred from his dozing, then let his head drop. Shenkin turned again on the bunk, the wound in his side pulled him back. '*It's alright Tommy I've got you,*' *he called out.*

'Tap on the rail Shenkin and keep on tapping, it will help guide us to you. But godsake be careful mind not to cause a spark, there may be gas in the air, if there is and it ignites we'll all be down here for the rest of eternity.'

Shenkin lifted a pick with his free hand and started tapping gently, very gently.

The fall had happened suddenly, a creak of pit props the timber yielding to the weight of tons of rock and coal, then down it all came. Not the first in Number 2 pit either. Two weeks previous 300 yards came down, killing all seven men in that section. This year alone had seen thirty-one killed by roof falls, and still only May.

Tap, tap, tap, tap, tap…

Shenkin took another lungful of black choking dust and coughed. It was like a tomb, one that was almost a mile below the surface of the earth with no beginning and no ending.

Tap, tap, tap.

Tommy stirred across Shenkin's upper body, where he had lain since the last of roof had crashed down on them his hands still tight around Shenkin's body.

'It won't be long now Tommy, hold on.'

'It's no good, I'm trapped under this big rock. I can't feel my legs, Shenkin, not a bloody thing, and I can hardly breath,' Tommy said, his voice weak the words coming in short rasping gasps. Blood covered Shenkin's shirt front. Not that he could see it, but it was wet, sticky warm, the side of his face throbbed.

TAP, TAP, TAP, dear god gently man, gently he said to himself. Tap, tap, tap.

'Don't give up now, damn it, I'll never buy you another jug at the Castle Inn, I bloody swear it. No movement came from him. 'Come on Tommy hold on, hold on they are almost here man, don't you want to see those snotty kids of yours again; lets feel you move eh?'

'I can't boy, it pains too much.' His voice now no more than a whisper between coughs. Shenkin's blood slicked hand gripped the pick firmer. Again he hit the iron track harder than he intended.

TAP, tap, tap, tap tap. The roof creaked, small bits of stone and coal fell around them like fine drizzly rain. Shenkin laid the pick down very gently.

'Jesus, for God sake don't move,' shouted Waldo, looking up at the roof in terror.

'What the hell are you doing Shenkin, tap gently for Christ sake,' Waldo called. 'We are nearly through and your father is here.'

'We'll get you out my son, as God is my judge, we'll get you out,' Idris Shenkin said. He no longer worked in the pits, but they could not stop him from going down in the cage carrying the extra men to help in the rescue. The roof creaked and moaned again, a prop collapsed by the side of the rescuers. Everyone stood still, afraid to move a muscle. For heartbeats, fear struck deep into every man's soul, if the remaining timbers went they were doomed, there would be no way forward or back. Only their rapid breathing disturbed the swirling clouds of coaldust. At last the roof settled back into place.

Tap, tap, tap.

A rat scurried across Shenkin's face making for a draught of air as the men removed a large piece of coal in the wall. Regan O'Hara kicked the rat out of the way killing it instantly. Both the O'Hara brothers stood at the wall.

Huge men both well over six foot with powerful physiques to match. They were smiling, as if it was all a great big bloody game, tossing rock and coal to one side as if they were pebbles. But the truth of the moment was in their ripped and bleeding hands from tearing at the wall. Regan O'Hara looked in at Shenkin.

'Well now aren't you glad us Irish work here now, and for less money too?'

'Shut up Regan,' said his brother Sean, throwing a broken prop onto the side.

'Careful boys don't start the roof moving. We don't want it's creaky voice singing again do we?' Waldo said, smiling at his own grim humour. No one laughed at the joke, as all turned nervous eyes upwards. Cracks appeared above them but by some miracle the roof stayed up. 'Right let's get on with it ,' said Waldo, in a hushed voice.

'Didn't I tell you they'd soon be through?' said Shenkin.

But this time no response came from Tommy his body too seemed heavier.

'Tommy, Tommy!' But Tommy had gone to a more peaceful place then the black tomb their bodies occupied.

Tap, tap, tap, tap, tap.

'No need to tap now boy we've got you,' Waldo said, his face streaming sweat, in the cold earth's air. They soon made a hole almost large enough to crawl through then Waldo stopped them.

'Wait, let me check for firedamp.'

Holding the Davy Safety Lamp steady in his hand Waldo pushed his arm through the hole. The flame in the lamp was surrounded by a metal-gauze screen that distributed the heat over a large area, so that the maximum temperature of the screen was below the ignition temperature of any flammable gas mixture.

'The flame looks good it seems alright, so in we go boys.'

The light from the lamp took in the scene. Shenkin was sitting upright, huddled tight into a corner and pressed hard against the side wall. Tommy Morgan his lower back pinned down by a large rock lay across Shenkin. Shenkin's left arm was buried under coal, splintered timber props covered them both.

Tap, tap, tap, tap, tap....

Waldo took the pick from Shenkin. 'Alright boyo it's over now.'

The roof shifted. Coaldust fell around them like dainty black flaked snow. 'Quick as we can now, before the roof becomes part of the floor,' said Waldo.

Spluttering and spitting coaldust out of his mouth Shenkin looked at Waldo Evans.

'He's dead Waldo.' Then turning to his father. 'He saved my life Da, he pushed me into this corner. He covered me with his own body. All the roof fell across his back and legs slowly pressing the life out of him,' Shenkin said

'I can see that my son.'

The O'Hara brothers lifted the large rock as others pulled Tommy Morgan off Shenkin. Freed he slowly followed the body out.

'Right let's have a look at you,' said Waldo, lifting the lamp up at Shenkin. 'Is any of this blood yours before we move you further?'

'Side of my face hurts, but I'm alright I think.'

Holding the lamp closer Waldo poured water over Shenkin's face. 'Bloody big splinter from one of the props has ripped into your face, boy. The owners will stop the cost of that wood from your wages, you see if they don't.' The tight smile on Waldo's face turned into a broad grin.

'Willy Stitch will get it out, then a needle and thread to close it up,' said his father. 'Now let's get them up to the surface.'

Waldo still looking at the splinter sighed. 'Well, it's not going to do anything for your love life mind. It's going to leave a hell of a scar,' said Waldo.

'Now don't go spoiling my day, Waldo.' Shenkin said, slowly getting to his feet. His father could not stop himself from hugging his son. Self-conscious, with the O'Hara brothers looking on, Shenkin pulled away.

'I'm alright Da let's get to the surface.'

He bent down to help carry the man who had saved the rest of his days out of their crypt.

Tommy was placed on a makeshift stretcher of timber props and belts. They began the mile journey along the main heading to pit bottom. Galleries to their left were eerily still, coaldust blowing out of them. Waldo turned. 'Long wall working in there, we'll never get the hewers out.'

Shenkin looked into the damp darkness of the tunnel. 'How many got out Mr Evans from the fall area.'

Waldo Evans the grin gone from his face now. 'Just you, boyo, eight buried under the East heading too, everything came down for at least 400 yards. It will take days to dig out the bodies, that's if it all stays safe.'

'And if the owners think it's not too costly,' added Sean O'Hara.

'Come on let's get to the surface,' Idris Shenkin said.

Including Tommy Morgan nineteen men were dead. The earth cashing in on its payment for its black diamonds.

At the surface a fine mizzle of rain was falling over the gathered crowd. It was a silent crowd one filled with pain and sorrow. The dark mountain shadows draping the valley in mourning. Shenkin saw his mother first. A rain-soaked shawl wrapped around her shoulders. She had a clean white mop cotton cap on her head, the rim was edged with wet coaldust. She was trying not to cry out at the sight of her son. Then he saw Tommy's wife, a baby tight to her body in a swaddling shawl. Another two children clinging and pulling at her skirts. Their bare feet standing in a pool of dirty cold water. Horror on her face when she saw only Shenkin with four men at his side carrying a stretcher with a covered body on it. She screamed. 'No, no, not Tommy please God no.' Family and friends held her back, as she tried to rush forward the two children falling in her wake.

Shenkin's mother ran over to her. 'Come on we'll get you out of the rain. Let them clean him up, you can go to him then my lovely.' With that Megan Shenkin lifted one of the now crying children into her arms. She took hold of the woman's hand and slowly walked her down the coaldust splattered road.

'I'll be home soon my son to prepare a hot meal for you all,' she said, touching Shenkin's arm as she passed.

'Yes mam,' said Shenkin, although he would not show it, he was grateful to be again with this strong woman he called mam but his voice portrayed him for it was tight with emotion.

His father placed his hand upon is shoulder.

Shenkin met his father's eyes. 'He saved my life Da, pushed me into that bloody corner and took the full weight of it across his back.' Emotion continued to tightening his throat as he spoke. The shock of what had happened now hitting him like a runaway dram, he staggered slightly, his father wrapped his arms around him to steadied him.

'It's alright my son steady now, let's get you home. I'll not forget what Tommy did, his family will not go hungry while I have breath in my body, I swear it. But for now I'll send for Willy Stitch to remove that splinter. Then we'll post it back to the mine owners.' They both laughed grimly.

Then in a more serious voice Idris Shenkin said. 'We must have change, that pit and the rest of them are death-traps,' he said, his voice shaking with temper. 'But first we'll bury our dead, then we will start a union to save the living, the rally meeting on the Waun will be the start.'

The siren whistle blew out to let the town know the accident was over. Not the wail that had brought them to the pit head so many hours before, but a sharp penetrating single sound. The crowd began to disperse. Many held old coal sacks over their heads to keep off the rain. The high shrill sound cut through their small village like the slice of a knife. It rattled the delicate bone china cups and saucers on the dining table of the big house, where they were about to have high tea.

***

The following evening Cathy O'Hara stood on the mountain above the town of Merthyr Tydfil. The late rays of sun shone in her jet-black hair that hung to her waist like a dark velvet mantle. Shenkin lifted his head and waved to her, his steps quickening to reach her. Cathy was the sister of the O'Hara brothers who had helped in his rescue the day before. If they knew that Shenkin was seeing their sister there would be hell to pay. But from the first time Shenkin had seen her he was drawn to her heart-stopping sensual looks. The face of a Madonna, dark olive skin, large blue eyes that flashed a most unsaintly gaze. The gaze stirred his manhood as no other woman had done so far, she was like a drug or drink to him. One taste and every nerve in his body was aflame. She was wearing a black swirling skirt that fell to her feet, with just enough petticoat showing to catch the eye. A white, well nearly white, blouse failed to conceal the swell of her breasts, they quivered with every move of her wide hips. A colourful scarf tied around her neck completed a tantalising voluptuous figure.

The shawl she carried covered hands that were calloused and marked by the iron filings she handled at the Dowlais ironworks, she hated Shenkin to see them for they marred her beauty. At last Shenkin was at her side pulling her to him, they kissed hungrily. Breaking from each other she stepped back.

'Don't you look a bloody sight worse than after one of your fights. What did that old pit do to you, my milis?' she said, using the Gaelic word for 'sweet' that she always called him.

'I forgot to duck this time, lost the round to a pit prop and half the bloody roof of Waun Wyllt's number two pit,' Shenkin said, the charm of his smile spread over her, warm and enticing.

'So I heard, and if my brothers knew about you and me they'd have pulled down the other half of the roof on you.' Then looking up at him she said in a small voice. 'So many dead Shenkin; I work with Tommy Morgan's wife, may the saints watch over her.' Cathy said, crossing herself as she spoke. She touched the side of his face running her finger over the wound then up on tip toe to kiss him there.

'Willy Stitch said it will leave a scar blue in colour because of the coaldust.'

'Colourful,' said Cathy. 'Let me make it better my milis.' Saying so she pulled him to her, as she did, she opened the front of her blouse, nestling his face onto her full breasts, her nipples erect with arousal. He cupped one of the heavy breasts in his hand and took the nipple into his mouth. His other hand searched beneath her skirt. Cathy never wore underclothes soon he touched the heat of her womanhood. Laying back on the warm earth, she brought Shenkin down onto her. Unbuckling his wide leather belt, she hurriedly opened Shenkin's trouser front. Searching out his erect penis she grasped her hand around the hard shaft and began to caress him, first slowly then in a quickened pace until Shenkin groaned with pleasure. Lifting her skirt above her waist she guided him into her. They both gasped as they melted into each other's body. Shenkin was glad to be just himself at last, and to make love to this Irish beauty who gave herself so completely to him.

Afterwards they stayed in each other arms on that mountainside high above the squalor of their dirty black town. For these few hours the world was uncomplicated. It was made pure by the honesty of their love and their need for each other. Their passion spent Shenkin finally knew peace. Below them in the distance they could see the Waun Fair being set up for the coming week, all colour and fluttering flags. It would also be the setting of their rally; straightforward workingmen would put forward their support for reform. Worker self-assertion would be the main objective, and how best to bring this about by a petition to the king and parliament. Large numbers were hoped for by Shenkin and all the other leaders of the cause. The rally would be made up of all the active industries in South Wales as far afield as Monmouth. Shenkin's heartbeat faster at the thought of bringing change to his valley, where men could vote on their own future and destiny. His thoughts were broken by Cathy kissing him on the side of his face, a smile of satisfaction in her eyes. He looked down at her. 'What cariad, what is it my milis?' Shekin said, joining together their two languages in words of endearment.

'I see your fight with the pit roof hasn't effected any other part of your body Daniel Shenkin,' she said, moving her hand down between his legs. Thoughts of the rally left him and he turned eagerly towards her, but she held him back.

'Sure now that was no invitation, I've got to get away home. Sean will soon be back and Regan too they'll be looking for their supper and wondering where I am.' Seeing the disappointment on his face she said, 'Don't fret now for I'll see you here on Saturday night, so I will. My brothers will be out for the evening in the Glebe or the Castle Inn sinking jugs of ale and rearranging some of the furniture, and a few of the faces. See you then my milis,' she said. Then with a kiss she started down the mountain, but turned and ran back to him. She took the colourful scarf from around her neck and going up on tip toe she placed it around Shenkin's shoulders. 'To keep you safe and to leave my scent upon you.' Cathy said, a wicked look in her eyes, and then she was gone.

Shenkin knew the scarf was something she cherished, a smile came to his face and he held it to him tightly. *There on his bunk in the sick bay, in the middle of a great ocean, in his fevered restlessness he touched the scarf with a sea damp cold hand. Then his mind drifted back again.*

A few days later the Waun Wyllt Number 2 pit was closed. More roof falls and flooding had prevented men from any chance of digging out the dead, the galleries were closed forming a permanent grave. And Shenkin was out of work.

'No bad thing out of that pit.' his father said. 'A bloody death trap, like most of them. I'll speak to Sid Slope Daniel, see if he can get you a job at the ironworks. He owes me a few favours, he'll do it if he can.'

Sid Slope had one shoulder three inches lower then the other due to carrying bags of coal when he was six years old. Sid was now foreman at the Cyfarthfa Works slope and all. Shenkin's father had gone there from the pits a few years before when they needed more labour to meet the increasing orders for rails. Sid Williams, to give him his correct name, and his father had been childhood friends suffering many hardships together.

'They have a big contract from Russia, so I'm sure Sid will find room on my working gang for you,' said his father.

So Shenkin had followed his father again. This time into the heat of the blast furnaces. Dressed in clothes that were no protection against the hot flying cinders of the metal. He did not know then that it would only last but a short time, days in fact leading up to the fateful rally that would become not a rising but a riot that would fill the air with musket balls, bayonets, and stabbing pikes. It would change all their lives for ever.

Slowly in the frenzy of his delirium his fears turned to anger. Anger against the people who had driven his countrymen to use force of arms, as the only way to get justice. Anger at the rape of his land to make rich men richer, paid for with the blood and sorrow of a once great nation. Not only his land but the peoples of many lands, whose only crime was that they had something that another stronger nation wanted. Land, cattle, seas, minerals. His father had told him it was ever so and would be till man drew the final breath from his fellow man.

***

He felt his mind wander drifting in and out of awareness. The cabin was spinning, his breath coming in short rasping sounds. Sweat flowed out of him, he felt as if he was drowning. The wound in his side became a red-hot poker constantly stabbing him. The chains banged against the bulkhead, voices screamed out. Iron against iron slamed from somewhere deeper in the ship. A ship that rode the waves on its tossing, dipping course. Taking him towards a life sentence in a penal colony or a hangman's noose. That's if he made it through the night. With a great effort he lifted himself up on one elbow his hair falling free from the once colourful scarf, his eyes came wide open and he cried out, 'To hell with you all I will survive' then he collapsed back onto his bunk unconscious. The guard outside came awake with a start. 'Shut up you Welsh bastard, or I'll drop a few more chains on you,' he said angrily.

Then finding he needed to piss the guard relieved himself against the bulkhead. A rivulet of urine seeped under the sick bay door to join the other odours of Shenkin's place of suffering.

CHAPTER 6

'Come!' This in response to the knock on the captain's door. Tarn entered. 'Good morning sir.'

Not looking up Moxey studied the chart laid out in front of him. 'Tarn I think I said at the start of the forenoon watch sir, we are now well into the day,' said Moxey, irritably.

'Duties sir.'

'And they were?' said Moxey, still not looking up.

'Sick bay man and one of the crew ill, running a high temperature.'

'Bloody grog or the clap more like it.'

'I believe I am the doctor. I promise to offer no opinion on the charts,' Tarn said, his Irish temper beginning to rise.

'How dare you question my remarks. Your defence of the convict's behaviour last night at supper, fuelled by an excess of wine, my wine I might add, was unacceptable sir.' Moxey was now standing, the chart curled itself into a neat roll, it journeyed along the chart table and on to the floor.

'If I cannot express an opinion, perhaps I should excuse myself from your table, and drink my own wine.'

'I am master of this ship sir, and will run the crew, soldiers, and convicts my way.'

'I think the War Office, or the Commissioners of Victualling may see it differently. Blurred lines I think, as to where one authority ends and another begins,' said Tarn. Both men were now shouting.

This had always been a difficult area for the government. Both Moxey and Tarn knew it. Who should have the final say aboard a convict ship on the officer's respective areas of responsibilities.? Move was afoot to bring the Navy Board back into administration to resolve this problem.

'I sail this ship sir,' fumed Moxey. 'I also own it.'

'Under contract to the government sir. My duties sir, are to see to the wellbeing of the convict's health, the Commander of the Guard, the soldiers, passengers and crew.'

'I will captain this ship as I see fit.'

'Within the terms of the contract you signed captain.'

'You damn papist upstart,' shouted Moxey, red in the face.

'Politics are bad enough sir, but religion is not an area to get into on a long voyage, and on such a small ship in the middle of a bloody big ocean.'

At that moment Elizabeth came into the cabin. 'You are heard on the quarterdeck uncle, both of you.'

'Knock when you enter my cabin,' said Moxey, still shouting.

'Please lower your voice uncle, I am not one of the crew.'

Both men said nothing for a while, reluctant in the presence of a woman, to continue in the manner and language they had been using.

'That will be all for the moment Tarn. Return to your duties,' said Moxey, his voice still shaking with anger.

'Sir,' said Tarn, slamming the cabin door hard behind him.

Elizabeth caught up with Tarn halfway across the quarterdeck. 'Doctor Tarn this is my fault I fear, I am most sorry.'

'No, not really it's an old quarrel aboard these ships, who has the final say, when and in what area. One I hope that will soon be made more clear in the future. So don't worry yourself I have been through it many times before,' said a resigned Tarn.

'Doctor Tarn?'

'Yes, my dear.' Forever entranced by this beautiful young woman.

'May I see the convict Shenkin?' she said, quickly adding, 'in your presence of course,' in a small voice.

'What! Why and for what purpose madam?' Tarn said, full of disquiet.

'I don't really know, I admire him he has a way about him,' she said then added. 'To think of him alone in a cold damp cell, is most disturbing.'

'It's the sick bay madam, not a cell.' But then Tarn hesitated, he had caught a look on the girl's face.

'Oh no I am not playing cupid to two so ill-matched a young couple. The captain, your uncle, would put me in irons. And he'd be right to do so.'

'I don't know what you mean Mr Tarn, I really do not,' said Elizabeth Moxey, blushing a deep red.

But Tarn had seen it. 'You may well blush you should be ashamed of yourself young lady, be off do some stitching or such.' Tarn said, making his way to below decks.

There he found Shenkin hanging off the side of his bunk. His right leg twisted badly around the chain. 'Guard!' shouted Tarn.

'Sir'

'Remove these leg irons.' the man hesitated.

'He's my patient I'll take responsibility. Damn it man, remove them.'

The guard dropped to his knee. Taking the irons away he lifted Shenkin back on to his bunk. Tarn examined Shenkin's right leg which was cut and badly bruised. He applied balm to both ankles. Shenkin was delirious, sweat ran over his whole body. Tarn felt his forehead, hot feverish, high temperature. 'It's a critical time, he'll either come through it or not,' Tarn said. Shenkin heard nothing, he was still in his own world, muttering something or other, that Tarn could not make out. Then Shenkin lifted himself off the bunk shouting some kind of threat or call. Collapsing back on to the bunk he drifted again into an incoherent flood of words.

Tarn left him to his pain and restlessness. Telling the guard he'd call in again during the afternoon watch.

'Right sir.' The cabin door slammed, lock clicked, darkness reigned. It made no difference to Shenkin, he was in another place, another time.

It was just as well for at that moment a scream went out that cut through the ship like a knife. It came from the well of the top deck where the chained convicts were being held in a line waiting to be branded. The men were covered in urine and excrement their skins puckered by damp, lice bites decorated their necks, arms and legs. Their hair a tangled greasy dirty mess. The rats had left even larger bites the wounds weeping and saltwater burnt. Surrounding them were the soldiers their muskets at the ready to quell any resistance or disturbances. Sergeant Ketch, cosh in hand, administered the proceedings.

Captain Moxey stood on the quarterdeck looking down. 'Lieutenant Feltsham this I think is a good time to hose them down.'

'Yes indeed sir. Sergeant hose them down.'

'Sir.'

Crew members began pumping seawater. Soon the whole deck was awash, chains clanged as convicts fell over as they became caught up in the links of chain. After a moment or so, the lieutenant called for fresh water buckets to sluice them down.

'Don't waste that water, Lieutenant.' shouted Moxey.

'No sir. Ketch bring up the fires.'

Two crew and two solders lifted iron rods that passed through a large brazier that they placed in the middle of the deck. Out of the main body of the fire poked two branding rods, at the end of which the iron had been twisted into the shape of the Government property mark. Each convict would be spreadeagled and leather strapped to a wooden framed triangle. The convict's right-hand palm was turned upwards, he was then branded in the soft middle of the palm. One guard stood by the side of the fire to hand the next iron to be used. On the quarterdeck, Lieutenant Feltsham stood by the side of Doctor Tarn. 'First time for me to witness the procedure don't you know.' Feltsham said, a vicarious look upon his face that caused his lower lip to tremble, which Tarn found disgusting.

'It is barbaric sir, it's out of the Middle Ages. To brand men for the rest of their lives is intolerable and a condemnation of a so-called civilised age. Also as a physician I find it completely unacceptable to injure the human body so,' said Tarn, his hand tight around the tin of balm that he held ready to treat the convict's wounds.

'But they are the property of the government sir and must be seen to be,' said the Lieutenant, the quiver still on his lower lip and now in his voice. In the line of men stood Collins his face a mask of terror. Behind him Regan O'Hara was supporting the lad with his arm. Collins had already collapsed once at the sight of what was about to happen to him. 'Sure it'll be over in no time at all,' said O'Hara.

'No! No! Regan don't let them do it to me,' cried Collins.

Ketch moved close to Collins. 'If you don't stop whining, I'll have them brand you on both palms, you snivelling little bastard.'

Regan shot a look of sheer anger at Ketch. 'You got something to say, you Irish bastard?' said Ketch.

Regan said nothing as they shuffled forward his arm still around Collins. Looking down he saw that the lad was urinating, the side of his leg led to a pool on the deck. Collins was trembling like a leaf. Regan squeezed his arm whispering. 'Soon over now lad couple more and we'll be through it.'

The air was soon heavy with the smell of burning flesh, scream after scream went up from the branded convicts. Then they pulled Collins forward, fear produce strength in Collins that took them all by surprise. Collins hit out at one of the guards then kicked the other and he was running across the deck towards the rails his leg irons banging at the side of his ankles. Ketch rushed across to him and brought the cosh down hard over his head. Collins went down in a heap. 'Get him on the triangle and get him done then throw him in his cell,' shouted Ketch. At this O'Hara swung the two guards that were holding him into one another, both went down. The nearest soldier came forward thrusting out his bayonet into O'Hara's belly. O'Hara tangled the bayonet in his shirt front then pulling the soldier to him he head butted him in the face, blood flew across the deck as Lieutenant Feltsham together with Tarn came hurriedly down the companionway. O'Hara was running towards Ketch who in panic fell across the brazier letting out a cry as his leg pressed against the hot side of the fire. Hot coals spread over the deck seamen rushed to the buckets of water that stood against the gunnels. By now O'Hara had his hands around the triangle and with one mighty heave he pulled the side of the triangle off the deck splitting the wood along the length of the frame. Then four soldiers were on him pinning him to the ground. 'Right screamed Ketch we'll do it the hard way. Get the iron straight jacket Burke and the spiked collar.'

'For pity's sake man can't you see that he is now held firm?' Tarn said.

From the quarterdeck Moxey called down. 'Stay out of this doctor the man is ours until we have finished branding him, then you can administer your balm not before. Lieutenant Feltsham carry on if you please.'

The Lieutenant gave a sharp nod. 'Do what is needed Sergeant Ketch.'

'Sir,' said Ketch.

Moxey continued. 'Then put the man in double irons and spiked collar also on bread and water rations for one week, for dangerous behaviour and damage to the ship's property. Place a grating against the rail Mr Lawson to spreadeagle the rest of the convicts for branding.

'Sir.'

'Remember we have two sick convicts, they too must be branded,' said Moxey

'I object most strongly captain those men are too ill for such barbaric treatment,' said Tarn.

'Are you questioning my orders once again sir?' said Moxey the anger raising in his voice.

'Can we discuss this in your cabin sir?'

'No sir, we can not. You heard me Lieutenant Feltsham I expect it to be done.'

'Then if the sick men die, I will state in my report that the branding contributed to their deaths,' said Tarn

Moxey paused.

'Sergeant Ketch the sick convicts will be branded, when they are deemed well enough.'

'Sir,' said Ketch, a look of dissatisfaction spreading across his face, his hand pressed hard against the burn mark on his leg.

Tarn straightened up with a look of resignation, at least the sick were spared for the moment.

So the morning into the afternoon went on, convict after convict was branded until only the men who were sick that day remained free from the mark.

CHAPTER 7

'We must have more say in our future, we must, we must...

'Take up arms like the farmers and weavers,' shouted Billy-one-leg, holding on to a fence pole while swinging his crutch. Billy had lost his leg in an underground explosion when he was only eight years old. Mind, he walked well enough after sinking a few ales in Castle Inn pub.

'And have the troops from Brecon barracks down on us like last time,' Idris Shenkin said. 'No! we'll not have this called a riot, a rising yes, but not a riot.' It was stated bluntly.

Regan O'Hara pushed forward. 'To hell with it, you and the whole bloody working committee. We are getting nowhere, so we are. I'm for destroying the owners houses, burn the bastards into giving us the vote.'

'You are not in bloody Ireland now, look what that got you,' said Shenkin, moving to meet O'Hara in the middle of the throng of men. Idris grabbed Owain Shenkin's hand to stop him following his brother. Owain pulled away from his father, but stood still as both men glared at each other. A furnace man from Dowlais Ironworks called out. 'They'll never listen to us, unless we cost them their profits.'

'YES! That's right,' came shouts from a great number of the men.

Shenkin and O'Hara backed away as the crowd shouted among themselves at what needed to be done next. On a grey overcast evening 2000 men had gathered on Waun Hill above the furnace iron melting, coal burning industrial town of Merthyr. The mass rally the largest ever gathered was held just a few hundred yards from the Waun Fair. A holiday atmosphere permeated the air, a carnival damp spring celebration this late Mayday. Men drinking beer, unfurling white flags with 'God Save William IV' and 'Reform Now' marked in charcoal across the sheets. Beer swilled down with the intoxicating talk of worker self-assertion, votes for the working man. Rebellion filled the air. They pushed and shoved each other to hear what their leaders were saying. Some men were there to report back to their masters the ironworks and coal owners. The leaders kept an eye on the ones they knew were scabs, knowing that to call them out would cause the crowd to lynch them. Idris Shenkin wanted to keep it as peaceful as possible.

'Will you all listen, just listen,' shouted Idris Shenkin. We are here from everyone one of the ironworks Cyfarthfa, Dowlais, Plymouth and Penydarren. Together with the men of the collieries and mines. Each representative has given their view, we are all agreed we must improve our lot. Well now is our chance to do this right. The Reform Bill is again in front of the new Whig Government, so we will put our petition to parliament and the works owners in writing. Firmly stating our needs, framed within the spirit of the Bill. We must act now while the political crisis on the Reform Bill is at its most critical time. The Lords cannot continue to reject the Bill, not in the face of mounting public demand for Reform, our petition will be a contribution to this pressure. All over the country working men are rising their voices, we must join them; we must be heard for the sake of all our futures.' The crowd roared their approval as Shenkin's father continued. His strong sober voice had a calming effect on the mass assembly of men, each straining to hear his words. 'We will be following the thinking of men of reason, of just reform this is the moment, this is the right time,' he shouted. Men pushed forward to get close to their leaders. Idris Shenkin turned to his son Daniel who was standing at his side. 'The committee have given a number of speeches but my son has also asked to say a few words.' At this O'Hara shouted out again his broad Irish accent cutting through the general noise like a ripsaw.

'Here we bloody go again the Shenkin family telling us what to do, they think they know it all, so they do. Well, they bloody don't and I'm here to say so.'

Daniel Shenkin grabbed O'Hara's coat and pulled him forward. 'Go on try it,' said O'Hara, itching for a fight. Daniel's father stepped between them. 'Fighting between ourselves that's just what they want. A rabble to deal with, and every justification to call in the army. We are not going down the catastrophic Irish route, starved out by their landowners, many forced to work for even less than before, famine and hardship to endure. An Ireland ruled over by a handful of wealthy men, all of them mostly living in London. Poor and poorer still, is not the way. Is that want you want O'Hara, well is it?'

Regan O'Hara said nothing.

Idris Shenkin continued. 'Listen to me all of you, this Reform Bill will go through even in the face of Wellington's resistance, even he cannot stop the tide of history. We now have Lord Grey pushing hard for it. They know without electoral reform the alternative could mean revolution. Please I beg you, let my son speak.'

The wind blew hard into the faces of the men assembled as they argued the merits of which way forward, then a hush as Daniel Shenkin moved onto an area of higher ground. An imposing figure powerfully built, his arms in the air to quieten the crowd. The scar from the prop splinter still vivid on the side of his face. His long black hair now tied back with Cathy's scarf. O'Hara was looking at it but could not connect it yet, but something about it troubled him. Shenkin let his gaze take in the crowd, more men were arriving all the time. I only hope I can find such words as my father, he thought to himself. Before he could say a word O'Hara turned to the crowd.

'I'll not listen, or wait any longer, all us Irish in China district are for taking up arms and torches. We'll burn the bastards into giving us the vote, so we will.' The group around him, Irish to a man, roared their agreement.

'China's full of loudmouths, pubs, and brothels. More into shouting and bragging what they can do, then what they are able to do.' This from Billy-one-leg who was now standing right by the side of O'Hara. O'Hara's huge fist flew sideways catching Billy on the side of his head, dropping him like a sack of coal. Falling down on him O'Hara pinned Bill's arms with his knees and began punching him in the face. Shenkin's arm came across O'Hara's throat pulling him off. Then dragging O'Hara to his feet, Shenkin spun him around all-in-one violent fluid movement.

'Right you bastard, let's see how good you are facing someone your own size and with a full set of pegs.' Idris Shenkin tried to stop his son, but it was too late, Daniel's temper was unleashed there was no stopping him now. He stood back and held on to Owain whose eyes were alight with excitement.

O'Hara was no stranger to a brawl. Coming level with Shenkin's face he head butted him, the force sent Shenkin reeling into the cheering crowd who were already forming a circle.

This was better than the fights outside the pubs in China Town on a Saturday night. Chinatown, so named by the Welsh because everyone who lived there was a foreigner. Nationalities of imported cheap labour, living in squalor and ignominy. These two men represented the two areas of the town. One like his father full of pride, determination, and rage. The other only in this black hellhole of a valley because his own country had starved him out of his beloved Ireland.

'I should have left you under that fucking roof fall Shenkin,' O'Hara said, throwing a solid punch at Shenkin's head. Shenkin ducked under it, hitting O'Hara in the kidneys, then the stomach. Surprise crossed O'Hara's face then he recovered and charged into Shenkin with swinging fists. They were well matched, both young and powerfully built with sledgehammer fists. Toughened by the demands of heavy labour in the pits. Hardened by the heat of the blast furnaces, tempered by the rain and numbing cold of the Welsh mountains and Irish bogs. O'Hara was the taller by a good six inches and heavier by at least four stone. He was a massive giant of a man. But Shenkin looked the fighter as he squared up to the Irishman. A bare-knuckle boxer fighting for money since he was eighteen years old. His father had taught him everything about boxing, every clean and dirty way there was to deliver solid damaging punches. His fists held high, perfectly balanced on the balls of his feet. Shenkin danced around O'Hara, hitting him with a combination of left and right blows. O'Hara's head jerked back in unison to the accurate delivery of the punches. He had to give ground pressing against the circle of onlookers, who pushed him back into the centre of the ring of men.

O'Hara charged forward, using his bulk to force Shenkin off balance and grabbed him in a bear hug. Shenkin gasped for breath as his legs were lifted off the ground. He pushed O'Hara's head back with the palm of his left hand, and drove the edge of his right-hand fingers into O'Hara's exposed throat. A gurgling sound came from O'Hara's lips as he let Shenkin go. Shenkin stepped back to give full shoulder and body weight to his punches. He counterpunched with left and right jabs, splitting open O'Hara's lips top and bottom, then a short right cross. The punch could only have travelled six inches, but in that short devastating distance it caused O'Hara's face to alter into a distorted mask, but the blow had not yet completed its journey of destruction, Shenkin followed through with his forearm then his elbow. His elbow crashed into the side of O'Hara's jaw. The grate of bone on bone was heard above the shouts of the baying crowd.

O'Hara moved back loose-jawed. In desperation he swung his head across Shenkin's head with all the strength he could muster. When they came out of the clinch Shenkin's scar was beginning to open, and blood was streaming from O'Hara's mouth. But again, it was Shenkin who had the look of cold control. With O'Hara lashing out in temper and frustration. Shaking his head to clear the blood from running into his eye, Shenkin crouched and went in for the kill.

The front row of the crowd was splattered with blood. Shenkin stepped in between O'Hara's swinging arms, driving a solid blow under his heart then another into his big beer belly. O'Hara's bent double bringing his giant frame down, arms hanging loose at his sides. Kill the body my son and the head dies, his father had told him many times. Shenkin let out an animal snarl and unleashed a right upper cut on to the point of O'Hara's jaw. A crack of bone resonated around the mob of men. O'Hara went down as if a trapdoor had opened under him. He hit the cold hard mountain ground with a sickening thump even then to his credit O'Hara tried to get up. Shenkin smiled in spite of himself. O'Hara got up as far as onto his knees, then with a grunt fell forward face down. It was over.

Blood streaming down his face Shenkin turned to the mob. 'Well! Anyone else in a hurry to join O'Hara? If so, now is the time to step forward,' said Shenkin, his legs apart in perfect balance, shirt sleeves rolled up, fists still clenched. No one moved, the crowd was silent.

In heartbeats laced with lust for more blood and the terror of the moment, the crowd shrank back from O'Hara crumbled body. Then the silence was broken the moment gone a few spots of light drizzly rain fell from the grey sky.

'That showed the bloody ugly swine,' Billy-one-leg said. Billy was on his feet wiping blood from his nose, his crutch jammed back under his left arm pit.

'Shut up you,' Shenkin said. 'What have we proved except that we behave as the gentry expect us to. Brawling amongst ourselves like the animals they believe us to be.'

Stooping down Shenkin helped O'Hara to his feet. 'Look at us, me with stitching opened that Willy needs to re-embroider and a black eye come morning. And you with probably a broken jaw. What have we proved, the owners are still calling the tune and we don't have the vote.'

O'Hara started to say something but his mouth could not form the words due to a swelling at the side of his face. He just nodded his head in agreement.

'Right,' Shenkin said, turning to O'Hara's friends. 'Get him to Willy Stitch, he'll soon wire the jaw up. At least it will stop him talking for a while.' A smile played across Shenkin's bleeding and bruised face as he spoke. In his favour O'Hara tried to smile too, but it came to the eyes rather than the lips, they were beyond making any shape.

The crowd gathered around Shenkin waiting to hear what he had to say. All eager for leadership.

Calm now and back in control Shenkin turned to address the crowd. 'My father and the others who have spoken for the Reform Bill are right. We must earn it by workers' votes, by petitioning the king and parliament for Reform, for the abolition of the Court of Requests, an increase in the poor wages in the iron and coal industries, safer working conditions. To do this we need to form a strong union now and show the owners that we stand together in solidarity. You have been petitioning Parliament for years but no notice has ever been taken of it. Now that Reform is in the air, we must show our unity by bring this to a head swiftly. I advise we strike at the earliest time.' A gasp went up. 'Yes! Damn it strike, stop work, close the works. said Shenkin. Shenkin's father gasped, he was not expecting this. Shenkin went on. 'Someone said earlier hit their profits then they'll take notice, I agree. While on strike we prepare a petition then vote for someone to take it to the owners and speak for us.'

For a while there was silence, some murmurings from the older men. A lone voice in the crowd shouted out.

'No need for a vote, Shenkin's our man.'

Then a steady pulsing cry rose up from the crowd. 'SHENKIN! SHENKIN! SHENKIN!'

Idris Shenkin turned to his son. 'The die is cast my son, it's you they want, no need for any vote. They will follow your proposal my son, they will strike and may God be with us all.'

'Amen,' said Shenkin.

One man close to Shenkin, a tethered goat at his side, tore off his white shirt. Bending down and taking a butcher's knife from his belt he slit the goat's throat. All eyes turn to the sound of the animal's scream. The man, a herdsman from Dowlais Top, dipped the shirt into the gushing blood. Then tying it to a spiked pole he held it high above him like a red flag. A second man a loaf of bread in his hand speared it on to the top.

'Yes,' Shenkin said. 'Our blood and our body the symbol of a workingman.' A Welsh hymn began in the crowd it swept through them like a wave. Slowly the mass of men began to make their way down the mountain.

O'Hara supported by his fellow countrymen walked towards Chinatown. The Welsh were by now chanting a warrior's song from an ancient battle. Pride swelled, the red flag waved, the Irish started up a Gaelic war song. The few Scots among began a reel, the Spanish clapped their hands and stamped their feet in tune with the beat of the voices. The ironmasters and works owners in their big mansions held their breath as they looked out of their fine bow fronted windows at the candlelit procession coming down the mountain side like an avalanche, the sound rattled the windows and their nerves.

Shenkin felt a shiver go through him as he watched his people making a stand for their future, he only hoped he'd made the right decision. Father and son stood with their backs to the valley. It was dark now their shoulders and heads were framed by the lights from the ironworks furnaces behind them, furnaces that would soon be shut down for the first time in a decade. Father and son appeared like giants casting their shadows over the whole mountain side. Dominant, strong, unwavering in the course they had set themselves. They turned to join the crowd and walked towards Chinatown. May their God indeed walk with them thought Shenkin.

The China district of Merthyr Tydfil was notorious. A lawless area of the town where a reputation was gained by hucksters, circus performers, boys doing tricks for beer money, ballad singers, gambling and the sexual predilections of every kind that the collective minds of a dozen or more nationalities could think up.

Here across the River Taff on bridges over the Morlais brook they brought their communal festivals and marriages that were sanctified across the bars of the many public houses that littered the Glebeland area. Blessed by beer and washed down with gut rot gin. Petty loans by unscrupulous moneylenders that trapped the inhabitance between the company truck shops and the Court of Request for unpaid debts. All excises in self-help and mutual mistrust, cloaked in fellowship and clouded by liquor.

Shenkin had collected Willy Stitch along the way. They came to a row of hovels dug into the side of a cinder tip, held up with stolen pit props; it was not much but the O'Hara's called it home. Shenkin ducked inside the one they carried O'Hara into. Inside the walls were whitewashed with lime, an upturned wooden crate served as a table. Straw beds on the floor, a few plates and the like, some rickety old chairs, a separate room for their sister Cathy. A worn-down broom stood forlornly in one corner. Cathy hurried to help make a bed for her brother, but without waiting for the straw to be plumped up the men dropped him on the earth floor. Lime flakes lifted around them like a small white cloud.

'Sweet Mary in heaven, what's happened?' Cathy said, placing some straw and rags under Regan's head.

She looked up as Shenkin came through the door way. 'Is it you that did this.'

'Yes,' said Shenkin.

At that moment Regan saw the scarf again then, looked at Cathy and made the connection. 'That's that's...' but the words were as mangled as his face.

Cathy also saw the scarf. 'My choice, my decision, so mind your own bloody business or I'll give you another clout,' she said, to her brother eyes blazing.

'But,' said Regan.

'Shut up or you'll have no one to care for you, so you won't. Leave this moment Shenkin, I'll deal with you later.'

Liam O'Toole, one of the six men that it took to carry Regan down the mountain smiled. 'More comfortable now Regan, bleeding here rather than on that dirty old mountain.'

Willy Stitched pushed passed him. Shenkin nodded to him. 'Do what you can Willy.' Then turned and left, passing Sean O'Hara at the doorway.

'Yes, Sean before you ask I did it.'

'Then step outside...'

Regan O'Hara called out. 'It was a fair fight... Sean, leave it,' he said, stumbling over his words.

Sean O'Hara looked down at his brother. 'Jesus, you look a mess man. I'm at work and I'm told my brother has taken on Daniel Shenkin. Dear God, didn't you know he beat every kind of hell out of Cardiff's bare-knuckle champion.'

Regan let his eyes do the talking, because the swelling on the side of his face prevented any further words

'Let me take a look,' said Willy. Willy Thomas was a small man with a shock of white hair that flowed down to his shoulders. Willy was not a doctor, in fact he had no medical training whatever, but he could stitch together a split eye, set a broken leg on man or beast, cure a hangover, hiccups, and toothache – usually with pliers – deliver a baby or a lamb, and all at a charge of six pennies and a bottle of gin.

O'Hara groaned as Willy pulled his head around to take a closer look.

'I understand this is young Shenkin's handy work.' Willy said, squinting at the swollen jaw. 'Good thing he was not in training, bare-knuckle fighting then see, and the Cardiff champion was in a hell of a worse state. I should know boyo for wasn't I the cut-man that night.' Heads nodded around him in remembrance.

'I was just telling him that Willy,' said Sean. 'The stupid bastard steps off the boat and thinks he can take on Wales. Dear sweet Mary and all the saints in heaven, will you just look at the state him.'

Regan O'Hara turned his eyes to heaven despairingly at the unfairness of life that had brought him to this black inferno, so far from the green hills of his beloved Ireland. Rubbing his first finger and thumb together as a sign that he wanted to know how much?

'Don't worry about it Shenkin dropped me the coins on his way out, also a bottle of gin at the Glebe Inn later.'

O'Hara made a mental note of his debt with a nod of his head.

'I'll square it Regan,' said his brother.

Willy leant forward. 'Open your mouth now for me to pour down a drop of this lovely gin. Some of you hold him down so I can get to work,' Willy said, pushing his coal dirt fingers into O'Hara's mouth. Having probed around Willy looked up at the men around him and smiled.

'Well can you believe it, Shenkin must be losing his touch the jaw's not broken, some teeth top and bottom have gone mind. It's just a dislocated jaw. I'll have it right in no time, but it's going to hurt like hell. None of us will feel it mind, just you Regan, so that's alright isn't it?' Everyone including Sean laughed. 'I'm going to push it back into place and bind it tight, so don't join in the laughing see, there's a good boy.'

Willy didn't wait for a response his nimble hands twisted his patient's head sharp to one side. A crack rang out that replaced the one lost on the mountain top. O'Hara's bones were back where they belonged.

'There now you're your ugly old self again,' Willy said, binding up the jaw.

But Regan O'Hara heard not a word, he had passed out. Willy let him hit the ground. Then wiping his hands on Regan's shirt, he stepped back to admire his work.

'Dear God why don't you jump all over him, call yourself a bloody doctor,' Cathy said, fussing around her brother to make him more comfortable.

Willy looked shocked. 'No one can say I've ever called myself a doctor, oh no. I'll be going now, if he is in any pain and he will be, just give him some gin. With that Willy was gone coins and all.

*How many would stop working, hundreds, thousands. He'd take the petition to the owners. Once we have the vote... once we .... 'If we get the vote...' Covered in sweat Shenkin turned again on his salty bunk of torment.

**

The permanent red glow from the blast furnaces against the velvet black sky was giving way to the grey of another day. Shenkin's face was home to two new stitches at the top of the scar. The scar prickled, but Willy had said not to scratch it. He felt that the itch was worse than the damn fight. Soon they'd start the strike, the valley would be silent for the first time in his memory. The cold early morning mist settled like a white shroud over the town. Shenkin shivered. The air was heavy with the pollution of industry. It clogged the throat and nose while hot cinders filled the air, red flying dust that burnt the eyes. But strange as it seems it cleared the minds of those who strived to get above the grime and squalor. But at what cost, one way or another this week would tell.

Shenkin looked up has he walked towards the dull red glow of the blast furnaces. The steady thump, thump of the hammers beat into the ground with a relentless ear-splitting rhythm. The clanking of the rolling mills and the confused din of machinery that worked twenty-four hours a day. Production was still high at the two main works. The railway boom all over Europe was demanding more and more of their high-quality rails. This ensured that the Shenkin family, at least at the moment, were on good wages but at the smaller works orders were drying up and wages were being cut. The truck shops still kept their prices high, even in the face of the practice being made illegal. Notices were already nailed up telling the workers, that to stay competitive the ironmasters would be cutting wages. Not profits, wages.

Larger profits at the expense of men's earnings. Cutbacks would be felt at the food table, on the lack of clothes and shoes of their children.

Top wages of twenty shillings a week for skilled men at the ironworks and in the pits were in many cases lower than a year ago. The cost of living on the other hand went steadily upwards hand in hand with despair and hunger.

Shenkin looked at the markings on the side of the rails. They read like an atlas of Europe, at least to those who could read. Read or not they stacked the rails as high as they could reach men, women, and children some as young has seven. Lifting, straining, drained of energy and dignity their faces as white as china cups.

There must be more for us then this, Shenkin was thinking as Willy Stitch came around the side of a coal dram.

'You are getting soft in your old age Shenkin, O'Hara's going to live. But he'll find it difficult to smile for a few weeks mind. Still, it was not much of a smile to begin with,' Willy said, with a grin. Turning to Shenkin he looked at the new stitches he'd put in the night before at the Glebe Inn.

'It's as fine a job as any surgeon in the country. But you will have a vivid blue scar mind, from the coaldust left in the wound. Willy shook his head.

'You'll be looking like a piece of embroidery from Jones the Drapes if you keep on fighting with fists and timber props, boyo.'

Looking up at Shenkin Willy changed the subject. 'I hear you and the other leaders will speak for all the men in the ironworks and pits, is that so?'

'Someone needs to.' Shenkin said, with a shrug of his broad shoulders.

'And you think its you do you?'

Shenkin turned. 'At least I'm one of them Willy.'

'Yes, and it's you that will be out in front when the trouble starts, just like your father was in the 20s.'

'The London political pamphlets are saying we must establish workers' rights, and to do it by democratic means.' Shenkin laughed at the futility of his own words.

'In the meantime?' said Willy.

'In the meantime, children die of hunger, women in giving birth, and men are old before their time. If that doesn't get them then cholera or typhus will. I think it's time we had a say in how we die don't you?'

Willy smiled for he had seen it all before. 'You will give them this say, will you?'

'A fairer one for my sons and their sons, if that means being out in front then so be it,' said Shenkin, walking towards the heat of the blast furnaces.

CHAPTER 8

Tarn swayed along the passageway with Elizabeth Moxey following behind him. The weather was now a great deal warmer. The sea a greenie-blue, the ship's calmer movements more pleasant after the violence of the past long weeks. The convicts were on the main deck scrubbing the planking, and cleaning up after the stormy weather. The soldiers had mounted guard around them, with Ketch shouting out orders to his men and convicts. First Mate Lawson watched with disgust from the quarterdeck at the brutal handling of the prisoners, but his orders were clear the military were responsible for the convicts' discipline and work routine. He turned to Tarn with a curt acknowledgement. 'Good morning doctor, Miss Moxey,' Lawson said, touching his hat.

'And a fine morning it is Mr Lawson but why the grim look, man?'

'I am all for discipline sir, but Ketch is hard on these convicts. The lash and that cosh fall too many times. Lawson paused has he looked down at the scene below them the distaste etched deep in his weathered face.' Turning to Tarn he said. 'Another of the crew became ill this morning doctor, and two of the convicts I understand. If we add injury to the sick list you'll be hard pressed sir.'

'Yes, you are right I'll speak to the captain. I'll see the sick crew members on the afternoon watch first, then I'll examine the convicts.'

'Ay, ay, sir.'

'Thank you, Mr Lawson.'

Moving to the companionway, Tarn turned to Elizabeth. 'It is a brutal world you find yourself in my dear. I would not have brought a young woman of breeding on to any convict ship. You must not judge your feelings against your own place in society. This is a desperate class of men, ruthless and unpredictable. They would not hesitate to resort to the most violent of behaviour.' Then he added, 'Ketch, while I do not condone his methods, knows this. However, I must say Shenkin seems to be a cut above the rest, with a strange sense of honour, if a dangerous one. But this request is not the right thing to do, the captain will have every grounds to reprimand me,' he said.

'Only if he finds out doctor,' Elizabeth said, with a flutter of her eyes.

'But why the interest, apart from the young devil's good looks. And have I not already said such an attraction is ill founded.'

'Please doctor, it is not such an indelicate thing as that. No, I simply wish to see how the poor man is. After all he was defending the young convict from great harm. I was also at risk at that moment, and many weeks have passed since the incident, has it not?'

'It's a mistake I know it is, I know it. You are taking advantage of a man's nature madam, so you are.'

'Come now doctor this is a long voyage, I am bored with the endless monotonous routine of the ship, indulge me in this please.'

At mealtimes Elizabeth Moxey had flirted shamefully with Tarn. Mrs Scrimshaw was embarrassed by the girlish laughter, followed by the womanly eyes that Miss Moxey cast upon the Surgeon-Superintendent. It did not seem to interest the captain who had spent more time at sea then in the company of his family. He regarded his brother's child almost as a stranger. Often as not he steered clear of any discussion with his niece. However, from time to time he would remonstrate with her, but to little avail. He contented himself that she took after her mother and that was an end to it. The captain had been against his brother's marriage and had warned his brother that strong willed women brought nothing but sorrow. Until their death from fever in India after twenty-two years of marriage the union had been a very loving and a successful one. The captain never referred to it, and let his niece's foolish banter with Tarn run its course, he had a ship to govern, and that was an end to it.

Lieutenant Feltsham was put out by Elizabeth's attention to Tarn, so had turned to his uncle for conversation. After dinner they had each gone to their cabins. Except for Tarn and Elizabeth. Who approached the companionway to the between decks. 'Can I not dissuade you from this folly madam?' Not waiting for an answer Tarn went on. 'It was the wine and those eyes that lead me to promise this, so it was. And don't go giving me that look of yours, I can feel them through my back bone, so I can.' Tarn said, shaking his head in bewilderment that he had agreed to this lunacy.

'Just one quick look and I'll go straight back to my cabin, I promise,' Elizabeth said, pressing a dainty silk handkerchief to her nose, as the stench from the convicts quarters greeted them.

Tarn shrugged. 'He is not an animal in a cage to be gaped at.'

'No of course not,' Elizabeth said, trying to cover her nose and descend the ladder at the same time.

At the bottom of the companionway, they found Burke. He was carrying a tin cup full of water. A look of embarrassment spread across his face, the scar below his right eye twitched, at being caught taking sustenance to a sick convict. This was added to further, as the flying petticoats and white muslin dress of Miss Elizabeth meet his gaze, revealing a shapely ankle.

Flustered Burke blurted out. 'Sir! sick man calling out for water, thought I'd just take some into him, so he'd stop his howling.'

Tarn nodded while turning to help the captain's niece down the last few rungs of the companionway.

'Very well Burke unlock the door or we'll be here when the captain makes his rounds, and not a word about Miss Elizabeth being here.'

'About who sir?'

'Good man.'

The guard stood to the side as Burke unlocked the sick bay door. They were met by a call from Shenkin for water. Burke moved to Shenkin's side.

'Not too much now, dip a cloth in the water and just dribble it over his mouth,' Tarn said.

Shenkin splattered over the offered water. His hair wet with sweat, his face blotched with fever. Elizabeth Moxey let out a gasp at the sight of the man and his horrendous surroundings. Shenkin made a gurgling sound as he managed to swallow some of the water. Then fell back mumbling incoherently. The headscarf was tangled with his hair, his right hand held it tightly.

Bending down Tarn bathed his patient's brow, then kept his hand on the forehead for a moment. Shaking his head, the doctor stood back. 'The fever is still upon him, but the crisis cannot be long now.'

'He must be moved from this filthy place at once,' Elizabeth said, each word she spoke was laced with pity.

'I fear the captain would not permit it madam. This is where all ill convicts are kept and for that matter any of the crew.'

'But the man will die down here. It's damp and cold, the air heavy with stench.

Tarn shrugged his shoulders. 'Then die he will for I have done all I can, but if the fever breaks, then he stands a slim chance.'

'Is that all you can do, or say?'

'What more do you think I can do?'

'Are you not the Surgeon-Superintendent aboard this ship?' Elizabeth Moxey said, her voice rising.

'Madam! May I remined you that you should not be down here,' Tarn said, irritability creeping into his voice. 'Also you will change your tone of voice when addressing me.'

Burke embarrassingly shifted his feet the scar at his eye twitching. The guard quietly closed the cabin door.

Apart from Shenkin's delirious murmurings, silence fell over the sick bay.

For a while they all listened to Shenkin ramblings as he twisted and turned. Then Elizabeth broke the silence. 'I apologise doctor,' she said, dropping her eyes, 'but upon my word I feel we must do something.'

Tarn studied the young woman; while she rubbed her bare arms against the chill of the damp cabin. This was more than idle curiosity or the need to break the monotony of a long voyage. Was it possible that a moment's gaze upon a stranger's face, a man who was a convicted felon, had struck at the heart of this woman? Perhaps this is what love is; he had often known lust but regrettable love had eluded him.

Taking a deep breath Tarn placed a hand upon her shoulder. He noticed there were tears in the beautiful eyes of Miss Elizabeth Moxey. A smile spread across his face as the sight of her tears touch his Irish heart. 'Young and in love, so you are,' said Tarn, he realised to his horror it was tinged with a little jealousy.

Placing his hand upon Elizabeth's shoulder he spoke in a tender tone, a tone he had not used in many years. 'Elizabeth my dear lovely girl, while I am envious of your regard for this young rogue, it's a hopeless state of affairs.

She looked up at Tarn and heaved a sigh. 'I know I am being foolish Doctor Tarn but I....' Unable to finish she dabbed at her eyes.

Burke could think of nowhere to look, so fumbled with the keys. The scar around his eye now twitching vigorously. Tarn noticed his discomfort and thought; what fools we men are, self-conscious in the presence of true feelings and to find them on a convict ship of all places.

'Listen my dear, not only you but Burke too should not be here either. Is that not so, Corporal?'

'If Sergeant Ketch knew I was here Miss, I'd be on a charge. Bleeding watch on watch it would be.' Burke said, then realising what he had said quickly added. 'Begging your pardon, Miss.'

Tarn turned to Burke. 'Alright Corporal, back to your duties, leave me the keys.'

'Sir.' Burke said, has he handed over the keys. Slamming the cabin door behind him he was glad to be out.

Alone Tarn held up his arms. 'This is madness, so it is.'

'I know,' Elizabeth said, in a small voice. 'But he will die if we do nothing.'

'Elizabeth, Elizabeth, he needs care. Dressings changed three times a day, his body dried, clean clothes, warmth. If not, he will become chilled, the fever will bring on pneumonia. If that sets in together with his considerable loss of blood then…' Tarn said, shaking his head. 'Frankly, I am surprised he has lasted this long.'

Tarn looked at Elizabeth as if expecting her to agree, if so he was mistaken.

'I will not see him die doctor.'

'Sweet Mary, don't you see that his condition is serious. Bad living conditions, poor food, prison, and now a knife wound, this is not the way to travel to "places beyond the seas". My dear young lady I have one hundred and nineteen convicts to care for and supervise, not to mention the health of the crew, soldiers, and passengers. I cannot spare the time to sit by this man's bunk, mop his brow, or hold his hand.' Tarn said, raising his voice. 'I do what I can, and that I have done. That he is still alive is testament to that, is it not?'

'Indeed it is doctor, however I do have the time to spare.'

'What are you suggesting child?' Tarn said, letting out a gasp.

'Let me help I can do it, really I can. My father was a missionary in India. I often assisted my parents in nursing the sick in our small mission hospital indeed when they became ill, I also cared for them.' It was delivered in a flat statement, an iron will formed the words.

Tarn began to realise there was more to this young woman then her beauty.

But he was determined to point out the difficulties. 'Dressings ideally should be changed three or four times a day, his body washed.' Seeing the look on Elizabeth's face he stopped. 'Yes! his body, all his body young lady. Then dry clothes, kept warm, hot soup, fresh water. All of this to be done while making sure the captain does not find out. Well! Miss Moxey answer me how would you manage that?'

Silent determination on the face of Elizabeth said it all.

'Elizabeth please I beg you,' said Tarn, raising his eyes to heaven. 'And they call the Irish stubborn,' said Tarn, shaking his head.

The pause that followed was palpable. Tarn could see the resolute look on her face. Shenkin mumbled and turned on the bunk, his face glistening with sweat.

Elizabeth bent and mopped his brow with her silk handkerchief. The gesture caring, pitying, loving.

Tarn threw up his arms in a gesture of surrender. 'Right and may all the saints in heaven preserve us both, now we need a plan.'

Elizabeth kissed the good doctor on his cheek. Causing the brash Irishman to have a foolish look upon his face.

'Away with you now, that's enough of your wicked ways,' Tarn said, but never the less there was a smile on his face.

Taking a deep breath Tarn turned Elizabeth towards him. 'Now apart from me calling into the sick bay twice a day you will be on your own, do you understand? Not waiting for a reply Tarn continued. 'Let us hope the fever breaks soon, say in another week or less with your care. I will have the guard removed and explain to the captain that the weakness of the patient does not warrant one. The captain is short of crew so he will welcome the extra man. I have the keys of which there are two I'll give you one, which you must keep safe. If the captain wishes to go into the sick bay he will ask me first.'

'Right doctor I understand, that also brings me to something else.'

'What! more demands upon my stupidity?' Tarn said. 'Well, what is it then, for we are already embarked on mutiny.'

Elizabeth took a deep breath. 'I fear my uncle was implicated in some way with the late Mr Kettlewell.'

Tarn had a look of incredulity on his face. 'What grounds do you have to make such an outrageous suggestion?'

Steadying herself against the roll of the ship she stared at the doctor as if hesitant to say more, then she continued. 'I do not make this accusation frivolously doctor, but I feel I must say something. During our first night at the George Inn near London Bridge our supper was disturbed by the landlord with a message for my uncle. My uncle having read the message advised the landlord to show the persons into a private room. He also enquired if Lord and Lady Feltsham had arrived. The Landlord said no, but that a coach was expected shortly. My uncle instructed the landlord that on their arrival he was to see Lady Feltsham to their rooms and to see to his lordship's trunks. He was then to escort his lordship into my uncle's private rooms together with a bottle of his best brandy.' Elizabeth paused, as if expecting a comment from Tarn, none came.

She went on. 'I was told to retire, that we had an early start come morning when a carriage would be collecting us at 6 am prompt for the short journey to Woolwich Docks. My uncle finished his supper then stood up wishing me goodnight, no explanation as to who these men were, nothing doctor.'

'I am a little at a loss my dear,' Tarn said.

'That is only the beginning, please bear with me. I was intrigued with this behaviour. The main door to the Inn was now open Lord Feltsham standing in the doorway. Doing as I was bid, I began to go up to my room while my uncle remained in his rooms. I came quietly back down the stairs and hid in the stairwell. The landlord showed his lordship into the private room. It was becoming dark outside and the darkened room was now illuminated by two large lamps. Two men now stood around the long black table upon which were placed a bottle of brandy and some glasses, the table was surrounded by half a dozen chairs. I was standing in the darkness of the recess in the passageway directly opposite. I had a clear view of the men doctors, one had removed his cloak. My uncle in a harsh voice told him to put the cloak back on. Do you know why doctor?'

'This is your story Elizabeth please continue, but I must say I can not see where this is leading, the captain would have many things to attend to before setting sail, would he not?'

'Indeed he would but you see the cloak had covered convict's clothes, but the government marks were very clear in the lamplight.'

Tarn had a look of shock upon his face. 'Impossible during the day all the convicts were secure on the hulk ready for boarding the *Runnymede* come evening. I supervised the arrangements myself, having spent the day examining each convict as to their suitability to be transported, all were accounted for. Late that day they were shackled and escorted by the soldiers to the between deck. Where they were again counted and made secure. So as the convicts, by then, would have been imprisoned in the *Runnymede* they would also have been in double irons to ensure no one escaped before sailing on the early tide. Is that not so?'

'I understand the hulk officials or the guards are not above a bribe. Is that also not so?'

'It is,' said the doctor grudgingly. 'But any convict would have made good his escape. Why go to the George Inn?'

'Wait doctor I am sure all you say is sound, but I can now identify the men,' said Elizabeth, leaving a pause for effect.

At that moment Shenkin called out for water. Tarn gave him a small amount and placed a fresh damp cloth on Shenkin's brow.

'Well, who were they?' said Tarn, a little tetchily.

'The convict was Kettlewell and the other, our very own Sergeant Ketch,' Elizabeth said, triumphantly. 'A strange gathering of fellows would you not say.'

Tarn was silent for a long time unable to believe what Elizabeth was saying. Never the less it was possible Moxey and Feltsham were somehow involved in something, but what? He had indeed been requested to hurry the medical examinations in order to catch the morning tide. He had explained to the captain that he needed more time, but Moxey was insistent saying that an important personage would be joining them and had requested an early departure. The final parts of the examinations were perfunctory at best.

Tarn stared at Elizabeth for a moment longer. Shenkin stirred restlessly, continually murmuring.

'Well doctor?'

'Tell me, did Feltsham join them?' asked Tarn.

'Yes, and appeared to be in full knowledge of who he was meeting. They talked for about an hour then Lord Feltsham opened the door, just slightly but enough for me to catch the conversation. His lordship was saying the he'd be damned, excuse me doctor, if he would wait longer. His creditors were close on his heels and given their business arrangement this might also threaten the ship, but that once in Australia all their fortunes would be made. They would be away from creditors, the stink of London, and the new epidemic outbreaks of cholera and typhus. Also he asked had anyone on the hulk seen any of Kettlewell's goods. Kettlewell replied yes, one of the convicts a man named Shenkin. Lord Feltsham said he was sure they would see to it that the man did not become a problem at a later date. Feltsham then opened the door fully and came out, calling for the landlord as he did so. My uncle told Kettlewell to forget the rest of the 'goods' that these would be secured at a later time on another ship. He then instructed both men to return to the *Runnymede*.' Elizabeth pause for a moment then went on. 'Kettlewell was angry at having to leave any of his "goods" behind, but Ketch grabbed his arm and pushed him out into the passage, and they were gone.' Elizabeth sighed, visibly glad to have shared the secret.

Then in a small voice said, 'Doctor until I boarded the ship the following day, I did not know who these men were. But then the knife fight and I of course immediately recognized Kettlewell. Since then, I have not known who to tell' Elizabeth said, turning to look down at Shenkin. 'He is in great danger doctor. Not only from the wound but regrettably from my uncle, Lord Feltsham and Ketch.'

Tarn considered what Elizabeth had told him and was silent for some time then spoke. 'First Shenkin may not recover from the knife wound, also I need time to observe and learn just how your uncle and Feltsham are involved in this.'

Elizabeth began to remonstrate. Tarn stopped her with a gesture of his hands.

'If what you say is true then Shenkin is safer here than anywhere else aboard. Also, we can control the matter between us if you are so determined to care for him. In the meantime, I'll try to find out what's a foot. Do you agree?'

Elizabeth gazed at Tarn for a heartbeat. 'Very well doctor, when can I begin?'

They made their arrangements and quickly left the sick bay cabin only just ahead of the captain's daily general inspection. Shenkin did not know it but he now had a beautiful guardian angel.

CHAPTER 9

In the deep nightmare of his feverish sleep Shenkin turned to address the men assembled at the bottom of his sick bay bunk. 'I have just heard that the Irish of Chinatown district will join us.' At this a cheer came up from the assembly of men in the small Welsh chapel where they were meeting. Shenkin raised his arms for quiet. 'The Irish will meet with me tonight at the cinder tips to discuss our plans for tomorrow. Their spokesmen will be the O'Hara brothers, who will decide how many men they will commit, once they hear our plans. If in agreement, they will persuade the gangs of China district to our cause,' said Shenkin, having to raise his voice above the chorus of cheers.

Idris Shenkin stood up. 'Quiet down, do you want the constabulary looking in at the Chapel to see what all the noise is about?' The noise became less, but still an excited hubbub ran through the crowd.

Hands on his hips, defiance in every gesture Shenkin continued. 'My father is right we do not want the news of our plans getting out, not when we are almost ready. It's only the full support of the Irish and the rest of China district that we need now. Every man must guard our cause with his silence.

'The owners already know something is afoot, but they don't know when or how it will happen. Tomorrow no man will report for work, petitions will be handed to the masters of all the iron and coal companies. The petition will state our demands, clearly and forcefully,' Shenkin said. He began to tick them off on his fingers.

'The main call will be for the Reform Bill to be passed in Parliament. A fair pay for a day's work, one that meets our living needs.'

'Yes!' shouted. the men.

'This to be negotiated by a committee of workers,' said Shenkin, having to raise his voice again above the noise.

'Yes!' shouted the men again.

'No more wages in tokens, but in hard cash.'

'Yes! Yes!' came the reply.

'Workers' rights and a union to enforce them, these to include safer working conditions.'

At this a steady chant of agreement rolled around the chapel like the growl of a primitive beast.

'One day a week off, this to be a Sunday, to cleanse our soul and regain our strength, at no loss of pay. No to the Reform Bill, if it means interference by Cardiff. We as a Political Union join the fight for Parliamentary Reform in the coming General Election. We stand for making Merthyr a Parliamentary Constituency in its own right, with the right to a vote for workers, not just the landowning gentry.'

At this a roar came from the assembled men, for this was closest to their hearts. 'SHENKIN, SHENKIN,' screamed the crowd.

'Finally, and most importantly, we want this right to vote to enable us to have a government that we trust. One that will speak for us. To secure our futures, and that of our families,' bellowed Shenkin, above the chanting.

Dear God thought his father we'll never get away with it.

Shenkin! Shenkin! chanted the men over and over again.

Well! It's too bloody late now thought Idris Shenkin turning to his son. 'You must quieten them Daniel or the whole town will know.'

But the cries went on, 'Shenkin. Shenkin.'

Again and again cheers of support rung around the small chapel. 'Quiet damn you, sorry Lord,' said Idris Shenkin, looking up at the rafters of his beloved chapel. The old organ in the corner vibrated to the raised voices, as if clearing its long tubes for a hymn. Then he gave in and joined in the chant of support for his son. Trepidation and pride mixing with his breath in equal measure.

At that moment one of the local special constabulary officers came in through the chapel doors to see what the noise was all about. The eyes of a hundred men met him, daring him to say a word. Taking in the scene, Shenkin in the pulpit with Willy Stitch at his side, he took off his tall black hat and from the pocket of his new blue Peeler tail coat, with its row of brass buttons neatly divided by a black leather belt. He took a flat cloth cap from his pocket and placed on his head. Then with a rather sickly smile he very slowly sat down.

Shenkin acknowledged the act with a nod of his head then continued. 'Willy Stitch will be our rallying point,' Shenkin said, turning to Willy.

Willy stepped forward, his white hair flowing around his head looking every inch one of the old Bible prophets. He called for quiet. 'Any man that fails to turn up at the rally point, or who gives away our plans, will have my little knife to deal with. I'll cut him from his balls to his throat in one slash,' Willy said, sweeping the assembled men with his piecing blue eyes. Slowly taking in each face has he did. For the first time there was quiet, no man moved or spoke. Willy finally fixed his eyes on Special Constable

Edward Mason or Edward the Squint as everyone called him. Mason shifted uncomfortably in his pew, his cloth cap pulled down hard. Both eyes more or less looking at Willy, then in a heartbeat he nodded. The silence reigned supreme for a dozen more heartbeats then exploded into shouts of support.

Someone called out 'Hurray for old Squint,' first in Welsh then in English for Edward was from Bristol.

An hour later saw Shenkin striding down towards China district's cinder mine tips.

'I hope we'll have no trouble with the Irish,' Willy said, running along beside Shenkin to keep up with his long strides. As the wind cut across an exposed area Willy brushed his long white hair out of his eyes, but to no avail the flowing hair swept back across his face like a curtain of snow. Cinder ash mixed its gritty fingers with the wind, causing both men to bow their heads against the abrasive blast.

Shenkin shook his head. 'If they don't all join us then we will fail, it must be a united front or God help us.'

'I understand God helps those who help themselves,' said Willy. 'Doesn't that bring us right back to the gentry?' Willy was now out of breath, his words coming in short gasps. He stopped 'For godsake slow down Shenkin, even this wind won't blow Chinatown away,' Willy said, between gasps. Coaldust and lungs do not go well together and Willy had been working underground since he was six.

'Sorry Willy,' Shenkin said, slowing his pace. Then it was Shenkin who stopped dead in his tracks, leaving Willy continuing to pant ahead of him.

Willy turned. 'What now?'

'We will march under a red flag Willy. Remember the white sheet dipped in the goats blood?' Not waiting for an answer, Shenkin went on. 'It will be our banner to a better future. Huw the Blast can play a marching chapel hymn on his trumpet,' said Shenkin, smiling. Huw Jones was a wonder on the trumpet he'd play all night if you let him, however it had to be said that his neighbours saw it differently.

Willy's eyes shone a brilliant blue, his hair swirling in the wind like a billowing white bed blanket. 'Yes! Daniel, an army of sinners marching to the tune of righteousness. A symbol of a people determined to give the only thing they have left to give, their blood. Yes! Daniel, yes!' Willy said, through a sob in his throat, as they walked over the tram rails into the cinder tips area.

'Now don't go soft on me, do you hear?' Shenkin said, slapping Willy on the back as he strode off leaving Willy in his wake still stifling a sob. Looking down the River Taff towards the iron bridge; built as a testament to the Town's

Iron Masters, Willy heaved a sigh. 'I remember the old Merthyr stone bridge before Crawshay and his lot replaced it with their iron one. Beautiful it was, all hand-dressed stone, arranged with loving care. Everything now seems to be hard unyielding metal, no soft lines anywhere. Where's the green and yellow of the fields? The fish that once darted like shots of silver in the once clear water,' Willy said, between gasps of laboured lungs and flying hair.

'Good god Willy stop it. You'll have me in tears in a moment, which the O'Hara's will not appreciate,' Shenkin said, looking down at Willy and then began he to laugh. Willy joined in their laughter which lifted above them into the course grit-filled air.

At last they came to the China area. Eyes watched them suspiciously as they walked on towards the Irish community. The O'Hara brothers were waiting for them at the door of their hovel dug into the side of one of the cinder tips. A dozen men stood around them, also a few of their women some with children in their arms, or holding on to their ragged skirts. Cathy O'Hara stood by her brothers, her hair the colour of coal, flying blue black and wild about her head like a midnight storm, her hands on her hips, a longing look in her blue eyes. If her brothers knew she had been seeing Shenkin on Waun Hill it would be the end of any agreement. Shenkin put the though firmly at the back of his mind. After tomorrow it would not matter anyway for the die would be cast.

Willy caught the look in Cathy's eyes. 'Oh God!' he muttered.

'What is it, Willy?' said Shenkin.

Willy said nothing he just shook his head but thinking to himself that women and politics do not mix.

'So, when do we start the riot then?' Regan O'Hara said, as they approached the door.'

'This will not be a riot, it's a rising. A revolt of ordinary working men to gain their rights. If you, or your men fail to understand that then we are lost.'

Regan gave Shenkin a look of disgust. 'Alright call it what the hell you like, but when do, we let loose,' Regan said, the words still mangled and mumbled through his bound-up jaw.

'What did I tell you Shenkin they are all temper and blabber but no discipline,' said Willy.

'We will hear you out Shenkin you'll have no trouble from me or mine,' Sean O'Hara said, turning to Regan. 'Is that understood Regan?'

'Alright, alright,' spluttered Regan.

Shenkin nodded his head. 'Then let's get down to business. First I do not want you standing or marching as an Irish group.'

'We stand and fight together, as always,' Regan said.

Shenkin looked exasperated. 'Dear God! Is there no end to your narrow view? Do you think the gentry spend their time in disarray, no they are always united in their resolve to protect their common interests. We must do the same not Welsh, Irish or Spanish or any other damn nationality but all of us workers demanding reform.

After a heartbeat Regan finally gave a grudging nod. Sean ushered Shenkin to a chair or rather an upturned beer crate, then handed Shenkin a pint of ale and one for Willy. They all shook hands. Shenkin took a deep drought of his ale and said, 'Can you get the rest of China to march with us?'

'I am meeting with them straight after this talk. But remember they are a mixed lot, out and out rogues mostly I regret to say, but good to have on your side in a brawl.'

'I hope it does not come to that,' Shenkin said. 'But they will look a persuasive element scattered among the rest of the men.'

He took a deep breath. 'The plan is this – over the coming days we will present our petition and hold a number of demonstrations in support of the Reform Bill. Mark these days well for they will establish all our futures one way or another,' Shenkin said gravely, a look of grim determination on his rugged scarred face. 'For the first time we will move into independent political action. At our rallying point above the town we expect to see thousands of working men gathered from all over the industrial areas of South Wales. These will be divided into four groups. One to the Brecon road, one to the Aberdare road and one to the Cardiff road; they will seal the town off from any outside interference. The fourth and largest group will march under a red flag down to the town, assembling around the Castle Inn. It is this group that will present the owners with our petitions. They will be told no work or business will be done in the town until our demands are met.' Shenkin paused to let them take it all in.

Silence hung in the air, as each man reflected upon the enormity of what they were about to do. The wind had finally died down making the silence even more heightened.

Finally, Sean O'Hara spoke. 'Sweet Mary in heaven! man we'll never get away with it.'

Hearing the plan again even Willy gasped now that it was becoming a reality. They were about to take the town over by force of arms if necessary.

Only Catherine O'Hara had a small smile on her wild Irish face. The smile was one of longing and belonging, for wasn't he her man had she not held him to her breasts, felt his warmth about her, inside her. In his whispering she had known the child within this strong man. She had known the thrill of his passion that took her breath away. Her eyes looked up at Shenkin she wanted him then, right that moment. The fierce excitement rising in her cheeks like the blush of a rose.

Regan O'Hara shook his head in wonder. 'Sweet mother of God.' His voice dry in his throat. Then the moment was gone and everyone was speaking at once.

'All of you shut up, I need to think,' Regan said.

'Sure now, it's not what you do best Regan,' said Jimmy Doyle, who was standing right by the side of Regan. Regan's fist sent the man flying, ale sweeping an arch across the lime white walls leaving a dark brown line.

Sean stepped in to settle things down, helping Doyle up he turned to them all. 'Just listen for god's sake give the man a chance to explain.'

Shenkin waited a few more moments. 'We need to close the town down see, that way we can talk to the owners without having to deal with reinforcements of the military or constabulary.'

'But take over the town Jesus man, they'll hang us all for treason,' said Doyle, blood at the corner of his mouth from Regan's blow.

'Yes! Jimmy is right this is the risk we are taking if it all goes wrong,' said Shenkin, trying to take in their mood. He felt he could be losing them. He waited. Time stood still, nobody spoke. Then Sean laughed out loud. 'Sure, it's a marvel of a bloody plan, why they'll never expect us to be so organised or bold.' Then he answered his own question. 'And why should they now for we never have been before.'

'Because it's never been done before. Not on this scale, or with so many men. I also believe this time they will listen,' Shenkin said.

'What makes you so sure?' said Sean.

Shenkin put a hand on Sean's shoulder. 'Because now is the right time Sean. Reform is blowing in from Europe and America. A Reform Bill is being put to parliament for the second time, they would not do so unless it was a possibility. They can see that property alone should no longer give a man the right to a vote. All must have the vote or the country may face a revolution of the working masses.'

Sean nodded. 'Let us hope you are right or we may all be facing the end of a rope instead. But I am with you Shenkin.'

Shenkin looked at the rest. Doyle stepped forward wiping the blood from his mouth. 'I was at Waterloo with Wellington, he called us the scum of the earth so he did. He is one who will never agree to Reform, and him Irish too. But the bastard's gentry first, so he is. So I'm with you.'

Sean spoke again. 'Isn't that what we are rioting for, sorry Shenkin, I mean rising for, to make changes to the old order of things?'

Thank god for Sean thought Shenkin. 'Sean is right, listen to him. We must not let our old angers fog our purpose.'

'Yes! This is the time,' said Regan and Doyle almost at the same time. They looked at each other and laughed.

'Right then, I take it we are in agreement Sean?' said Shenkin.

Sean nodded. 'I'll pass the word to our people tonight. No one will turn up for the morning shifts tomorrow. I'll also speak to the rest of Chinatown asking them to join us on Waun Hill at first light.'

Sean took Shenkin's hand. 'I promise, you have my hand on it.'

'Then goodnight to you. Willy and I have much to do before we meet again,' said Shenkin, then turning to Cathy he said, 'Goodnight Cathy.'

'Goodnight Shenkin and may our God go with all of us in the coming days.'

Regan gave a strange look at them both. No, he thought it can't be, or can it?

'Amen to that cariad,' said Shenkin. All the Irish crossed themselves. Shenkin tapped Willy's arm. 'Let's go Willy and get ourselves ready.'

Willy nodded. 'Right you are, onward we march with the red flag flying.'

They started to walk slowly back up the hill then across the iron bridge over the Taff River. For some time they walked in silence, each deep in their own thoughts at the chain of events they had put in place. The wind was now only a light breeze, the world seemed at peace for a few precious hours, only the ironworks machinery disturbed the night. Tomorrow would be a different story for all would be silent, but for the voices of a determined people.

Shenkin rolled to the motion of the ship. His eyelids flickering to the changing images in his mind. He mumbled in his fever. 'So many risks, so many lives. A town holding its breath for the coming light. So many, so very many…'

***

The sun peeped through the heavy dust-filled clouds that warm June morning in the sky above Merthyr. It looked to see for itself this historic call to arms of ordinary working people. Machinery in most of the works stood still, as if the turn of their wheels may change the course of the events these men had set in motion. Furnaces blew cooling smoke gently on the morning air. The brick walls cracked to the chilling of their bellies, and the greater cold the day may bring. The mass rally of the men above the town milled and talked excitedly about the day ahead. They had gathered before to voice their grievances but never in such numbers. Red-stained cloths acting as flags flew from long spiked poles. On the top of each were speared loaves of bread, symbols of their blood and bodies. The Waun Fair was a perfect cover for the rally, although by now the owners would know that the men were on strike. They began to form the last and largest group that would ever march on the town. The leaders had told them to look hostile, but to avoid violence. Many were armed with makeshift weapons, clubs, bludgeons, pit props. Slowly they began to move off. Someone began to sing an old Welsh battle song, which was soon taken up by the rest. They marched not in the name their Anglo-Saxon conquerors had given them, but as the Cymru.

As they marched Shenkin wondered if the barracks at Brecon had been contacted, and if so had they been able to stop them on the road into the town? He had given Sean this task a few hours ago. Regan came running up to him at that moment.

'Sean looked every inch the fucking general leading his troops into war, so he did.'

'Not a war, not a riot, a bloody rising for the hundredth time,' said Shenkin

'Alright man a rising it is, but look around you I hope when the time comes they all see it that way'

Shenkin tried to gauge the mood around him has he swept his eyes over the column of demonstrators that had now been joined by their women with tugging, crying, laughing children. He hoped to God that Regan was wrong.

Willy caught up with him and with breathless speech said. 'What a-bout t-he roads to Brecon and Aberdare then?'

Shenkin looked down at Willy slowing his pace as he did. 'The groups left over an hour ago while you were checking names and faces,' he said sharply, the tension of the day already making its mark.

The vanguard of the crowd, its banners flying in the morning wind turned into Foreman's Field near Penydarren House a large mansion of one of the ironmasters. Outside of which, standing to attention was a detachment of Highlanders numbering around a hundred soldiers. To the side of them stood their officer and William Crawshay the Second, known as the 'Iron King' – the most powerful of the ironmasters stood defiantly beside him. Crawshay had just announced wage cuts that came into effect that very today also many redundancies making many in the march already out of work. So the crowd booed and jeered Crawshay while marching both through and passed them. Then on the order of their officer the detachment of the 93rd Highlanders also began to march. People at the side of the road hissed and shouted. 'Reform now!' Gangs of women and children mocked the soldiers. 'Look how few they are, we have them beat already,' they shouted, with jeers and insults at the uncomprehending soldiers. But muskets were shouldered, backs were straight, discipline was intact. Many of these men had faced the French Imperial Guard, a rabble harmed with makeshift weapons posed no problems.

As they continued towards the town Shenkin took in the moment. They were now facing the naked power of the state, against a well-trained detachment of soldiers, far more disciplined than them. If we are being escorted into town, how many more were waiting for us? Shenkin thought.

Willy caught up with him again. 'So Sean didn't stop the troops from Brecon then?'

'They may have got here last night,' said Shenkin, trying to justify his decisions.

They were now passing Quarry Row. Idris Shenkin fell into step by his son. 'You sure you've got enough men boy, there must be thousands here. Good of the owners to give you a military escort mind,' he said, shouting above the noise.

'That's what is worrying me Da, how many more are in town?'

His father looked up at his son. Shenkin's hair was tied back with Cathy's scarf. His face close-shaved, the scar on his face part blue and part red where Willy had put the new stitching from the fight with Regan O'Hara. Concern etched deep into his brow. His father needed to change his son's mood.

'Well, don't you look like a gypsy from the fair with that scarf. Only a gold earring you need now and I'd buy bloody pegs from you myself.'

The men around them laughed at the remark. One that only Shenkin's father could have got away with. Their tall imposing leader joined in the good humour, and in so doing it restored his spirits. After a moment Shenkin said, 'Let us hope we can all smile at the end of this day.'

Idris Shenkin turned to his son. 'Amen to that and to the better future these coming days will bring. But today is the most important of them all my son, for we stand or fall by this demonstration of our solidarity.'

Men around them voiced their agreement. They were now entering the town where the noise was deafening, from every street corner more and more were pouring into the town centre. Shops were closed, the doors and windows barred and barricaded against the coming storm of men.

Shenkin acknowledged each leader as they came up to their assembly point outside the Castle Inn. The troops had formed two ranks along the wall of the Inn, and in front of the main door. The rest manned each window, standing still by the side of the coal-stained curtains. The officer was shouting at the crowd to disband immediately, but to no avail as the press of men lined up man for man in front of the Inn.

One of the other leaders, Lewis Lewis, was shouting to the crowd. 'Stick together boys until we get the terms we demand.'

A shopkeeper waved his fist at him. 'Never, never, we'll see you all in prison every man here.' At this the crowd lunged forward causing the soldiers to move back against the wall of the Inn. Terms must be met thought Shenkin but what terms? Did the owners have the authority to meet them? Would this rising give them Reform? Will it close the Courts of Request which demand all debts must be paid for by the workers few possessions? Shenkin reproached himself, this was not the time to have doubts. He put it all at the back of his mind and raised a hand of greeting to Thomas Kinsey and James Bird, both hard men who had led the Reform demonstrations at Dowlais. Shenkin then saw Richard Lewis, a young miner in his twenties full of political ideals, come striding down the main street pushing his way through the mass of workers to get to the front. Dic Lewis had thrashed a special constable during one of the demonstrations over the last few days. The constable had sworn to get his own back somehow. Behind Dic Lewis, who now stood at the front, marched even more men women and children all shouting laughing or singing, as if they were off to the now deserted fair. Some of the gypsies from the fair had also joined in the march. Abbott the barber was trying to save his barber's pole, but was being pushed away from his premises, in the end he hurried back into the shop. By now the rear of the march had arrived in the town spilling over into every side street and lane. They took in the line of soldiers at the Castle Inn. More soldiers were also lined across the lower part of the main road leading into the town. All the soldiers' muskets were at the port position, bayonets fixed and ready.

Shenkin turned to his father. 'Well Da, this is the moment we have been planning for, the moment we present our petition. If they want to know who the ringleaders are then just look around you,' said Shenkin.

'It's all or nothing now Daniel, and may our God have mercy upon us and guide us through this day,' Idris Shenkin said.

'Amen,' said Shenkin.

At that moment Megan, Rachael and Owen Shenkin together with Cathy O'Hara joined their menfolk. Idris pleaded with his wife to go home. Looking up at the man she loved Megan gave a small but determined smile. 'We have lived through good times and very hard times. I have borne you two sons and a daughter; we have worked one for one throughout the years. Idris Shenkin would you deny me the right to stand by your side now?' Megan said, tears of pride running down her pale but still beautiful face. Idris said nothing, he straightened his back then clasping her hand he gave it a gentle squeeze. Steadily they marched forward hand in hand. Cathy pushed her brother Regan aside and stood by Shenkin. I knew it thought Regan, I bloody knew it and himself not a Catholic his fists beginning to clench. Cathy sensed her brother's tension.

'Don't make the mistake Regan of questioning me or the man of my choice.' Then turning to Shenkin she said. 'That's a nice scarf so it is, who loves you enough to give you that then?'

Shenkin a smile on his face looked down at Cathy. 'A gypsy girl I just met at the fair,' said Shenkin, getting a punch in the arm for the remark.

His sister Rachael was holding on tightly to her small brother Owain's hand to stop him from running forward with the other children. The mass of demonstrators fanned out each side of the road in front of the Castle Inn, where they were now many lines deep. A deafening noise as a wall of sound wrapped itself around the town. Fists and weapons were raised up in defiance at the armed soldiers and the Iron and Coal masters who were now standing at the doorway of the inn.

Chants of 'Give us the vote', 'Reform now', 'Where are the owners to take our partitions?' 'Come and face us,' roared the crowd. Shouting children danced while making fun of the soldiers. But the Highlanders remained unmoved, disciplined, waiting for orders.

Shenkin again gave a small prayer. 'God help us if we have got this wrong.'

He now faced the main door of the inn. Petition in hand he stepped forward to hand it to ironmaster William Crawshay who was only an arm's length away. Soldiers barred his way with crossed seventeen-inch spike bayonets. The blades sharp and gleaming in the now midmorning sun. Their war-hardened faces stared him down. They had been disciplined on the drill grounds of the British

Army and the bloody battles of the Napoleonic wars. In the back rank one soldier pushed his bearskin helmet back off his eyes. Shenkin saw that he was very young, no more than eighteen years old, his uniform too large for him the fur of his bearskin damp with sweat. His eyes big and alarmed with the fear of the moment. Shaking hands held his musket a nervous finger on the trigger. A sergeant standing beside him muttered, 'Steady lad,' for the sergeant had seen it all before from the front ranks at Talavera to Waterloo, screaming FIRE! FIRE! into the French advance of their Imperial Guard. Shenkin noted the contempt on the sergeant's face for this rabble in front of him. Shenkin stood face to face with this unflinching soldier of the realm, they held each other's gaze, the hard steel of the sovereign state shining bright between them, unyielding, steady. The town magistrates stood behind the lines of soldiers, huffing and puffing full of self-righteous authority. Having barred and barricaded their places of business, the shopocracy of Merthyr Town were now armed as special constables ready to defend their rights to make excessive profits from the poor.

The three main ironmasters stood by the side of the man they had helped put in office the High Sheriff of Glamorgan. All were looking towards the officer commanding the 93rd Argyll and Sutherland Highlanders. The officer, a major, stood resplendent in his uniform erect and calm, his kilt swishing about his legs. He turned to his men. 'Steady men no sudden moves or levelling of muskets.' The major then turned and confronted the mass of protesters who now numbered some 10,000.

'Fall back now and return to your places of work peacefully and allow the town to function in a civilised manner,' he said, his voice steady and firm.

At this the front row did step back but were pushed forward by the press of workers behind them.

Shenkin his eyes still locked on the sergeant in front of him shouted out. 'Put down your arms we have no fight with you but with the owners of the ironworks and mines whose cuts in wages are starving our families,' Shenkin pleaded. The sergeant remained impassive. Again the major asked them to disband. But to no avail, if anything the mass of protesters pushed further up to the line of soldiers. The special constables behind the line of soldiers also pushed forward. It was now difficult to tell where the military line was formed and the crowd began. The old hatred of the town shopkeepers by the workers was being stirred up into a fury. These same people now waved truncheons at them goading the demonstrators to screaming pitch. Clubs, iron bars, pitchforks and hammers were held high as a great surge moved towards the front of the Castle Inn. Fear slowly spread across the faces of the people at the inn windows. The company owners flanking the High Sheriff pushed a chair forward. Holding a paper in his hand the High Sheriff stepped up to the chair, then with the help of one of the managers from the Dowlais Ironworks he climbed on to the chair raising him above the mass of the crowd.

Shenkin noticed that the paper in his hand shook. The man's brow was damp with sweat, his legs trembled causing the chair to wobble slightly. He hesitated a dozen heartbeats, as if this was the last chance he might have to breath. A black crow landed on one or the three chimneys of the Castle Inn, as if to sit in judgement on the assembled workers. A hush settled on the protesters.

'They've given in,' shouted a stone miner behind Shenkin. 'They'll increase our wages, we've won.'

'Is that so?' said Cathy, turning to Shenkin. But before he could answer her the High Sheriff began to speak.

'I have here in my hand the words of the Riot Act,' he said, his voice dry with nervousness. 'Once... I have... read it out,' he faltered again.

'For God's sake get on with it man,' said one of the mine owners.

'Once I have read it out... you will have one hour to disperse,' he said, in a rush of words the chair rocking precariously beneath him. A second man moved forward to help steady the chair. The High Sheriff continued. 'If after one hour you fail to disband the full weight of the law will come into force,' he said slowly, lifting the paper up to read.

They had won nothing. The mass of marchers were now face to face with their sovereign.

'Go on man, read it,' urged the gentry and shopkeepers from the front of the inn and its windows.

Abbott the barber next door, having tried to save his barber's pole had also climbed into the inn by a side window. A boy in the crowd threw a stone at him, it missed but smashed the window causing a soldier to duck back. The boy's father clipped the child's ear.

Shouts started again in Welsh then English but by now no one was listening everyone was waiting to hear what was on that trembling piece of paper. The major held his men firm by glancing up and down the red line.

'Get on with it,' said Crawshay.

'Yes, yes sir,' said the High Sheriff. And so with a shaking voice he began.

'Our Sovereign Lord the King chargeth and commandeth all persons, being assembled, immediately to disperse themselves, and peaceably to depart to their habitations, or to their lawful business, upon the pains contained in the Act made in the first year of King George 1st for preventing tumults and riotous assemblies. God save the King.' The High Sheriff stepped off the shaking chair; it was then read again in Welsh. For heartbeats the crowd stood, the silence spread over the mass like a stifling blanket.

CHAPTER 10

Both Tarn and Elizabeth watched Shenkin as he twisted and turned on the bunk. He now had a rasping cough with no sign that the fever was abating.

'Is there nothing more we can do for him doctor?' said Elizabeth, her voice full of concern and anxiety. Elizabeth had been nursing Shenkin for the last three days but still the fever raged. When her uncle slept, she spent as much time as possible in the sick bay, changing the dressings, bathing and caring for Shenkin, who she now regarded wholly her patient.

Tarn turned to her. 'We have done all we can my dear. My worry now is that the infection has gone to the lungs, hence the coughing. It is now adding complications to his fever causing shivering and the sweats. We can only continue to sponge him down with tepid water and keep him warm.'

'Do you not have any medicine that will help stop the shivering and increased fever?'

'I have nothing to stop it, we can only keep him warm. Hopefully he will ride out the fever,' said Tarn, shaking his head. Before Elizabeth could say more the doctor continued.

'Even if we were in a London hospital Elizabeth, nothing more could be done many people die of fever. I saw more die of fever from their infections in the war then ever did on the battlefield.'

'I will not let him die doctor,' said Elizabeth determinedly, while placing even more blankets on Shenkin.

'The next few days will tell my dear. He is putting up a brave fight and must have a very strong robust constitution to have battled the fever this long. It will be in his favour, but I am afraid it is now up to him and his God.'

'And me doctor, and me.'

Tarn could not help but smile. 'Yes, my dear, and you. But come we need to leave, I will call in again later and keep you informed, are you able to be with him tonight?'

'Of course doctor.'

With one final glance from Elizabeth, they left Shenkin to his personal battle.

***

Shenkin moved on the bunk in a bath of sweat. The wound in his side seeping blood through the dressing that Elizabeth had placed there only a short time before. The sick bay lifted and fell to the swell of the sea as he fought again his fever and his yesterdays.

The Riot Act had been read, only the silence prevailed. The commanding officer stiffened as he waited to see what would happen next. The Castle Inn and its occupants also became still, expectant, hopeful that the reading of the Act would bring an end to the rising. The crow flapped its wings and crawed its dry call, as if impatient with the slow reaction of the once raucous crowd. For what seem like a moment frozen in time, the attackers and the attacked took in the last fatal chapter of their day. Heartbeats raced through the words they had just heard. Men shifted their feet waiting for their leaders to make a move. The soldiers in front of them waited for orders that seemed to take an age in coming. Yet it was only seconds that had passed. Then someone in the crowd, no one would ever know who it was, called out, 'So they've read the Riot Act so what, we have nothing to lose and this chance will not come again.'

All grasped the words. Before Shenkin or any of the other leaders, who still held the petitions in their hands, could say anything all hell broke loose.

The men at the front grabbed at the musket's of the soldiers, fists slammed into faces, clubs came crashing down on heads and shoulders. One or two of the troops managed to bring their muskets down and jabbed at the crowd with heir bayonets. One soldier levelled his musket as if to fire. The major screamed, 'Do not open fire, do not fire!' A stone hit the major has he spoke causing him to stagger back falling over the steps of the inn.

'Now press home the attack lads,' called Lewis Lewis, as the line of soldiers faltered at the sight of their officer going down. Bearskins were knocked or pulled off, some uniforms were covered in rotten vegetables thrown by the crowd. Windows were being shattered by flying stones and bottles. Men on the opposite side of the street began tearing slates off the roofs of shops. These sliced through the air like many sided knives, hissing and screaming as they cut their way towards the Castle Inn. Children's voices matched the screams of the flying slates, as their laughter changed to sobbing. Mothers stooped to collect their children into their arms and away to safety. As they did many were pushed to the ground and trampled on. Flying missiles that fell short of their target ploughed into the mass of people in front of the inn, cutting heads and arms. Fathers shouted at men to give way to young children but to no avail, the day was now the riot that Shenkin had dared not call it.

A bayonet prodded forward by the side of Shenkin, it found its spot in the chest of an ironworker next to him. The man fell to the ground, blood spurted forward trying to catch up with the steel blade that was first expertly twisted then pulled from the man's body. Shenkin drove his fist into the soldier's face as a stone passed his head the wind of it lifting the scarf holding back his long hair. A troop of reinforcements charged their way to the Castle Inn. The Royal Glamorgan Light Infantry, their muskets steel bright with fixed bayonets, cut a path through the mass of workers slashing out and clubbing their way forward. Their officers on horseback slashed down with their sabres, the broad blades a lethal cutting edge of cruel unforgiving bright steel. While many fell in the face of this advance even more workers were now coming from the surrounding ironworks to swell the mass of protesters. All armed with axes, iron bars or clubs, some managed to disarm the soldiers taking their muskets from them they used the bayonets to stab at the reinforcements. Hand to hand combat spread into the road and nearby streets. Shopfronts were smashed the long shards of glass used as weapons. Shenkin found himself at the far side of the inn, a miner lay with his back against the wall of the inn, his hands pressed against his stomach to stop the blood and intestines from slipping through his fingers; he looked up at Shenkin in disbelief. Turning Shenkin fought his way back to the front of the inn where he saw his father go down on his knees to help a wounded worker. Shenkin rushed forward as quick as he could to pull his father up. To late he watched his father kicked then stabbed with a bayonet. Hitting the soldier with a powerful blow to the jaw that sent the man backwards into his comrades, Shenkin lifted his father into his arms his mother screaming beside him.

'Idris! Idris dear god my love, my cariad,' she cradled his head to her as the crowd pushed and fought around her. Regan O'Hara came to their aid, between them Shenkin and Regan cleared a space around them. Covering both with his body Shenkin pulled his father to the wall of the inn. While Regan protected them Shenkin looked for Willy Stitch. Seeing his flowing white hair only yards from him Shenkin called his name, then Willy's back was turned by the melee of workers and soldiers around him. And Shenkin saw that one side of Willy's head was no longer white but stained red with blood. Willy stood only by the press of the crowd around him his face was as white as his once flowing hair, that no longer blew in the wind like Jones the Washtub's sheets on a Monday morning. Even at this distance Shenkin could tell that Willy Stitch was dead.

All this in less than a few minutes, and it seemed to Shenkin that it happened in slow motion. His heart seemed to skip a beat, or perhaps it did. Nothing was real he would wake up from this nightmare, please God let him wake up. But there was no waking up. The big sergeant still stood firm in front of the inn he now had a sneer on his face. He lunged at Shenkin with his bayonet causing him to move away from his father's side. The young soldier Shenkin had seen earlier had lost his helmet, a piece of the fur stuck to his sweaty face, he looked both comic and tragic at the same time. A slate came screaming through the air and it struck the young soldier in the face, he went down into the mud of the road. At the sight of this the sergeant moved into action, the blood of battle now rushing through his veins. He became the well-trained killing machine he was, two workers went down in quick succession to his bayonet, he swung again at Shenkin who avoided the main thrust. The blade scraped passed Shenkin's arm slicing open the skin. Then the butt of the musket, in a well-practised action, slammed into the side of Shenkin's head sending him to his knees. The sergeant stepped forward and swung the musket upwards under Shenkin's chin. Shenkin was flat on his back, the sergeant walked over him and into the crowd chopping down a line of workers; unstoppable he cut men down in front of him like wheat. Head spinning, Shenkin fought to get up, he felt an arm around him it was O'Hara.

'What about my father is he alright?' shouted Shenkin, shaking his head as a swelling came up at the side of his face.

O'Hara looked down not wanting to see the pain in Shenkin face. 'He's dead,' said Regan, bluntly. 'Your mother will not leave him, but she is safe. I pulled them both against the side of the inn wall. She is rocking your father in her arms.'

'Thank you,' said Shenkin adding, 'Dear god what about my sister, young brother, and Cathy what about her?' said Shenkin, anxiously.

'I don't know,' said Regan, shouting above the yelling and screaming around them. Shenkin was numb with shock his eyes took in the window opposite the curtain rail inside was hanging at an angle, all the glass gone. A soldier, his musket at the ready, stood in the frame of the opening.

Shenkin felt he could not breath, the air around him was still, as if it too was bewildered by the death and devastation of the day.

'Shenkin we must move,' Regan shouted, urging Shenkin to his feet.

'I must go to my mother,' said Shenkin, struggling to his feet but they were being swept away by the charge of the soldiers. The workers renewed their attack on the inn. The High Sheriff was again calling out the Riot Act but no one was listening or caring, they were too busy killing or dying. A child cried out from somewhere in the middle of the road, which was now churned into a mix of mud, blood, cinders, broken slates, glass and horse shit. The child's mother called out in vain, the butt of a musket slammed into her face. Axes, pick handles and rocks clashed with cold steel in violent frenzy. A stone hit a horse pulling a wagon of hay, the farmer desperately tried to control the beast. The animal reared up in the air; a woman turned to look transfixed at the frenzied hooves towering above her. Screaming the woman tried to avoid the hooves but was trampled into the ground and out of Shenkin's sight. Soldiers were now all around them, schooled in the art of killing they moved in disciplined formation. They had faced the beating drums and the battering columns of French voltigeurs, and they had beaten them. The protests of these poorly armed, ill-organised workers were no match for them. The workers' dream to take on the iron and coal masters and win their small battle for fair pay and enough to eat was being crushed beneath the boots and hooves of the crown's military might.

But they refused to give in and again and again rushed the front of the Castle Inn. Gentry, owners, magistrates and special constables, shrunk back into the inn. The commanding officer, blood running freely down his face from the wound the stone had caused, could see that the state of affairs was now critical. Grim-faced, he took the only course open to him in the face of an assault in such large numbers. Shenkin, still dazed, charged forward with O'Hara in the final assault on the inn. His head spinning from the blow to his head he felt as if he was in a fog.

The officer braced himself then stepped forward, unsheathing his sword as he did; he stood calm and upright, running his eye down the line of his men. In the fog that slowly descended on Shenkin, his arm stretched out with the petition still grasped tight in his hand, he took in the scene in front of him. The officer screamed an order. The front rank dropped to one knee, the back rank remained upright their backs against the front wall of the inn. Each man raised his musket to the firing position. The workers halted in panic at the obvious intention, those in the front of the crowd were trying to turn back, but too late. The officer dropped his sword arm indicating one final unspoken order.

'Front rank fire!' shouted the sergeants. 'Back rank fire!' 'Front rank fire!' So it went on in a well-drilled action that ruled a third of the world.

Shenkin heard the reports of the musket fire as he sunk to his knees pulling O'Hara down with him. The fusillade ripped through the workers. Streamers of hissing white metal passed over them like a murmuring moving wall. Bodies fell across them as they flatten themselves into the mire of the road. In that short violent space of time it was all over. Throughout those terrible moments some had lost their lives, but all had lost their futures. Nothing would ever be the same again.

Dear God murmured Shenkin, the bunk creaking under him has he rocked himself dear, dear God…

CHAPTER 11

They had had no time to discuss further what Elizabeth had seen or overheard at the George Inn at Woolwich. In the last few days Tarn had been busy with a number of convicts and crew that had been taken ill. Meanwhile Elizabeth had been nursing Shenkin early morning and again at night. They had watched him slip in and out of delirium. But Elizabeth had been true to her word she had bathed, fed and cared for Shenkin over these last few days. If Tarn had been concerned about the delicate matter of Elizabeth sponging down Shenkin's body, it was soon dispelled; she did it with care and tenderness.

That evening they were again attending to him.

'I am concerned with his feverish chills, he must be kept warm, the perspiration is chilling on his body it is also causing salt loss,' Tarn said, turning to Elizabeth.

'I have put so many blankets on him already doctor, including two from my own bed.'

After a few moments Tarn said. 'I must leave you my dear a number of crew and convicts are now ill, in fact the symptoms are giving me great cause for concern.'

'Of course doctor. I will attend to him as I have for the last week.'

'You have done well young lady. Shenkin is very fortunate, but do not let yourself become too involved my dear. He is a convict and will stand trial for the killing of a fellow convict when we get to Australia,' Tarn said, rather sternly.

'No doctor,' said Elizabeth, looking up at him with her deep blue eyes.

'Why do I not feel reassured by that quick reply?'

'Go along Doctor, see to your other sick patients. As you have observed I can care for our patient on my own,' she said, with pride.

'Indeed you can, the effort you have put into the duty does you great credit my dear. All these early mornings and late nights while ensuring you were not missed by your uncle has been remarkable. But remember Elizabeth do not get to involved with your patient,' Tarn said, pressing a hand upon her shoulder.

Closing the cabin door firmly behind him Elizabeth was again alone with her patient. It always sent a quiver of excitement through her young body which shamed her. But has she looked down at Shenkin, she just could not help herself.

Shenkin was shivering uncontrollably. In that moment of concern with the compassion and love she felt for Shenkin, she turned to the cabin door.

Locking it firmly, she began slowly to undress. Speaking out aloud she said. 'Convict or not I will not let you die, the warmth of my body will keep you warm, my wild wicked Welshman,' she said, laughing. 'I know there is good in you, I knew it when you protected that young convict that led to the knife fight. I knew it. You shall not die.'

Bonnet gone, her hair fell loose to her shoulders. Then Elizabeth removed her high-buttoned shoes followed by her muslin gown. Unbuttoning her corset, she let it fall to the moving lifting deck. Quickly now, almost in a state of sexual excitement, she was down to her loose-fitting shift. Her breasts, free from the restrictions of the corset, fell firm and full as they pressed against the thin cotton shift. She blushed at the realisation that her nipples were hard. She softly touched the tips and trembled. Checking again that the cabin door was locked she pulled back the blankets and slid in beside Shenkin's hot perspiring body. She felt the tautness of his muscular physique shivering next to her. Soon she was as wet as Shenkin, who still murmured to himself.

'Hush, hush now, sleep, sleep my dear,' Elizabeth said, as if it was a child she held in her arms. She felt that she was freely giving herself to him, willingly, her body, her warmth, and yes her love. This night she would hold him to her, willing his fever to abate. While Shenkin continued to relive his nightmares, over and over again.

'How is he Burke?' asked O'Hara.

'The fever is still in him Irishman but he's putting up a hell of a fight. The doctor doesn't know how he's still alive.'

O'Hara looked up from his task of collecting their scrubbing brushes. 'Thank the merciful Mary in heaven for that,' said O'Hara, crossing himself as he said it.

'It's Surgeon Tarn you have to thank, not any saints in this world or the next,' Burke said, moving the line of convicts back to their cells.

Collins tugged at O'Hara's arm. 'Does that mean he'll be fine then?'

'He's a good man so he is, didn't I tell you so? Hard as nails is Shenkin, I should know for haven't I the marks to prove it,' said O'Hara, a smile playing across his broad Irish face.

The cosh of Ketch smashed across O'Hara's kidneys. 'Shut your mouth you miserable Irish bastard, or do you think you are still a fucking altarboy back in that country where your mother spawned you? That's if you ever had a mother,' said Ketch, scowling. 'Wait till I get that Welsh pig back from the sick bay, he'll wish he'd died from Kettlewell's shiv. The bleeder robbed me of a mate, he did, and booty as well, I won't forget that I won't,' Ketch said, turning to another convict to vent his malice.

O'Hara stared after Ketch as he swayed down the file of men. As he did, he made free with his cosh on everyone that was close enough to strike.

'I'll have that little man before this ship sees God's green land again, so I will.'

'Tell me tonight Regan,' said Collins, fear in his small youthful eyes as he watched Ketch kick a man who had fallen over a pail of soapy water.

'Swab it up! You useless piece of shit!' screamed Ketch. 'It's no wonder your country don't want you. I don't want you. Your mother don't want you, no bugger wants you,' Ketch said, striking down with his cosh on the man's back has he stooped to lift the pail upright.

First Mate Lawson came down the companionway from the quarterdeck to investigate the trouble. 'What's all the bother about Sergeant Ketch?'

'No trouble, sir! Just making the ship neat, tidy and free from utensils being left about, dangerous like. Sir!'

The First Mate looked down at the convict who was holding his back from the pain inflicted by the blow. 'I'm watching you Ketch. Now get these men back to their cells.'

'Sir!' Ketch had learnt a long time ago to always say 'sir' loud and confidently when an officer questioned you.

The Mate turned his back and made his way to the above deck. Ketch smirked turning to the nearest guard. 'Bleeding officers I put pay to a few of them on the fields of Spain and France.' Then looking down at the convict he had struck. 'What you looking at, want another kiss of the cosh do you?'

'No sergeant, not me,' said the man, quickly swabbing up the last of the spilled water.

'That's alright then,' said Ketch, kicking over the pail as he passed.

Turning to the guard next to him he said. 'Put that man in double leg irons with only bread and water for three days, for wasting water.'

'But its seawater, we've got a bloody ocean of it, Sarge!'

Ketch moved threateningly towards the soldier. 'You're not arguing with me are you, private?'

'Sir! Leg irons and bread and water for wasteful use of provisions. Sir!'

'Right, teach the bastards to be careful it will,' said Ketch, pulling down his tunic over his gut. Turning sharply all military like Ketch saluted up to Lieutenant Feltsham who now stood above them on the quarterdeck.

'Sir! All correct. Sir!'

At this the first mate shook his head in disgust. Lieut. Feltsham nodded his head. 'Good man that.' then shouted down to Ketch. 'Very well Sergeant take them down.' Full of himself in his fine trimmed uniform the Lieutenant turned to Lawson. 'The nights are getting warmer Lawson, do you not think?'

'We are approaching the Canary then Cape Verde Islands with West Africa on our portside Lieutenant. Barmy nights ahead for us at last, but it will be hot below decks, very hot. Which is why I think you should have a word with Ketch.'

'Why so?'

'The man's a sadistic bully, Lieutenant. We don't want a riot on our hands do we?'

The Lieutenant looked sternly at Lawson. 'I cannot think what you mean sir. The man is carrying out his orders, my orders to be precise, which is to ensure that we have strict discipline among a dangerous group of convicts. A little fear will hold them in check, don't you know. Also after branding them, they need to be in no doubt as to the consequences of any resistance.'

'Fear and cruelty can also push them too far. One hundred and nineteen men living in a confined space discontented, rebellious, and outnumbering us.'

'This is not a leisure cruise Lawson it's a bloody convict ship,' said the Lieutenant, red in the face.

'What do you know of hardship. Your lack of experience shows in every order you fail to give. Ketch has a free hand.' Lawson regretted the retort, but it was too late.

'Let me worry about the convicts, while you see to your ships' duties. I feel sure Captain Moxey would agree with me on that, also my uncle, don't you think?' Both men stared at each other for a heartbeat. Then Lawson gave a nod of his head.

'As you say we each have our own duties, if you'll excuse me, I will get on with mine,' said the First Mate, turning on his heel to join the helmsman.

'Pray do so sir,' said the Lieutenant, in a huff. Returning to his cabin he was already preparing a speech in his mind to tell the captain and his uncle.

O'Hara and Collins were finally shackled for the night. Collins had cuts all over his hands from the hard bristles on the scrubbing brushes. The saltwater had swollen his fingers to twice their size, the branding mark was all inflamed, the ulcers on his ankles were weeping as tears rolled freely down his young face.

'Its bad lad isn't it, but it will pass, even pain passes,' said O'Hara.

The boy was curled up in the corner of the cell sobbing softly, while rocking back and forth to comfort himself.

'Yes, Regan thank you, Regan,' he managed between heavy sobs.

At that moment Burke came to the front of their cell rationing out the evening meal. 'Wash your hands in fresh water nipper,' said Burke, pouring extra water into Collins's tin cup.

'Thank you, sir,' sobbed Collins. 'You're very kind.'

'We'll not forget Burke, I promise you,' said O'Hara.

Burke nodded. 'Stay clear of Ketch Irishman he's out to get Shenkin and anyone close to him.'

'But why?' said O'Hara.

'Ketch seems very protective of boxes in the hold. He's forever back and forth checking them. Also I'm sure Kettlewell was carrying something on his person when he came on board. Ketch was watching out for him all the time, making sure he came to no harm. Then your mate Shenkin goes and kills him, so be careful, he's a malicious bastard,' said Burke, moving further down the line of cells.

'What do you think he's on about Regan?' said Collins.

But O'Hara was remembering the hulk back at Woolwich. Kettlewell had been missing from their cell a few nights then from the ship on the first night. 'So that's how he got out at night, had help from Ketch,' said O'Hara, out loud.

Collins looked at him. 'What do you mean? Where did he go and why did he always come back?'

'Good questions lad. Where and why?'

When O'Hara didn't say any more Collins moved back into the corner splashing more fresh water over his hands, while sobbing quietly.

O'Hara looked over at him. 'Come on lad first few weeks, or is it a month already, anyway they are the worse, so they are. We'll soon be in warmer waters. The Canary Islands they say, where ever the hell that is, sure now I thought that was a bloody bird. Pain passes Collins you see if it don't. I remember when Shenkin put my jaw out of place, hurt like hell it did.'

'Thought you were friends you and him.' Collins said, the words jerking out between sobs.

'So we are, so we are, but not in the beginning. No, we didn't see eye to eye until the fall in the mine, then the fight on the side of a bloody cold black mountain,' said O'Hara, a faraway look on his face.

Collins was now alert to every word. 'Go on Regan tell me, tell me,' for a brief moment his burning hands forgotten.

'How did he get that scar?'

'What did he do to get sent to "a place beyond the seas"?'

'Why were you fighting?'

All the questions coming out in a rush, broken only by a few sobs.

'Hold on boy we have plenty of time,' said Regan.

'Come on Regan tell me, tell me please.'

O'Hara settled back on his bunk, the chains pulling at the skin around his ankles.

'Bastard iron and coal masters it was. First Number 2 pit, a bloody death trap, tons of rock and coal fell every few weeks.'

'Was Shenkin down there Regan?'

'He was so, we were both down there me brother too when the roof in Shenkin's section came down. That's when the scar on his face mapped his past, nearly died he did. He was the only survivor, sitting in a corner with a dead man across his lap.' O'Hara's tough strong face saddened by the memory of it.

'Go on Regan.'

'After the fall, Shenkin's father got him a job in the Dowlais ironworks. Some of us Irish including me and my brother Sean also went. They had to close down Number 2 pit see, sealed it off they did, dead men and all. But it was at the ironworks that I got to know him better, me and my brother worked in the same gang as Shenkin. Cocky bastard he was, but your man had a way with him, so he did. Men much older than him seemed to listen to what he said, which was always about forming a union for workers' rights. One day towards the end of our shift Sean stepped in front of a runaway drum, heavy with iron scrap. Don't ask me how Shenkin got there so fast, but he did. He hit Sean flying out of the way, saved his bloody life he did. Do you know what he said when I thanked him?'

'No what?'

'Shenkin just looked at us both, Sean still on the ground as white as a sheet. 'He'd have done the same for me, so don't feel you or him owe me anything.' Regan O'Hara smiled. 'Proud as hell so he is.'

'What happened then?' said Collins, but a guard's voice cut him short.

'All secure, sir.'

'Right every other lantern out and be bloody quick about,' bellowed Ketch.

The hold plunged into semi-darkness. Men groaned, swore, called out for water or pulled at their chains and argued with their cellmates. A rat scurried out across the gangway to feed on bread dropped from the upper deck through the grating. A kick from one of the guards sent it squealing back into the blackness of the hold.

'Move your bleeding leg off my bunk before I break your toes.'

The voice that answered was as cold as steel. 'The rats will be feeding on your yellow balls if you push my leg again.'

'Shut up the lot of you,' said the guard, walking down the length of the cells on the starboard side.

Silence for a moment then someone coughed a deep grating cough, spitting out the phlegm through the bars of his cell. It landed full on the stove, which was being stoked by one of the crew, the man jumped back as the spit sizzled on the hot plates. The convict laughed.

'Bastard! You won't laugh tomorrow I'll wager, when the blazing sun burns all the spit out of you,' said one of the guards.

'What does he mean Regan?' said Collins, distracted from Regan's telling of Shenkin's past.

'Just trying to worry us,' said O'Hara, but he had noticed that the sun was getting hotter. Scrubbing the decks from now on was going to be gruelling, also their hands were still painful from the branding.

If Collins believed him or not, O'Hara was not sure, the boy just nodded. 'Go on with telling me about Shenkin.' But O'Hara saw that the lad was holding his hands again and had recommenced rocking himself.

So Regan O'Hara in a whispered voice told him everything, the roof fall, the fight, the riot, until finally Collins fell asleep.

Through the timbers of the ship Shenkin shivered in Elizabeth's arms while he ran down the dark lanes of his nightmares.

'Shh, shh,' said Elizabeth, cooing softly.

***

I will not be ground into this shit and mud, no I...

Shenkin turned on the ground to look up at O'Hara – the cold anger in his face made O'Hara gasp. The noise and screams around them deafening. Shenkin struggled to his feet pushing O'Hara's arms away from him. He swayed on his feet. O'Hara again made to steady him but was pushed away.

'There's nothing you can do man, it's the fucking riot I told you it would be,' he said, shouting at Shenkin while firmly holding him by the shoulders.

'How long have I been unconscious?' asked Shenkin. A child cried beside them, the mother face down in the mud not moving.

'About quarter of an hour, that sergeant gave you a hell of a blow with the butt-end of his musket, but I caught up with the bastard,' said O'Hara, pointing to the crumbled form of the sergeant laying side by side by the fallen mother. Screams, shouts and shots filled the late afternoon men bleeding, dying in the face of a crushed cause.

'I must get to my mother,' said Shenkin.

But before they could they were surrounded by soldiers. 'Put these two with the others' shouted an officer. One miner turned to run but a bayonet in his stomach from a large Scots soldier brought him down. The soldier stepped over the body and pushed Shenkin and O'Hara forward. Shenkin struggled to free himself but the fixed bayonets now formed a circle of steel around the group. Everywhere the scene was the same, struggling groups of miners and ironworkers, some of them already in chains. They were soon herded into waiting farm carts that the army had acquired. Horses restless in their harnesses strained to get away from the congested raucous crowd. One broke lose, the driver pulled off his seat. The horse trampled over the wounded and the dead before being brought under control. Shenkin was pushed up onto one of the carts, he slipped on the straw and sheep shit that lay at the bottom of the cart. Out of the main street they began to climb up the hill in the direction of the workhouse. Unloaded, they were shoved into makeshift cells, the poor former residents sent out into the street. Some of these were on crutches, others in rags. Destitute mothers held babies to their thin frail bodies, all wailing to no avail. Soldiers brutal in their handling of men, women and children continued to separate the poor from the rioters.

'Dear God what have we done?' said Shenkin as he was pushed into a room.

'We took on the gentry, the government and then the crown,' said an old man blood running down his face.

'What?' said Shenkin turning.

'We gambled and lost, a brave gamble, a noble gamble. They will note it down in their ledgers while reckoning up the cost. Properties damaged, production output down, military and police expenses, the possible spread of civil unrest. They will not want it again. So the next to protest may, just may, find it easier. All is not lost young man we progress one faltering step at a time.' the old man said, in a trembling voice. Then slowly he slumped down onto the floor.

Shenkin went to help him. Meeting the old man's unwavering gaze, Shenkin felt a lump in his throat, it could have been his father speaking. He rolled up his jacket and placed it under the old man's head.

'O'Hara, do we know how many died?'

'Only rumours but some say at least twenty or more in the town. More on the roads leading in,' said Regan. Then in a small voice that Shenkin could scarcely hear. Regan said. 'Sean is dead Shenkin, he lies somewhere on the Brecon Road. They say he took three with him, so he did,' said O'Hara, his eyes clouding over, the look was so at odds with his strong Irish face.

'I am so sorry Regan,' said Shenkin. It was the first time Regan remembered Shenkin ever calling him by his first name.

'It's been a bad day, so it has. The bastards, the bloody, bloody bastards of hell. I was in the cart behind yours Shenkin as it travelled up to the workhouse at the back of the Castle Inn. It stopped to collect two miners. It was then that I saw your mother she was down in the mud still cradling your father's dead head in her arms. She was not weeping mind, for she wouldn't give them the satisfaction, you… you bloody Welsh and your damn pride. At her side was your brother Owen his face buried in your sister's skirt weeping. My sister stood there too her hands on her hips rebelliously, just daring anyone to touch them.

'Willy Stitch you know about. Daft Billy-one-leg is dead too, stopped a bayonet, so he did, while hitting one of the soldiers with his crutch. I've told you about my brother, so I have.' Regan stared into the space of their bleak workhouse room. 'God bless them all,' he said, crossing himself. 'Sure now I didn't even know Billy's last name. Isn't that a sin not knowing the name of a man who dies beside you?'

For a few heartbeats it was quiet, then Shenkin said. 'Thomas.'

'What?'

'His name was William Thomas,' said Shenkin. 'His mother will miss that four-pence a week pension he got for the loss of his leg. Mind he always said it was a big save on socks.' Shenkin said, tears running unashamedly down his face into the line of the blue tinted scar. Stinging, bitter, salty tears shed for all the people that he loved and had left his life for ever.

O'Hara shrugged his broad shoulders. 'They can't find Lewis Lewis, but Dic Penderyn is being held at the courthouse charged with seriously wounding a soldier and insurrection, as we all are.'

Shenkin looked at O'Hara. 'But it was not a riot!' he said, knowing in his heart that it had become just that. At that moment the door was swung open a body thrown in. Shenkin recognised the voice of Lewis Lewis as he shouted abuse back at the soldiers. The last of the leaders had been captured. Shenkin helped Lewis to his feet. 'How many are here?' asked Lewis.

'How many of us are here, call out your names,' shouted Shenkin. So the roll call began together with Richard Lewis of Penderyn; up in the courthouse Shenkin made it nineteen – 'Sixteen voices, one absent, two unconscious,' Shenkin said, looking down at the old man. But he had slipped away taking his wisdom with him. Shenkin covered the old man's bleeding face with his jacket. O'Hara made the sign of the cross. 'God rest his soul,' he said.

Shenkin sighed, 'Eighteen then.'

'A reckoning will happen old man, but first we must survive,' said Shenkin, as he covered the old man's face.

Others died in the night, come morning those who were still alive were lined up outside. They were now down to fifteen. They had been given no food, water or a doctor to tend them. A number of rattlers and carts stood ready for them to be loaded into.

'Where are we being taken to?' Shenkin asked a sergeant.

'You'll know when you get there, so shut your bleeding mouth.'

The soldiers began the loading. This time the drivers were all military. Stern and unsmiling, just waiting for the opportunity to open fire. The day before resting uneasy on their minds.

Shenkin tried again as they were pushed forward towards the carriages. 'Our fight was never with you, sergeant, it was with the iron and coal owners who make vast profits while we go hungry.' The sergeant began to turn away but Shenkin held his arm. 'I see you wear the Waterloo Medal, do you see that ironworker over there. He was bayoneted in the stomach, he's been calling out for water all night, he too was at Quatre Bras and Waterloo but had to sell the medal for food. You may even have fought next him. Would you watch him die now, answer me that?'

The sergeant looked over at the man who called out again for water. Turning to Shenkin he said. 'I have my orders Welshman, so start getting into the carriages.' Then added. 'We are taking you all to Cardiff gaol for trail, the living and the dying.'

'Thank you for telling me,' said Shenkin. The sergeant nodded. 'Right! get moving. McCoy, don't bloody stand there get these bastards onto the carriages and carts and be quick about it.'

'Yes! Sergeant.'

Shenkin and O'Hara together with three others including the wounded man, who was still crying out for water were bundled into one of the carriages. No room to stand, they were crammed in, packed like animals. Officers on horseback rode each side of the transportation column.

O'Hara turning to Shenkin said. 'It's going to be a long day.'

They began to move off, the military in a hurry to clear the town of the leaders of the riot, and as many of those that they had arrested as possible.

As they moved away the sergeant opened the door of their carriage. Throwing two full canteens of water to Shenkin. 'I hope he lives Welshman, but they are going to hang you all anyway,' said the sergeant, slamming the door.

Before Shenkin could say anything, they were moving off at a fast pace.

'Move! Come on man, move. Keep loading them you lazy bloody Scotsmen,' screamed the sergeant behind them.

The voices faded as they jolted their way out of the town. The Rattler was well named as the iron rims of the wheels hit every cobble stone, jarring their bones, as if to break them.

Shenkin lifted the wounded man's head. 'There you are Bryn, take a deep gulp.' The man did, then coughed it all out with blood and his last breath.

'Fourteen now,' said Shenkin, banging on the roof of the Rattler. 'Stop! we have a dead man here.'

'Sling him out, we are not stopping,' said the officer, riding at their side.

Shenkin looked at O'Hara and the other two men. 'Do it!' We can't have a dead man lying on us for the next God knows how long,' said O'Hara, starting to open the door.

The officer drew his sword. 'Careful now I just want to see the dead man. I'll cut down anyone else who shows himself.'

Bryn Evans, late of Merthyr and the Dowlais ironworks, went out of the door. His body rolled to a stop, the last of his blood mixing into the mud of his town.

'Close that carriage door,' called out the officer.

'Have we really come to this,' said Shenkin.

'Yes!' said O'Hara.

***

127

Dead men, dead cause, no, no...

'Hush, hush now,' said Elizabeth, as she rocked Shenkin in her arms. Both of them sweating profusely from the heat of their bodies, and the increasing temperature of the climate, as the *Runnymede* lifted and sank into the swell of deep blue water.

CHAPTER 12

A dead town Regan, a dead town.....

In what seemed no time they were at the Court of Requests building.

'Stop,' called the officer in charge. 'We have a man to collect.' Carriages and carts came to a juddering dust coal clouded halt.

'Sergeant! pick two men and bring the prisoner out.'

'Sir.'

'McClean! Thomson! follow me.'

In minutes they were back out. A man was being held up between the two soldiers.

'Right, get him into the nearest cart,' said the officer.

It was then that Shenkin, looking out of their carriage, saw that it was Richard Lewis from Penderyn his head lolled over to one side. The face was the colour of fresh dough, drawn, drained and bloody.

The man looked up and seeing Shenkin called out. 'It was not me that wounded that soldier Shenkin, I swear it on my mother's sweet life.'

'Shut up you murdering swine,' said the big Highland sergeant, swinging his musket into Dic Pendryn's bloody face sending him down onto the cobblestone road. He lay there unconscious. The big sergeant kicked him in his side. 'Get up you lazy bastard.' At the sight of it, O'Hara was through the carriage door. The officer reined his horse to stop him but too late. O'Hara drove his fist into the sergeant's face sending him reeling across the road into the side of the carriage. Shenkin chopped his fist down into the man's throat. They were surrounded by soldiers all swinging their musket butts. The officer screamed an order, 'Constrain and manacle the prisoners get the unconscious man into the same carriage also manacled. Sharp now.' At the same time the officer swung the flat of his sword across O'Hara's head bringing him to his knees. Several soldiers held Shenkin and O'Hara as others fixed the manacles on them. Soon they were again on their way.

'He's in a bad way,' said O'Hara, blood running down his face.

'Give him some water and let's try to make some room for him to lay.' Restricted by the manacles, they struggled with their tasks.

Dic Pendryn gurgled on the water and opened his eyes. 'It's alright you are with friends now lay still,' said Shenkin.

Looking out Shenkin saw that the streets were lined with soldiers. Muskets with crossed fixed bayonets formed a line of steel along the road out of the town. Moving slowly down the High Street the town silent but for the horse's hooves clip-clopping over the uneven cobblestoned road. It was a funeral march for a lost cause. People stood calm and hushed behind the line of soldiers. Many of the women were crying, children held tight to sobbing breasts. Few men stood among them most of which were old. Shenkin realised many were still in hiding. He could see groups of armed soldiers going into the row of houses that led to Chinatown.

So many soldiers everywhere, officers on horseback watching for any trouble. They need not worry thought Shenkin, the town no longer had any leaders. It could only lick its wounds and watch its men being driven away. They jostled for space on the bone-breaking boards of the carriages and carts. The subdued procession made its way through the deathly still town of Merthyr Tydfil. Broken men looked out on a broken town. Young women sought out their menfolk, while the soldiers pushed them back behind the line. All were weeping into shawls that cradled babies. A hushed farewell came from their tear-filled eyes. Shenkin looked for his mother, finally seeing her in the lined road of weeping people. Their eyes locked in an unspoken understanding. She was dressed in black her face full of sorrow. His sister Rhiannon and young Owen stood at her side. Owen pushed forward. 'I'll kill them all Daniel,' he screamed, a soldier used the butt of his musket to push him back. Megan Shenkin pulled him to her, wrapping him in her arms. Shenkin thought his mother looked so much older, although it had only been a few days since he had last seen her. A sigh escaped his lips.

Cathy O'Hara was also standing close by, nodding to her brother, then threw a kiss at Shenkin and mouthed the words. 'I love you.'

Shenkin turned to look at Regan O'Hara. A smile came to Regan's bloody face. 'Sure now, haven't we all known for some time?'

Shenkin said nothing he just nodded his head. Then in heartbeats he said. 'Dear God! What have we done Regan?'

'We tried to change the world, our world, but that is not what they want.'

No thought Shenkin it is not. The rising was over, the power of the state had restored the rule of law. The workers were back in their rightful place.

The column made its way out of the town on their way to Cardiff. These men who had dared to question the sovereign state would be taught a lesson that their town and its people would never forget. The government in far away London would guarantee it.

After many hours of bone-jarring travel, they arrived in Cardiff. The news of their arrival had spread fast. Crowds swarmed the streets, some cheering their new political martyrs, others shouting abuse. Fights had broken out in the crowd. Constables and soldiers were trying to keep civil order but losing.

In the leading cart, one of the Dowlais men was near to death, no care was administered, no expression of concern. The man died among the shouting, cheering abusive, indifferent crowd. All the prisoners were hungry, thirsty and exhausted. They gazed upon this mass of baying people with a look of confusion. Many had never been to Cardiff before, indeed they had never been but a few miles outside of their black mountains of coal and iron. A man in the crowd called out to Richard Lewis, 'We are gathering a petition Dic. Do not worry the truth will save you.' Another voice called 'You too Shenkin or we swear Cardiff will be the next to see a riot.' Both men were pulled from the crowd and frog marched into the gaol ahead of the prisoners.

One of the officers shouted an order. 'Disembark these men, smartly now.'

The crowd pushed forward jostling for the best view. 'Get these people back,' called a sergeant. 'Form a barrier around them, move it.'

A soldier's helmet fell to the floor, crushed under foot, the bareheaded soldier gave up trying to collect it.

'McDonald I'll have you on a bloody charge for that, you useless bastard.' screamed the sergeant.

'Get on with it man.,' called the officer.

'Sir,' said the sergeant.

Finally they were through the big doors. Soldiers formed a line across the opening. The doors crashed closed they were in, but they were now down to just thirteen.

Standing on a raised platform they were greeted by Governor Woods. Puffing out his chest to appear a man of importance as appropriate to his office, he began to address the prisoners. Hardly heard above all the noise inside and outside of the gaol. He nonetheless persevered, hurriedly telling them that he expected good behaviour. That their trials would begin as soon as all the facts were marshalled. Without further delay they were marched into cells located on two floors. The Governor gave a sigh of relief as the sound of cell doors slammed shut the keys scraping metal to the locked positions. Richard Lewis and Lewis Lewis were placed into separate cells on the ground floor, guards mounted outside each cell. The rest into a large common cell on the top floor. Windows high up the walls were crossed with iron bars, letting in very little light but all of the outside noise.

Doors slammed closed. They were finally on their own. Each man took in his surroundings, a collective murmur began.

'Shenkin, will they give us water?'

'What about facilities, I mean somewhere to piss?'

'How long will we be here do you think?' said one ironworker, to no one in particular.

Regan O'Hara stood his legs apart hands on hips. 'We could start lifting these flagstones, you never know we maybe above the kitchen.' Men laughed but it was strained laughter.

'How deep would we need to dig before we found out?' said Shenkin, shaking his head. 'It may also be above the guardhouse.'

'Sure now, that's a good point, so it is.' replied O'Hara.

'Seriously Shenkin will they give us food?' said a man at Shenkin's side. Tom Williams came from the same street as Shenkin, they had grown up together.

'God knows Tom,' said Shenkin, 'and he's not telling.

'Perhaps they think if they keep us starved, we won't have the will, or strength to try anything,' Shenkin continued.

'We must try something to get out,' said O'Hara. 'If we don't, they are going to hang us anyway, so what have we got to lose?'

A chorus of yesses echoed around the room.

'What about the iron bars?' said Tom Williams, a sound of desperation in his voice.

Then to their surprise from the other side of the wall came a woman's voice. 'Is that the Merthyr rioters?'

'Yes,' came a chorus of shouts.

'Welcome to Cardiff gaol my brave ones. My name is Sarah Murphy, counterfeit coins a speciality.' The voice was rasping and coarse.

'Me friend here is Mary Jones, thievery and a few other little services best not to mention. We were sentenced to hang but they decided to transport us instead. And me not knowing how to make those funny foreign coins, I'll be lost so I will.'

While she was talking Shenkin found the crack in the wall to the next cell. 'How long have you been here Sarah?' said Shenkin, looking through the crack. Shenkin saw broken black teeth and smelt the reek of her breath as she pressed up against the wall.

'Too bloody long. I need a bottle of gin before I die of thirst, so I do.'

'Do you know when the next session of assizes is being held, Sarah?'

'I heard the Turnkey say they are holding special trails for you lot. The two murderers first, so they can hang 'em. The crowd will love that so they will, bless 'em,' said Sarah, an edginess in her voice. 'The trial will come before Mr Justice Bosanquet, as early as possible. Then its good luck to you, rioter, for you'll need it.'

Sarah was silent for a moment then said. 'Mind, it's the Turnkey you need to watch out for, he's a mean bastard. Sells bread, beer and mattress so he does. But you'll have neither in that common cell they've been and put you in no water either, am I right?'

Shenkin took a slow look around. 'Plenty of dust, dirt and piles of shit watered with piss in the corners. Some mattress all of which are soiled. The smell is foul enough to strike a tinderbox on, but no, no water,' said Shenkin, looking at Regan as he spoke.

'Do you have coin on you?' asked Sarah.

Shenkin turned out his pockets and gestured the others do the same. After a moment Shenkin said. 'Some yes, but only a little, we left our homes in rather a hurry at the point of a bayonet.'

'Right.' Tell him you have much more then you show. That you want fresh bedding, water, food,' said Sarah. Then added. 'Oh, and a bottle of gin. That's for me, cos I gave you the wink see, and more if you want to get out. Well! Do we have a pledge rioter?'

All heads around him nodded. 'Yes,' said Shenkin. 'But how do we know we can trust you? Perhaps they want us to try and escape, a few musket balls are cheaper than trials or the truth.'

'That's simple,' said Sarah. 'We need your help we've loosened these stones but can't move them, cos they are too big. Now you sound like strong men, easy for you to pull and lift them out wouldn't you say?'

Shenkin thought for a moment, Regan nodded his head and said, 'What do we have to lose?'

'Show us the ones you've already loosened,' said Shenkin.

'I will so,' said Sarah, in an excited voice. At this, a big stone began to move towards Shenkin. Grunts from the women, heavy and laboured. But slowly the big stone started to move further towards them. As the edges began to appear Shenkin motioned to Regan. Taking hold of the stone they lifting it clear from the wall.

Sarah Murphy's face poked through the opening in all its glory, to the gasps of the men. 'Sure now, wasn't I saying how strong you'd be.'

A chorus of laughter rang out from the men of Merthyr. They looked upon a face that had seen the inside of every liquor parlour from Dublin to Dowlais and back again.

'What you looking at my sweet things haven't you seen a pretty face before?' said Sarah, with a smile full of black stumps of teeth, as decayed as her wrinkled countenance. When all was quiet Shenkin bent to the opening. 'One stone going from cell to cell will not get us out of here Sarah.'

'But now, haven't we loosed a number of these beauties from the outside wall? Enough to give an opening to let us all out into Sweet Holy Mary's good free world. Just a twenty-foot drop and we are away to the nearest Inn,' said Sarah, licking her lips at the thought.

Shenkin looked at Regan in amazement. 'How did you work the stones loose?'

'Now that's a clever woman's ploy, so it is. They searched us well enough before they dropped us into these quarters, but we still had corsets, didn't we?'

The men were silent at this. Shenkin looked blankly at Sarah.

'The bones that hold the girdle in shape man! Didn't we pick them out of the garments? And weren't they perfect to work the mortar free? Good and long so they are. They goes right through they do seeing how the lime and mortar between the stones is old.' After a while as Shenkin and the men were digesting this Sarah added. 'Why the whole bloody place is falling down, so it is.'

'Well I'll be damned,' said Shenkin, beginning to laugh as he took in the moment.

'They're thin bones of course like a long knife but one that bends to the shape of the joining just as they do to a woman's shape,' said Regan.

'They do that,' said Sarah, holding up a thin blade of bone.

Regan shook his head in disbelief. 'Hell! we should have had her at the riot.'

Shenkin shot him a look. 'Alright, alright the bloody rising. All I'm saying is it's a stroke of genius,' said Regan.

'Um,' mouthed Shenkin turning back to Sarah. 'So, where's Mary?' asked Shenkin.

Sarah moved to the side and Mary Jones appeared. A girl of no more than sixteen or seventeen years of age. Her pretty dirty face leered up at them, hair bedraggled and matted. Her eyes spoke volumes of experiences older than her years. Her dress was soiled, torn and revealed an ample bosom, the deep cleavage swelled to her breathing that both Shenkin, Regan and the rest of the men found difficult to ignore.

Sarah hand pulled Mary away from the gap in the wall. 'Isn't she a sight for sore eyes then, and that's a fact, so it is. Works the docks does Mary, better than any ship on the water, she can say yes in five different languages, so she can. Isn't that so my pretty one?' Not waiting for an answer Sarah went on. 'She don't want to leave her trade for foreign ports when she knows Cardiff port so well, do you darling? No course you don't,' said Sarah, still not waiting for a reply.

With a gap in Sarah's flow of words, Mary spoke at last. 'Pigs they are, yes! dirty pigs! for sending me to places I don't want to go to,' said Mary, then she began to cry.

'Alright Mary we're not on our way yet,' said Sarah. 'Dear God will you just listen to her, we'll have the gaolers here in the moment, so we will.'

After a moment while Mary was being calmed down by Sarah, Shenkin spoke. 'How many come to tuck us in for the night Sarah?'

'The Turnkey with two of his men, they make the rounds for the night, checking locks, lights and a head count. They carry muskets they do, so careful does it see,' said Sarah, wiping a snot off the end of her red veined nose.

'Don't forget your pledge rioter, in the morning we'll put our plans to work. Now lift that stone back into place before they are here.'

Shenkin and Regan replaced the stone. Before it went into place Shenkin looked into Sarah's eyes. 'If you cross us, I'll wring that chicken neck of yours.' A rasping laugh came from her lips. 'Now don't be fretting yourself and I'll be saying a goodnight to you all.'

The stone finally in place, Shenkin turned to look at the their surroundings. A cold flagstone floor stopped at big jumper stones that formed damp walls. High up were two iron barred windows. Difficult to reach and by what means for there was nothing in the room. Some of the men had rolled up their coats to use as pillows. One man whose condition had become worse over the last few hours had stopped coughing he lay his back against the stone wall head slumped. He was dead. 'Now twelve of us,' said Shenkin, to no one in particular. Regan nodded. 'Well! They just went sooner, that's all.'

'We are not beaten yet my Irish friend; if Sarah is right about the stones, then we'll chance it, now let's find a place to settle.' Before they could find a place keys turned in the locks and three gaolers came into the room.

'Right let's have a head count, every prisoner stand and line up into a single file,' said the bigger of the three men. He was obviously the Turnkey Sarah had spoken of. Burly unshaved, hard of face and manner he stood apart from the other two.

With shuffling grunts, they slowly moved into the centre. One gaoler went left the other right counting out has they did.

Passing from right to left they came back to stand by the Turnkey.

'Twelve,' they said, in unison.

'One missing, sir.'

'One dead' said Shenkin, pointing to the slumped body against the far wall.

'Right! drag the corpse out Williams, then let's get them locked up for the night'

'Sir.'

The Turnkey turned to the standing men. 'Any of you got any money?'

'Some,' said Shenkin.

'Right, you'll be a little more hungry and thirsty come morning, we'll talk then. Lock 'em up.'

The two men grunted, the bolts slammed into place.

Shenkin sat back against the wall. 'Right let's get some sleep.'

The night drew out like a sharp knife across stone. Everyone was restless uncomfortable, cold and hungry.

Come first light after a miserable night almost every man was fully awake. Shenkin had slept little. Turning to Regan he prodded the big Irishman's in the side. 'You awake Regan?'

'Well, I am now, what is it?'

'That church clock strikes the hour, next time will be for 6 am,' said Shenkin.

'So?'

'So, the gaolers will be back for the morning check. We need to be ready for them. Collect whatever coin we have, while I wake Sarah from her beauty sleep. If they are planing an early trial, it could be tomorrow or even today,' said Shenkin. 'So we go for it as soon as we can, tonight if possible.'

Regan was already collecting coins. Shenkin called out to Sarah.

'Sweet Mary in Heaven what's all the bloody noise about,' said Sarah, early morning croak in her voice making it sound even more rasping.

'Sarah we are going to make a break for it tonight,' said Shenkin. 'Start work on the stones straight away, both on this wall then the outer. You'll need to loosen enough stones for men to climb through, so two big squares. Can you and Mary do it?'

'Most of them are already done my sweet thing,' said Sarah, chuckling.

'Right, if you need help pass the end of one of the bones through these inner walls and we'll saw down with you.'

'Yes my lovely rioter that's a good'un, we'll start as soon as the gaolers have been.'

'It's going to take all day but come nightfall we should be ready, unless we are brought to trial today, then it's all too late,' said Shenkin.

'No, it will be tomorrow or the next day earliest. They need to make a show of it, so they do.'

'Knows her law does Sarah,' called out Mary.

The church clock struck the hour, the key turned in the cell door.

'Right let's have you,' said the Turnkey. 'Are any more dead?'

After a moment. 'Twelve it is sir,' called out both gaolers

'Good! All well and healthy then with a good appetite.'

Two of the men put down two large bread baskets with water containers at each side of them.

Shenkin went over to look into them, all were empty. The Turnkey stared hard at Shenkin. 'Well?' he said.

'They are empty no more than a few crumbs and a damp base to the water containers,' said Shenkin, then added, 'Which means?'

'It means if you or anyone complains of no bread or water, we simply say we gave you some this morning,' he said.

With a smug smile the Turnkey came up close, his bad breath covering Shenkin like putrid mist. 'Who do you think they will believe, the murdering rioters, or the gaolers?'

Backing back Shenkin nodded. 'Point taken how much will it cost?'

'How much coin have you got?' asked the Turnkey, greed in his eye.

Shenkin opened his hand. 'This to start.' Shenkin's hand held mostly farthings, halfpennies and a few copper pennies.

'No silver?' said the Turkey,

'It's what we were fighting for,' said Shenkin. 'Higher wages.'

The Turkey said nothing just looked at the hand and the money it held trying to count out its worth. Before he said anything Shenkin dropped a silver coin into the pile of coins. The man looked at him

'Its for a bottle of gin as well,' said Shenkin.

The Turnkey laughed. 'Bottle of gin you rebellious bastard. Are you crazy?'

'No gin, no silver,' said Shenkin, taking it out of the pile of coins. Looking hard at the Turnkey he said. 'It's all we have at the moment but family and friends are coming to see us and they will be bringing some coin,' he said.

In heartbeats the men watched the Turnkey come to a decision. 'How do I know more coin will be brought to you?'

'You don't,' said Shenkin, with a shrug. 'But for now, this is all we have.'

After another long silence the Turnkey spoke. 'Right! One loaf of bread, half a container of water and a small flask of gin.'

'For twelve men?' said Shenkin. 'No, we may as well wait for more coin to arrive.' Shenkin was betting that an early trial date would make the Turnkey take what he could get at that moment.

'Bastard! One and a half loaves of bread, one full container of water and a bottle of gin for the silver,' said the Turnkey.

'Done,' said Shenkin. Then added 'Bring in the bread, water and gin first.'

The two assistants went out. 'We'll need a while to get the gin,' said the Turnkey, pointing a loaded musket at Shenkin. They waited. Finally the bread basket and water was placed inside the door. The Turnkey held out his hand for the money. 'And the gin?' said Shenkin. The Turnkey smiled nodding to one of his men by the door who handed the bottle to Shenkin. Shenkin dropped all the coins into the Turnkey's outstretched hand, who checked that the silver was included. Satisfied he nodded to the other two, turned and they walked out. The door slammed shut the key turned in the locks, the bolts slid into place, they were alone.

In that moment the men made a dash for the food and water but Shenkin moved quicker. 'Wait! We need to ration it out so each gets a fair share,' said Shenkin, daring anyone to defy him. One of the miners made a grab at some bread. Shenkin chopped down with a brutal fist to the man's jaw dropping him to his knees.

'Anyone else want to try?' nobody moved. Shenkin helped the miner to his feet. 'Get in line Thomas.' he said. 'Regan cut the bread up in chunks each man to have a fair share. After each man is given his bread, he goes to the back of the line and eats it while waiting for one cup of water, agreed ?'

'Yes!' chorused the men pushing the miner Shenkin had hit, to the back of the queue.

They worked steady all day. By the time the Turnkey come to lock up for the night they were ready. All the outer wall stones had been loosened except for the outer line of mortar which would be removed when they were ready to go.

After lock up, Shenkin turned to the men. 'We'll sleep for a few hours, let it all go quiet then we make the break,' said Shenkin. All agreed they began to settle down to sleep, but there was an air of excitement in the room that made sleep impossible. The men moved around speaking to each other in whispered voices. The moment was broken by Sarah's voice. 'What about the gin you promised me after the work was done?' cried Sarah, both her and Mary had worked side by side with the men all day.

'Fair enough,' said Shenkin passing the bottle through the wall.

Sarah seized the bottle with shaking hands. The cork popped the glass neck rattled on her rotten teeth has she drank down the first deep draught.

'She'll be drunk by the time we are ready to go.' Regan whispered. 'But much easier to handle,' retorted Shenkin.

'She will so.' Regan said, with a smile.

The church clock struck three times. Shenkin began to stir the men, most were already awake. They removed the stone blocks between the cells and one by one they squeezed through into the women's cell. Mary was aglow with excitement, gazing at Shenkin with unabashed pleasure. Pulling on his arm she said. 'Sarah's done for, the bottle's empty and she's full of its joy.'

Shenkin looked at the corner of the cell where Sarah was slumped against the wall mumbling to herself, the empty bottle gripped tightly in her hand.

Regan called from the outer wall. 'Sweet Mary! We'll never get the women down that drop it must be all of twenty feet. I am not even sure about us,' he said, pulling in his head from the opening.

'Get all the bedding and cloths we can find, including our topcoats; drop them down to break our fall. Then two men down first to catch the women, Sarah first,' said Shenkin.

'Mother of God we just can't drop…'

Shenkin cut Regan short. 'Damn it man, it's now or never, we wait till she sobers up and god knows what the morning will bring. He turned to the gathered men. 'Well! What do you all say, are you with me?' Every man nodded their assent. 'Right!' said Shenkin, turning to Mary. 'And you what's it be, go or stay?' Mary looked up into Shenkin's eyes and smiled. She'd follow him anywhere. 'I'll take that as a yes,' said Shenkin, as Regan walked over to Sarah. 'She's as drunk has an Irish squire on market day, so she is.'

'At least she won't feel the ground as she hits it,' said Shenkin, lifting Sarah to her unsteady feet.

'Right! Who's going down first, it'll need two strong men?' said Shenkin. No one moved all aware that the first down could break a leg or worse. 'Come on, Regan and me have agreed to stay to the last in case the jailers come back, we can fight them off while you make your get away,' said Shenkin, exasperation creeping into his voice. For heartbeats the place was still, most of the men looking down at their feet. Finally, Thomas Timms the miner Shenkin had hit pushed forward; he'd been very quiet since the incident, the others had not spoken to him all the time they had worked during the day. 'I'll go first,' he said.

'Good man,' said Shenkin, turning to the others. 'Come on we have not got all night.' Billy Sheeps, a farmer from Dowlais, stepped forward.

'Right,' said Shenkin. 'Let's do it.' Soiled bedding, blankets and coats went out of the opening, a thud welcomed the flying beds to the ground. Shenkin raised his hand and called for quiet. No jailers came, all was peaceful.

'Right down you go boys and good luck, remember once the women are down run for the chuch yard.' Both men nodded.

Down into the dark space they went a few curses after the wind was hit out of their lungs, but they were down. In moments both were on their feet and looking up waiting.

'The women next, Sarah first,' said Shenkin. 'Remember scatter into the church and into the surrounding streets as fast as our legs will go,' he said, then added. 'And God help us all.'

'Amen!' murmured the men, Mary added the sign of the cross to the prayer.

The women went down safely even the gin bottle, which they were unable to wrench from Sarah hands without her making a sound, arrived to the ground unbroken.

'So far so good,' said Shenkin.

Soon only the two of them were left. Regan jumped, his six foot four frame scattering the bedding around. After he had pulled them back together Shenkin jumped and found Mary at his side helping him to his feet. Sarah still laying on the ground was singing an Irish ditty. 'For god's sake, shut her up,' said Shenkin.

Mary put her hand over Sarah mouth, both men lifted her up and began to run through the market area out into Trinity Street. Then like blowing leaves they crossed into the graveyard of St Johns Church. Men were running in every direction; it was each man for himself now. A whistle from the gaol, the bird calls of the early morning dawn gave way to shouts of alarm as the big doors of the gaol swung open. The game was up no need for silence now. A yellow finger of light flashed along the walls of the church, alarming the angels and bowed heads of stone. Rats scattered from their coffin homes, squeezing passed broken slabs of marble headstones. Seagulls screamed in the dawn's lighting sky. In the nearby houses and taverns lights came on windows flew open, as heads craned out onto the streets and cobbled lanes, adding their voices to the general commotion.

'Over to the graveyard. Muskets at the ready, follow me, and be careful not to bloody fire on one another.' This from the officer of the guard who dressed in rumpled uniform, bedraggled, helmet askew, eyes blurred with sleep, he took Trinity Street at a run, cursing as he realised he'd not put his boots on.

'Sergeant send a man back to the barracks to get my boots at the side of my bed.' then added, 'And bring more oil lamps, men and the dogs.'

'Sir,' said the sergeant, turning to the nearest soldier. 'Hutton back you go you heard the officer and be smart about.'

Meanwhile Shenkin, Regan, Mary and a loose-limbed Sarah moved deeper into the cemetery searching for a way out.

'Where's me bottle? I want me bottle, so I do.'

'Sweet mother of God will you just hear her,' said Regan, between gasps. 'I'll give her the bottle in a moment, over the bloody head so I will. Let's leave her Shenkin let her go and to hell with her.'

'No! If it was not for her, we would not be out here. The first dark doorway we'll have met our pledge,' said Shenkin, his breath coming in gasps as they scrambled over gravestones and bushes, the sweep of lights just yards behind them. A dog's bark split the air with a deep howl another joined in then another.

'At least they're in tune,' said Shenkin, cursing has he fell over a tree root.

'For the sake of my saintly mother and her beloved son where the hell is the way out?' said Regan.

'Mary which bloody way is it?' Shenkin said, holding his knee.

'We are almost there.' As she spoke, they came to a gate, they were in open ground at last. Behind them they heard a soldier call out. 'I've got one of the bastards, sir. The sound of a tussle broke out then the soldier again. 'Right, how do you like the taste of steel?'

'No! don't kill him for Christ's sake.' But a scream went up in the night that chilled the morning air. After a moment the officer's voice was heard loud and condemning. 'Damn it man he's dead. I want these men caught alive, do you all hear?' screamed the officer. Captain Longstaff sighed; he would need to write a full report on the death of this bloody man all because these bloody, bloody soldiers he commanded were the dregs of the army. Also the sharp stones of the cemetery had torn his feet which were now cut and bleeding. 'Where is that damn man with my boots Sergeant?'

'Coming sir coming.' They ran into the still dark winter morning.

Ahead the three of them stumbled forward. 'Eleven,' said Shenkin to himself, he wondered who it was, as he ran on.

Coming to a tavern doorway they dropped Sarah, pushing her body as far into the dark recess as possible. 'Thanks woman for your help,' said Shenkin, but it fell on deaf ears, Sarah's wits swam in a sea of gut-rot gin.

'Thank God for that,' said Regan, straightening up.

In the distance behind them the soldiers had caught another of their number. 'Shackle him! No, the legs first you damn fool' The officer's voice cut across the cemetery, has he gratefully pulled on his boots over bloody feet. Now many yellow fingers of light probed, searched and separated the stone figures from the shrubs.

'This way.' called Mary. 'We need to go down Working Street towards the docks,' she said not breaking her stride.

'I hope you know where we are going,' said Shenkin, as running boots hammered the cobblestones behind them.

'Hold on to the dogs, don't let them loose.' shouted the officer. We must catch them unharmed, if possible. The court will raise hell if they are cheated of passing sentence.' His voice rasping in the cold dawn air.

'Quick! We must get to the docks,' said Mary.

Running faster now without the encumbrance of Sarah they were soon down into the Hayes area of the town. Led by Mary they crossed a canal bridge at the bottom of the road, disturbing the wildlife as they did. Ducks and seagulls scattered in confusion. Rats moved in for the kill as the fowls were startled by the early morning men, dogs and musket shots.

'Aim high damn you!' called out the officer.

The three fugitives raced into Bute Street as fast as their legs could carry them Mary her dress flying in the wind, her hair wild about her dirty face, Shenkin was sure she was laughing has she ran for her life.

Up over Bute bridge, the dark outline of the docks just ahead of them. It was not the first time Mary had run down these grimy cobbled streets and she knew exactly where she was going. It was difficult to keep up with this slip of a girl as she darted into and out of side lanes then jumping over streams of mucky slow-moving water. Both men were breathless, their talking down to a minimum, but in spite of their plight Shenkin, as he watched Mary run, had a smile upon his scarred rugged face. Go girl, go, he said to himself. Regan said 'Dear Mother of God if they catch us there'll be nothing left to hang at the rate she's running. And I don't know what the hell you are laughing at, so I don't,' said Regan between breaths, as he looked at Shenkin. 'You are not a fit man that's your trouble, too much beer around your waist,' said Shenkin. At that moment Mary stopped dead in front of them, so suddenly that Shenkin could not stop in time – he hit Mary to the side and went headlong into the canal. The officer heard the splash. 'They are in the canal towards Bute get some bloody light over there, we've got them now.'

***

The water so cold... so cold... Shivering Shenkin twisted and turned on the bunk. 'Hush, hush,' said Elizabeth cradling Shenkin tighter.

CHAPTER 13

A knock at Tarn's cabin door disturbed his reading on the symptoms of the recent outbreak of illnesses. Grim-faced he put the medical book. 'Come!'

Burke stood at the door. 'Begging your pardon sir, Captain's compliments sir. Would you join him on the poop deck?'

'Very well Burke.'

'Sir.'

Moxey was pacing the deck as Tarn came up the companion ladder.

'You wished to see me captain,' Tarn said, steadying himself against the rail.

Moxey's face was dark his eyes full of hate. 'I am not a man to be trifled with sir! Have you or have you not allowed my niece to go into the sick bay?'

'May I ask who made such an accusation?'

'The guard you removed from his post reported to Sergeant Ketch, who reported it to Lieutenant Feltsham. Well sir?! Yes or no.'

'Yes,' said Tarn.

'The hell you did and on whose authority sir. Answer me that damn you!'

'As the Surgeon-Superintendent of this ship, sir.'

'What's that you say?!' blustered Moxey. Both men were shouting the crew on the quarter-deck turning to look up.

Seeing this Tarn raised his hands in protest. 'Sir, I suggest we continue this discussion in your cabin, not in full glare of the ship's crew.'

Moxey was red faced with anger he was unaccustomed to being told what to do on his own ship.

'Do you sir, do you?! I'll have you in irons you insubordinate papist upstart.' Moxey's voice was almost a scream as Lord Feltsham came up the companion ladder.

'What's this captain, further entertainment for your passengers?' said Feltsham, in a voice mixed with aloofness tinged with sarcasm, as only the aristocracy seem to manage.

'You will please stay out of the affairs of the ship sir!'

'I am glad you mentioned that Moxey. I would say that the affairs and good running of a ship facing a long voyage needed a doctor free from the restraints of irons. I feel sure the owners would agree, in fact sir I am positive they would.' The last words were given heavy meaning by Lord Percival Hugo Feltsham. Moxey took a step back from Tarn.

Standing by the gangway Feltsham turned to look back at the quarterdeck.

'Come now a glass of your excellent madeira captain. Let us settled this in the comfort of your cabin, what say you?' said Feltsham, not looking at Moxey but fixing his eyes on Tarn, who he felt was the more dangerous of the two.

For heartbeats all was still then Tarn also moved to the gangway. Standing to the side he turned the captain. 'At your convenience sir.'

The captain shot a look at the first mate. No words left Moxey's lips as he struggled to hold on to both his temper and dignity. The first mate saved him from further embarrassment as they came onto the quarterdeck.

'Sir! I have the ship.'

'Thank you Mr Lawson, keep her on this course, if you will.'

'Steady as she goes sir. Helmsman, steady as she goes, if you please.'

The helmsman, hands tight on the wheel, dropped his eyes to check his course. 'Steady it is sir.'

The chill of the past few moments eased. The helmsman's shoulders relaxed as the wind blew them further into warmer climes, with the promise of fresh water and fruit at their first stop, the Cape Verde Islands.

***

The climate in Moxey's cabin was anything but warm. Each man poured his own glass of wine. Moxey's hand shook with temper so much so that some of the madeira spilled over the top of the glass. The wine puddled on the table then began to flow to the side as the ship swayed to the motion of the sea. Tarn watched the liquid run to the edge of the table. It come to rest against the raised lip, where it welled up then poured over the top.

Moxey turned very slowly then called out, 'Steward.'

'Sir!' the man was just outside the cabin door clearly eavesdropping.

'Clean up this mess smartly now. And if I find you snooping behind this or any cabin door I'll have you flogged and put ashore at the next port. Do you hear me?'

'Yes sir! Sorry sir won't happen again sir, I swear it.'

'Then get on with it man.'

'Sir!'

The three men took advantage of the moment to calm down. By the time the steward left they had downed their wine. Both the captain and Feltsham were seated. Tarn stood before them.

'His lordship has intervened on your behalf Tarn,' said Moxey. 'Both he and I take the good running of this ship very much to heart. But sir! I will not tolerate situations developing that as master of this ship I know nothing about. Do I make myself clear?'

Before Tarn could answer Feltsham spoke. 'Yes, yes captain you make yourself very clear. And you are quite right, but first let us hear the good doctor's explanation. Doctor, please sit down you are not on trial.'

Tarn looked at Moxey, 'Sir?'

'Sit man, for god's sake sit,' said Moxey. 'Let's get this over with.'

Pulling a chair towards him Tarn sat. He then crossed his legs, folded his arms and leaned back. Moxey bridled at the impertinence displayed in the gesture.

'Firstly, are you questioning my authority, captain?'

'Damn you I am asking the questions here.'

Feltsham lifted an elegant well clad arm. 'We captain, we are asking the questions, are we not?' The question hung in the air.

'If you say so,' said Moxey, through gritted teeth, wishing he had handled this better.

'I do my dear captain, I do,' said Feltsham. Then turning to Tarn. 'Not questions doctor but the reason behind your decision. Now what say you?'

After some pause Tarn took a deep breath. He let it out slowly.

'A number of crew and convicts have become ill,' said Tarn, but before he could say more Moxey again interrupted.

'The result of inactivated, grog or the clap. I have seen it many times before particularly among convicts, it will pass.'

Tarn exasperation on his face, again heaved a sigh. 'I wish it was that commonplace. But when you called me to join you on the poop deck I was reading up on the symptoms. I now suspect it could be worse.'

'But this is why you are aboard doctor to attend the sick and the convicts' general wellbeing, is it not? said Feltsham, still adjusting his cuffs.

'Indeed it is my Lord, but I can not be seeing to everything and everyone.'

Moxey shifted in his chair. 'What does this have do with my niece in the sick bay? That is what we should be discussing, is it not?'

'Quite so,' said Tarn. 'Having enquired after the state of the wounded man following the knife fight, I have kept your niece informed as to his condition.

'With his condition deteriorating, he required around the clock care if he was to survive. I could not give it with this outbreak of illness occurring. Your niece offered her services to help, she had much time on her hands and had cared for the sick in her father's missionary in India,' said Tarn, not giving the details of the care needed, but never the less he paused for any comments. Before Moxey could say anything Feltsham said. 'His condition now doctor, how is the man is he improved or not?'

'I called into the sick bay this morning and found him greatly improved. The fever has abated, his breathing is regular, and he sleeps soundly, if rather restless.' then added, 'Thanks to your niece's care captain.'

'Excellent! 'Then she is no longer needed in the sick bay doctor, is that so?' said Feltsham giving Tarn a knowing look.

'That is so.'

'There you have it captain,' said Feltsham, pulling a silk handkerchief from the underside of his right sleeve. For a short while the three men said nothing. Feltsham flicked an imaginary speck of dust off the front of his coat.

Tarn smiled at the affectation. Moxey seeing the smile jumped to his feet. 'You insolent Irish bastard I'll have you lashed within an inch of your life.'

Feltsham pulled at the captain's coat. 'Sit down man this is not the seventeenth century. Reason, understanding and a dash of humour will serve us better.'

For long heartbeats Moxey did not move. The silence was tangible, only the sea made a sound. The afternoon bells rang out. 'Lunch I think, also we have more pressing plans to consider, have we not?' Fetsham said, annoyed at having to explain himself. 'Sit down sir.'

At that moment Tarn knew both men were involved in something that tied them together. Also that whatever it was, it was Feltsham who called the tune.

Looking at Tarn Feltsham recovered his demeanour, then smiling said. 'Right gentleman we all have our duties to attend to, have we not?

'You captain to the ship. Doctor Tarn to your ailing patients. And I to the well-being of Lady Edith.' Both he and Tarn left the captain's cabin. Moxey still sat red faced in his chair.

Back on the quarterdeck Tarn breathed in the fresh salt air and gave another sigh.

'Doctor Tarn.'

Turning Tarn found Elizabeth Moxey at his side. 'Good morning my dear, or rather good afternoon.'

Her face flushed with excitement she said. 'Doctor our patient is much improved, is he not?'

'Indeed he is I was just telling your uncle the captain the very same thing,' Tarn said. Then looking at the helmsman he walked over to the starboard side of the ship, holding her arm he took her with him.

'Elizabeth you are not to go to the sick bay again.'

'He knows then, but how I have been most careful?'

'The guard told Ketch who told Lieutenant Feltsham who eagerly told the captain.'

'I see I have given you trouble again doctor I am so very sorry.'

Tarn smiled. 'It will pass soon we may have much more to worry about.'

'What, doctor?'

But Tarn would not be drawn. 'Let us be grateful that the young convict is recovering. A long less disturbed sleep and we can return him to his cell and Ketch's good care, but I feel we may have to watch Ketch.'

Elizabeth looked sheepish. 'My uncle said nothing more doctor.'

'About what my dear?'

Shyly Elizabeth looked out at sea, then after a moment said. 'Last night.'

'What about last night young lady.?

After a moment she blurted out. 'I stayed the night in the sick bay doctor, in the bed in fact,' she said, covering her face with her hands in embarrassment. 'I wanted to give him warmth, to stop the shivering, to break the fever.'

Tarn looked down at this lovely creature who was prepared to defy the social conventions to save the life of the man she had fallen in love with. While the man in question was not even aware of her sacrifice. He wondered what Shenkin would make of it.

The smile on Tarn face said it all. 'Well, lest said the better my dear for our patient or should I say your patient is most certainly recovering. You may well have helped to break the fever.

'Thank you doctor.' then added. 'To save you further problems, although I want to, I will not go down to the sick bay again,' said Elizabeth, tearfully.

For a while neither said anything, then Tarn spoke. 'I must get to my books to see if this malady we are experiencing can be explained, so if you will excuse me my dear.'

'Thank you again doctor for your understanding and now your discretion,' said Elizabeth. At that moment Lord and Lady Feltsham came on deck, both were in good spirits, laughing at a shared joke, It seemed the earlier disagreements in the captain's cabin were forgotten. However, Lady Feltsham seemed none to steady on her feet. The sea was now in calmer waters which made Tarn suspect it was madeira rather than 'la mer' that caused her Ladyship's ungainly progress across the quarterdeck.

'Sir, I must ask you to escort Lady Edith to her cabin, given how rough the sea is becoming.' This from the captain has he came up the companionway from the forecastle deck. A bemused Mr Lawson looked out on the calm sea for they were entering the Doldrums he shrugged his shoulders. 'Mr Lawson if you have little to do I suggest you stride the forecastle to ensure the convicts are busy.' Moxey's sharpness told of a temper that was still just below the surface.

'Sir!' said the first mate has he moved quickly down the companion ladder.

'Captain I see your temper has not improved, it now extends to Lady Feltsham. I would urgently request you improve by supper sir,' said Feltsham. 'I meant, I…' blustered Moxey but Feltsham was gone. Tarn also turned to go but stopped, walking over to the captain he said. 'Miss Elizabeth is aware of our discussion sir she will not be going to the sick bay again,' said Tarn, feeling it was best to keep everything on as even a keel as possible.

'Thank you Mr Tarn I am obliged to you,' said Moxey, with some effort.

Tarn called into the sick bay on his way to his cabin. 'Well my riotous convict maybe you are oblivious to the world about you but you are causing a hell of a stir aboard this ship. Now let me take a look at the wound.'

Shenkin winced at the doctor's touch and called out. 'We'll get Sarah down first,' he said out loud. 'Sarah is it? Well you seem to be having fun you young devil,' said Tarn. The bandages off, the doctor leaned in close. 'Sore, tender yes but clean, it looks much healthier. Apart from some restlessness I'd say you were on the mend, thanks to your guardian angel.' Tarn smiled. 'You can not hear me but it's not Sarah that's saved you my friend, but a young woman of beauty and courage. I only hope you are not going to be a disappointment to her. Well I must see to my other sick patients, so sleep as best you can Welshman, I will see you in the morning.' Tarn redressed the wound and quietly left the cabin.

He came up to the forecastle deck to the sound of Ketch's voice. 'Move yourselves you lazy bastards, or I'll put every third man on the flogging list.'

To say Michael Patrick Tarn did not like Ketch was like saying the Pope was not sure about Satan's true character. Brutish men fashioned by cruel times of poverty and the battlefields of the British Empire, Tarn had meet men like Ketch during his time in the Peninsula Wars and right up to Waterloo, men who put themselves first before King and Country or the men in their charge.

'What is the problem Sergeant?'

'No problem sir, they're swinging the lead aren't they? They say they have a headache, or the cramps all the time. But don't you fret sir I'll cure them, dirty bastards they are I'd give them a taste of the cat. Now take these two, sir,' said Ketch pointing down at the men doubled up on the deck. 'They have gone and fainted on me this morning sick all over the place, making a mess of my clean deck.' As Ketch spoke another man fell to the deck, his face grey and drawn. Ketch kicked the man has he lay in a foetus posture, his arms across his stomach he was twisted up in pain. 'Get up you rotten bag of shit,' screamed Ketch, about to kick the man again.

'Stop damn you these men are ill,' said Tarn, going down on one knee to examine the man who had just collapsed. Turning the man over Tarn was met with a spray of vomit. Feeling for the man's pulse Tarn could hardly detect a beat it was so faint. The man's face was shrivelled, drawn tight across the skull, his lips blue. Tarn quickly lifted the man's shirt; his whole body was dehydrated the tail of the shirt was covered in diarrhoea. One of the other men had gone into extreme cramps, screaming out in pain, the muscles in his arms were twisted into knots, he finally collapsed. Tarn stood up. 'Sweet Mother of God,' he muttered.

At this Ketch let out a gasp. 'Dear God it's not...'

'Shut up!' said Tarn cutting him short. 'Get these men to sick bay, and be quick about it.' Ketch stood as if rooted to the spot. 'Move damn you, move,' said Tarn, turning on his heel and hurrying to his cabin.

'Sir,' said Ketch, but he had no intention of touching the sick men himself. 'Burke, Johnson get these convicts to sick bay, on the double,' said Ketch wiping his hands on a filthy handkerchief he had taken from his pocket.

Tarn pushed passed the captain without a word. 'Ignorant of good manners too, are you doctor?' But Tarn was gone a look of concern etched deep on his face and mumbling to himself. 'Please sweet Mary in heaven, let me be wrong.' His mind was racing, first he'd need to move Shenkin out of the sick bay back to his cell. Then clear the sick bay cabin to take as many of the sick as possible. Calling out to two of the nearest crew he led them to the sick bay.

CHAPTER 14

The two seamen lifted Shenkin off his bunk none to gently. 'Easy men easy now.'

'Sir,' called one of them.

'Right, back to his cell and inform Corporal Burke I'll be along shortly.'

'Ay sir.'

Disturbed, Shenkin tried to turn but strong hands held him firm.

***

We must keep running damn it, run man run. Hell the waters cold, so, cold... Were the hell's Mary?

Regan pulled Shenkin out of the canal up onto the slimy bank, a look of disgust on his face. 'Man you stink to high heaven, so you do,' said Regan, laughing out loud in spite of the men and dogs that were closing in fast. They both looked up in time to see Mary disappear to the right into a passageway of timber crates.

'Quick if we lose her, we are lost,' said Shenkin shaking the foul-smelling water from his body' then added. 'Wait! Jump in the water Regan, hurry.' Regan hesitated. Shenkin pushed him in then bent down and pulled him out. Regan blustered and splattered, his Irish temper about to explode. Shenkin held him firm. 'Regan think, it will throw the dogs off the scent.' Regan was still about to hit out, but at the same moment what Shenkin said registered on his face. Shenkin nodded.

'Am I right?'

Both stood still the lights almost up to their feet. They dived into the stacks of timber boxes after Mary. To Shenkin's relief, she was waiting at the furthermost end of the crates. 'Quick into here,' she said. A gap between the last of the boxes let them into the depth of the stacks. 'This one,' said Mary pulling a panel open on one side of an old crate. The three of them wriggled into the case. Once inside Mary dropped a thick timber plank across the opening then down between four large nails bent to keep it closed.

'They'll never find us,' she said triumphantly 'And the dogs will never pick up the scent.' added Shenkin. The three fell to the ground exhausted but laughing. 'Be quiet,' said Shenkin, as the dogs closed in. 'They sound as if they are at the canal,' said Regan. A splash, then another.

'Control those dogs damn it,' shouted the officer. The yelps and howls went on, as the soliders fought to control the animals. 'The bloody things are going around in circles, pull those two from the water. Use the damn leads man.'

'They've lost the scent sir.' This from the Sergeant. 'It's the water sir the dogs are trying to cross over, perhaps the prisoners did sir?'

'Is there a bridge nearby?'

'Further up, I think sir.'

'Right lets us get across.'

The voices carried in the morning air but slowly they became less audible as the men and dogs moved away.

Shenkin grinned. 'We've done it, as God is my judge, we've done it, thanks to you Mary, but where are we?' Mary looked at them with pride on her face. 'It's my home from home my lovelies, it's where I entertain my gentleman friends at sixpence a time or more if the evening is slow,' she said, pointing to a makeshift bed over in one corner. 'Comfy it is see? No old cold or rain and better then under the bridge it is. I'll light a candle for you to look around.' The candlelit Mary threw her arms around in pride. 'It's a bloody palace, snug as my corset it is,' said Mary, pulling Shenkin to an upturned small box. 'Sit yourself down, I've even got some bread and a little gin.'

The inside was large. Apart from the bed of straw with some rags for sheets, there was a small table, a bottle with a candle stuck in the top some sandpaper and friction matches, together with a few tin cups. The table had two small boxes around it for chairs.

Regan stood still looking around him in wonder. 'You're a good girl, so you are, pretty, clever and as sweet as the dew on the mountains of Kilkenny,' he said, his eyes clouded with admiration or lust. Shenkin looked at him with a frown. There was little doubt in Shenkin's mind which it was.

'What are you going to do Regan? Ask her to bed down, do you think you'll have enough time with dogs and men breathing down our necks?'

Regan smarted. 'I was just thinking.'

'I know what you were thinking, but now is not the time. We can't stay in this bloody crate for ever can we? Mary where are we on the docks?'

Mary sighed her moment of glory over. 'We are on Jenkins Boat Yard, he has a shack at the end of the jetty. He stores these cases, for the trading schooners that plies their trade across the channel to England,' she said, pointing in the general direction.

'What about this case?'

Mary looked around her. 'It's an old one waterlogged and rotten in places, not used anymore.'

Shenkin nodded his head. 'Right, so we are safe for the moment, if we stay holed up here until the hunt dies down then we have a chance.'

'Now what about food, water, and tell me about the ships,' said Shenkin

Mary was pleased to be back in the centre of their plans. 'Docks here for cargo twice a week, Jenkins has his men load them up then they sails back across to England.'

Shenkin was thoughtful for a moment. 'Will Jenkins help us get away?' he asked.

'No, not you,' said Mary. Both Shenkin and Regan frowned. Then Mary smiled up at Shenkin.

'What?'

'He'll do it for me my lovely. she said, winking at them both.

***

The officer, limping has he walked, turned. 'Stop talking and quieten those dogs.' The sergeant threw some strips of meat onto the ground. The animals fought for a moment then went quiet as they ate the meat. The officer strained to listen to any sounds, there was nothing but birds and lapping water.

'Damn! Where are they, they just can't vanish?' said the officer. He could see his leave cancelled, his promotion delayed and an end to his marriage plans.

'The bloody, bloody rioters where are they?' he said out loud.

At that moment a young private came running up. 'Compliments of Mr Wood sir would you return to the gaol sir, I was to say they have recaptured all of the others except for two who are dead sir, one from a bayonet, and one drowned in the canal sir,' said the soldier all in one hurried breath relieved that he had delivered the message correctly. Then took a deep breath quickly adding, 'Also the trial starts this morning at 9 am sir, with or without the two who are still at large, sorry sir, I forgot that bit.'

The officer closed his eyes in consternation. 'Is that all private?'

'Yes sir.'

'Are you sure man?'

'Yes sir.'

'Right,' said the officer pleased that the responsibility had been taken from him.

'Sergeant I want three men stationed at the start of this jetty, muskets at the ready, also leave one of the dogs. They are to report any sighting, is that clear?'

'Sir.'

Shenkin did not know it but they were now down to nine.

Finally, after much discussion their plan was agreed, except that Regan disapproved. He did not like the fact that Mary would have to offer herself to Jenkins in return for food and securing places on one of the ships. Shenkin had explained to Regan that Mary did this long before they had met her. That this was just once more for a cause that would enable them to get away. But didn't it worry Shenkin that they were using her, Regan had asked. Shenkin admitted it did, but could they undo all the other days and nights in Mary's young life? No, so in the end it was settled Mary would slip out of their hiding place at first light find Jenkins then proposition him.

'He'll still be in bed at 5 am, I knows he will, he enjoys certain things at that time he does. And with the promise of more the night before we get on board he'll do it. So let me get to work.' Mary said. That decided they settled down for the night.

In the morning Shenkin moved stiffly. It had been a cold uncomfortable night, but they were still free. Standing Shenkin looked down at the other two then at the timepiece Mary had on the table. Which she told them she had stolen from a real gent when he was in his cups. It kept her customers to their payment times since she charged by the half-hour. Picking it up Shenkin saw it was 4:30 am, time to get things started.

'Regan, Mary, shake yourselves,' said Shenkin, kicking Regan then gently pushing Mary's shoulder.

'What the hell, where are we?' said Regan. Shenkin watched as Regan's memory slowly fell into place with a groan.

'Oh! Sweet Mother of Jesus wasn't I dreaming of a beautiful colleen and me back in Ireland too.'

Shenkin grinned, 'Well you are not in Ireland, with any woman or surrounded by your fellow heathens. You are on the run from a gaol that wants to hang you.'

'Alright, alright now! Sure there's no reason to let your usual good humour slip,' said Regan, smarting

'Damn it! I'm just saying we need to get things moving,' said Shenkin with equal testiness.

Mary had the alertness of an animal, she was already fully awake and on her feet. 'I'll go now to see Jenkins I'll make him sweet. Then get some food water or wine, whatever comes to hand,' she said, making to remove the timber plank from the loose panel, Shenkin stopped her. 'Be careful Mary they will still have soldiers out there.'

'There's nice my lovely, concerned for me is it?' said Mary, looking up into Shenkin's eyes.

'You going to ask her out Shenkin, do you think we have time,' said Regan, with a grin.

'Just be careful girl that's all I'm saying,' said Shenkin.

'I will, don't you worry I'll be back soon, it will not take long to bed Jenkins, no staying power see,' said Mary with a wink. 'I'll offer him something he's never refused yet when I've needed food or money.'

Regan swept her up in his arms. 'Why you're a lovely wicked girl, so you are.' She struggled free then like a wisp of smoke she was gone. Within minutes she was back. 'What the matter?' said Shenkin, 'Is it the soldiers?'

'No but I can't move the rowboat to cross the canal to the yard, it's so heavy.'

'Damn it to hell we'll have to go out let's hope we are not spotted,' said Shenkin.

Outside they soon had the boat in the canal. All was still with not a sign of the search party to be seen or heard.

'We'll risk it Regan by rowing her across, it will give us a chance to see this Jenkins at the same time,' said Shenkin. 'What do you think?'

'Let's get on with it,' said Regan, lifting Mary into the boat. In no time they were across to the jetty and walking towards the shipping yard office.

'You two stand behind these timber cases out of sight, while I knock to wake him up,' said Mary.

She started hammering on the door to the shack and shouting out at the same time. 'Rhys Jenkins, wake up you lazy bugger it's Mary.' No movement from within so Mary starting kicking the door, hammering and shouting.

'Sweet Mother of God they'll hear her back at the bloody prison, so they will.'

The door swung open. 'Who is it and what the hell are you up to, are you trying to wake the dead?' said Jenkins, then seeing who it was called out, 'Mary it's you girl.' From the shadows they both saw the look of lust in Rhys Jenkins's eyes. They had little doubt that they would get what they needed, or rather Mary would.

After only a short time, in keeping with Mary's predication that Jenkins had no staying power, they both came out. Mary smoothing down her skirt and pulling at her blouse, Jenkins was buckling his belt. The man was tall, thin about forty-five or fifty with a sour looking long face topped with sparse grey hair. His clothes hung loose on his thin frame, like most tall men he stooped slightly. Hurried introductions were made while the morning light stirred the day awake.

'So, from the County Jail is it, those bloody Merthyr rioters are you?' said Jenkins.

'Shenkin stepped forward about to hit the man but Regan stopped him. 'Well let's say it was a difference of opinion we were having, seeing how we need your help, isn't that right Shenkin?' said Regan, holding on to Shenkin. Shenkin said nothing but lowered his fists stepping back as he did.

'There's been all hell let loose looking for you two. They are bringing more solders in today to search the area again. Word has it that the trials start today to get sentences doled out quick like.' The words came in a rush as if he did not want to be part of it. But his eyes kept going back to Mary who fluttered her eyelashes at him while holding his arm under her full breasts.

'Rhys is going to help us to cross the channel, aren't you my lovely boy,' said Mary, tickling Jenkins under the chin.

'Now wait a moment I said I'd see I didn't say I would,' said Jenkins

'What?! After the lovely cuddles we just had and more to come tonight isn't it,' said Mary, pulling the top of her blouse down a little lower. 'Come on Rhys you will won't you I'll make it up to you tonight, you see if I don't. I promise all the things you like, honest.

Jenkins looked self-conscious while glancing quickly at Shenkin. Then unable to help himself said. 'Well alright, but I need to be careful see.' His eyes rarely leaving Mary's ample breasts. Mary did not wait. 'We need food and water now to take back to our safe place, then you can make arrangement to get us on the Packet. We'll be here an hour before she's loaded so you and I can have some time together my naughty boy,' said Mary, giggling.

Shenkin shook his head in despair as Jenkins went to get the food. 'Can he be trusted Mary?'

'He's always kept is word to me in the past,' said Mary, shrugging her shoulders. At that moment Jenkins came back out of the shack loaded with food and water. Poor fare thought Shenkin, mainly bread, cheese some apples, but better than nothing.

'There you are Shenkin isn't Rhys a fine-looking man, good in bed too, aren't you my tall lovely,' said Mary.

In a dry voice Jenkins motioned them to a larger boat. 'We'll use this to get further down the jetty,' he said. 'We'll row down this side of the canal to one of my old warehouses, it'll be safer there, you can see anyone coming across the canal, and it will be easier in the morning to get you up to the Trader.'

Makes sense thought Shenkin, turning to Regan who nodded.

'Alright,' said Shenkin. 'But if you cross us I'll kill you,' said Shenkin.

'No, he won't,' said Mary. 'Rhys and me we are bosom friends, if you knows what I mean.' Mary said, with a wicked wink while lifting her breasts a little higher.

Regan grabbed a pair of oars both he and their new found friend dipped and lifted their way towards the warehouse. As they went, they scattered the morning ducks, causing the gulls to scream across the lighting dawn. Soon they were alongside the warehouse. Jenkin's turned to Shenkin. 'Bonded warehouse this is, see I'm the keyholder,' he said, pulling a ring of keys off his belt. The ground about them was wet and gave off a heavy salty smell, the sea mist was rolling back with the tide and for the first time Skenkin saw the sea, or at least the Bristol Channel, he stared in wonder at the vastness of the water before him, he was a man of the valleys and mountains. This was his first sight of the sea, any sea. He was brought back to the moment by Jenkin's voice. 'This is Dowlais Iron Wharf so you should feel at home here its where all the iron you produced in Merthyr comes to.'

'A lot of blood, tears and empty stomachs are stored here too. Big profits for the owners, and children with small cold feet and no shoes,' said Shenkin, his voice shaking with anger as he continued. 'A lot of burn marks and deaths went into these bundles of iron my friend, I hope you treat them kindly'.

Jenkins glanced at Shenkin. 'Just goods to me man no different to any other cargo.' Shenkin moved threateningly towards him only to be blocked by Regan. 'Leave it man he knows no better and we need him, so we do.'

Shenkin backed away as Jenkins walked further into the main part of the warehouse.

Shenkin looked at Regan the anger still present in his gaze 'See this is what it comes down to, minerals and money not men and mountains.'

Regan grunted. 'So, was it worth the lives we just spent trying to change it?'

Shenkin closed his eyes in pain. 'I hope to God it was Regan, I hope to God.'

They climbed over some bundles dropping into a space between the stacks of iron. Once inside they were completely hidden from view. Mary did not join them, they could hear her talking to Jenkins.

'No not yet Rhys they need food and so do I then we can, I promise.' Jenkins swore in frustration, then sighed in resignation. 'Right I'll get some bloody food but don't expect a fucking banquet,' Jenkins said, in frustrated anger. From their confined space they heard the door slam in temper then the key turn in the lock. Again Shenkin felt trapped as yet another door closed shut on them.

A small unkept man in his early forties met Jenkins has he stepped out of the skiff onto the jetty. 'Where the hell have you been, we'll have the Trader here soon.' Rhys Jenkins shrugged his shoulders. 'For God's sake Numbers can't a man have a quiet shit without you throwing a fit?' said Jenkins, still irritated by Mary's delay in meeting her promise.

'I'm just saying it will be here soon and us with no paperwork ready,' said Numbers. Numbers was a worrier and continued to fret about how late they were as they walked towards the small lean-to building that served as office, kitchen and Jenkins' bedroom. No one knew Numbers' real name but he was good at counting anything that stood still long enough for him to record it in his tally book.

'For Christ sake shut up Numbers we'll be ready in time there's another hour yet I'm having something to eat first,' said Jenkins.

'But I think we should make a start.'

'And I bloody don't,' said Jenkins slamming the kitchen door behind him. It swung loosely on its hinges and remained open. I must repair that door thought Jenkins, but knew he never would.

In the outer office Numbers began to prepare his ledgers for the incoming and outgoing cargo. He called out to Jenkins. 'Heard about the escaped prisoners, some of those Merthyr rioters they are. I read a notice on the wall of the gaol, offering a reward they are. Five guineas it said for information leading to their capture.' Jenkins was back at the doorway. 'How much did you say?'

'Five guineas, not the old gold piece, but it's worth in coinage, £5 5s, a tidy sum to rattle in the pocket if only I knew where they were,' said Numbers. 'Why that's a 105 shillings, 1260 pennies, 25–'

But Jenkins cut him short. 'For Christ sake, stop counting,' he said, trying to think.

'What's the matter with you this morning too much gin last night or were you unsuccessful in your whoring?' said Numbers, laughing at his own jibe.

But Jenkins was balancing lust against greed, his mind racing. He'd have Mary first then turn them in, yes but he'd need to play along with them until then. He sighed to himself pleased with his decision. He started to put some food together, a small amount of food, no point in wasting good food on men on their way back to gaol to be dangled. The humour of it made him laugh out loud.

'What the hell is wrong with you?' said Numbers.

'Never you mind boy,' Rhys Jenkins said, slyly. 'Never you mind you just keep counting numbers, Numbers.' A joke that always annoyed Numbers.

***

At midday, Jenkins held out the food and flask of water. But as Mary grabbed for them Jenkins pulled them back. 'Let's see some appreciation girl a kiss, a hug, a feel of those tits' said Jenkins. Resignation slowly spread across Mary's face. 'Come here then,' she said, holding Jenkins close and kissing him on the mouth, while he ran his grubby hands over her breasts. He began to remove her blouse but Mary pulled away. 'No not yet Rhys, the food first then we can go into a quiet corner to do it proper like.' Jenkins was beside himself with frustrated lust. 'Quick then or the bloody Trader will be here.'

Hurriedly Mary climbed up to the top of the stack and called out to Shenkin.

'Are you alright girl?' said Shenkin.

'Yes, I'm fine. Nothing I haven't done many times before,' said Mary, dropping the food and water down to them. O'Hara caught the bag of food and angrily looked up at Mary. 'We've got the food and something to drink so I could send him to his forefathers, if he has any, with no trouble at all.'

'I gave my word and we still need him to get on the ship don't we?' said Mary, honest indignation cut into every word.

'Yes, you are right my girl, take no notice of him he'd find fault with the air if he didn't have to breathe,' said Shenkin.

'Alright! Alright,' said Regan, opening the bag of food, then letting out a cry. 'Does he call this enough food for two grown men and a girl?'

Jenkins heard this and called out, 'That's all I could get my hands on this time of the morning its left my place empty, if you are not satisfied give it back.'

'It will do,' said Shenkin, tight-lipped.

'Right, I'll be back for you when its dark and get you two aboard the Trader but Mary will have to service the old captain to do it.' At this Regan was halfway out of their hiding place before Shenkin could stop him. He came face to face with Mary at the top of the stack of material.

'Do you want to ruin our escape Regan, well do you?' Regan jammed his big shoulders against the iron bars and stared into her young face. 'But we can't let you do it,' he said, as Shenkin pulled on his long legs.

'For God sake Regan, come down we'll take her with us if that's what you want, but we need to get away first. If we stay here then its recapture and back to the gaol. How will that help Mary she'll go back too, to God knows what future?'

Regan dropped down to the floor beside Shenkin. 'You'll take her with us?'

'Yes! we'll talk to her later about it, I promise,' said Shenkin.

'If you don't, I will,' said Regan.

'I know.'

Footsteps moved away from where they hid. The door to the warehouse slammed shut and they were alone, all that would happen was outside their control now.

They slowly ate the food that the girl was paying for, first with Jenkins and then the captain of the schooner. They ate in silence and guilt. Finally, Regan said. 'Dear sweet Mary in heaven has it come to this. I can't swallow the bloody bread.'

'We're alive and free aren't we so shut up and eat, it's costing enough.' They bit into their food in guilt, anger and hunger.

Having finished their food, they then set an amount aside for Mary. Shenkin turned to Regan. 'Even if we get off this wharf and across the sea to England then what, where do we go? Can we ever get back to Merthyr?'

'We could try for Ireland I know where to hide and where to get help,' said Regan.

'Right! Starve on the bogs of Ireland, that's a great idea. Said Shenkin, shaking his head. 'I was thinking what if we joined the army, at least, if they'd have us we'd be fed wouldn't we?'

'Fight for the bloody English, never!' Regan said, in disgust.

'Well! We'll need to come up with some plan or other.'

Their conversation was cut short by the door opening and voices. Mary was speaking urgently to Jenkins. 'You've had your enjoyment Rhys now remember you promised more grub and getting us on the Trader when it leaves in the morning.'

'I said I would, didn't I? How many more bloody times?'

'Good just you do it, tell the captain I'll see he's well satisfied if he'll see us right. I'll give him a time to remember tonight, better than those English girls.'

'And me mine,' said Jenkins.

'You bloody men you think of one thing all the time, yes! and you, at the same time if you like.'

'No, I'd rather just you and me,' said Jenkins.

'I was joking you bloody fool. Now get to work on the food and talking to that captain,' said Mary.

Mary turned to go to go back to their hiding place while Jenkins walked out of the door, locking it behind him. All tucked away they are and me with the key thought Jenkins, Mary tonight then the captain in the morning, after that I'll lead the soldiers to them and claim the reward. Jenkins was laughing to himself has he stepped into the skiff for the journey back to the incoming schooner, and Numbers sat fretting on the opposite jetty.

Shenkin looked at Regan as the door to the warehouse slammed shut. Then they heard Mary call out. 'Are you both alright I'm coming over the top to you?' said Mary, grunting has she heaved herself to the top of the iron bars. Dropping into Regan's open arms, he held her for a moment longer than was needed. Shenkin sighed. 'You can put her down now man.'

Regan placed her lightly on the ground. 'There's a good girl, all worn out are you?' Shenkin shot him a look of despondency. 'For God sake haven't you any bloody sense in that lump of a body?' said Shenkin, putting some bread, cheese and a rotten apple on a up turned crate.

'Now what have I said?'

'Never mind it would take too long to explain,' said Shenkin. 'Sit girl, and eat what you've earned, it's not much but it will hold us till tonight.'

Looking at the food Mary said. 'It's not much is it, but he promises more tonight when he comes with the captain. We need to be careful they don't go back on their words after they get what they want.'

'If they do, I'll kill the bastards, I'll tell them so, so I will,' said Regan.

'That may be a good thing to point out to them,' said Shenkin, then after a moment said. 'What if we hold Jenkins here over night as a safeguard? The captain needs him to sign papers for the cargo release or something doesn't he, so he'll need to come back to the warehouse in the morning. It should be easy some gin and your charms Mary. What do you think?'

'Yes, I could do it, it would mean an all-night session, but I'll do it if it makes you safe Shenkin,' said Mary, looking up at Shenkin with unabashed love in her eyes.

'Sweet Mother of God are we pimps now?' said Regan. 'Why girl, why do you do it, this selling of your body.'

At this Mary's eyes filled with tears. 'Why did you leave Ireland Regan?' she said, between sobs.

Shenkin turned to the big Irishman. 'Are you satisfied now, but go on tell her why did you leave your beloved Ireland, go on tell her,' said Shenkin, his voice growing in temper.

For a while Regan was thoughtful then his great head dropped and speaking in a low voice he said. 'To survive, to survive, anyway I could.'

After a moment Regan put a large hand very gently on Mary's slim shoulder. 'I'm sorry Mary darling, so I am.'

'It's alright Regan, I know you mean well but life is hard and at the moment your lives are in the balance and mine facing transportation to god knows where.'

'Right!' said Shenkin. 'Now that's settled, are we agreed about holding Jenkins here?' Both nodded their heads.

'Then let's see if we can get some sleep while we can. It's going to be a long night.'

Mary gazed up at Shenkin. 'Does this mean that you'll take me with you Shenkin?' Tears had left clean run marks down her dirty face. At that moment she looked to Shenkin like a small child, which after all he thought, that is what she was.

Shenkin looked at Regan and smiled. 'Yes, damn it! we'll manage somehow won't we Regan?'

With a smile as broad has his face Regan said. 'So we will, we will so.'

Reaching up Mary flung her arms around Shenkin's neck. Self-conscious Shenkin disentangled himself. 'Sleep! or none of us will have the strength to go anywhere.'

They tried to sleep. Each drifting in and out of their dreams of fear, famine, and freedom, while one dreamed of this man who had come into her life. She'd never let him down or betray him no never, till her very last breath, she would love and protect him whatever the cost.

CHAPTER 15

Aboard the *Runnymede*, Shenkin had been returned to his cell the sick bay turned into a ward. Makeshift bunks filled the floor space. The symptoms were manifest in the three men that lay before Tarn. The men's soiled clothing had been removed, blankets covered the bodies. Tarn had been back to his cabin to read his medical books, one more time. He began again to re-examine each man in turn. Under his breath he spoke to himself. 'Go over it again man, slowly.'

'Weak pulse, yes.'

'Fever, yes.'

'Vomiting, yes.'

'Diarrhoea, yes.'

'Dehydrated, yes.'

'Skin drawn tight over the skull, eyes sunken, lips blue?'

'Yes! Yes! Yes!'

'Extreme stomach cramps?'

'Yes!'

'Overwhelming thirst?'

'Yes!'

'Cholera?' said Tarn, this time out loud. 'Classic physiognomy, damn it to hell!' said Tarn, cursing himself for speaking out loud.

Crew members around him stood back from their tasks. Fear in their faces, as they stared down at the writhing men they had just carried into the sick bay. One wiped his hands down his shirt front.

'Back to your duties, and keep this to yourselves until I've spoken to the captain,' said Tarn.

'Yes sir,' said the men in a rush, eager to leave the cabin. But Tarn knew the news would spread like wild fire. 'Damn it,' said Tarn.

At that moment one of the sick men sat bolt upright. 'Water, for pity sake water.' The man was in shock his whole body shaking uncontrollably, he had soiled himself and the faeces contained parts of his gut. His face was withered and drawn as he collapsed back onto his bunk of straw. Tarn lifted the man's head, the eyes were open but lifeless. The first of how many, thought Tarn.

'Sweet Mother of God, have mercy on us all,' said Tarn, crossing himself, as if the genuflection would protection him from what was to come. Tarn the man of medicine knew better.

Rumours like disease spread fast in a ship. Tarn met Ketch as he made his way to the captain's cabin.

'Well sir is it what I hope to god it isn't.'

The Surgeon- Superintendent of the convict ship the *Runnymede* looked at the sergeant. A heartbeat hung between them, beating out their dread. It was Tarn who recovered first. 'I want you to inspect the rest of the prisoners Ketch, report to me their condition, we'll separate any that are ill with fever or the like,' said Tarn, in as quiet and as controlled a voice as he could muster.

'But that's not for me to do sir, no sir, that's not my job, sir!' Ketch's voice was laced with undisguised terror.

'Don't talk such bloody bilge man, we are in a confined space on a ship in the middle of a bloody ocean, no one is going to avoid contact with it,' Tarn said in a cold chilling voice, leaving no room for Ketch to protest further.

'Sir,' said Ketch, already thinking who he could order to do it. 'Burke, Thomson follow me at the bloody double,' screamed Ketch.

Tarn made his way to the captain's cabin to break the news to Moxey.

'Come.' Moxey looked up as Tarn entered the cabin. 'Well, what is it?' said Moxey, his words clipped and sharp at being disturbed. Tarn stood in front of the captain's desk which was covered by a chart, compass and dividers. If he was right about the cholera, and he was. Tarn thought how useless plotting the route may become.

'Out with it man, can't you see how busy I am, damn it.'

So Tarn got straight to the point. 'Cholera captain, one convict dead another two dying.'

The colour drained from Moxey's face. 'Cholera!... are you sure?' Tarn said nothing, which said it all. 'But how from where?' said Moxey, with alarm.

Tarn looked down at the captain and sighed. 'There is divided opinion as to the how, or the where, with the treatments just as diverse and controversial. But the bacteria is either in water, airborne or both. What is certain is that filth, poor diet and the lack of good sanitary conditions spreads the disease. This is aggravated by an overcrowded living environment. I have read all I can find in my medical journals together with my notes from treating typhus and cholera during the recent war. The field hospitals were breeding grounds for such fevers, the view is that there are two kinds of cholera, simple and malignant, during the war doctors who had served in India were able to diagnose which was which,' said Tarn, pausing for Moxey to ask the obvious question.

'Well man, which do we have?'

'Malignant cholera without a doubt,' said Tarn, in such a deliberate a voice that it left no room for questioning. 'I saw a great deal of it in the charnel houses from Spain to France. It is, as the name suggests, the more severe of the two. The contagion-miasma concept maintains that the disease-bearing agent is communicated directly from person to person. The anti-contagions however believe it is due to environmental causes, particularly the water source. I believe it's a contribution of both. This will necessitate an immediate quarantine policy, isolation of the sick, fumigation of goods and the environs. Fresh water ideally; none of course is available, so we must boil what we have. These measures as I say to take immediate effect.

Moxey seemed confused by the medical jargon. 'Plain bloody English man.' He didn't wait for a reply. 'Dear god! we must prevent it from spreading. Damn it! I order you to control it. Dispose of the bodies overboard, without delay. The convicts are to be confined to their cells. They are to be watered and fed through the gratings. At all other times the gratings are to be shut and locked day and night. Is that clear doctor?' said Moxey, stopping to take a breath. 'Is that clear doctor?' he repeated in a louder voice. Every tone of word spoke of his terror of this disease, one that he had heard of and seen many times in his travels of the world's oceans and ports, particularly in the Indian subcontinent, now it was on his ship.

Tarn too had seen this disease in the charnel houses of the war, where he had amputated arms and legs only to lose his patients to these very fevers in the stench and filth of battlegrounds. For heartbeats, both men said nothing the silence broken only by the creaking of the ship's timbers, then Tarn spoke in the same slow deliberate voice.

'No captain this is my responsibility, I will decide which is the best course of action you will continue with the good running of the ship, plotting our course to the nearest port for fresh water, food and any assistance they can give,' said Tarn, then after a moment added, 'That is if they'll have us, you will need to fly the yellow flag captain to let them know we have fever on board.'

Moxey nodded his head. 'Of course, I'll have Lawson run it up when we approach any harbour.'

For a moment Moxey just sat staring at Tarn aghast, while he considered what other action he needed to take. To begin with he was fully aware of the charge placed upon the Surgeon-Superintendent by the Transport Commissioners London. Tarn would prepare a full report on the voyage as to the care and final condition of the convicts and the cooperation of the captain in the implementation of these duties. The captain in turn would add his comments to the report, the number of convicts embarked and disembarked, their condition of health before, during, and at disembarkation, together with the satisfactory joint execution of these duties. Finally, the report would be agreed by both men and would carry their signatures. The report acted as checks and balances for both Moxey and Tarn. To do otherwise, or fail in these duties would cost Tarn his position and Moxey the loss of any future government contracts. Moxey fought to regain his composure, after some moments he looked up again at Tarn.

'Yes, your decision of course, as to the best course of action in containing this fever,' said Moxey. All his overbearing manner had been sucked out of him. He looked as limp as a sail that had lost the wind. Tarn could see the captain was struggling to regain his position, to come to terms with the situation. The ship rolled them in a slow dance of time, the timbers creaking the minutes away. Orders bellowed to the crew drifted into the cabin as the two men took in the moment. Finally, Moxey cleared his throat. 'Very well doctor what steps have you taken, or will you take?' Tarn took a deep breath. 'The convict Shenkin has been removed from the sick bay and returned to the between decks back into his cell, while still suffering from delirium he continues to recover. The sick convicts and crew are now in the sick bay and the cabin rearranged to take any further cases. As I have reported one has already died, the other two have high temperatures, vomiting, diarrhoea and cramps consistent with the disease. I have given orders to Ketch to check all the convicts, Lawson to do the same with the crew and Lieutenant Feltsham and the soliders.' Tarn paused seeing the look upon the captain's face. 'There was no time to lose in this matter captain while I reported to you I...' Tarn corrected himself. 'We needed to know how far the disease has spread,' said Tarn, again pausing for Moxey to speak. The captain said nothing he merely nodded his head. Tarn went on. 'All water must be boiled before being drunk, or used in cooking. The sick must be given copious amounts of boiled water. I'll need oil for rubbing into muscles that will go into spasms. On checking our cargo, I find we have an amount of camphor on board. This together with all alcohol, oil and sugar is to be stored in a safe area. The cabin is to be locked, the key to be in my possession, any other items I might need will also be held there' Tarn again waited for Moxey's comments.

'Very well,' said Moxey, but not without some difficulty.

Tarn went on. 'We must have an area set aside for quarantine; this will hold all, I repeat, all, who succumb to the malady. Malignant cholera is a deadly disease, as I am sure you are well aware of captain, consequently I can give no guarantee as to how many of us will be alive by the end of this voyage.'

The chilling words hung between them like a death sentence. It would creep over the ship day by day, hour by hour, minute by dreadful minute. Finally, Moxey spoke. 'But you can not mean convicts, crew and God forbid possible passengers, will be placed together. Tarn I will not hear of it do you understand?'

'Captain this is not open to discussion. I must have complete control of the situation if we are to have any chance of getting through this.'

'But all crowded together Tarn, it's just not acceptable.'

'Captain Moxey there is much that will become difficult to accept as time goes on, but I assure you we will be forced to accept them.'

Again the silence between the two men was palpable. Moxey strained to keep control, then in a clipped voice said. 'Very well doctor do what must be done, but I am to be kept informed at all times is that understood?'

Tarn was not going to argue the point. As the disease spread the captain would have no option but to accept whatever Tarn said.

Tarn simply said, 'Sir.'

As Tarn was closing the cabin door Moxey called after him. 'Give my compliments to Lord Feltsham and would he join me here.'

'Right sir.'

***

Throughout the ship alarm ran rampant. Tarn did not have to search for Feltsham, he was waiting for him on the quarterdeck. 'Well! Tarn is it true?'

Tarn studied his lordship's face. 'Is what true, my lord?'

'Don't be obtuse man, this rumour of fever that is going around,' said Feltsham, in a small whispered voice, as if that would ward the evil off.

'Ah! You mean the cholera?'

Feltsham shrunk back from the very word, but before Tarn could say more Ketch came up the companion ladder. 'Three ill, six say they feel hot and weak, two others have the cramps sir.' Then added. 'It's camp fever sir isn't? Not waiting for a reply he went on. 'Saw it during the Peninsular campaign, I did, then again in France. killed more on both sides then ever died on the battlefield. Both us and the frenchies built huge bonfires to burn the dead. The arms and legs the surgeons had chopped off, the dead from the fevers, typhus, typhoid, the worst of them all was cholera. It marked the battlegrounds it did, the stench was a smell that never leaves any soldier. Please god tell me it's not what I think it is sir.' Ketch said, in a rush of words, as if the very saying of it would tempt it close

Tarn looked at the Right Honourable Lord Percival Hugo Feltsham and the coarse, battle-hardened Sergeant Thomas Ketch. They were equal now in the face of a disease that did not differentiate between the high born or the lowly.

Tarn sighed. 'Yes, it's cholera also known as camp or gaol fever. The likely cause is overcrowding, unwashed bodies, bad water and food, poor sanitary conditions together with lice merrily hopping from person to person. An accurate description of this ship wouldn't you say?' said Tarn, looking at them both. 'Or of the hulks at Woolwich Docks, that you were so in a hurry to leave Lord Feltsham.' Tarn's voice coloured his words with irony and bitterness.

Feltsham alarmed by Tarn's words busied himself by pulling at his cuffs. 'Are you saying that I contributed in any way to this?'

Tarn turned slightly to look into Feltsham's eyes. 'Your haste to leave on the next tide gave the hulk prison authorities the opportunity to get rid of any suspect illnesses, they may have had. London has seen outbreaks of both typhus and cholera over the last few months.'

'If anyone is at fault sir, it is you sir. As the Surgeon-Superintendent of this ship were you not responsible for the examination of all the convicts before they are allowed to be transported?'

This was indeed true. Tarn had examined all the prisoners but the last group had been hastily checked so they could make the next tide. All at the insistence of the captain. Tarn sighed. 'Yes that is correct, but I was not advised of any illnesses or deaths from cholera, typhus or any other disease by the hulk medical staff. If they had sir!' Tarn paused, he was trying to keep himself under control. 'If I had then I would have isolated all the convicts marked for transportation for at least one or maybe two weeks in the hulk hospitable ships. Which would have been most inconvenient for you, would it not?'

Feltsham stiffened visibly. Then his cultivated manners slipped and Tarn saw the ruthlessness beneath the veneer. Forgetting the sergeant Feltsham scowled at the doctor. 'You bloody Pope loving Irish upstart you forget your station.' His voice tense with malice and contempt.

'Ah! your true colours, my lord. I assure you we will need all the candour we can muster in the coming days, creditors will seem as nothing compared to a pox ridden ship.'

The moment slowed to an unreal time, heartbeats quickened at the fear of what may lay ahead of them. To his credit, breeding or both Feltsham recovered his pose quickly fully aware that the doctor, and only the doctor, stood between him and cholera.

A forced smile spread across Feltsham's face. 'Come now doctor let us not fall out, surly this fever can be contained?'

Tarn turned to Ketch. 'Sergeant in the charnel houses of the battlefields what happened when camp fever broke out, whether cholera or typhus?'

Ketch who had been enjoying listening to his betters arguing brought himself back to the present. 'Spread like wildfire it did. We burnt corpses with their clothes on. You could smell the stench everywhere. But try as they did they could not stop it. It spread across the entire battle front like raking cannon fire,' said Ketch, the look of terror back in his eyes.

Tarn looked at Feltsham. 'We, Lord Percival, do not have the benefit of open space. We breathe, eat, drink, and sleep in the close confines of this ship. One hundred and nineteen convicts, a crew, the men at arms, yourself, Lady Feltsham, the Captain, his niece, the Lieutenant and the Wilkes. A total of one hundred and ninety-seven souls, with one doctor in attendance in the middle of a vast bloody ocean with no fresh clean water or fresh food. All things considered the charnel houses of the battlefields in Spain and France seem the better of the two options wouldn't you say?'

Feltsham said nothing bringing an end to any further discussion on blame or otherwise.

The Surgeon-Superintendent turned on his heel. 'Ketch follow me and bring two able-bodied men with you.' The term able-bodied was not lost on Feltsham it was plainly going to get worse. The watch bell rang out like the sound of a burial service. Burke and Thomson were still close at hand. Without waiting for Ketch they both fell in behind the infantry sergeant. The king's shilling had hammered discipline and obedience into these men. It had been driven home by the lash and officers of the line. They acted instinctively, regardless of cholera or any other pestilence just as they had across the plains of India, the rugged mountains of Spain and the killing fields of France. The only difference on this ship was the rolling tilting floor beneath their feet.

***

Regan and Collins were pushed and manhandled back into their cells. Where they were both delighted but surprised to find Shenkin laying on his bunk. He was asleep laying in a pool of sweat but seem to be breathing in a steady regularity. 'Well would you look at that now sleeping like a baby and him with enough sins on his conscience to keep a priest busy for a year,' said Regan, smiling down at Shenkin. That he was pleased to see him was obvious. 'Sure we'll not disturb him, let him sleep it out.' Then added 'God knows how many of us will still be alive to welcome him back.' Regan looked down at Collins. Who was trying to ease the pain in his hand from the branding, the scar was inflamed from all the saltwater. Then Collins looked up at O'Hara. 'I don't think I can take much more Regan the cholera will see the end of me. All that's happened so far and now fever on board. Whatever it is it will get me I know it will,' said Collins, wrapping an old piece of dirty cloth around his trembling hand.

'Sure you and I will be fine, so we will. And now that Shenkin is back, why we'll soon figure how to get through this,' said O'Hara. Collins smiled a thin faint smile, but said nothing.

Ketch shouted from the gangway. 'How many feel ill? How many thirsty? How many vomiting? How many dead?' Check them all Burke you take the portside Thomson you the starboard side. No! To the bloody right man. Jesus some of you deserve to die. Report to me quick has you can,' said Ketch, wanting to hurry up the companionway into god's clean air.

Burke and Thomson approached each convict slowly, scarves tied over their noses and mouths. Only their eyes betrayed the fear in their faces, as one at a time they looked into each cell. Halfway down the starboard side the soldier called out.

'Anyone sick or got the cramps in there?' said Thomson. No one replied. 'Come on, we can't treat you if we don't know, now can we?'

A weak voice came from a convict in the next cell. 'They've been ill all day mate, can't you smell the stink of shit?'

'Four here sergeant it sounds like the next cell too,' said Thomson. At the same time Burke called out, two ill here one dead. It was the cell next to O'Hara and Collins. 'We're for it now Regan its creeping towards us.' Collins said, in a flat toneless voice.

'What fever is it Burke?' called Regan. Burke stopped for a moment then said. 'It's fucking cholera Irishman, two are already dead, no three now counting this man. The sick bay is filling up quicker than a pub in the Eastend on a Saturday night. Surgeon-Superintendent Tarn is doing all he can but how do you stop cholera, saw it in the war it spreads fast. But I see Shenkin is sleeping well enough, the lucky bastard, even missed being branded. What about you two any sickness or the shits?'

'We're alright so far,' said O'Hara, crossing himself.

O'Hara studied Burke's face or rather his eyes, the fear was clear. 'But there must be a remedy or a linctus, there must be something he can do?' said O'Hara.

'I wish to god there was Irishman for we are all prisoners now. I'll let you know how things are going,' said Burke, moving slowly down the line. O'Hara turned back to Collins. 'Now don't go worrying lad we're not dead yet, at least I don't think we are,' said O'Hara, giving the lad the best smile he could manage. He looked down at Shenkin still sleeping, if a little restless. 'You stay where you are, for this is the hell they told you about in chapel, and where the Jesuits told me I'd end up. Collins' eyes were wide, his face twisted in pain has he held his stomach. 'Regan I...' but he collapsed in the corner of his bunk, vomit spilling from his month. 'Oh no Sweet Mary not you too.'

'Burke, Burke! It's Collins.'

'I'm alright Regan I just feel weak. I don't want to go to the sick bay, please don't let them take me I'll never get out,' said Collins, in a strained voice.

Burke turned to go back to their cell. All the time saying, 'Yes, yes its cholera.' to everyone who asked.

Chains rattled as the convicts took in the fearful news. Whispers began that turned into shouts of alarm. A chant went up. 'Let us out, let us out.'

'Call Ketch we need more soldiers down here or we'll have an uprising on your hands'

Thomson went up to the top deck, but Sergeant Ketch was already on his way back with several armed men. Lieutenant Feltsham called from the safety of the quarterdeck. 'Restore order Sergeant, shoot if you must.'

'You bloody fool the convicts are frightened men, don't you understand that?' Lawson said flatly. But before the Lieutenant could answer down in the back black corner of a cell someone screamed.

CHAPTER 16

Through it all Shenkin slept, sweat running freely off his body. Then with a shudder his eyes flickered and a garbled sound came past his lips, he twisted on his cell bunk. Collins, sick as he was, moved to help him. 'Leave him!' said Regan, the sharpness of his words startled the youngest. 'I was just going to make more him comfortable Regan, that's all,' said Collins, falling back in a heap. O'Hara was fearful of him touching Shenkin, of spreading the fever, then he felt guilty.

'I know lad but he's safer in his mind of yesterday, then he is in this hellhole of today, he'll join us soon enough. Let him dream it out, you rest yourself save your strength.'

But Collins face was already becoming drawn and pale, his eyes the biggest feature of his face. 'I need water Regan, please I need water.'

Burke came into the cell. 'Get this man to the sick bay on the double.' His voice muffled by the large red handkerchief over his mouth.

'No please Regan, stop them.'

'You'll be better off there lad, some medicine from the doctor to stop the cramps. Isn't that right Burke?'

'Yes, yes now get him out of here.'

Collins screamed.

***

We need to wake up, wake up, wake up!!!

'Come on wake up. Jenkins will be back here soon,' Shenkin said, first kicking Regan then shaking Mary gently by the arm. Shaking the sleep out Regan grumbled to himself. 'Now what?' said Shenkin.

'I'll kill the bastard if we are nothing more than easy payment for his lust, so I will.'

'I'm worried too that that is all we are to him,' said Shenkin, looking at Mary for reassurance. Before Mary could say anything, Regan struck his fist into the side of one of the timber crates. 'Right let's beat the shit out of the little sod.'

'Shut up someone's coming,' said Shenkin. The three of them looked up at the top of their pit of crates and metal rods.

'It's me, Jenkins.'

'Right,' said Mary, beginning to climb her way up with the help of Shenkin.

'Do you have some more food Rhys, and is all arranged with the captain of the Packet?' said Mary, has she struggled to the top

'Yes to both questions that's if you are still ready to give me what I want.' Then added, 'and old Jack as we agreed. He says he can get them on the Packet by mid-morning, on the next high tide; the old bucket needs as much sea under her as possible,' said Jenkins, by way of explanation. It was lost on Mary but Shenkin agreed from inside the stack of materials. 'Right but tell him the three of us are going. So Mary will need some men's clothes, large enough to disguise her female form.' Jenkins laughed. 'I'll do that once I've seen it all myself,' he said.

Regan was halfway out of their hiding place before Shenkin managed to stop him. 'Steady Regan.'

'Rhys the lovely man has brought more food,' called out Mary. 'I'll bring it to you before I go to work.' The door to the warehouse clanged open and another, older, voice greeted Jenkins. 'So this is our girl is she, nice young and rounded she is too.' His English voice strange upon Shenkin's ear has he strained to hold Regan back.

'Right! Who's first?' said Mary.

They both sat looking at each other as the time dragged while Mary paid for their crossing to England. At last Mary's voice called out. 'The captain says he'll be back in two hours with old clothes for us all, so be ready.' With that the door slammed shut. 'I'll just see him to the skiff. I'll be back for the empty food containers also with paperwork for your crossing, which you'll need for the other side to leave the docks,' said Jenkins. The door opened and closed again with a loud clatter as metal hit metal. 'Damn we wanted to hold him with us,' said Shenkin, in anger.

Then after a moment. 'But I had not considered the need for paperwork, so I suppose it works out alright,' said Shenkin, a little apprehensively.

'No he's right. Shenkin didn't I have to show paperwork leaving the boat from Ireland before I could joined you heathens in Merthyr?' said Regan.

'Well! Let's hope so because we're trapped here Regan. I just don't trust him regardless of what Mary says.'

***

Jenkins had already put his plans into operation. Sexual satisfaction on his face, money in his pocket from the captain for the use of Mary with more to come from the authorities at the gaol. Bidding old Jack a safe crossing back to England on the evening tide Jenkins turned to face Captain Wagstaff and his men who had been waiting for him on the jetty.

'Good morning, Captain, do you have the reward?' said Jenkins, holding out his salt-stained sinful hand.

'On the capture of the prisoners that is what the notice says man, so where are they?' The captain was in ill mood from the search of the night before, lack of sleep and painful feet. Having returned to the gaol the captain had been told about the hurried sentencing of all the main leaders of the uprising, including the two still at large. Dic Pendryn would be the scapegoat for them all and would be hanged.

That afternoon carriages would be waiting to take the rest to the hulks in London. There they would await transportation to Australia. So the news that someone knew where the last of the leaders were had the captain again limping down into Cardiff Docks. The officer turned to his sergeant. 'This cur of a man Jenkins has brought us right back to where we ended the search in the early hours of this morning. I'll teach him to hold out his grubby hand for money if the bastard has us on a wild goose chase, I'll have him in the bloody gaol with the rest. And remember sergeant, the girl is of no consequence but one of the men was one of the main leaders of the riot. I want both men alive, do you understand Sergeant?'

'Yes Sir.'

Wagstaff's commanding officer, a lieutenant-colonel, together with the governor of the gaol had both left him in no doubt that if he failed to recapture Daniel Shenkin, alive if possible, then he could say goodbye to any chance of advancement. His future bride's family would take a poor view of their daughter marrying a man of low rank in the Royal Glamorgan Militia. Captain Albert Cuthbert Wagstaff stood six foot tall, every inch the English officer and gentleman. He was the son of a vicar of a small church in Sussex. His stifling church upbringing had made him determined not to go into God's ministry he had spent to many days listening to boring sermons by his father, when he could have been out foxhunting with the local gentry not crumpling his trousers while bent in prayer. He had missed the war and with no chance of swift promotion had reluctantly taken a commission in the Glamorgan Regiment. To add to his discomfort, he had been forced to wait on this bloody informer on a cold windswept jetty. His soft upbringing had left him with a permanent petulant look upon his face, much to the ridicule of his men and the despair of his sergeant.

'Well man are we to stand here all day, I need to get back to the gaol as quickly as possible?' said Wagstaff. How he hated Wales and everything Welsh. This illiterate grubby man who had kept him waiting was typical of his kind.

Not waiting for a reply, he went on. 'Well! Have you no tongue in your head as well as no brains? Speak up damn you.'

'Don't fret yourself your honour I have them all locked up ready,' said Jenkins, swinging a key in his hand then turning towards the warehouse.

'Follow me your honour we'll have them back in the gaol in no time.' Led by Jenkins they marched their way along the jetty. The captain still limping slightly while cursing under his breath. His men shuffled and sneered behind his back, while the sergeant wished he was back with his old Scottish regiment.

As they marched the short distance to the warehouse, the captain went over in his mind the events of the morning. The trials had started early with the sentencing of the rest of the rioters processed as speedily as possible. 'We must get it over with Wagstaff, if not London will send a judge of their own choice,' said the prison governor, which would undermine his position. He was determined not to let that happen.

At that stage two, of the leaders had been sentenced to hang Richard Lewis, aka Dic Penderyn, and Lewis Lewis. This was later changed, only Dic Penderyn would hang. While both were regarded to be among the main instigators of the riot, the government did not want martyrs. Letters had been sent to the Marquess of Bute, who owned large tracts of industrialised land in South Wales which gave him considerable sway with the Whig government, he suggested that Mr Justice Bosanquet would request in his report that the sentencing of Lewis Lewis should be commuted to transportation for life. Lord Melbourne, Home Secretary in the Whig government, made the decision not to prosecute the rebel leaders for treason, but that one man would hang as an example. That man was Dic Penderyn, convicted for the wounding of a soldier.

The hanging would also criminalise the action of the Merthyr men rather than give the riot any political significance. The law and its officers acted with speed and purpose. The rioters one by one or in groups were brought before the hastily arranged courts both at Merthyr and Cardiff.

David Evans, eighteen years old, taken into custody at the riot. Sentenced to ten years transportation.

William Thomas twenty years old arrested holding an offensive weapon (a sweeping brush handle). Sentenced to ten years transportation.

Liam O'Toole, twenty-two years old, charged with damage to property and spitting at a shopkeeper. Sentenced to fourteen years transportation.

On and on it went the gravel slammed down like the ticking of the tower clock on St John's church that stood in the churchyard outside the gaol. Striking off men's lives, as it ticked its way through the morning. Most were sentenced with transportation to a penal colony in Australia. The rest, those of lesser crimes, were sentenced to hard labour at local prisons. A number, as young as ten or twelve, were given sentences of five to eight years depending on whether they had resisted arrest.

The punishment was indeed swift, all the leaders apart from Richard Lewis known as Dic Penderyn would be sent to the London Hulks to await transportation. All that is except Shenkin and O'Hara – however, the governor assured the court that they would be recaptured that morning. This in mind, Captain Wagstaff snapped at Jenkins as they entered the warehouse. 'If they are not here you'll get the sharp end of a bayonet not money.' Jenkins had lifted out his hand again, hoping for payment. But dropped it quickly at the officer's words. The officer's voice echoed around the warehouse the words plainly heard by the fugitives.

O'Hara turned to Shenkin. 'Damn the bloody man he's betrayed us, well that's it we fight our way out.'

Shenkin nodded his head slowly. 'Looks like it, Regan' he said, already starting to climb out of their hiding place eager to let loose his anger on Jenkins and whoever else he had brought with him. Regan was close behind him. Mary scrambled after them sobbing has she climbed. They landed squarely on top of Wagstaff and his sergeant. The officer spun around but too late Shenkin drove his boot down the side of the man's left shin. Wagstaff screamed in pain then collapsed in a heap as Shenkin hit him full in the face. One down.

Regan grabbed the nearest soldier and used him has a battering ram to take down another two, he used his boots to render them out of the fight. Four down.

Shenkin headed for Jenkins reaching him as he ran for the door. Shenkin turned him around in one ferocious move driving his clenched fist into Jenkins' jaw has he did so. As Jenkins went down the soldiers rushed them.

Wagstaff wanting to make sure of the recapture had brought a quarter of his company with him, twenty-five together with the sergeant.

Regardless of being outnumbered soldiers were falling to the fierce fighting of Shenkin and Regan. Jenkins began to get up but Shenkin hit him with an iron bar that was resting up against one of the crates. Shenkin gave a grim smile as gristle and bone disintegrated. He turned to face the rest of the soldiers who had now formed a circle around them, bayonets fixed. Mary trembling and sobbing had stayed close to Shenkin. For a moment all was quiet save for Wagstaff who was groaning on the ground. Shenkin and O'Hara now stood back-to-back, daring the soldiers to charge. 'Come on let's have you, one at a time, or all of you bastards at once,' shouted Shenkin. No one moved. 'Too yellow are you, I'll mark you for life, come on which one is first?' Shenkin, said again, swinging the iron bar as he spoke. Unlike his officer the sergeant was no vicar's son but a burly man who had earned his stripes the hard way. His officer down, the sergeant's Glaswegian voice cut through the silence like cannon fire. 'Seal the exit and move this bloody officer out of the way.' Then he turned to face the cornered men. A street fighter from the slums of Glasgow and the battlefields of Spain and France. Recognising a fellow brawler Shenkin smiled has he moved to meet the sergeant head on. Pushing a young soldier out of harm's way he closed on the sergeant fast, grabbing both the man's ears. Shenkin pulled his head forward while smashing his own head upwards. The sergeant's right eyebrow split open but he never murmured just grunted as he hit Shenkin in the face with the butt of his musket. The blow opened the old scar above his own eyebrow. The young soldier was hanging from Shenkin's neck while two more pinned his arms. Shenkin kicked one in the groin and headbutted another, both dropped to the ground. Seven down.

The sergeant, his face covered in blood, brought his musket down hard on Shenkin's foot then drove the butt into his stomach. The wind left Shenkin's body. Four soldiers had Regan pinned to the ground another two charged forward, bayonets extended directly at Shenkin, who now lay breathless against one of the crates. Mary shrieked out Shenkin's name and ran forward between the points of the bayonets and Shenkin's body. She was pushed forward on to Shenkin. He felt the tip of a bayonet protrude from Mary's stomach. She looked up at him a smile on her dirty pretty face then sunk to her knees blood flowing from her mouth as the musket was twisted free from her body. Mary's body fell sideways, the life gone from her young eyes forever. In the moment it took Shenkin to take in the horror in front of him the soldiers were all over him. The officer had finally got to his feet, but still groggy, blood running down the side of his petulant face. The big sergeant had Shenkin pinned down three bayonets pointed at his throat he twisted and turned, but it was useless. Regan had got to his feet but was still held firmly by the soldiers against the wall of the warehouse, straw fell around them from one of the opened crates. Regan stood braced against the wall, a look of sadness on his strong Irish features all the fight gone out of him at the sight of Mary's lifeless body. The sergeant leaned close to Shenkin. 'Give in lad it's, all over.' Blood from both men pooled at their feet. Then turning to his officer, the sergeant said. 'Right sir, we've got the bastards.'

'Get out of my way let me at him,' screamed the captain; drawing his sword he rushed at Shenkin. Moving sharply across his path the sergeant knocked the officer off balance. 'Sorry sir but I thought for a moment that you were going to kill him and us with orders to bring him back alive to the gaol for sending to the hulks in London. Captain Wagstaff, sniffling in frustration and anger, turned quickly to look at the sergeant bloody face. In fast heartbeats, the officer tried to regain control. The girl was dead, so be it, no loss there. The informant Jenkins lay bleeding and fighting for breath through a broken nose, good I'll pocket the reward. The two men recaptured possible promotion secured. Right.

They returned to the gaol more like returning troops from a battlefield then an escort for prisoners. Nine were covered in blood, a number had uniforms torn, all were in disarray. Captain Wagstaff called a halt. Their prisoners swayed but stood upright. Both bloody, both with mean hard looks upon their faces. Ropes tied their hands behind their backs, which had dug deep into their wrists. The officer limping forward proceeded to knock on the gaol door while a crowd of people shouted insults at him. The small window in the door opened, the guard seeing the officer quickly swung the main door open. Inside carriages and carts lined the courtyard. Men were being organised into groups of six then packed into the waiting carts or carriages that the governor had been able to muster at such short notice.

Governor Woods stood mopping his brow, a look of nervousness on his face. He stood on the steps that he had only a few days previously welcomed them to the gaol. Turning to the big studded doors of the gaol he smiled a sickly smile at the sight of the recaptured men. 'Do not take them to their cell captain keep them tied up for placing in one of the carts.'

'Which cart sir?'

'Any damn cart, just get rid of them.' Woods said in a flurry of words.

'But they are not chained sir just the ropes.'

The governor exasperated shouted out. 'Dear God man they have been sentenced in their absence to twenty years transportation and must be on their way to Woolwich Docks Hulks with the rest. Just load them, they are now the responsibility of this armed London detachment,' he said, adding under his breath, thank God.

Up into a cart they went to be greeted by the other men.

Bloody dirty hands still tied behind their backs and saddened by the death of Mary they began their journey to London. Shenkin gazed in wonder at the passing scene outside of the gaol. Never had he seen so many people gather together, some shouting encouragement while others screamed abuse. Fighting had broken out among the factions, a mix of soldiers and the constabulary trying in vain to maintain order. One man called out to Shenkin, a man he knew slightly from the Merthyr Ironworks.

'We'll not forget you Shenkin,' he said, emotion catching each word. Shenkin was sure there were tears in the man's eyes, but he may have been mistaken. What he was not mistaken about was the woman standing beside the man. It was Cathy O'Hara tears streaming down her beautiful face, she must have walked the twenty-five miles from Merthyr for her last sight of the man she loved. Regan saw her at the same time he called out to her, leaning over the side of their cart as he did so. One of their Dragoon escorts pulled his horse over to the cart then drawing his sword struck Regan across the side of his face with the flat of the blade. Cathy screamed out abuse at the dragoon and went to throw a stone but the man at her side stopped her. 'It'll only make it worse for him my lovely,' he said, holding Cathy's arm. Regan swayed but stayed on his feet fresh blood running down the side of his face. He looked at the dragoon while Shenkin held on to him. The Irishman had hate etched deep into his face, the horseman shied away from Regan's fearful stare. It was the last they saw of Cathy O'Hara as the convoy of misery slowly made its way out of the town.

In the long stop start week it took to get to London another three died, one of which was Liam O'Toole, a close friend of Regan's who had fought by their side during the rising. On a stretch of open country road the escort of soldiers threw the bodies into a ditch. Large black crows began to circle as their cart moved away. Shenkin's hate mounted with every jolt of the cart and passing mile. They were given little food or water, slowly even the strongest among them were beginning to weaken. If the plan was to keep them weak, and in so doing make them easier to handle as they approached the great city of London, the plan was working. Finally, on a smoke-filled early September evening they arrived in the breath-taking city of London. Through the smog the place began to take shape, then all of a sudden it was all around them. Dirty, raucous, impressive, overwhelming. If Shenkin thought Cardiff was large, it was a village compared to the sprawling English capital. Great buildings climbed into the thick heavy dirty smoke. While people hustled and bustled for space to move, to breathe. Pushing into each other with no forgiveness in their rough gestures. It was a place to survive or to go under in its crush of humanity. Shenkin saw a man selling hot pies, another bread, while a third sat in the middle of the road, as drunk as a lord.

Two of the soldiers dismounted and threw the drunk into the path of the milling crowds, who walked around or over him in unconcerned interest. Life was precarious in this city, a city that commanded so much of the world's wealth and military power. We, thought Shenkin, are but pawns to be pushed aside in its tide of progress. Their efforts for recognition in their black Welsh valley a mere fleabite to be scratched with contempt, nothing but a small irritation that all these people probably didn't even know or care about. Their government had dealt with it swiftly, harshly. It was now sweeping it away to a land beyond the seas far from this capital of the British Empire.

As Shenkin pondered upon this, painted women shamelessly flaunted themselves in front of each carriage and cart calling out to soldiers and felons alike in the most profane language. They stood brazen skirts lifted, blouses undone to show their wares. At their sides sat limbless soldiers begging for coin or food, their unconnected limbs now lay like decaying monuments on the battlefields of Europe. Back in his valley chapel Shenkin had once read a description of hell, how well it fitted the sight before him. His reverie was broken by a pail of foul-smelling liquid cascading over them from a window high above them. A woman's toothless smile framed by greasy hair shouted abuse to be joined by handclapping from the whores. The contents fell over the convicts, most of it covered the man by the side of Shenkin. The soldiers joined in the laughter as they watched the last vestiges of the man's dignity drip away. The man turned to Shenkin. 'Is this what we fought for Shenkin?'

Shenkin looked at Tom Thomas, piss and shit sliding down a once proud face. 'Hold on Tom we'll get through this,' said Shenkin, trying to clean the filth from the man. 'Leave it damn you.'

As Shenkin closed his eyes in sad bitterness and self-knowledge of their dire predicament the lead rattler turned into a narrow street where high buildings towered menacingly above them. In a few hundred yards they came to a juddering stop. The dragoons dismounted, eager to rid themselves of their prisoners, their commanding officer quickly exchanged the necessary paperwork with the hulk overseer who stood waiting on a small jetty that thrust out into a dark river, a number of long boats bobbed on the rise of the water. Shenkin now out of the cart was pushed towards the jetty. The felons were lined up by the soldiers who in turn were replaced by the hulk guards. They were then grouped into eights chained together at their legs their hands made free. Each group filed down steep stones steps into the waiting boats, there to be seated twofold, their legs fastened to the boat. The rattle of chains across the cobbled wharf rang out along the river. The evening was foggy, cold, a miserable mean wind blew across the water. This did not stop a small crowd from gathering to see the convicts loaded. The guards cursed every man they had to handle, as if they were to blame for the foul weather.

One guard kicked a convict who hesitated at being placed in one of the boats. 'Move you bastard or I'll make you swim out to the hulk,' he said, making to kick the man again. The overseer came over beside them. 'Now, now you mustn't hurt them for they are the property of the government, with this he hit the man across the back with a heavy knotted rope that sent him crashing into the boat. The boat load swayed dangerously as water drenched all in the boat. 'Bail the water out of that boat,' screamed the overseer. The guards and crowd laughed at the sight of the convicts struggling to empty out as much of the water as possible before the boat sunk. Shenkin seated at the stern of his boat took in the scene as he called out to a man coiling a rope up on the jetty.

Cupping his hand at the side of his mouth he shouted. 'What is this place my friend?'

The man stopped coiling the rope looking astonished at a convict who dared to speak. 'What is this place why its Woolwich and you're in the Warren, and I'm not your bloody friend,' he said, spitting black tobacco expertly on to Shenkin below.

Regan seated just in front of Shenkin turned as far around as he could. 'Friendly bastards aren't they?' he said, the words coming in a rush the first he had spoken for a long time.

Shenkin nodded his head. 'Well! Speaking again are we?' said Shenkin. Hearing voices from the boat the overseer called down. 'Shut your bleeding gobs or I'll have every other man over the side and towed over to the hulk.

Shenkin felt an ice-cold grip in the pit of his stomach. Dear God, he thought what is to become of us?

CHAPTER 17

Tarn had not slept for the past two nights, he had been dispensing to the living, tending to the dying, and committing the dead to the deep. At last he found time to see how Shenkin was progressing. O'Hara had been tending to Shenkin since his return to the cell and turned to greet the doctor as the guard unlocked the cell door.

'How is the situation and young Collins sir?' said O'Hara, grim faced.

Tarn shook his head in despair. 'Bloody awful we've lost another two this morning and Collins died last night, I'm sorry Regan.'

'The poor lad he never had a chance in this world, may he find it in the next,' said O'Hara, crossing himself.

'Miss Elizabeth held his hand as he died. She told me he called out his mother's name and yours Regan.' On hearing this the big frame of Regan O'Hara trembled slightly, a small sigh broke from his lips.

'God rest his young soul,' said O'Hara, fighting to control his emotions. 'What of the others, doctor?'

'Lord and Lady Feltsham refuse to come out of their cabin, as do the Scrimshaws. The captain insists we burn or throw overboard all contaminated clothing and bedding. In fact its only Miss Elizabeth Moxey that's keeping calm. She insists on helping where ever she can, much to the captain's annoyance.'

On hearing of Elizabeth Moxey, Regan had told the doctor he was not surprised by her attention, that women had always been attracted to Shenkin.

The doctor nodded. 'She wants to know how Shenkin is recovering. I told her I'd let her know after my rounds of the cells. If it was not for her nursing, he may not have recovered at all.'

O'Hara smiled. 'Women just can't leave him alone, the lucky bastard,' he said, adding, 'As for Collins I think he'd been ill for a few days. Fear hung about the boy like a black cape, he had been feeling unwell but did not want to admit it, then on hearing about the cholera he realised the terrible truth. He should not have been here at all doctor.' They were both silent for a moment.

'No he shouldn't have been here, perhaps many of us should not be here.'

Regan nodding in acknowledgment. 'That Elizabeth Moxey she's a strong one, so she is. She was down here yesterday holding a convict's hand and bathing his forehead,' said Regan.

A look of alarm spread across the doctor's face. 'I hope the captain does not hear of it. Although he has much on his mind at the moment to get the ship to Rio hopefully for fresh water. That's if they let us into harbour with us flying the Yellow Jack. Cape Verde refused us entry making our stores of food and water very low. We are killing the animals for fresh meat but it'll be a close-run thing. And this slow passage in the Doldrums isn't helping, how many more will die before we get there is impossible to answer,' Tarn said.

'You can't go blaming yourself doctor for your doing all you can.'

Tarn sighed in resignation, tinged with a sense of hopelessness.

Regan looked around him, gaps were appearing in each mess as one by one convicts became ill or had already died, then his eyes settled on the stove. 'At least Shenkin was saved that,' said Regan, looking over to the now cold stove.

The doctor followed his eyes. 'Yes, for the time being anyway,' he said. Running his eyes over O'Hara he looked for any signs of the fever.

'Sure I'm fine doctor, and that's a fact.'

'Good and how is Shenkin?' said Tarn, placing a hand on Shenkin's brow which seemed normal, his breathing slow and steady.

'After sleeping peacefully he's been a little restless for the last hour,' said O'Hara. 'I've feed him bread milk sops and some soup we were given, though god knows what it was.'

'Has he spoken at all, does he know where he is, or what has happened to him?'

'Not a word, if he recognises me then he's keeping it to himself, so he is. Mind he's cursed a few times in English and Welsh while throwing a couple of right crosses,' said O'Hara, smiling. 'I think he'll be back to his old self in no time now, if the bloody cholera don't get him. If he does it will be thanks to you and that guardian angel of a girl, so it will. I thank you for it, doctor, we've been through a lot him and me.

When Regan O'Hara starts to compliment the gentry, you know it is a deeply felt sentiment. The Surgeon-Superintendent gracefully accepted the praise. 'Coming from you O'Hara I regard that as better than a handsome fee.' They both smiled. They had come to know each other over the last terrifying days as the cholera spread throughout the ship. 'As for our friend here,' said Tarn looking down at Shenkin. 'He seems to have no symptoms of the malady, nor do you O'Hara, no vomiting or stomach cramps?'

Regan continued to smile. 'Me not a thing wrong sir except for some sea sickness like a lot of other convicts, not that much comes up since they don't give us much to go down. Tarn nodded. 'I'll speak to the captain again, but I can't promise anything.'

Tarn was still looking hard at O'Hara. 'Collins was in the same cell as you, are you certain you are alright, though I can see no sign of it on you.'

'Yes I'm fine, but then didn't I see it back home sir when I was just little. Lost a brother and two cousins, so I did.'

For some time Tarn was deep in thought at O'Hara's reply, as he again checked O'Hara over.

Still thinking of Collins, O'Hara said, 'I've been so busy watching Shenkin I never noticed how quiet the lad had gone. I blame myself.'

If Tarn was listening he did not comment, instead he asked O'Hara if Shenkin had ever been in contact with cholera.

'Sure now they had a bloody graveyard full of cholera victims back in his black valley so they did, as well as those that died of typhus, and a host of other unspeakable ailments.'

'Did they now?' said Tarn. 'That's interesting, most interesting O'Hara. Let me know when Shenkin is fully conscious. I'll be back to see to you with some boiled water to drink. I am also making up a compound called the Calcutta Remedy,' he said, not waiting for a response, not that he expected one. Tarn impatiently called to the guard to open the cell. Preoccupied, Tarn hurried to the upper deck as if all hell was on his heels, he made straight for the captain's cabin.

***

'Come,' said Captain Moxey.

Seeing it was Tarn who entered the cabin Moxey sighed. 'Well how many more?'

Tiredness filled Tarn's words has he spoke. 'Two, yes they are over the side, and yes their bedding is burnt.'

Moxey glared. 'Be careful of the tone you take with me sir.'

'Captain we may all be dead within a short space of time unless we can contain this fever. The polite words we use to each other will mean little as the time draws nearer.'

'Contain it, you said yourself it's impossible to stop it spreading, did you not?'

Not answering, Tarn considered his next words carefully. 'Captain Moxey have you ever been in contact with cholera or typhus before?'

'Good God man I've been around the world a number of times and have encountered it in many of the places I've been to,' said Moxey, tetchily. 'India is full of it as is the Slave Coast of Africa. Since a young man I've seen men die of many diseases the world over. Get to the point sir.'

'That I think is the point captain, you are not infected are you?'

'No! So what are you saying?' said Moxey, a puzzled look upon his face.

'Bear with me a moment longer sir. What of Lord and Lady Feltsham?'

Moxey sighed. 'Very well, as a young man Lord Feltsham served in India at Seringapatam having bought a commission in the 33rd Foot. Wellington was Colonel Wellesley at the time, serving as acting deputy commander of the British forces. Discipline was very strict under Wellington. Major John Shee, also a scrupulous disciplinarian, commanded the 33$^{rd.}$ There was some talk of mess funds being misappropriated or the like,' said Moxey, wishing he had not mentioned this. 'Nothing proved mind you, but Lord Feltsham returned to London. A few years later a vacancy came up in the 23rd Light Dragoons and Feltsham, a fine horseman, was soon a Major in the Peninsula War. I believe you too saw action there, Tarn, so you know of the many fevers that raged across most of the battlefields, including cholera, do you not?'

Tarn just nodded. 'And Lady Feltsham?'

'As far as I know she has never left England, until now.'

'Finally, sir you niece has she ever been in contact with cholera or typhus?'

A light was beginning to cross the captain's face. 'She spent her childhood in India, her parents were missionaries in Jaipur were they run a hospital for the sick.' For heartbeats neither spoke, then Moxey said. 'Good God! do you think?'

Tarn cut him short. 'I don't think anything yet captain, but we must try whatever we can to prevent the spread of this deadly disease. A number of the convicts have also been in contact with cholera, at some stage of their life, they too are not infected. I am sure that is the same for members of the crew,' said Tarn.

'So?!'

Tarn took a deep breath. 'So captain I want all on board to be separated again into two groups. Those who have been in contact with cholera and those who have not.' The captain looked hard at the doctor. 'You mean the convicts?'

'No I mean all on board, passengers, crew and convicts.' Before the captain could say a word Tarn went on. 'Also they must not know why we are asking the question. Those who have been exposed to it will hope for better attention, those who have not will expect to be helped. Whichever way I can certainly confirm those who are now infected,' said Tarn, again he did not wait for the captain to respond. I'll isolate Lady Feltsham straight away, then speak to the Scrimshaws. We will draw up two lists without delay, then arrange places of quarantine,' said Tarn, pausing for the first time.

Moxey stood up hands clenched to the table. 'Are you insane! Its unthinkable sir, quite unthinkable.'

Tarn sighed. 'The unthinkable is already happening captain we are watching each other die.' This statement of fact hung in the air between them. The doctor's words giving substance to just how dire their circumstances had now become. Moxey went very pale as he slowly sunk into his chair.

A knock on the cabin door broke the spell. 'Come,' said Captain Moxey, the dryness of his voice gave away the serious of the moment.

It was the steward that came into the cabin. 'Will I serve dinner now sir?'

'What?'

'Dinner sir, shall I serve it sir.'

Moxey was still trying to come to terms with the consequences of what the doctor was proposing. 'No, I'll call you when we are ready,' said Moxey, including Tarn into the later meal.

As he spoke the doctor held the captain's eyes. When the steward left Tarn leaned forward. 'Let's begin the lists with Lady Feltsham at the top of the ones at risk.'

Captain Moxey was many things but he was not a fool, very quietly he said. 'Yes, the lists.' Slowly he placed two plain pieces of paper out in front of them and began to write.

On the list of exposed Tarn wrote the names of the Captain, Miss Elizabeth Moxey, Lord Feltsham, Shenkin and O'Hara. 'Right, that's a start we'll now work our way through the ship. If you will captain, please question the crew and I'll see to the convicts and the Scrimshaw's. After speaking to Lt. Feltsham he can question his men. I will then prepare a compound of the Calcutta Remedy recommended by doctors who had served in India. Fortuitously I have both tincture of rhubarb and laudanum in my medical box, but I'll need all the lavender that the ladies have, also cinnamon from the cook,' said Tarn. He was thinking about what else needed to be done when the captain looked up from writing.

'Calcutta Remedy! What the hell is that Tarn?'

'I'll explain it later captain let us get the separations under way first,' said Tarn, as the captain called for his steward. The man came to the door quickly. 'Ready for dinner sir?'

'No damn it!' heard Tarn, as he hurried passed the man. 'Give my compliments to Mr Lawson and that I want to see him here in my cabin immediately,' said Moxey.

'Aye aye, sir.'

As the steward come on deck Lawson was tending to one of the crew, the man was vomiting violently. The mate called out to Ketch, who was coming up from the forecastle. 'Give me a hand here Ketch.'

Ketch looked at the sick man and quickly stepped back a look of sheer terror on his one-eyed face. 'Not my responsibility Mr Lawson. I only see to the soldiers and convicts.'

'You cowardly bastard,' said Lawson. But Ketch was already scurrying back down the companionway. The steward who was also keeping his distance called to the mate. 'Compliments of the captain sir, would you join him in his cabin.'

Lawson lifted the sick man into a sitting position. 'Bosun get two men and take this man to sick bay.'

'Ay ay, sir.'

At the captain's voice Lawson entered. 'You wanted to see me sir?' said Lawson, turning to acknowledge the presence of the doctor.

'Firstly, are any more of the crew ill?'

'Two within the last hour sir. Ordinary Seamen Barrett and Paisley.' Tarn spoke quickly. 'I will list all the ones in sick bay captain.

'Very well,' said Moxey, turning back to the Mate.

'Mr Lawson, I want to see every man, on their own, in my cabin without delay. Send them in to me as their duties allow. In case there is a change in the weather leave the top-men aloft I'll see them last.

'Aye aye, sir,' Lawson said, leaving the cabin smartly. Sensing the urgency in the captain's voice he did not waste time in asking the reason.

'A good man that captain,' said Tarn, who had now returned.

'Yes, he's been with me a long time, including the Slave Coast, so I think he can go on your "exposed list" doctor.

'Indeed,' said Tarn, writing the mates name onto the list. Come morning, thought Michael Patrick Tarn, how many on these lists would be dying or dead. He needed to speak to Lt. Feltsham then the Scrimshaws. He must also prepare the compound for treating the one's already sick, then check that plenty of water was being boiled. It was going to be a very, very long night.

CHAPTER 18

Shenkin turned on the bunk in the cell. *'Black cold water, cold...'*

Regan looked down at him. 'What's that you're saying?' Regan shrugged his broad shoulders. 'If it's food you are after then I can tell you there's no more and isn't feeding you the very devil of a job.'

***

'Black water, black dirty cold water... the boat will sink...' continued Shenkin, drifting back into his troubled nightmares.

At last all the long boats were occupied. They swayed to the floundering movements of the shackled men. Oars dipped and lifted to the cursing of the hulk guards, resentful at having to come out on such a damp miserable night. With a grunt the overseer settled himself into the boat that Shenkin and O'Hara were in. 'Keep still you treasonous bastards or the Thames will swallow you up and make the rowing lighter. You wouldn't say no to that lads, would you?' he said, turning to the guards. The guards gave a shout to throw all of them over the side. It had the desired effect causing the convicts to grab their seats tighter as the boats pulled away from the wharf. Shenkin's fingers tightened on the timber under him has he swayed to the rhythm of the great river. The river was black, cold, ominous and stinking. An open sewer for the filth and decay of an overpopulated metropolis. The journey was short and wet. Shenkin became aware of a timber wall of blackness that loomed above them smelling of rot and mould. High above hurricane lanterns cast dirty yellow fingers along the side of the timber wall. Somewhere a bell tolled sending out a metallic menacing sound into the night. The longboats bumped their way alongside the slimy wet timbers of a large ship that creaked out its lament at being so abused.

A number of rope ladders came into view as the overseer shouted out. 'Ship oars and look smart about it. Let's get these swine settled into his Royal Highness's comfortable home for the realms' felons.' This raised a laugh from the crew, although they had probably heard it many times before.

Standing up swaying with the rock of the boat the overseer announced, 'Gentlemen welcome to your new home the *Stanislav*, one of his Majesty's finest prison hulks,' he said, swinging his left arm in a wide sweep. 'You'll be snug here I promise you, anyone who complains will be introduced to our Punishment List, you'll find it includes all manner of complaint remedies. Is that not so lads?'

'Yes sir,' came the chorus.

'Right then you convicts of the crown, up on the ladders quick and nimble like. But don't forget your shackles will you?'

This raised another peal of laughter from his men.

So, is this where it all begins, thought Shenkin gazing over at O'Hara. The big man had a grim determined look upon his face, as if to say, right you bastards whatever you have to hand out to be me had better be your best, because given the chance I'll be over the side and gone. 'Careful Regan they hold our lives cheap,' said Shenkin. O'Hara nodded with a sour smile that did nothing to reassure Shenkin.

'Come on get to your feet you stinking wastrels. We'll get you aboard then we are going to strip you, wash you down with cold water, and give you new clothes, ones with little arrows on so we know who you belong to. So move your arses, guards a little persuasion, if you please.' With that, knotted ropes fell on the prisoners who hurriedly tried to stand as the blows rained down on them. The boat swayed violently, making the shackles that held them together bite deep into their legs. Slowly, rung by slippery rung they began their ascent up the side of the once great ship of the line. All her dignity gone, the glory of her battles forgotten. She was now home not to heroes but to the unwanted of her country, as she herself now was. Let's hope no one falls off thought Shenkin has he fought his way upwards. As if in answer to his thought a splash behind him, together with a severe biting pain around his ankle, signalled that a man was in the water. It was the man at the end of the line. He had pulled the convict in front of him hard against the side of the boat, causing him to scream out as his leg twisted over the side of the boat. The overseer already on deck called down, 'Cut the bastard free from the next man or we'll have them all in the drink.' The guard unlocked the shackle on the man. Shenkin felt the chain go slack. The guard lent over the side looking for the man. 'Where the hell is he?' he said, lifting an oil lamp to search the black water. 'Over there,' called one of the guards from another boat, as a lantern's yellow finger picked its way across the water. About ten yards from the boat the light showed the convict struggling to keep his head above water. The fast flow of the river was moving him further and further away. Soon he was out of reach of the beam of light. But still he called out. 'Help, help.' Then a number of gurgles, then nothing.

The overseer shouted to the guards. 'To hell with him, I'll put him down as trying to escape and that's an end to it.' In thundering heartbeats both convicts and guards looked at one another.

'What you lot waiting for, a fucking invitation to come aboard?' called the overseer. 'Get them up here, do you hear?'

The scramble for the ladders resumed, but now each convict was very careful with his footing. Shenkin heaved himself over the rail and fell on to the deck with a thump at the feet of the overseer.

'On your feet, you filthy piece of shit,' the overseer said, kicking Shenkin in the side has he spoke. Pain shot through Shenkin has he stumbled into the man in front. The man cursed has he fell forward into the next man. O'Hara chained behind him also landed heavily onto the swaying deck. Taking in O'Hara's size, the overseer hesitated to be free with his boot; he simply pushed O'Hara along. Most were now aboard. The line of men moved steadily along the deck. Ducking under torn frayed washing that hung from makeshift lines, each man stared about in disbelief. Shenkin saw some crude huts built of rough timber planking, a chimney stuck out of the top of the nearest one, out of which dirty smoke fought to be seen against the black night sky.

All the masts were cut down to about a few feet off the deck. Long-handled brooms and mops stood piled against them, alongside of which were a number of buckets mostly of wood with rope handles. Bigger ropes, coiled neatly, hung from wooden pegs on an inside rail. Some rotten vegetables had spilled out of one of the buckets causing one convict to slip bringing down a number of men with him. This brought laughter and jeers from the guards who swung their knotted ropes or kicked out at the fallen convicts. In the shadows Shenkin saw a dark object swaying to and fro. As the line drew nearer Shenkin saw it was the body of a man hanging from a gibbet. A creak came from the taut rope as it swung the body in time to the lift and fall of the ship. The overseer stepped forward. 'Stop gawking, unless you want to join him,' he said, giving the corpse a push has he passed. Creak cried the rope louder, while the corpse stayed silent. Is life so cheap thought Shenkin. He knew the answer without thinking too hard about it. He also knew, that from what he had already seen, it was going to get worse, much worse.

After being kicked and pushed along the deck they came to a companionway that went down into the belly of the ship. Armed guards stood aside as they came down to the between decks. Their chains made their progress difficult but finally, after part sliding and part falling, they reached bottom. They were greeted with shouting from convicts already incarcerated in cells of timber and iron.

'Shut your mouths you bloody miscreants another sound and I'll have you all scrubbing decks for the rest of the night. The noise stopped as if a tap had been turned off. Shenkin noted this effect, it indicated the kind of punishment that was metered out to anyone who disobeyed. The overseer turned to the newcomers. 'Get a bloody move on you useless morons.' Then noticing that the end man, who had been dragged down the ladder had fallen he quickly moved back to him.

'Up on your feet or I'll cripple you for life.' The man struggled to his feet in seconds. Yes, thought Shenkin we are learning fast. In shuffling steps, they marched forward until the overseer called halt. 'Unlock tethering chains,' he shouted. The chains that held them together fell away leaving only their legs in irons. 'Open port and starboard cells.' At this order the armed guards stepped forward muskets at the ready. Shenkin looked around him. On both sides were heavy wooden doors. They had large metal hinges top and bottom. Halfway down the doors were metal plates fixed to which were bolts that slid into the pillars of the cell. Keys hung on metal rings at the side of each door. As the door in front of him swung open Shenkin saw figures move in the darkness.

'Right in with them, two to a cell quick about it now,' shouted the overseer. Shenkin and O'Hara were pushed forward into the cell. O'Hara's bulk drove one of the occupants into the bulkhead opposite.

'Lock doors,' bawled the overseer. Metal ground on metal followed by deep sounding thuds as the doors embraced the timber frames. They had arrived.

***

Out of the darkness someone grabbed Shenkin's arm. 'Well now is you the new meat?' Not waiting for a reply to the obvious question the figure went on. 'If you is, I'm the mess captain of this bleeding cell see and I say what's what, got it?'

Shenkin's eyes were gradually becoming accustomed to the darkness. The figure before them was a rat-faced miserable man with bad breath. O'Hara had his large hands around the man's throat in a flash, only to feel the point of a knife dig into his stomach. 'Go on!' he said. 'Keep your hands there while I rip you open from belly to throat, you'll need your big hands to hold your guts in,' he said, giving the knife a slight twist causing O'Hara to flinch.

'Leave him Regan,' said Shenkin.

'Smart your friend, smarter than he looks, he's giving you good advice he is.' Slowly Regan removed his hands from the man's throat and stepped back. The man was much smaller than O'Hara but there was a coldness about him that spoke of cruelty and viciousness.

'That's it, no profit in getting a shiv in you, this being your first night and all,' he said, smiling has he spoke. 'Just so we understand one another like. Don't want to get off on the wrong foot do we?' he said, lowering the knife he placed it inside his shirt.

'I'm in charge here see, so don't you both forget it.' But Shenkin had moved very close to the man, so close that the man was pinned against the bulkhead. Shenkin spoke very quietly. 'Can I ask you something?'

'What,' said the man, he was pressed so hard against the timber that his breath came in gasps.

'Do you ever sleep boyo? If so I'd be worried about not waking up one morning,' Shenkin said, his voice as cold as the steel of their new cellmate's knife. A chill fell over the small damp cell. For heartbeats, no one spoke then Shenkin said, 'I'll take the knife my friend, handle first. Careful now.' Giving just enough room for the man to hand over the knife. The man smiled, if you could call it a smile, it spread across his face like an ugly rash. 'Now let's not get off to a bad start,' he said, My name is Kettlewell, Ebenezer Kettlewell owner of the most nimble fingers in old London, and this piece of leftover is Collins. Out of the shadow stepped a lad of indeterminate age. A spotted face stared out from under a mop of ginger hair. If he weighed more than Regan's pair of arms Shenkin would have been surprised.

Kettlewell grabbed the boy's hair dragging him out into the better light, 'Ugly little bastard ain't he, but he does my bidding he does. Don't you shit face?'

The lad shuddered at Kettlewell's touch. 'Yes sir,' he said, as Kettlewell clipped him across the ear. The youngster scurried back into the recesses of the cell.

'Bloody young isn't he?' said Shenkin.

'Young!' said Kettlewell. 'He ain't young, he ain't, some on the hulks are as young as six years old, hardly able to dress themselves.'

Shenkin looked incredulous at Regan. 'What the hell could they have done to end up here?'

Kettlewell the twisted smile still managing to hold on to his mouth, gave a grunt. 'Stole something or other, a bleeding loaf of bread, a handkerchief, who fucking cares they're here ain't they.'

The look on Shenkin's face was cold and hard. 'See Regan society needs to change. Children should be cared for, not abused,' said Shenkin, turning back to Kettlewell he pressed hard against him. 'We fucking care, lay a hand on the lad again and I promise you pain, a great deal of pain. That's what's what, got it?' Kettlewell tried to move but Shenkin held him fast against the damp timbers. 'Have you got it, speak up?'

Kettlewell hesitated for a heartbeat. 'Got it.'

'Louder so the lad can hear.'

'GOT IT!' shouted Kettlewell.

'Good, very good,' said Shenkin, moving slowly backwards. You'll get the knife back in the morning if you behave yourself, now let's get some sleep, lad come over to this side of the cell. What's your name?'

'Collins sir.'

'I'm Shenkin and this is Regan,' Shenkin said, holding out his hand.

'I am pleased to meet you sir.'

'Shenkin lad, not sir.' Collins visibly relaxed. Regan smiled his broad Irish smile as they settled down for the night. Kettlewell cursed his way into the darker recess.

Throughout the night the men and hulk moaned the hours away. At last it was daylight; a few shafts of light struggled to penetrate their cells. A bell rang, keys rattled, doors slammed open. Harsh coarse voices screamed out orders. 'Move yourselves you lazy bastards,' said a guard, pushing his musket into their cell. Their first day on the prison hulk was about to begin. It would be an experience Shenkin would never forget. He let Kettlewell go out first, he had given him back his knife. Better to have him in front where he could keep an eye on him.

Their chains clanked their way towards the companionway. Musket butts and bayonets urged them along, some of the older convicts fell over, their legs stiff from the cold night. They were soon brought to their stumbling feet by kicks from the guards. 'Get a move on, next man to fall gets no bloody grub,' shouted the guard near Shenkin. No one else fell. Kettlewell pushed Collins forward; he almost went down had Shenkin not held his arm. Shenkin shot Kettlewell a threatening look then whispered. 'Just once more, do you hear, and you'll never make it to the top deck.'

Kettlewell quickly shuffled forward. Men argued and swore at each other as they made their way up into the greyness of the morning. 'Shut your talking or the cat will quell the next convict who utters a word,' said the overseer, who stood on the upper deck to greet them to the morning light. The river gave off a chill wind that caused Shenkin to shiver. 'Right, last night's newcomers strip then stand in a line, the rest continue to the mess deck and be smart about it, move.' The column of inmates clanged their way down into another part of the between decks the grey garb of convict cloths blurred them into the grey morning, only the black government arrows outlined their stumbling movements.

The overseer turned to the line of naked men in front of him. Their bodies were tinged blue with the cold, their cloths in a pile at their feet. 'Right! You lot are going to wash in clean water, disinfectant soap, and the fresh morning air of dear old Father Thames. I'll stand no snivelling any man to make a sound or move away from the hose of water will get the lash across him. He won't feel it at first due to his cold body but as he warms, up he'll scream with the pain of it, when he does he'll feel the lash again,' he said, turning to the two guards at his side. 'Start pumping I want a steady stream and make sure you wash behind their ears.'

The freezing water snaked towards them. Shenkin braced himself but as it hit his body it took his breath away. It reminded him of the cold-water regions of Number 2 pit back home, while the smell of the soap was reminiscent of washing in the tin bath in front of the fire in Quarry Row after a shift in the bowels of the black earth, only there was no fire here. Compared to the cold water underground this trickle wasn't even close. The man next to him tried to fend it off. Out of the curtain of water a whip uncoiled its way on to the man's hands. A gasp left the convict's lips. The hands dropped away as he hurriedly began to use the soap. O'Hara his teeth clenched gave a rebellious look at the guards, while rubbing the soap over his body, as if he was bathing in a warm summer spring.

Shenkin smiled at the sight of him and joined into the rebellious moment. Turning as the water began to fall away, Shenkin saw that the overseer had noted the act of defiance. They were becoming marked men. To hell with it he thought there are few pleasures to be had here, let's at least show them that they cannot break us. Rough burlap rags were thrown at them. 'Dry yourselves then turn left in a line, and walk forward,' shouted the overseer. As they came to the companionway hatch, each convict was given his prison clothes, chains were unlocked, trousers climbed into. Guards with cocked muskets watched every move. Some clothes fitted some didn't but wear them they did grateful at least to have their bodies covered again. In the cold early morning every man was soon shivering except for Kettlewell he had had a heavy coat placed over his shoulders by one of the guards. So that's the way of it thought Shenkin pointing his head to Kettlewell so Regan could see. Dressing as fast as their chains allowed, they began to descend into a large mess room. One convict spoke, expressing his thanks that at last they were going to eat. 'Shut your mouths, any more talking and the cat will come out.' 'Yes sir we hear you sir,' said a convict in a broad Irish accent that turned O'Hara's head. The whip cracked its way across the line of men laying open the side of the man's face he went down on his knees screaming. 'Who's next for a gentle morning kiss?' said the guard. First lesson learnt. Now only the rattle of chains, the shuffling of feet, the clatter of spoons in bowls disturbed the morning mess room. Tin mugs, wooden bowls and spoons were handed to each man while a guard intoned. 'Lose or break your utensils you'll get no food for a week,' he said, pushing each man towards a number of long mess tables, while another guard shouted out. 'You will clean your utensils after each meal. In future you will fold your blankets on your bunks and leave your cells tidy. Failure to comply with this will mean every man in that cell will receive ten lashes.' Second lesson. In the corner of the room was a large black stove belching smoke out of a chimney cut into the top deck. A cook, ladle in hand, slopped a gruel like mess into each convict's bowl. Another old convict next to him filled their mugs with hot tea.

Shenkin turned to look at Kettlewell. The cook spooned two helpings into Kettlewell's bowl. Shuffling forward the convict in front of Shenkin dropped his bowl of food, picking it up he asked for more. The whip snaked out in front of Shenkin catching the man across his ear. splitting it open from top to bottom. The man screamed falling to his knees, tea and blood flew in a crescent shape onto the next man.

'Pick up your utensils, you useless piece of shit,' barked the guard, coiling the whip to his side. Third lesson.

Shenkin sat at the top of one of the tables where he was better able to read a notice nailed into the bulkhead at the top of each table. The convict next to him asked what it said. The words were hardly out of the man's mouth as the whip struck him across his back. 'Eat in silence, or you don't eat at all,' growled the guard. Fourth lesson.

Shenkin made out the words between mouthfuls. In bold letters at the top, it read **Rules of Convict Establishments**. Shenkin's eye quickly run down the list.

3.00 am. Cooks (long-term men) rise to prepare prisoners food.

5.30 am. All hands on deck; breakfast; Then one of the decks is washed each morning.

6.45 am. Each prisoner brings his hammock/blanket stows it and then proceeds to his allocated daily labour. On leaving the hulk their irons are examined by the guards, who also search their persons to prevent anything improper being concealed; each guard will be held responsible for the prisoners they search. The convicts are divided into sections of ten, and delivered into the charge of the Dockyard Labour Superintendent. The felons will be overseen by the First and Second Mate to prevent them from straying, or attempting to escape.

At a quarter of the hour before returning to the hulk the prisoners will board the boats at the jetty line. Guards on board the hulk will ascertain that the returning numbers are correct.

12.00 noon. Prisoners return for dinner and are counted and searched. Prisoners are served and locked up in their cells to eat.

1.20 pm. Prisoners return on shore for labour.

5.45 pm. On board again. Irons are examined and prisoners are searched.

6.30 pm. School commences. All prisoners are examined to assess if they can read and write. Religious instruction forms the main area of learning. Arithmetic will not be encouraged.

7.30 pm. Prayers in the chapel; then all prisoners mustered and locked in their cells for the night.

9.00 pm Lights out.

Shenkin smiled, thinking to himself that he had never had a proper education. It had taken a rising to do it, perhaps after all it had not been entirely in vain. Another smiled crossed his face has he finished the last of his thin salty gruel. He lifted his mug of tea in a salute to the notice. The leather coil of the whip stung into his fingers, he grunted but kept the mug firm in his hand as the welt mark traced the coil around his hand. The temptation to grab it was almost as unbearable as the pain, but he resisted. He just gave the guard a look of indifference. The guard slowly wound the whip in, his face registered astonishment at Shenkin's self-control. Shenkin looked over at Regan, as if to say, it's the way we'll play it, right?

Regan's broad Irish face broke into a grin has he nodded. He had just finished his gruel, some had dribbled down onto his new tight convict clothes the seams almost at bursting point over his big frame, causing the grin to broaden even further.

'Prepare prisoners for labour parties,' called out the overseer. In Shenkin's section were Regan, Kettlewell, Collins and Fred Williams, together with three others from Merthyr, two Londoners and the Irishman whose ear had been slit. It was still bleeding the blood running freely down over the black arrows on his convict top, but he didn't dare try to stem the flow for fear of another kiss from the whip. Regan moved up next to Shenkin. 'Since I can't read, what did the notice say?' Shenkin dropped his voice. 'You're about to learn boyo,' he said, as he quickly told Regan the main points of the notice. At least they'll know the times of day thought Shenkin, if only they knew what date it was. But thought Shenkin, as they clanked their way to the long boats, his father used to say, 'All things flow my boy, nothing abides.' No, time passes even in this godforsaken place. The sway of the boat bobbed its way to the banks of the Woolwich Docks for their first day's work. They would be the first of many hard labouring days and weeks.

***

In the offices of the Chief Superintendent of Convict Establishments, that grey winter morning of 5th January 1832, sat John Henry Capper a good administrator and loyal servant of the crown. He had succeeded Aaron Graham in this position at the handsome remuneration of £400 a year, together with an allowance of £131 a year for the use of his home. He considered himself to be a reasonable man, resolute in his duties, but always fair in their implementation. Since his appointment in 1814 he had brought about a number of reforms that had made the establishments far more humanitarian in the care of the country's felons. Capper was mulling this over in his mind when his clerk knocked on the door of his office, which was a room at the Home Office, while he still claimed for his home allowance.

'Come.'

'A letter sir, by special delivery.'

'Thank you, Johnson,' said Capper, reaching for the letter. He noted it bore the wax seal of the crown. He slowly began to open the letter which, he thought, may contain the government's approval of his reforms. He felt he certainly deserved their acclamation since all convicts were now held in greatly improved surroundings. Not least of all by dividing all convict ships into compartments, making the sentences of felons a good deal easier to bear. It's possible a week or even a day in one of his Majesty's rotting hulks would have changed his view, but Capper never strayed far from his office or the comfortable inns that served the area.

The letter was not affirmation of his endeavours but rather from the Home Secretary, instructing him to despatch without delay the political prisoners involved in the previous year's riots at Merthyr Tydfil. It went on to state that the government wished to see the back of these felons on the first available convict ship bound for Australia. That following questions in parliament, both sides of the house felt that after several months the rioters should have been despatched at an earlier date than now. Further, the ship or ships should also contain all other high-risk felons, in particularly, and as a priority, ones found guilty of political crimes. That given the discussions now afoot on the Reform Bill the Government would prefer a clean slate at the Convict Establishments as convicted political dissidents might form rallying points for the discontented in the country if the Bill failed for the second time. It ended with the sentence, 'We expect sir a report on the favourable execution of these instruction within forty-eight hours.' It concluded with the Home Secretary's name and Seal of Office.

Far from acclamation, this read like a reprimand that these felons were still on British soil. Capper's smug face took on a sour look.

'Johnson,' he called, in an irritable voice.

'Sir.'

'Get me the files on convicts involved in the riots of last year in South Wales a place called, wait…' said Capper, as he referred to the letter. 'Merthyr Tydfil,' he said, slowly spelling out the name. 'Also the present standing list of high-risk convicts currently on London hulks,' his words tumbling out in a rush. Then added, 'Quick as you can Johnson.'

'Very well sir,' said Johnson, already on his way to his small file-lined office.

In readiness Capper began to clear his desk. He had been preparing a report to the Penitentiary Committee of the House of Commons. He would now incorporate his swift actions regarding this letter of instruction into the report. He would show them just how proficient John Henry Capper could be at attending to the business of State.

'Come,' he said, in answer to the knock on his door.

'The files you requested sir.'

'Thank you,' said Capper, taking the files. 'I'll have a report for the Penitentiary Committee ready by this evening Johnson. I want a copy sent to the Home Secretary.'

'Yes sir, will that be all sir?'

'No,' said Capper, referring to the paperwork. He was a man of little imagination but with a dogged determination to carry out his orders to the letter. He quickly found that the rioters were being held at Woolwich Warren. 'Send a runner to the superintendent of the hulk ship *Stanislav*. The message to read: "I intend to visit you very early tomorrow morning before the convicts are put to labour. You are to have ready the list of all convicts currently awaiting transportation." Top and tail it in the usual way ready for my signature,' said Capper, looking up. 'Well! Get on with it man.'

'Yes sir, right away sir,' said the clerk, scurrying out to do his master's bidding. Capper didn't acknowledge the leaving, he was already going through the list of contractors whose ships the government hired for the convict trade. He needed ships that were preparing to sail over the next 48 hours. His eyes ran quickly down the London Woolwich list.

Exmouth Sailed March 3rd 1831 New South Wales

Camden Sailed March 28th 1831 New South Wales

Elizabeth 111 Sailed October 7th 1831 Van Diemen's Land

Gilmore Sailed November 27th 1831 Van Diemen's Land

Captain Cook Sailed January 8th 1832 New South Wales

Surrey Refit no date set – -

Runnymede Sailing 7thJanuary 1832 New South Wales

Exmouth Sailing March 2nd 1832 New South Wales

He stopped. The *Runnymede* it is. 'Johnson!' he shouted. He'd show them the man he was, he'd have it done in less than the given time. Returning to the list of felons he first selected the Merthyr rioters, then every other political dissident, together with the worst of the criminals. At the end he had 100 convicts that he would ensure were on the *Runnymede* within forty-eight hours or less. The convicts already scheduled for this ship would be moved to a later departure.

'Sir,' said Johnson.

'I want another message sent. This time to Captain Moxey, Master of the *Runnymede*, by fortunate circumstance also at Woolwich Docks, message to read: "I require to see you in my office tomorrow afternoon at 4 pm regarding convicts due for departure," said Capper.

His clerk waited for any other instructions, when none came, he made for the door. 'Very good sir.'

Capper studied the list of convicts. The leaders of the riot headed the list, together with the remaining rioters of whom there were six, eight in all. Capper penned his signature to the list. The power of the pen prevailed. Shenkin's life was duly processed, stamped and signed away to a dubious future. He then completed his report with a copy to the Home Secretary drawing his attention to the relevant paragraph regarding political dissidents.

Finally, Capper sat back in his chair, sighed while congratulating himself on a good morning's work. He stood up and went out of his office for a well-deserved lunch at the Lion Inn. The smug look was back in place.

***

After a day working on the docks some unloading ship's cargo, others filling wheelbarrows with the mud of the Thames to keep the bank clear, the convicts finally stopped for food. Hard labour hour after hour had begun to take its toll on the old men and young boys. Back in the hulks they were given hurried meagre meals that did little to renew their energy. Some quarrelled amongst themselves while eating while others stole the weaker convicts' food. The guards laughed at the sight of these dirty, unshaved men fighting over small scraps. Shenkin had Collins sitting between himself and O'Hara. Kettlewell sneered at them over an extra helping of food. Then back to the dockyard where free labourers and foremen were waiting to separate them into work gangs for various parts of the dock. Darkness found them exhausted, covered in the filth of the river and chilled to the core. Shenkin wondered how long they could survive. He was to learn, has they piled into the boats for the return trip, that Phil Thomas had dropped dead while loading sacks of coal onto a Thames barge. Of their original number from the rising, only seven were now left. How long indeed before they were all dead. As if in answer to his thoughts the prisoner next to him whispered. 'What you here for mate?'

Shenkin stared across at a bent fragile figure, the face no more than a skull held together by hollow cheeks, wisps of lank hair fell across his skeletal brow.

Shenkin hesitated then he too whispered. 'An uprising back home for better wages.'

The emaciated figure grunted. 'A riot is it? They don't like that they don't.'

Shenkin sighed over the word riot, but said nothing. 'How long have you been here?'

'Six months I think, the names Henry Tombs. Stole some vegetables for the family, starving they were. The shopkeeper brought a charge against me so here I am,' said the man, as the boat bumped into the side of the hulk. He pulled Shenkin's sleeve. 'How do I look?'

Looking into the man's face again Shenkin tried to keep the horror out of his expression. 'I've seen worse,' he said, quickly turning away. Dear god was he gazing into his own future. Slowly they began their climb on to the hulk. Shenkin had to help Tombs to the top, telling him he would make sure he was close by to help him at the end of each day's work. 'Thanks mate it's becoming more difficult for me day by day now,' said Tombs his legs hardly able to lift the weight of his irons. 'I'll watch out for you, we both will isn't that right Regan?'

'We will so.'

'Shut your talking or there'll be no food for the three of you,' shouted a guard. As they moved away from the guard, Henry Tombs lent over to Shenkin whispering. 'I've got a store of food hidden away I'll see you both won't go hungry,' he said holding out his skeletal hand. Shenkin took the hand each small bone as delicate as china. Their first day's work was over, more hard lessons had been learnt. They had also made their first friend, a ghost of a friend it was true but a friend who they could learn from. After what passed as the evening meal they were lectured on the goodness of God, in the most ungodly of places. On their way back to the cells Tombs pushed forward to Shenkin pressing some cheese into his hand as he passed. Turning he gave Shenkin a wrinkled wink. Shenkin nodded a silent thanks.

CHAPTER 19

On board the *Runnymede*, Lord Feltsham was finally lost for words. He had, over the last hours, blustered, bullied and even pleaded, but in the end screaming hysterically Lady Edith, together with Lieutenant Feltsham were taken to the quarantine area for those that had never been exposed to the fever. True both her and the Scrimshaw's were given some privacy in the form of a blanket draped over a wooden frame. It separated them from those men who had also never been in contact with cholera. Lt. Feltsham would supervise this area while maintaining the best possible order in the circumstances. Tarn finally determined that the ship must be divided into three quarantine areas; those who were already ill, those who had never been in contact with the disease but might succumb, and those who had been exposed to cholera. Those who had, which included Shenkin, were placed in the stern of the ship. This enabled the captain to run the ship, albeit with a mixed crew, which would now include the convicts. A short speech called by the captain, but given by the doctor, made it clear that they were fighting for their lives. Any misdemeanours or shirking of duties would result in that man or men being placed with the ill to perform tending duties, including disposal of the dead. This was met with a hushed silence. The crew looked at the soldiers, who in turn looked at the convicts who now stood at their sides free men for the time being. Earlier in the captain's cabin, Tarn had had a long difficult argument with Lord Feltsham and Moxey. Firstly, regarding Lady Feltsham then that everyone would comply with these rules. All duties required to sail the ship together with containing the disease would be shared. The captain, with reluctance, had reinforced the doctor's speech by making it clear there would be no exceptions. But still he turned to Feltsham. 'I will make your duties as light as possible my Lord,' he said, looking at Tarn in defiance. It was the best Tarn could hope for, so he said nothing. If Lord Feltsham was appalled at the thought of having to soil his hands while mixing with the lower social order, he kept it from showing on his face. However, a number of the convicts sniggered, while his lordship adjusted the sleeves of his coat.

The captain placed the responsibility for the mixed crew in the hands of his mate Lawson. Sergeant Ketch would continue to be in charge of the soldiers. The doctor had determined from the ship's records that it was possible to tell, at least to a degree, those that fell into which separated area. Over half of the convicts had been in the war, almost all of the soldiers had served in Spain or France together with some who had served in India, which would have exposed them to cholera, typhoid or typhus. Possibly all three hoped Tarn, if his theory was right. If not, then God help us he thought. For the first time in many years, he crossed himself with a fervour he had not felt in a long time. He noted that Elizabeth now had her wish. She was quite openly tending to Shenkin, who while still weak was slowly returning to full awareness.

The captain was busy with Lawson assessing which of his new 'crew' had sea experience or worthwhile skills. After a glance over to his wife's makeshift blanket-covered accommodation, Lord Feltsham retired to his cabin grateful for the fact that at least the cook was in their group. Ketch had been sent to inspect the cargo then report to the captain of its safety. Why not one of the crew thought Tarn, but that would have to wait, those who were still alive when they reached Australia may find the answer. Tarn turned his thoughts to dealing with the crisis at hand. The quarantine procedure had not been easy. The ones in the suspect group were near to panic. The ones already infected were too ill to complain, and had to be carried into the extended sick bay that now included the between deck cells. In the end it was achieved at the point of muskets, with Moxey ordering a continuous guard on the possible future cases. After much searching Tarn had gathered together the ingredients he needed to make a compound of the Calcutta Remedy. Gathering them all together, he retired to his cabin and began preparing it. One ounce of cinnamon and water from the cook's store. Cinnamon alone is habitually prescribed in powder form, but when combined with water together with the other medicines, it not only eases, but can stop vomiting. Fifty drops of laudanum from his medical supplies, to relieve pain. One drachm of spirits of lavender, from Elizabeth's bottles of essential oils, lavender acts as a restoration drug against faintness, weakness or even spasms. Two drachms of tincture of rhubarb, that by good fortune was also in Tarn's medical box that he kept for the lessening of stomach pains. The doctor only hoped it would work, or at the very least ease the suffering.

Earlier the ship had sailed past the coast of Africa. While still many miles off the portside the stench of rotting vegetation was carried on the wind. It added to the general aroma of sickness. By the following few days, they were out of the doldrums into the South East Trades. The continuous lack of wind had contributed to the tense atmosphere on board. Everyone was edgy, a tinderbox of human emotions ready to explode. But they were getting more organised, the burial services were quick unceremonious affairs. Each quarantine area had settled into a routine of sorts. At night the dying called out for water, while the living tried to close their ears to the possible future that awaited them all. Tarn had administered his made-up medicine and was waiting to see the results, but so far only the dead seemed to have found any peace. Regan O'Hara had been tireless in his efforts to help wherever he could, but his main concern remained Shenkin's recovery.

One evening under a black velvet sky the stars hanging over them like brilliant white glittering diamonds. O'Hara spoke to the doctor. 'Do you think he is getting stronger doctor?'

Tarn looked down at Shenkin. 'He's a remarkable man to have survived at all, so I see no reason why he should not make a full recovery. With your care at night and Miss Elizabeth's during the day, he'll probable outlive us all,' said Tarn, a broad smile spreading across his tired face. As if in answer to their discussion Shenkin in a weak, but determined voice, spoke lucidly for the first time since the knife fight.

'I intend to doctor, I intend to.' Shenkin was back among them his right hand still holding on to Cathy's old scarf. A wicked smile lit up his rugged face as he looked up at the bright bejewelled sky. Slowly he lay back closed his eyes and drifted off to sleep, his breathing steady. The doctor smiled at O'Hara. 'That answers your question, so it does.' Both laughed out loud in the midst of a place that had long stopped laughing. After some hours Lord Feltsham came out of his cabin onto the quarterdeck. He had been drinking. He walked unsteadily towards Tarn who, with O'Hara, was carrying a crew member into the sick bay area. He looked forward to where his wife was ensconced. All was still and quite there, it reminded him of the family crypt. He shuddered, his hand tight on the rail to steady himself, as he continued to look down at the forecastle. O'Hara came up the companionway closely followed by the doctor. 'Good evening my Lord,' said O'Hara, touching his forehead. His lordship ignored him, but turned to Tarn swinging his arms unsteadily. 'By God, sir! you had better be right, for you have possibly sentenced my wife to death.'

They both stared down at the blanket-covered area. The whole of the forecastle was a series of makeshift huts of every shape and size. The whole ship had been turned into a jumble of dwellings marking out the three areas that Tarn had called for. While in the doldrums they had stitched together some spare canvas sails to form canopies across the open decks. It was hoped it would offer some protection against the blazing daytime sun. After a long silence Tarn spoke. 'This way her Ladyship maybe saved from the fever my lord, if not then I will tend her daily, as I will everyone on board who is ill,' said Tarn, while trying to gauge how much boiled water they had left before another day began.

Feltsham spun around his face flush with gin. 'You will do more than that sir!'

The doctor gave a long hard look at Feltsham. 'Talk sense man I don't even know if this quarantining, or the medicine I am administrating, will make any difference to the outcome.'

'Don't know, don't even know,' shouted Feltsham, his face turning puce with alcohol and temper. 'Yet you submit us to such indignities while putting all our lives at risk.' The words slurred from his mouth as he fought to keep upright.

'I have explained all this to you Lord Feltsham. I am an ordinary general medical practitioner with no experience of cholera epidemics. If I am wrong then we are all doomed. We will not see our destination sir.'

Lord Feltsham fell silent for some moments then turned to the doctor, panic in his voice. 'She must live, everything depends upon it. My whole financial future is in the balance,' he said, turning away from the doctor. Then realising he had said too much he turned back to Tarn. 'I mean to say...' but he said nothing further just walked ungainly back to his cabin. He walked past Elizabeth Moxey. Bumping into her, he gave no apologies for his uncouth manners, just a grunt of slurred words sheathed in an cloud of alcohol. She watched in disgust as Feltsham disappeared into the cabin he now shared with the captain.

Shaking her pretty head, her hair was not at its best while her clothes were stained and dishevelled. Nevertheless she still retained that energy that comes from youth. She spoke in a clear calm voice that had so impressed Tarn over these past weeks.

'What is going to happen Doctor Tarn, surely there is more we can do?' For heartbeats, only the sound of restless stirring men together with the few crew that were about their duties disturbed the moment. Tarn took a deep breath. 'We are doing all we can do, or all I can think of to do. As to your other question of what will happen...' said Tarn, gazing portside to where he imagined the South American port of Rio de Janeiro awaited them, but he suspected not with open arms. 'During my time in the army Elizabeth I met a surgeon who had served in India. He told me of an outbreak of cholera in Calcutta in 1817. The fatalities in the population as a whole was never known, but the British Army counted 10,000 dead among its imperial troops. Based on that fact he estimated hundreds of thousands of natives must have fallen victim to the disease,' he said, letting the numbers register. Elizabeth Moxey said nothing knowing the strength that he had already witnessed in this young woman, he went on. 'First they will vomit violently which will be accompanied by diarrhoea until nothing but liquid will emerge. This will be followed by cramps, so severe their muscles will go into spasm. We must then massage their limbs with oil. This will happen many times my dear it will be very hard work. Some will dehydrate before we can get enough boiled water into them. As you have already seen, these will be the first to die. So it is a race against time,' he said, making his way back down to the sick area to count the dead. At the lower deck he called back. 'See how Lady Feltsham is then come down to the cells as quick as you can. And bring O'Hara and two other men with you to help lift the bodies.' All sociability of departure gone. It was an order, not a request.

The moment was broken with a call from the crow's nest. 'Rio! Two points off the port side.' Captain Moxey came hurrying across the quarterdeck. 'Come late morning we'll be off the harbour entrance,' said Moxey, turning to the mate. 'Mr Lawson we'll lay off at the mouth of the harbour, make sure we hoist the yellow jack. I'll verify the charts for a safe place to drop anchor,' said Moxey, making for his cabin at the same time calling out Lord Feltsham's name as he entered.

'Aye aye, sir,' said Lawson, calling for two men as the dawn began to cast its light over the ship. It was a light that displayed the miserable horror of cholera in all its drab deathly colours. The faces of the dying were a deep pinched grey. Skin pulled tight over shrunken skulls. It was a scene best left in the dark or jettisoned into the sea.

CHAPTER 20

Amid all of the suffering aboard the Runnymede *Shenkin still went in and out of a less restless sleep. His mind troubled by a dream of that last day on the Woolwich hulk. He turned in his sleep on a soft mattress, placed there, had he but known, by Elizabeth. He was now in less pain and his temperature was almost normal, so the dream became much clearer. The images were almost touchable. He slept, but his senses were fully awake.*

That evening Shenkin and his fellow convicts continued to be lectured on the milk of human kindness that God-fearing men brought to their fellow man. This was read out to them in a loud monotonous voice by a small stooped, black-suited, white-collared man in his seventies. Who coughed after every other sentence.

'God is good, he watches over us with love in his heart,' he said, coughing into a handkerchief that had once been white. After a short while Shenkin blanked him out. He was just glad to be sitting down on the hard pew, after the heavy labour of the day. Hard treatment with lessons spelt out by the guards from their constant use of the whips, or lead weighted coshes. But no man uttered a word, they had learnt that much during their first days aboard the hulk.

In their cells later Kettlewell boasted how he had skived off during the day. 'The three of you aren't going to last. I give you a few months at best, the boy will be the first to go under. I'd take a bleeding wager on it.'

They all turned to look at Collins. 'I'll be alright,' said Collins, his face a deadly white, his voice shaking has he spoke.

Kettlewell laughed. 'Alright! All fucking alright, you're dying on your feet you are. They'll throw your body to the river rats they will. Good bloody riddance, say I,' said Kettlewell, hitting Collins hard across the face. It sent the lad to the floor blood pouring from a split lip.

Shenkin grabbed Kettlewell by the throat, smashing his fist into his face. He felt bone collapse as blood poured from Kettlewell's broken nose.

'I swear I'll kill you, Shenkin,' said Kettlewell, with difficulty.

Shenkin grabbed him again, but at that moment the door swung open.

It was a guard they had not seen before. The man was in the army uniform of a sergeant. A black eyepatch covered his right eye. The jacket of his uniform kept raising up over his beer belly. Behind him stood the guard who had placed the heavy coat on Kettlewell's shoulders earlier in the day.

The sergeant had a sneer of a smile on his face that struggled through black broken teeth.

'Step back you three. Kettlewell! Come out.' Kettlewell staggered forward. The door slammed shut, the key turned. Only the sound of disappearing footfalls broke the silence. Shenkin and Regan lifted Collins gently onto his bunk.

It was late when Kettlewell returned to the cell. The smell of gin sat upon his breath like sour milk. His noise was now badly swollen, traces of caked blood streaked his face. He pushed Collins out of his way then began to unroll his bedding. When he was done, he sat down heavily, looking up at his cellmates.

'You lot don't know nothing. I've been drinking with the toffs I have.' The alcohol loosening his brain and tongue.

'How did you get off the hulk?' said Shenkin.

'None of your bloody business.'

O'Hara moved towards him, but Shenkin stopped him. 'Leave him Regan he's drunk.'

With that Kettlewell fell back on his bunk and passed out. In his drunken state he had urinated, the foul-smelling liquid ran down onto to the cell deck. To the other's disgust the smell of urine began to fill the cell with its acrid aroma.

'To hell with him let's try to get some sleep,' said Shenkin

But even though it had been a hard day Shenkin found it difficult to sleep. Images of the day together with the thoughts of the day's yet to come, kept going around in his mind. The night drew out like a knife, finally he dozed off. In the early hours he was disturbed by a noise close by. He awoke to find Kettlewell sitting on the edge of his bunk. He was counting something in his hands.

'What you doing you miserable bastard?' said Shenkin, swinging his legs to the floor.

Startled, Kettlewell moved quickly to cover a brown leather pouch on his lap. The sudden movement caused him to drop the pouch onto the deck.

'God help!' screamed Kettlewell, dropping to his knees to collect the contents that were now scattered across the planking of the deck. Shenkin stooped to help him 'Keep back or I'll do for you.' shouted Kettlewell, pulling his knife from out of the inside of his shirt.

'What the hell are they?' said Shenkin. Then from the light of the lantern outside of the cell in Kettlewell's hand Shenkin could see small brilliant pieces of glass, no not glass, thought Shenkin, instinct told him they were diamonds.

By now Kettlewell was frantic in his search to recover the rest of them. Slowly he began counting to himself. 'Dear god one's missing, the big one's missing.' He was tearing at the decking his fingers were beginning to bleed. Shenkin was also on his knees searching. But again Kettlewell called out. 'Get back, get back.' With that Shenkin stood up. 'You are no more than a filthy thieving bastard Kettlewell,' said Shenkin, shaking his head in repugnance. But Kettlewell continued to count. 'Ten, eleven, twelve! Bloody hell where is it, the pendant where, please God, where is it?'

'No God this side of hell is helping you Kettlewell. It's probably dropped between the planks. Look man a number have gaps in them,' said Shenkin, as Kettlewell tried in vain to lift one of the boards.

Regan jumped down from his bunk. 'What the hell is all the noise about?' Collins too was now wide awake his lips badly swollen from Kettlewell's blow of the night before. The lad's face was so pale it almost shone in the reflection of the lantern. All the while Kettlewell was becoming more and more agitated. 'I must find it, there should be thirteen,' he kept repeating over and over in a mantra of despair.

'Well?' Regan

'Kettlewell has lost a pretty stone and is all upset.'

'You bloody fool, you don't know nothing you don't ,' said Kettlewell.

Shenkin shook his head. 'Forget it, you'll never find it now, it's gone down one of the cracks in the decking.'

Kettlewell was close to tears of despair while still trying to lift a plank. The clang of metal, accompanied by screamed orders from the guards announced the start of another day.

'No, no I've got to find it,' cried Kettewell. 'It's the pendant, the most valuable piece.' The guards were not listening to his ravings only Shenkin heard his comments as the others gathered up their bedrolls tin plates and mugs.

'Well it's no worth now, no more than any other stone,' whispered Shenkin, as the guards began to shout again. The guard at their cell door was no friend of Kettlewell's. 'Move your arse or I'll open your skin, you lazy bastard,' he screamed, pulling Kettlewell out of the cell. But Kettlewell broke away and again rushed back into the cell dropping to his knees he continued to try to lift one of the boards.

'Right you shithouse, give me a problem would you.' The whip hissed its way into the cell. Kettlewell went on looking oblivious to the pain as the whip slashed across his back leaving a red stain across his dirty shirt.

Kettlewell was beside himself incoherent. He was blabbering on his knees in the centre of the cell. Another guard went into the cell, both guards dragged Kettlewell out. The man was a sight. Tears of frustration run uncontrollably down his face. His fingers were bleeding, the skin torn to ribbons, his eyes large staring out of his thin hatchet face in pure panic. He looked at the guards his voice pleading. 'Please, please, dear God I must go back in, you don't understand.'

'Get moving!' screamed the guard, hurling Kettlewell along the passageway.

Kettlewell continued to scream as they were pushed along the gangway to the mess rooms. Breakfast ran it's normal pushing and shoving meal. Then they were again rowed ashore to labour in the filth of the Thames, by then they had lost sight of Kettlewell. They were sure he was by now talking to his friendly guards. Finally, as the days hardships wore on they put him out of their minds That evening, as the chaplain read from his bible on the righteousness of a god who, they were told, cared for them all. Collins had fallen into an exhausted sleep. His arms were folded, hands crossed into a pillow. His fingernails were full of the riverside mud together with other filth that would be hard to put a name to. At the end of the long drawn-out sermon he began to snore. Hearing this, the guard standing between the row of pews turn his head at the sound. The chaplain in an uncaring irritated manner tut-tutted at the noise The guard sent his whip expertly across Collins's grimy hands. The boy cried out in pain. The whip snaked out again to reinforce the point, but it never landed Shenkin caught it in mid-flight. The guard was taken by surprise as Shenkin pulled him off his feet. Up out of his seat, Shenkin wrapped the whip around the guard's throat. Before anyone could move the guard's face was already turning blue, his eyes bulging from their sockets. Then guards were everywhere, the chaplain cowered in his pulpit. Two guards rushed at Shenkin but Regan beat them to it. Dropping one with a chopping blow to the jaw while headbutting the other in the face. By now the convicts had found their voices, egging Shenkin on.

'Kill the bastard, Shenkin.'

'Choke the life out of the bloody ugly swine.'

Whistles sounded, feet pounded the upper decks, as more guards scurried down the companion ladders. Regan hit another guard into the opposite bulkhead splitting open his head. Shenkin increased the pressure on the guard's throat. The overseer pushed a musket into Shenkin's face. 'Stop or you're a dead man.' Overwhelmed by six guards, Regan had been beaten down. Shenkin slowly let the guard go. The man was fighting for breath the whip cord covered in the blood of his throat, he began to cough frantically.

'Take these men to the solitary confinement cell. All other prisoners to the main cells,' barked the overseer.

***

They were pushed into a dark cold cell that had no porthole, no hammocks, no bunks or mattresses, just damp timber walls. The door had a small iron grill at the top. It was a place designed for contemplative thought. One of the guards looked through the grill. In a broad cockney accent, he bawled into them. 'So you want it the hard way do you? Well wait till the superintendent hears about this in the morning, it'll either be the noose or a flogging. If it's the cat then you'll be begging us to hang you,' he said.

Left on their own at last Regan turned to Shenkin blood running down his face his shirt hanging on by threads.

'Well now, how do you feel the first few days have gone Shenkin?' he said, a crooked smile spreading across his Irish face. Not waiting for a response, he added. 'It's been different, so it as. Now what?'

'We need to escape,' said Shenkin, holding his hand has he spoke, the palm had been cut open by the whip cord.

'Do you feel we're in the right place for that Daniel?'

Shenkin thought for a moment then said. 'If they hang us, then the decision is made for us. But if we are flogged then they'll need to take our leg irons off. Regan looked confused. Shenkin went on to explain. 'Henry was telling me that to flog you they spread-eagle you across an upright grating.' Regan winced. 'I'm glad I know that, so I am. And how does our free legs help us?' said Regan, with a shrug of his wide shoulders.

'Henry said it's the only time when you are completely free of chains. It will be the first time Regan that we will be free to move quickly.' Before Regan could say anything Shenkin continued. 'The grating is placed against the top rail.'

'Well?' said Regan.

'As soon as our feet are free, we go over the rail into the river. Once in the water we make for the bank on the far side. That's if we...' began Shenkin looking up at Regan.

'If we what?'

'If we can break free cleanly, don't hit the side of the ship or drown,' said Shenkin in a flurry of words, adding. 'Can you swim?'

'And wasn't I raised in Wicklow, and didn't I swim most summer days off Wicklow Head?' said Regan, pulling himself up to his full six foot four but having to bend due to the low timbers.

'Good, because I can't,' said Shenkin.

'What?'

'No sea up in Merthyr was there, just bloody pits and iron works,' said Shenkin, by way of explanation.

'Sweet Mary in heaven, you'll drown.'

'Not if you keep me afloat, after all it's not that far. That's if…'

'If, again.'

'If they don't shoot us when we are in the water.'

'Or we drown because you'll be hanging around my neck.'

'Right,' said Shenkin.

For heartbeats neither said anything. Shenkin untied the scarf that held his long hair back from his face. It was a habit he had developed whenever he was thinking. 'There you go again with that scarf. Does it bring back memories of home and my sweet sister?'

But for the moment Shenkin was deep in thought then turned again to Regan. 'Yes it does Regan, it does. So we must not end our days here at the end of a rope.' Then in a deep strong voice he said. 'If they mean to flog us then we take our chance and jump for it. Agreed?'

'You're a devil, so you are. I've known nothing but trouble ever since I've met you,' said Regan, a smile stealing across his face, then he nodded his head.

After a miserable night the cold light of day found them standing on the open deck. That morning the Superintendent of the hulk told them he intended to make an example of them with fifty lashes each. The punishment would be witnessed by all the prisoners before the start of the day's work, which they would also be sent to do. Failing to work they would receive a further ten lashes each hour until they completed their allotted work.

Shenkin knew this was nothing more than a slow death sentence. Come what may they would make a break for it. Better to be shot or drown, for it would be much quicker than the lashings. Regan agreed, if the moment presented itself, they would go over the side regardless of the consequences.

'Stop your talking,' screamed a guard.

The forecastle deck was surrounded by convicts on all sides. On the quarterdeck, the superintendent stood ready to give the order to commence punishment. Two gratings were propped up against the ships top rail. The gratings had leather thongs laced through the frame ready for arms and legs to be tied in place. Two guards stood, stripped to the waist, holding cat-of-nine-tails in their hands. A third guard waited ready to call out the count.

A hush settled on the ship as first Shenkin then Regan made ready. As the leg irons came off Shenkin screamed out.

'Now!' in two strides they went over the side. On their way down Regan caught his leg in some ropes but his weight pulled him free. They hit the cold water in a flurry of arms and legs. For heartbeats the guards froze but finally rushed to the rails. Muskets primed they waited for heads to break surface. At that moment a voice called out from behind the superintendent.

'Hold your fire, I want those two men alive.'

The superintendent of the hulk *Stanislav* swung around to demand who it was who gave such an order. He came face to face with John Henry Capper his cloak billowing in the morning wind his face set to the task.

'Sir I...' spluttered the superintendent, then to his credit he recovered quickly. 'Put up your weapons launch the boat recover those men alive, jump to it damn you.'

In the water, two heads struggled to keep above the waterline. Shenkin his arms tight around Regan's neck, who was spluttering for breath. It took almost half an hour, but in the end the half-drowned bodies covered in flotsam and mud were pulled into one of the boats.

Capper explained what was required. Quickly a roll call of one hundred men was complied. By the afternoon closely guarded they were shackled together. These most feared men of the British realm were ready to be moved to the *Runnymede* for shipment to a place beyond the seas.

Regan lent forward to Shenkin the chains pulling the man behind him with a sharp jerk. 'You're a lucky bastard, so you are.' Then added, 'Thank God.'

They stood like that for the rest of the afternoon waiting for the other guards to come back to the boat after the day's work. The superintendent was taking no chances with any more attempts at escape.

At last a guard called out. 'Get moving.' As darkness enveloped them, they were ferried to the waiting transportation ship.

Collins smiled nervously at Shenkin. The lad had the Tolpuddle men to thank for being included in the group. Further along the line Kettlewell was scowling back at them waiting for his chance to get even. He made a cut across his throat at Shenkin.

CHAPTER 21

'*I'll be ready for you Kettlewell*, I'll be ready,' shouted Shenkin, lifting himself off the bunk. Regan pressed a hand on his shoulder. 'Well! So you're back in the land of the living, so you are.' Regan said, a look of relief on his face. 'Not that it is the land of the living, more like the dead and dying, which includes Kettlewell by the way.'

'Where are we? What's happened? How long have I been sick? said Shenkin in a rush of words

Tarn was walking towards them as Shenkin plied Regan with his questions

'Good you're fully conscious again,' said Tarn. 'You are a very lucky man, we thought we would lose you a few times over these past weeks. The answer to your questions can wait until your mind catches up with your body,' said Tarn,

Shenkin pinned the doctor with an intense look. Slowly it was all dropping back into place. The hulk, the convict ship, his fight with Kettlewell, the sick bay. Shenkin turned towards the doctor. Then in a firm strong voice said. 'I owe you my life, thank you doctor.'

Tarn smiled. 'Sure, it's others you need to thank, not least of all Miss Elizabeth Moxey. For it was she who nursed you through the worse moments. She fed you, bathed you, yes bathed you,' said Tarn, seeing Shenkin's shocked face. 'She brought your temperature down in a way that I envy you for. But don't tell her I said that.' Tarn was a man long past blushing, but at that moment he was very near it. It was all confusing to Shenkin so he continued to ask questions. He wanted to know everything.

'It's enough that you know we are glad to see you back. For we need all the help everyone can give, after you have had some food fresh water, then later I'll tell you everything. In the meantime I have much to do,' said Tarn, turning to Regan he said. 'And so do you.'

'Yes doctor,' said Regan, in a voice of compliance that Shenkin had never heard before. Which made him even more confused. Both walked off to do whatever they had to do leaving Shenkin alone to came to terms with the chaos around him, why for instance was he laying here on the open deck.

Meanwhile the doctor entered the sick bay and took in the scene. Bodies lay every which way, the stench of vomit and excrement was overpowering.

Men called out for water, for attention, for their mothers. He'd heard it before on every battlefield he had ever been on. He gazed down on two frail forms in front of him. One was Mrs Scrimshaw who had contracted the disease three days ago. Beside her sat Alfred Scrimshaw who had refused to leave her side. Tarn never ceased to wonder at the frailties, or strengths, of the human spirit at such a time. Had he been too late with the medicine, was the remedy of little use? Was he completely wrong in his treatment? His thoughts were broken by Elizabeth standing at his side. She had lost her girlish look over these last weeks. She was now a woman, a strong woman, not afraid to look death in the eye. He told her that Shenkin, thanks to her, was fully recovered. Immediately Elizabeth Moxey turned on her heel and hurried up the companion ladder, before Tarn could say more.

She found Shenkin still pressing Regan for answers whenever he passed by. This man she had come to know more intimately than any other man before was now looking directly at her. He exuded sexuality, not by intent, it was simply just there. It took her breath away, she blushed thankful that the shade of the canvas covered her physical excitement. And then he spoke his voice deep, husky, intimate.

'I understand I owe you my life, Miss' said Shenkin, running his eyes over the beautiful young woman before him.

'I... I...' stammered Elizabeth, much to Regan's amusement. 'I was only doing what I could,' she finally, managed to blurted out. But the sexual charge in the air spoke stronger than any words. It was as if Regan or the ship were not there, their world had diminished to just them. After heartbeats of embarrassing silence Regan spoke. 'Well, I have things to do, so I do,' said Regan, picking up a coil of rope not knowing what he was going to do with it. But Shenkin held Elizabeth's eyes.

Finally, Shenkin broke the spell. 'I am told we have cholera on board.'

'Yes.'

'Where I come from, we had an outbreak a few years back, many died. I helped bury my mother's brother and three of his children. We were burying them in mass graves in the end,' said Shenkin, regretting he had spoken so bluntly.

'I did not mean to alarm you,' he said annoyed at being so forthright.

'I am aware of the seriousness of the situation sir, for the past days I have been tending the sick,' said Elizabeth Moxey, in a tone of rebuke.

Beautiful but feisty thought Shenkin, good.

'Miss! is this what you call helping the doctor?' Captain Moxey barked from the bottom of the companion ladder. The moment was broken Elizabeth stood looking down at Shenkin then made her way back to the sick bay. She did not even look at her uncle as she defiantly walked pass him, her head held high. A woman of spirit thought Shenkin, bringing a smile to his face.

'Give this convict something useful to do Mr Lawson.'

'Ay ay, sir,'

That evening the doctor answered all of Shenkin's questions. Regan nodded his head as Shenkin took in the moment.

Finally, Tarn told Shenkin that at least they now had fresh water fruit and vegetables, also some extra meat. This was thanks to the captain who had, after some augment with the authorities at the port of Rio de Janeiro, secured the victuals for gold coins. Tarn sat back letting Shenkin take it all in. Satisfied that it had indeed registered with Shenkin, Tarn continued.

'We then again picked up what was to be the tailend of the trade winds. We are now passing the Cape of Good Hope. So you have the moment Shenkin while we continue on our voyage to Port Jackson.

Shenkin looked hard at the doctor. 'It seems I have been saved either to die of cholera or be hanged. When, or rather, if we get to our destination,' said Shenkin.

'Now that's about the depth and width of it, so it is,' said Regan.

'Well I think you might both have a little more faith in my treatment,' said Tarn, continuing. 'We may just survive if what I have put in practice works' said Tarn, more in hope then conviction.

Having taken it all in Shenkin sighed. 'In Merthyr, doctor, we lit fires that had soaked rags of wood tar or coal tar in it. It was used to treat the timbers in the pits. Miners who had a chesty cough, sore throat or cold would breathe in the tar. It seemed to help, so when we had an outbreak of cholera or typhus, we lit fires around the town with tar treated wood or rages. Do we have any timber treatment on board doctor?'

The doctor thought for a moment, at last he burst out. 'Of course! It's a chemical compound called creosote. It has a long history as an antiseptic, I should have thought of it. I suppose the carpenter must treat the wood repairs with something. I'll ask the captain,' said Tarn, grateful that someone else was also thinking how they could prevent the disease from getting worse.

Having explained this to Moxey the captain consulted the cargo inventory. After some time, he was able to confirmed that they had a few barrels of tar wood treatment on board the main constituent was a chemical compound called Kreasoter

'That is it, captain, we call it creosote,' said Tarn, excitedly.

'But surly we are not in the hands of a convict Tarn?' For a brief moment the doctor considered the captain's words. 'Captain in the place that he was born this man has seen cholera a number of times. He has nursed those who contracted cholera and more importantly he has lived through it. I will try any remedy that seems to have been successful, never mind from who or where it comes from,' he said flatly. Without another word Tarn turn on his heel and left the cabin. He immediately had the barrels brought from the storeroom to the forecastle deck. Shenkin took charge from there. 'I'll start making fires in any metal containers we can find,' he said in the voice of a born leader, if still one that was a little unsteady on his feet.

'Well it may help, anyway there's nothing to lose in trying,' said Tarn. 'I'll keep the captain informed.' Regan joined Shenkin in the task, once they had them alight, they dipped rags into buckets of creosote. They placed the wet cloths across the flames. The smoke was soon everywhere men's eyes were burning everyone was coughing. Soon the air was like a fog.

Lord Feltsham came storming out of the captain's cabin coughing. 'Fires as well as cholera. How long is it to go on for Tarn or should I ask a convict?' Shenkin pushed passed him a lighted torch of coal tar in his hand. His lordship moved quickly to the side as the heat from the flame fanned his face. 'I demand to know what going on, where is Captain Moxey?' Instead of an answer Regan placed a fire bucket in his hand. 'This way your lordship.'

'How dare you speak to me in such a manner, you Irish waster?' Tarn just got to Regan in time has he was about to hit his lordship with the full bucket.

'We must put our social positions and prejudices to one side. We are sir as I must reminded you again, fighting for our lives. Now pick up the bucket and follow this man to where it is needed,' said Tarn.

'Damn you, I refuse to.'

'Very well then help in the sick bay to tend to the dying. For I have no time to argue any further sir. It's the open deck or the sick bay your choice,' said Tarn, flatly.

The captain had now joined them from the poop deck 'You cannot expect his lordship to work like a common labourer,' said Moxey.

'But I do sir, I most certainly do. I have this moment come from the sick bay another four have died regardless of my treatment captain. Do you and his lordship wish to join them?' The silence that followed was palpable. Shenkin a bucket in one hand, a torch in the other watched to see the outcome. The rest of the men crew, convicts, and soldiers did the same. This was a defining moment, everyone sensed it.

'Give me the bucket you… you…' But Feltsham did not finish the sentence he stood mutely looking first at Tarn then Shenkin. 'Well what now, damn you?' he said.

'We work sir, we work,' said Tarn.

The *Runnymede* sailed on towards the westerly winds of the Roaring Forties they were at latitude forty-two degrees south of the equator, the Southern Hemisphere.

For Tarn it was inconsequential. At his feet the dead and the dying lay side by side in close companionable communion. The *Runnymede*'s human cargo becoming lighter with every sea mile that passed under her keel, regardless of her position on the chart.

CHAPTER 22

Mrs Scrimshaw died as meekly as she had lived. Her husband died a few hours later, he had never left her side. Finding at the end the courage that had eluded him all his life. Of the passengers, only Elizabeth Moxey, Lord and Lady Feltsham and Lt. Feltsham were still alive. Tarn went over the last few weeks again in his mind. The captain had finally negotiated for fresh supplies at the port of Rio de Janeiro. At first they had been refused permission to land, but after a great deal of hailing across the water an agreement was reached. Three longboats were brought alongside with provisions of fresh water and fruit. These were winched aboard in exchange for an exorbitant amount of gold coin money Moxey had stood swearing on the poop deck the whole time the supplies were winched aboard.

Tarn came to his side as the fresh water butts were rolled into position on the quarterdeck. 'I want those to be put under guard, captain. We must ration out the amount of fresh water we have. Those who are now in the last stages of the disease will continue to be given the boiled water only.' The captain looked sharply at Tarn. Michael Tarn held the captain's stare then spoke in a steady tone. 'The dying will call out for water captain, this will trouble the living. But we should not waste fresh water on the dying. The boiled water will ease their way to their maker. The rest of us will be given sufficient fresh water to flush out any impurities we may have, or are developing,' said Tarn, in a flat statement that left no room for discussion. However, Feltsham had overheard the remarks. 'I expect my wife to receive fresh water together with the fresh fruit sir, if it saves her life.' Over the last twenty-four hours Lady Feltsham had succumbed to the fever.

Tarn addressed the captain directly. 'Captain Moxey anyone, I repeat anyone, who is beyond help will not be given our precious fresh water supply. I have just left Lady Edith, regrettably she is sinking fast.' At this Feltsham winced, then regained his composure.

'Captain, may I remind you who your benefactor is, together with the lucrative business we have in hand? May I remind you that Lady Feltsham's father will grant rights of manufacture to us for the production of his soap, is that not so sir?' said Feltsham, infuriated that he was forced to speak so openly about their plans.

Before Moxey could reply Elizabeth came up the companion ladder. Her face was drawn pale with fatigue. 'Your lordship, Lady Edith is calling for you.

I fear she will not last long sir. I should hurry to her side,' said Elizabeth, as a slight sob broke from her throat. She moved instinctively to Shenkin's side as he placed further rags on the fire they had on the poop deck.

Lord Percival Hugo Feltsham the current baron of a grand, if debt ridden, estate in Norfolk stood rooted to the deck, a cloud of coal tar steam shrouding his cowardly figure. Elizabeth Moxey turned as the smoke cleared. 'Lord Feltsham! She needs you, please hurry.' Feltsham finally moved but not in the direction of the sick bay but down to the cabin he now shared with the captain.

For heartbeats no one spoke then Shenkin touched Elizabeth's shoulder. 'Take me to her miss,' said Shenkin, in a tone so soft it was hardly audible. The captain looked aghast but before he could say anything both had disappeared down the companion ladder hurriedly heading to the sick bay.

Shenkin on entering the cabin was taken aback by the stench. 'Dear God! Miss have you been down in this nightmare of a place all this time?'

'We must all do what we can Shenkin,' said Elizabeth, using his name for the first time. Shenkin stood looking at this beautiful slip of a girl with a deep sense of admiration, also he had to admit, with a great deal of longing.

'Please Shenkin, follow me.' They made their way past the horrors of the last stages of cholera. Two crew members, one of whom was Burke, were carrying a dead body towards the far companionway. The waxed face of the only woman there identified Lady Edith to Shenkin. Shenkin knelt beside her and held her hand. 'Is that you Percy?' she asked.

'It is,' said Shenkin, in a small whispered voice hoping it would fool her.

'I knew you would come to me my dearest, I knew you always loved me. Tell me it's true.' Her breathing a harsh rasping noise in her chest. Shenkin leaned forward. 'I have always loved you my dear.' The yellow skin of Lady Edith face was pulled tight over her skull. She smiled, her lips curled taut around her teeth. For a moment her eyes lit up, then just as quickly went blank. Shenkin gently placed her hands across her skeleton body, put his hand to her eyes and closed them.

This is a remarkable man who I will always love thought Elizabeth Moxey, as she put her hand on his shoulder.

'She's gone Miss,' said Shenkin

'Elizabeth please.' As she pressed forward kissing him on his cheek. In the hellhole of the sick bay with the dying all around them, they held each other. Defying anything to come between them, even cholera. Burke came back into the sick bay startled at the sight of Shenkin with the captain's niece in his arms he started to turn around. 'No need to leave corporal, we are forgetting ourselves in the midst of this sadness and horror, please go about your work,' said Elizabeth, her voice slightly out of breath. 'Thank you Miss I was bringing a full bucket of boiled water down to these poor souls,' said Burke, still embarrassed by the moment. Shenkin recovering his composure placed a burlap cloth over the body of Lady Felthsam. 'I'll give you a hand to carry the body up to the deck, corporal.'

Elizabeth gazed down at the wasted remains of Lady Edith. 'We must tell my uncle to inform his lordship before you complete the burial Shenkin.'

'Right,' said Shenkin already lifting the body with Burke. 'We'll wait at the rail on the forecastle deck, but not for long, she needs to be over the side without delay,' said Shenkin, it was not a suggestion but a fact. 'Up with her corporal let's at least get into the fresh air.'

'Yes,' said Burke. Then added 'It's my fourth bleeding burial today, excuse me Miss.'

Later Elizabeth knocked on the captain's door. 'Come.'

As she entered, Lord Felthsam moved into the recesses of the cabin. Tarn stood facing the captain's table. He turned to Elizabeth. 'How is Lady Feltsham?'

'She is dead doctor.' At this a gasp came from his lordship, who seem to fold himself into a foetal position in the corner.

'Shenkin with Burke are at this moment attending to her burial. Do you wish to be present Lord Feltsham or do we commit her to the deep with no one of her own to bid her a last farewell?' said Elizabeth, bitterness edging every word.

All turned to look at Feltsham who still crouched in the dark corner.

'On deck you say, yes I will. I'll look down from the poop deck to stand witness to my dear wife's departure,' said Feltsham. Even his business partner the captain winced at the words.

They slowly made their way to the quarterdeck somewhere the tip of Africa lay off the port bow. But even at this great distance the wind carried the strong scent of decaying vegetation. Lawson stood at the helm his head turned up to the billowing sails. Seeing the procession walk towards him he lashed the helm in place. His lordship climbed up to the poop deck. Coming out of his cabin Moxey turned towards the helm. 'We are gathered to attended the burial of Lady Feltsham Lawson, have all hands on deck to remove their caps for a short prayer which I will give.'

'Aye aye, sir.'

By this time another covered body now lay beside Lady Edith. Both were covered in dirty shrouds of burlap that were now used so frequently that it allowed no time to clean them, not that Tarn would have allowed them to waste the water. And no one wished to touch the soiled sheets anyway. Shenkin and Burke waited for the order to lift while two other men – one was a soldier the other a hard faced convict both joined in this ritual of death – also waited.

The captain had gone down to the forecastle deck to stand at the top of the corpse. He began the pray. 'We commit Lady Edith Feltsham…' He stopped. He had no idea which body was Lady Edith. He restarted. 'We commit these souls to the deep in the knowledge that at the coming of the Resurrection we will again be reunited in the presence of God.' Without his Book of Common Prayer he was not sure of the correct words, but felt these would answer the moment. Finally, he said, 'Amen.'

No word came from Lord Feltsham, who at the sound of the twin splashes returned to the dark corner of the captain's cabin. 'Thank you Mr Lawson, please return the crew to their duties.'

'Sir.'

Shenkin caught Elizabeth's eye. The look spoke more eloquently than any words he could say. She saw in his look a response to her touch, to her warmth, to the woman within her. She blushed at her need for this man, this wanting that stirred deep inside her. Then the moment was broken Ketch was at Shenkin's side. 'Get back to work you're still a convict and don't you forget it, you Welsh bastard.' Shenkin spun around so fast Ketch had to step back. 'I'm not in a cell anymore Ketch, so I'd be very, very careful if I was you,' he said, his hand closing on Ketch's arm muscle. Ketch grimace as the fingers tightened on the muscle. Shenkin let go, the blood rushed back into the arm. It caused Ketch to call out. Lawson's head came over the top deck rail. 'What's going on there?'

'Nothing Mr Lawson, Ketch caught his foot on an iron bar,' said Shenkin. Regan shouted from the starboard side. 'It should be his bloody head.' A group of soldiers and convicts laughed at the remark.

'That's enough!' You are prisoners on this ship, we work together due to necessity, but you will all be mindful of your positions.' This from the captain who had just come back onto the quarterdeck. 'Mr Lawson you will keep order aboard this ship. You too Sergeant Ketch do you hear.'

'Yes sir.' cried out Ketch.

'Aye aye, sir,' said Lawson moving back to the helm.

'Ketch I need to see you in my cabin, now.'

'Sir,' said Ketch already climbing the companion ladder. 'It's not over yet Shenkin,' said Ketch, over his shoulder.

'Well, you know where I am Ketch, I'll not be going anywhere.'

Elizabeth watched with concern as Shenkin made his way to the sick bay, collecting more boiled water as he went.

In Moxey's cabin, Lord Feltsham was in deep conversation with the captain. 'Everything has changed I tell you. We must consider what we do next. We now need all of Kettlewell's loot.' A knock on the door then Ketch entered rubbing his right arm as he did.

'Go to the cargo hold Ketch we need you to search for that pendant stone. We need the complete necklace,' said Moxey. Ketch looked lost. 'But all that was on Kettlewell's body were the smaller stones. Kettlewell kept that necklace on him at all times. Do you think he hid it in with the rest sir?'

'It's possible, the thieving swine was not to be trusted,' said Feltsham, from the corner. 'Remember Ketch your cut is at stake as well, without the necklace we are short by a great deal of money, on this first consignment.'

Ketch shook his head. 'Kettlewell, put up quite a fight to go back into his cell to find it. He swore it went down between the decking boards. I saw his fingers sir, raw and cut they were from the splinters.'

'Just do as you are bloody told man,' said Feltsham. 'Also make sure everything else is secure.'

Captain Moxey lent forward towards Ketch. 'All our futures are in the balance Ketch. To begin with, search the men that shared the cell with Kettlewell.'

'On what grounds?' said Ketch.

'Find one man, find one,' said Feltsham. Tarn had been about to knock the cabin door when he heard the conversation. He paused his raised hand to listen. Moxey heard movement outside of the door. He jumped up out of his chair. 'If it's that bloody steward again I'll throw him overboard.' But instead he was met by Tarn's raised hand. 'Ah! I was just about to knock captain, may I come in.'

'Why are you lurking outside my cabin doctor?'

'Lurking captain for what reason? Indeed I wish I had time to loiter sir.'

'Well, what is it,' said Moxey, then turning to Ketch he said. 'That will be all Sergeant get on with it and report back.'

Moxey looked back at Tarn.

'Well?'

'I am glad you have taken over the command of the soldiers captain, because Lt. Feltsham just died.' For heartbeats no one spoke. 'I regret the double tragedy my lord, it must weigh heavy on you,' said Tarn. If Feltsham caught the sarcasm in the remark he did not rise to the bait.

'However, I can report that the coal tar appears to be reducing the spread of the disease, that, and I hope, the compound I have been giving to everyone.'

Lord Feltsham saw his chance. 'Even the ones who have died doctor?' he said with a slight flourish of his monogrammed handkerchief.

You bloody buffoon thought Tarn. 'Yes! Lord Feltsham even those, but regrettable it came too late.'

'Obviously,' said Feltsham.

Before he lost his temper Tarn crossed to the door. 'I have kept you informed captain. Lt. Feltsham's burial is in ten minutes, so if that is all, I will return to my duties,' said Tarn, slamming the door just a little too hard behind him.

Lieutenant Charles Hugo Feltsham sunk below the waves, a soldier who had never raised his sword or fired a musket. His only claim to being alive was his recorded death aboard the convict ship the *Runnymede*. His uncle remained in his cabin. His lordship felt he had witnessed enough burials for one day.

The cargo hold was hot and musty. Barrels of salted meat, baskets of fresh South American fruit gave off a sweet aroma in counterbalance to the dry straw, ropes, tar and coiled cordage. Shenkin was oblivious to it all has he held Elizabeth to him. Breaking away she looked up into his dark brown eyes, strands of his hair falling loose over his proud forehead. It took her breath away. For a moment neither said a word. To break the difficult silence Elizabeth said in an unsteady voice. 'Why the scarf Shenkin? Is it a keepsafe, did a woman give it to you?' said Elizabeth, not wanting to know the answer.

'Yes,' said Shenkin, 'But that was a long time ago now, it seems like another world, another life. A time before I knew you or dreamt my dreams of you.'

Pleased with his reply Elizabeth smiled. 'Well then! why continue to wear it?'

'It is a personal remembrance of a past time,' said Shenkin, in a tone she had no wish to question. He was here with her that is all that she wanted.

'Alright, at least let me wash it clean.'

'The dirt is part of that past I prefer to leave it, but thank you for offering.'

'I am sorry to pry Shenkin please forgive me.'

'There is nothing to forgive cariad, we are alone that is all that matters. It states our feelings much more than the past ever could,' said Shenkin, smiling.

'Yes it does. But we must be careful Shenkin, if my uncle finds we are meeting like this he will place you in irons and me to my cabin regardless of how short-handed he is,' said Elizabeth, breathlessly.

'No one will harm you or take you from me,' said Shenkin fiercely, as he took her into his arms again this time eagerly seeking her lips. He felt his manhood stir, it had been so long, so very long since he had held a woman. Sensing her inexperience, he gently guided her hand to his now hard erection. Then nature took over and she knew instinctively what to do. Hungrily she unbuckled his belt then her hand was holding his engorged penis. Excitement rushed through her body, as it had when she was alone with him in the sick bay, her nipples rising hard against her bodice. A small whimper broke from her throat as Shenkin laid his hand on the ripeness of her breasts. Small pert firm breasts that felt so warm and yielding to his hand. They were now eager to explore one others bodies, hands flying up and down impatient with the moment. They needed release from the heat, the building passion that held them prisoners. On top of folded sails, they let the moment take them. Elizabeth gave a slight shudder as Shenkin entered her, then a deep moan came from her as he, almost violently, plunged into her body time and time again. She felt has if she was going to explode her heart beat faster and faster, then both let out a near animal sound has they both climaxed together. For heartbeats Shenkin lay on top of her feeling the tension of all these months leave his body then he rolled over pulling Elizabeth into his arms. Tears streamed down her face falling onto his cheeks.

'I hurt you cariad. I'm sorry I just…'

But she put her finger to his lips. 'No my love, the tears are of joy,' said Elizabeth Moxey. 'I will cherish this moment till the day I die.'

They both knew that to say more would break the spell so they lay in a close embrace. The hanging ropes swung to and fro, the timber creaked out their rhythm with the sea. Slowly with a deep feeling of satisfaction they began to drift off to sleep.

Shenkin woke with a start. Ketch a twisted smile upon his face was looking down on them. 'Well now isn't this a pretty sight. They'll hang you for rape Shenkin for I'll stand witness to it.' Elizabeth was aware her petticoats were still around her waist her womanhood was covered but her breasts were exposed to this man's uncouth gaze, quickly she covered herself. Shenkin was on his feet standing toe to toe with Ketch.

Ketch stood, the smirk still fixed upon his face 'I thought I heard noises but thought it was rats or the like so I went on with my task. But then I caught sight of a pretty ankle on my way out. Imagine my surprise in coming across you Shenkin, raping the captain's niece,' said Ketch. He turned his gaze again at Elizabeth. 'Mind I wouldn't mind a go myself Shenkin, then it would be our little secret. What do you say?'

Shenkin hit him with an explosive right, sending Ketch into the barrels of salted meat. Ketch brought up his musket fast and hard it caught Shenkin across his arm as he protected his head. Shenkin's knee went up into Ketch's crotch causing Ketch to double up. At the same time the musket went flying out of his hand. Down on his knees Ketch realised he was no match for this man, he needed a weapon. Before Shenkin could stop him, Ketch picked up a grappling hook that lay on a coil of rope. He swung it wildly at Shenkin the point sinking into a bale of hay. Ripping it out he went forward swinging at Shenkin. Shenkin feinted back then pulled Ketch to him, driving his fist into Ketch's throat. As Ketch went down Shenkin kicked him in the side then again in the head. He had Ketch by the throat, slowly he tightened his grip. Ketch his arms flaying his legs kicking out. Slowly his life was ebbing away has Shenkin continued to close his grip.

'Shenkin! Stop please stop,' screamed Elizabeth.

He had almost forgotten she was there. Pulling back Shenkin stood up, it was over.

Ketch his breathing coming in short gasps, staggered to his feet then falling back onto the bales of hay. 'I'll see you hang Shenkin, mark my words if I don't. And you Miss, why involve yourself with an enemy of the crown, a rioter, a killer?'

'Yes! That's right Ketch, a killer. So help me I'll kill you if you breathe a word of this to the captain, I swear it Ketch, remember what happen to Kettlewell.'

'To hell with you Shenkin I'll bide my time, we are not out of this cholera yet and we have a long way to go before we get to Port Jackson,' said Ketch, rubbing his throat has he made his way to the companion ladder.

Elizabeth had alarm and fear still on her face after witnessing the violence this man, who she loved so much, was capable of.

Shenkin watching Ketch disappear turned to her. Seeing the look on her face he lifted his hands in supplication. 'We come from different worlds

Elizabeth mine is one of survival, yours a caring genteel world of love, safety and a promise of a good future. But for me it is a daily fight mentally and physically, as it is for Regan, and was for Collins and is even for Ketch,' he paused then went on. 'Indeed as it is for all of the convicts that find themselves here aboard a ship of disgrace.

'You speak well Shenkin, not just from the heart but from the mind.'

'Blame it on my father, his love of words, his belief in a better society. To my mother who believed in him and loved me.' He told her about the rising that became a riot, about his father dying in his mother's arms. The tears this time were ones of sadness, so Shenkin held her close again until finally she stopped. Looking up at Shenkin she said. 'I believe in you too, I always will regardless of class, we are now in our own world. Together my love, we can make a future.

Shenkin bent down and kissed her tenderly, gently, not in lust, but in love.

CHAPTER 23

'I thought you had decided to swim, so I did,' said Regan meeting Shenkin coming up from the between decks. 'We need to get some more tar on these fires. The doctor says they seem to be helping. We've had only two more cases since sunrise,' said Regan, but with a pained look upon his broad Irish face.

'Well!' said Shenkin

'I was thinking of Collins buried back there in the wake of the ship,' said Regan, making the sign of the cross.

Shenkin nodded then added with a sigh. 'What a life the lad had; drinking a pint of milk that was not his own, no father, a mother scrubbing the floors of the local gentry's mansions, then he's sentenced by mistake with a group of unionists to transportation. And you cross yourself in the belief in a supreme being who is supposed to be watching over us. What will help us to survive, Regan, is in not believing that we can't,' said Shenkin, dipping a rag on the end of a piece of timber into a barrel of tar and creosote.

'I tell you sir I searched everywhere there's not a sign of the stone. Kettlewell was certain it went down between the deck boards, his fingers bore witness to his words,' said Ketch, still holding a hand to his throat.

'Where did you get the welt across your throat from Ketch?' asked Moxey.

'Walked into a rope, some fool had stored across the gangway.'

The captain seemed surprised; he inspected the cargo hold daily as part of his routine checks of the ship and was about to say something when Feltsham spoke. 'To hell with the man's injuries, what about searching Kettlewell's cellmates?' A knock at the cabin door stopped their further conversation.

'Come.'

Tarn entered the cabin. 'Captain I intend to have all aboard, apart from the sick or dying, remove their clothing, these are to be placed in boiling water. All will then wash themselves in seawater which will then be rinsed off with fresh water. One half bucket full to every three men. Miss Elizabeth will of course change and wash in private.'

'Yes! An excellent idea doctor,' said Feltsham, to everyone's surprise.

'Very well Tarn, do it.'

'Thank you sir,' said Tarn, turning for the door.

Once Tarn had closed the door Feltsham turned to Ketch. 'Now is your chance man to search the clothes and belongings of Kettlewell's cellmates.'

'Of course,' said the captain, standing up from his chair. 'But one of them died sir.'

To Ketch's horror the captain said, 'Search the dead man's clothes or count yourself out of your share.'

Ketch left the cabin, fear etched in every line of his face. He almost walked into Tarn who was talking to Lawson. 'What's that red mark on your throat sergeant?'

'It's nothing doctor,' said Ketch, pushing past. Tarn shrugged his shoulders and continued to explained his intentions to Lawson. Two cauldrons of boiling water were ready for the first batches of clothes. Soon everyone was stripped, the soap and seawater had produced a reasonable lather the decks covered in suds. Shenkin had even dipped his scarf into the boiling water and proceeded in scrubbing the scarf in his hands.

'Sure I don't recognise you Shenkin without that scarf on. You look naked, so you do. Why! You are naked,' said Regan laughing. Strange to be laughing amongst all the dying but laugh they did. While they were washing, Ketch went through every piece of their clothing. Except for Collins who he was told had already gone over the side clothes and all. Thank God for that thought Ketch.

Rinsing down with clean fresh water seem to do wonders for everyone, many even combed and brushed their hair. Their wet clothes soon dried in the afternoon sun. They all returned to their duties in better spirits than before. The doctor also noted that not one new case of cholera had developed. Were they through it, if so, was it due to the Calcutta Remedy or the creosote drenched air? What did it matter, they had survived. Then to everyone's astonishment the Surgeon-Superintendent let out a holler 'Dear Sweet Mary in Heaven I think we've beaten it. Regan O'Hara let's give them an Irish song.'

Everyone watched as both Surgeon-Superintendent Michael Patrick Tarn and Convict Regan Liam O'Hara sang 'Bold Robert Emmet', the Irish Rebel Song of 1803. Then they danced an Irish jig. At that moment Elizabeth came out of her small cabin freshly washed, her hair glossy, her cheeks pinched red. She wore a dress of the most delicate colour of blue that matched her eyes. Her slim waist was wrapped by a sash of a deeper colour blue, while over her shoulders she wore a short spencer jacket of white silk. The floor-length dress showed just a hint of a petticoat. She had the eyes and breath of every man aboard. Lord Feltsham took her hand, as the captain stared in wonder. 'My dear you are a vision of beauty. May I escort you to the captain's cabin for our evening meal. Allow me to take you away from these men of poor manners and uncouth ways. Also, if you would allow me, I'll pour you a glass of my excellent madeira,' said Feltsham, with all the charm and assumed rightful claim of his superior position.

'You may sir, if those who have brought us through this dreadful time accompany us,' said Elizabeth, her eyes outshining the glow of her hair.

'Of course Doctor Tarn will join us, regardless of his misplaced loyalties, will you not sir?' Before Tarn could release himself from the jig with Regan to respond. Elizabeth added, 'Sir I mean all that saw us through, the convicts Shenkin, Regan O'Hara, Mr Lawson and Corporal Burke, if duties allow. she said, turning to her uncle for support.

'You trade too much upon your beauty madam. I am not accustomed to dining with felons,' said Feltsham.

'Due to them you are fortunate to be dining at all Lord Feltsham are you not?' said Elizabeth sarcastically.

But Feltsham had already turned back towards the captain's cabin beckoning Moxey to join him, who in turn called Ketch.

When they had gone Elizabeth turned to Tarn. 'Well doctor, it is a beautiful balmy evening surely we can make a table of sorts to dine upon.'

Tarn smiled. 'We can so. Regan lend a hand here, Shenkin some upturned barrels if you please, while I go to fetch a bottle or two of claret from my cabin.'

'Do you not have something a little stronger doctor?' said Regan.

'I'll ask the captain to break out some rum for all his motley crew,' said Tarn, with a wicked smile.

However, Moxey was not pleased either by the suggestion or Tarn breaking in on his discussions with Feltsham and Ketch. 'This is a convict ship sir not a bloody merry get together.'

'I see captain I'll instruct the convicts be return to their cells including crew and soldiers who are recovering from the fever,' said Tarn.

'Wait,' said Feltsham, quickly. 'Let us be charitable captain there is yet a long way to go. You told me you would not be stopping at Cape Town, since you are still flying the yellow flag and it is very doubtful they would have let us dock anyway. So we will need every hand, will we not, if we are to safely cross the Roaring Forties,' said Lord Feltsham, waiting a moment for Moxey to reply. When the silence stretched out Feltsham added 'Is that not so Captain Moxey, no point in putting our ship at risk, in fact I insist it is not sir.' Lord Feltsham was many things but he was not a complete fool, thought Tarn.

'Alright, but watered-down rum,' said Moxey

'After what they have gone through, I'll not give these men grog sir! They deserve the full 140 proof Caribbean rum, of which we have two tubs.

Moxey, red in the face, stood up. 'Very well damn it! Issue one, I repeat one, tot of rum. Is that understood Tarn, half a gill only to every man,' said Moxey, through clenched teeth.

'Thank you sir, I'll attend to your orders immediately.'

'I can do without your insolence sir…' But Patrick Tarn had left.

Coming back onto the quarterdeck. Tarn was met with the news that the last of the very ill had just died. Tarn had given him boiled water only an hour previous. He had been a thief from London's East End. His name was Harry Tombs and he had been with Shenkin and O'Hara on the hulk; he had given them bread and cheese when they had first arrived at Woolwich. He had also guided them through those first few days on the hulk.

'God rest his soul, for he found none in this life,' said Tarn, crossing himself.

The burial party was a small one. No other was to be buried Tombs, would thankfully, be the last. It was Shenkin together with O'Hara who insisted on being the burial party. Shenkin murmured a Welsh prayer, Regan an Irish one as they tipped the corpse of Harry Tombs the cockney over the side.

From the bridge of the quarterdeck Elizabeth with the doctor looked down on the scene. 'Is it really over doctor?'

'Yes, I believe it is, we have buried the last one. In which case young lady, I suggest we celebrate the living, for there is nothing we can do for the dead,' said Tarn, placing his hand on top of the rum tub. When all had their tin mugs filled, Tarn raised his glass. 'Gentlemen! And lady,' said Tarn, bowing to Elizabeth. 'I give you a Samuel Johnson saying, "The future is purchased by the present." Well you have all purchased our future in plenty, well done.' A cheer rose from the strangest of crews ever to sail a merchant ship. Even the captain from the doorway of his cabin, if a little reluctantly, nodded his agreement.

Feltsham smiled. 'Good, captain, very good, we must show we are with them until we reach Port Jackson then we can call in our account, can we not?' he said, removing the still non-existent lint from his coat. It was not a question it was a statement of vindictive intent.

Tarn had drunk three glasses of claret together with a tot, a large tot, of rum. He was becoming very mellow, being an Irishman he was also becoming sad and emotional. By his side Shenkin was sipping his rum slowly, while Elizabeth cut up some bread and cheese, together with a little meat.

'Shenkin!' said Tarn, a little too loud his voice slurred, his movements unsteady. 'Doctor! can I help you to your cabin?'

'Good God no. Excuse me my dear.' Turning to Elizabeth who smiled caringly. 'No need doctor you have had a very difficult time. When did you last sleep sir?'

'I am fine, it's just that I wanted to say to you Shenkin that I do understand the cause that brought you to this sorry state. It is indeed the right of every man to have the vote, and so have a say in their and their children's future. The last time I spoke those words it cost me my inheritance. You doubted me when we first met. I think you said my sort never understand, but I do Shenkin, many of us do.'

Shenkin shook his head. 'I have seen it doctor in your actions, in your statements, in the fairness of your care for all on board. It is I who should apologise,' said Shenkin.

Tarn sighed. 'Thank you Shenkin you are most gracious. So let me give a toast to the cause of suppressed men everywhere. I'll quote from the man we just sang about, Robert Emmet of the United Irishmen.' At this point there were tears briming in Tarn's eyes. 'Please raise your full mugs, the second ones I hope.' After steadying himself on the now empty tub of rum Tarn continued. 'Emmet was hanged drawn and quartered in 1803. When he was sentenced, he said this from the dock,' said Tarn, raising his glass up high to the evening sky.

'"When my country takes its place among the nations of the Earth, then and not till then, let my epitaph be written.' Tears rolled uncontrollably down Tarn's face.

Regan Liam O'Hara, sagging on a row of belaying pins, was sobbing like a child. 'That's the truth, so it is, it's the god's honest truth.' Slowly he sunk to the deck.

'Doctor let me help you to your cabin,' said Shenkin.

'Thank you Shenkin,' said Tarn, turning to the assembled group. 'Goodnight gentleman, Elizabeth.' Then lifting his hand off of the rum tub he allowed Shenkin to take his arm.

A roar of approval came from each man as they downed their last drop of rum.

CHAPTER 24

They made sweet passionate love till the early hours of the morning. Shenkin lay back on the straw bedding they had made in their hideaway corner of the ship's cargo hold. 'Elizabeth, I have learnt much during this voyage. Mainly, that I should not believe only the poor and oppressed see the wrongness of life. My father knew that but I wanted to sense the burning within my own soul, that no one else could share. You are educated, was I wrong?' said Shenkin, looking into Elizabeth's piercing blue eyes, that always caught his breath.

'No my dear it must start somewhere. That you begin to understand the broader implications shows that you have an open mind that is prepared to accept the views of others. That is good because it brings maturity to your reasoning,' said Elizabeth, holding his hand to her breast.

Shenkin gazed at her in wonder. She was like no woman that he had ever met before. He pulled her fiercely into his arms. Her lips were full, moist eager for his. A small moan escaped her, as she came down on top of him. They were lost in the passion of each other, as the rest of the ship woke to the day's tasks.

Ketch moved around the ship more freely now that the cholera was waning. He spoke to Burke in a low voice. 'Burke, now that that snivelling so-called officer of ours is gone to the land of the other chinless wonders, I'll give the orders now,' said Ketch, adding 'as I always did. There'll be no more sharing our moments with the convicts, they will be given work to do and no bloody tots of rum to reward them. Got it?'

'Sir,' said Burke, stifling a sigh.

'I want some order back into our duties. To start with that bastard Shenkin is not to go near the captain's niece, that's an order straight from the captain. So if you see him near her I want to know about it. Right?!'

'Sir.'

'I want the cells cleaned out by the prisoners, the decks scrubbed, those on crew duties to look sharp about it,' said Ketch, pulling the waistcoat under his tunic down hard. Burke watched as it slowly travelled back up Ketch's stomach. 'Well don't bloody stand there get on with it man.'

'Yes, sir.'

Of the 198 souls who had set out from London in January only 155 remained. Most had been victims of the cholera outbreak, two had died of malnutrition, one had been killed in a knife fight. Thirty-three were slowly recovering from their bout of cholera, thanks, Tarn believed, to the creosote and the Calcutta Remedy. But this still left the *Runnymede* well under-crewed.

Slowly the ship began to return to normality, and with it all the former social order. Feltsham strode the poop deck full of his rightful place in the world. He looked down upon the activities of the convicts and crew with distain. The captain had placed half a dozen soldiers to guard the prisoners at their work. Ketch resumed his bullying of both his men and the prisoners, while all the time waiting for his chance to get even with Shenkin.

Tarn tended the sick with the help of Elizabeth who he was well aware saw Shenkin at every opportunity. Let the young be young he thought, if this was a strange place to fall in love or lust then so be it, life was short at best and terminal for certain.

They had rounded the Cape of Good Hope with little trouble; some sail and sheets needed repair, but given their reduced crew the captain was relieved. He had stood at the helmsman side for many hours conning the ship while passing the Cape. An overbearing, arrogant man but a good sailor who issued orders with the confidence of years of experience. Tarn grudgingly respected his seamanship, Feltsham on the other hand continually interfered. After rounding the Cape they sailed into the last and most dangerous part of the voyage, the Roaring Forties. With the wind off the stern quarter, they made good progress. Then as their course took them around Van Diemen's Land, they entered latitude forty-six degrees. There the strong west-to-east air current began to blow up a storm. The westerly winds tore at the sails and rigging with a ferocity that took Shenkin's breath away. Moxey had already changed over to heavy sails, nevertheless he soon ordered reduced sail. In only a short space of time the wind was so strong that he called for the sails to be taken in. As the wind strength continued to increase the captain shouted out. 'I want to see bare poles Mr Lawson, sharply now,' called Moxey.

'Ay ay, sir.'

Moxey's eyes swept the deck and sails. 'Bosun attended to your locker for fast repairs where necessary if you please.'

'Ay sir.'

Lord Feltsham came on deck but then thought better of it disappearing back into his cabin, that had been the first cabin to be reinstated. However, given the now violent motion of the ship his lordship looked decidedly pale, as he tottered back inside.

Water came pouring down the gratings into the cell areas. Shenkin stood in pools of water shouting for the guards to open up the cells, that was again used to hold the convicts who were not on some restricted crew duties.

An order soon came for all hands, including the convicts to the top decks. The scene that confronted Shenkin was a maelstrom of wind and water he had never witnessed before. Men were desperately holding on to the life lines, but still their legs were taken from under them, as the ship lifted then bucked to the rising waves. Shenkin clawed his way to Elizabeth's cabin but Ketch blocked his way. 'Where you going then? You're needed down on the forecastle deck, not making a call to your dolly-mop.' Ketch began to say something else, but Shenkin hit him once then a second time that sent him crashing into Elizabeth's cabin door. Elizabeth opened the door ajar seeing Shenkin she opened the door further. 'Shenkin please don't worry about me, I'll be alright,' she shouted above the roar of the increasing wind. Satisfied that she was indeed safe Shenkin turned back. Stepping over Ketch he made his way to the lower deck companion ladder, where men, sails, and halyards fought one another first to port then starboard, then bow down and stern up. This cauldron of nature seemed to Shenkin to make the very waves stand up and walk across the sea towards them. The waves were gigantic forty, fifty-foot high walls of water that seem to stand like a barrier across their bow. Everything that could, or might move was battened down. Cargo was rechecked and lashed into place. The live animals that were still left stared wide-eyed, kicking at their pens. Straw flew about the air like demented creatures. Shenkin saw two crewmen on the portside trying to lash some sheets that were flying loose, when a wave from the starboard side hit the ship causing her to be in danger of broaching. The captain bellowed. 'Keep her heading into the wind, damn you. Bring her head into the wind, for god's sake. Mr Lawson I want two men on the helm,' said Moxey, hardly audible and red in the face.

'Ay, Ay sir'

When Shenkin made his way to help the men they were gone. Lashing in the flying sheets he turned to help Regan tie down some shrouds that had come loose from the foremast. At that moment a thunderous crack that sounded like cannon fire brought down the top foremast. Shearing off at the iron bands, it came crashing down onto the deck missing them by inches. The section of mast fell across the starboard side rail smashing the top timbers. The rigging tangled around their feet like spiderwebs while the top spar with its rigging was now in the sea dragging the ship around. 'Cut that rigging free,' shouted Moxey. Sailors rushed forward, axes in hand they began chopping at the rigging. The ship was now slewing about, as the mast together with the water she was taking on began listing her to starboard. Shenkin joined in to cut her loose. He was soon standing up to his knees in seawater, hacking and slashing wildly, finally they cut the rigging free. The mast was dragged overboard, hitting one man on the side of the head as the mast whipped up into the air. A coil of halyard wrapped itself around another the man's foot taking him over the side with the mast. Slowly the ship began to right herself. The helmsmen, with Moxey's help, pulled spoke by spoke of the wheel to bring her about. But the ferocious wind kept changing direction, as they struggled to keep her head into the wind. The yards chaffed in their slings until finally they had her head-on. Putting another seaman on the wheel to help the helmsmen, Moxey returned to the poop deck. The hours stretched on but the storm did not abate. Shenkin turned to look up at the captain who was at the poop rail over viewing the full forward length of the ship, not that he could see forward far. He glimpsed the shiny wet blurred movements of the crew, the tops of hatches battened, companion ladders straining at their fixings, swinging halyards and clouds of spray. His eyes screwed up against the blasts of wind and freezing water as he strained to see how his ship was performing against this ferocious onslaught. Standing back for a moment the captain held on to rigging from the mizzen mast, while the wind battered him as he fought to stay upright. The scuppers were not dealing with the water as more and more sea flooded the decks. Moxey moved to the overhang of the poop deck and lent over the rail. 'Mr Lawson, rig up pumps to bail out the water. Lend as many men as you can spare to it,' shouted Moxey.

'Ay, sir.'

Ketch had been staying close to the hatch on the forecastle deck ready to dive down it, if the need came to it. When he saw Shenkin move to the portside rail, he felt this was his chance to get even for all that had happened. He made his way with difficulty over to the rail. Picking up a belaying pin as he passed the base of the mainmast. The turmoil of plumes of spray and fog around him covered his intentions as he moved up behind Shenkin who was still busy clearing the deck of timber and rigging that had come down with the top foremast.

Ketch raised his arm to strike down on Shenkin, but Burke seemed to come out of nowhere and wrapped his arms around Ketch. They both fell in a tangle of rigging and splintered wood as a wave broke over them. The violent movement of the ship sent them over to the listing starboard side.

Their arms and legs were locked around each other as they fought to gain their balance. Struggling to his feet, Burke moved unsteadily to Ketch's blind side. Ketch, his eyepatch now on his forehead, struck out at Burke's knees with the pin, feeling bone break he brought it viciously back the other way. Burke mouthed a scream but not a sound was heard above the raging storm. They were now near the damaged rail left by the mast, the gaping space a mass of splintered wood. Ketch rammed Burke's head into the opening. The jagged timber sliced into Burke's face as Ketch lifted his legs and heaved him over the side. Regan turned in time to see that a struggle was going on but the sea spray and fog obscured his view. Then he saw Ketch walk out of the spray as another wave washed him back to the foot of the mainmast. Pulling himself up Ketch looked one eyed at Regan. 'What you looking at, you Pope-loving Irish bastard, get back to lending a hand, do something useful,' said Ketch, placing his patch back over the empty socket. Pulling down his waistcoat he made his way unsteadily back to the relative safety of the hatch. Crouching behind the hatch cover he looked to see if anyone else had seen him push Burke overboard. Satisfied that no one had, he pulled a small flask of brandy from his hip pocket. Before he drank he shouted at a soldier who had stopped to cover a badly bleeding arm. 'Afraid of a bit of blood are we, get back to work you idle slob.' At that moment all went calm the wind dropped. The very air seemed to stand still as an unnatural silence fell about the ship. For heartbeats no one spoke, even the bleating animals were quiet. Then from the poop deck the captain called to Lawson. 'Mr Lawson we are in the trough of two high waves get a man up the lower foremast to secure that mainstay before we are across it and back into the full force of the storm.'

'Ay sir,' said Lawson, blood running freely down his face from a cut to his forehead. Many of the crew and prisoners were by now cut or bruised as they waited to continue their struggle with the storm. The strong west-to-east currents were caused by the air being displaced from the Equator towards the South Pole, causing Moxey to steer away from a southerly course when he was able. The wind's chill factor cut to the very bone of the men has they carried out their duties. The intensity of the cold was beginning to have a marked effect on the crews' performance. All were wet to their skins, while the biting cold sapped their last reserves of strength. 'You man! Open that rum tub,' shouted the captain down to the quarterdeck,' throwing the man the key to the padlock. 'Fill some bottles, then a swig to each man, quick about it now, before all hell breaks loose again.'

'Ay ay, sir.'

'Mr Lawson keep a weather eye on the allocation of the rum. A swig per man mind, no more I want them on their feet and seaworthy Mr Lawson.'

'Sir.'

They hit the wall of the storm again as three men, holding desperately on to handrails, moved as quickly as they could among the crew, passing the bottles from man to man. The captain watched as the men moved forward into the curtains of spray and disappeared. At the forecastle hatch, Ketch lifted his hand for the bottle, but the seaman a big Irishman kicked out at the hand. 'Scurry back into your corner you Limey bastard, crew first then those who are trying to keep us afloat,' shouted the seaman, scrambling over to the portside where faces and hands were turning blue, as wave after wave crashed over the rails.

An old shellback took his swig then looked up to the water filled sky. 'Hadley Cell they calls it, but it should be Hades Cell, what say you shipmate?' The bottle carrier nodded, said something, but it was lost in the wind.

Shenkin had known cold in his black valley, but nothing to compare to this, his very blood seemed to be turning to ice. Putting the bottle of rum to his lips it rattled on his teeth uncontrollably, spilling some of the rum down his chin, which he fingered back into his mouth. The broken top foremast was finally lashed securely, the pumps had cleared some of the seawater from the decks but she was still awash as the wind picked up the sea and threw it violently onto the ship. Regan, his legs swept from under for the hundredth time, looked over to Shenkin. He mouthed the words Sweet Mary, his breath burning out of his mouth in a cloud as it met the cold air, while on his knees he genuflected. Shenkin nodded. When will it end he thought? It had begun so suddenly, from a moderate sea to a cauldron in minutes as yet more waves crashed over the ship. Then with immense power the seas lifted the ship forward and up onto the crest of a wave, the rudder clear of the water, the helmsman tossed to the side. For heartbeats they seem to hang in the air, then finally they crashed down violently into another trough. All around them the sea surged one way then another hurling itself up into a fury of bitterly ice spiked spray. The combination of hot and cold air had caused more fog to form, which further hindered the crew in their efforts to hold some sort of course. The binnacle holding the compass seemed alive as its brass cover bobbed up and down making the reading of the compass card difficult. In spite of the cold the light from the housing showed sweat gleaming on the helmsmen's faces has they fought the wheel to again hold a steady course. It was now 1 am, the sound of the bells hardly heard above the cacophony of noise. Moxey had gone back and forth to his cabin to consult his charts, his last sightings were just before they hit the storm. Given the now poor visibility he did not want to run into any land mass. While there, he noted that the storm glass reading continued to fall. He changed watches when he could to give the crew a moments respite, but with a reduced crew it became difficult to spare anyone. Men cursed the sea, the wind, and for being born at all into such a world of wind and water, as the ship slewed and see-sawed her heavy way forward. Suddenly the wind fell as the *Runnymede* went down into the deepest of troughs they had yet experienced. The crest of the massive wave loomed over them like a black cape. All hands gripped the nearest solid part of the ship that they could find. As the ship began to climb the curve of the wave, it suddenly broke over them. The wave crumbled in front of them, torn down like a black curtain, shredding itself into tattered strips of hanging water. It came down on them with a thunderous crash. The *Runnymede* creaked as she began to flounder under the weight of water, when another rising wave caught hold of her, tossing her cork like into the air. She came down with a bone jarring thud onto an open sea, where, mercifully deep swells carried her forward away from the vortex of the storm. Incredibly they were though, men and ship beaten, battered, and bruised, but alive. The captain, his hands still gripping the rail, called down to Lawson. 'Muster the crew, if you please, give me a count together with list of injuries, and a damage report.'

'Ay ay, sir.'

'Sergeant Ketch! Where the hell are you?' said Moxey.

From behind the hatch combing out of the now lighter fog came Ketch, limping his way forward.

'Sir.'

I want a count of your men sergeant–' but before Moxey could finish, Ketch spoke up. 'One missing sir! Corporal Burke sir! He's gone sir!' he said, in a rush of words. Realising his error, he added 'That is, I think sir.'

'Accuracy Sergeant, that's what I require.'

'Sir.'

Regan standing by Shenkin's side turned to him. 'That's what I saw, the bastard pushed him overboard.'

Shenkin stared at Regan. For a moment neither spoke then Regan explained what he saw. 'But why?' said Shenkin, a puzzled look upon his face.

They searched everywhere for Burke, but he was nowhere to be found. Guilt hung on Ketch like a coat as he joined the search. Shenkin came up very close to him. 'It was you wasn't it, you bastard, why?' Ketch sneered. 'Interfering he was, with my plans for you wasn't he?' he said, close to Shenkin's ear.

'I'll tell the captain Ketch I'll make sure the two of us stand trial for killings.'

'Prove it, the word of a loyal soldier who has fought for his King and Country against that of a convicted convict for rebellious treason against the Crown. I'll swear you were out to get Burke for not giving you fresh water when you were in the sick bay,' said Ketch, the smug look breaking into what passed as a smile.

'I have a witness. Regan saw you fighting with Burke during the storm.'

'What?! The word of another convict they'll never believe him, he's your fellow rioter isn't he?'

For some moments they stared at each other but Shenkin knew Ketch was right. He had no credibility with the captain and certainly not with Lord Feltsham, as he knew he would not have with the men who would judge him for the killing of Kettlewell. 'We'll have our day of reckoning Ketch I swear it, one day it will just be you and me.'

'That's if they don't hang you first Shenkin, there's a rope waiting for you remember,' said Ketch, walking away. 'And I'll be there to watch you dance on the end of it,' he said, over his shoulder.

Back in their cells Regan grunted. 'We could of course send him over the rail one evening.'

'It would be a noisy affair, with these chains back on us,' said Shenkin, gazing down. They were fettered again, even those on limited crew duties shuffled about the deck with difficulty, their inexperienced hands holding cautiously onto the life lines. The men they had lost were gone, they had vanished unheard and unseen in the white topped fury of the sea.

CHAPTER 25

In the days that followed the storm, the *Runnymede* took on a more leisurely pace. Repairs were made to the splintered timbers on the starboard rail, while convicts threaded twine through needles as the crew mended sails and sheets. The starboard deck boat had been smashed to tinder the timber pieces gathered, lashed and stowed. A jury rig now stood ungainly above the sheared foremast. Slowly the *Runnymede* became again the convict ship she was, if rather battered in appearance. However, the warmth of the sun gave way to a more peaceful sail. With even some balmy evenings, which after the hardships they had endured, seemed to lull most into a sense of wellbeing whether they were chained or not. Cholera patients were gradually recovering, some had even returned to light duties fresh water was issued together with the fruit, now on the ripe side, which they had taken on board at Rio. There seemed no sign of any significant scurvy from their salted meat but Tarn was taking no chances, all were given a daily number of limes. At Lord Feltsham's insistence, they had only fresh meat on the captain's table, to which Tarn was again invited.

Shenkin wanted to know all he could about the ship and sailing. He continually pestered the crew with questions, what was this called, what was that called and what were they all for? The sailors liked him so they spent time instructing him in the ways of the sea and sailing. He began to learn about knots; first he practised with a piece of thin lanyard, which he used on his scarf to tie his hair back. He began to master a bowline, a reef, a clove hitch, a half hitch and the toughest of all for him, the monkey's fist. At every opportunity during the day he'd send Regan crazy, practising over and over. The sailors told him when he could do them with his eyes closed then he would really know how to do them. And in the end, with great flourishes, he could indeed do most with his eyes closed, even the difficult monkey's fist. This always drew a cheer from the sailors who would check the knots and declare them perfect.

In case the convicts were needed for crew duties, the cells were left unlocked and lightly guarded. While all were asleep Shenkin would leave his cell. To the sound of Regan whispering. 'You'll get caught one of these nights, so you will.' Elizabeth would sneak from her cabin and they would spend their nights in passionate embraces until the dawn light parted them.

In the early light one morning, a call went up from the lookout swaying in the barrel of the crow's nest. 'Land on the port bow!' Captain Moxey who had wasted no time in taking a sighting after the storm knew they were on a course that should find Van Diemen's Land; nevertheless putting his telescope to his eye he was relieved to see it. They would continue to sail in a wide curve that led the *Runnymede* into the Pacific Ocean and on towards Port Jackson. Seabirds began to appear, of a species that Shenkin had never seen before; large fish escorted them in great numbers. The whole sea and sky became more and more alive. A week later in brilliant morning sunshine, their chains rattling while being marched around the deck to Ketch's usual bullying, birds alighted on the rails. Their feathers an array of brilliant colours, they were in the 'land beyond the seas'. Their voyage was over, the penal colony awaited them. Of the 120 convicts that had embarked only seventy-three were still alive. Of the eight Merthyr Rioters, only five remained Shenkin, Regan O'Hara, Thomas Williams, John Lewis, and Dewi Davies of Dowlais Top.

Shenkin had tried to encourage them during their ordeals, but it lay heavy on his conscience that of the eighteen he had fought side by the side with during the Rising only these men remained. What had they achieved? Would there someday be a union back in that black Welsh valley where his mother, sister and young brother now lived a subjugated existence, his father buried in the cold wet ground along with so many others?

Regan saw the tormented look. 'Sure now you cannot weep for the past even God cannot change the past Shenkin, what is done is done. Who knows one day it may make a difference, at least, let's bloody hope it does,' said Regan, turning to their cell door he called out, 'Any regrets lads?'

'I always wanted a sea voyage I did,' said Tom Williams.

'A lovely spot of sunshine mind,' said Dewi.

'Complete with painted bloody birds as well, now there's clever,' said John Lewis.

Regan looked back at Shenkin. 'There! they are all delighted to be here, wherever the hell here is. Also you have met Elizabeth, so you have, she'd have never come to Merthyr Tydfil would she?'

Shenkin smiled. 'No Regan, that's a fact.'

Captain Moxey had all convicts secured, their cells locked once more. He had mustered what was left of his crew, as he brought the ship to stand off Sydney Cove. 'Hoist the Yellow Jack, Mr Lawson. Bosun, I want everything shipshape and Bristol fashion, if you please.'

A chorus of 'Ay Ay, sir' came up from the two men.

Lord Feltsham stood at the captain's side on the poop deck. 'You have secured Kettlewell's boxes captain, have you not?'

'Ketch has them set to one side all have a small K on the top right-hand side. The boxes are marked Moxey Chandlers & Shipwright Company, for delivery to the Moxey warehouse on Kings Wharf. This will also be the method by which all the boxes will be sent from England, during the coming year,' said Moxey, then added. 'In all we have, together with the three in the hold, a total of ten boxes,' a smile spreading across his face.

'A good haul indeed sir we are soon to be rich men; mind it is a great shame that that fool Kettlewell lost the pendant stone, for it was a fine valuable piece, it would have brought a pretty price, don't you know,' said Feltsham.

Moxey nodded. 'It would have indeed but we are well suited my lord. We must now turn it into cash as quickly as possible.'

'With Kettlewell gone, thanks to that damn man Shenkin, are you sure Ketch can find and deal with this fence Kettlewell spoke of?' said Feltsham.

'He was recommended to Kettlewell by Ike Soloman, who has sent much pilfered goods over here my lord. Ketch is confident of contacting this man Isaac Goldspick for he's well known in the Rocks. I'll send Ketch to make himself known to Goldspick and he'll arrange a meeting place for us. The goods will stay in my warehouse until we agree terms and conditions.

'Very good Moxey, yes very good, but what of this convict Shenkin who remember saw Kettlewell with the diamonds. I don't like loose ends, Moxey, never did, never will,' said Feltsham, tapping the side of his nose.

For a moment the captain turned his gaze midships. 'Let go the anchor Mr Lawson let her swing with the tide.'

'Ay, sir.'

The Bosun already had the sails furled, the captain nodded his approval. They were anchored and made fast. Moxey turned back to his lordship. 'I have prepared a letter that will be sent ashore to the Deputy Superintendent's Office at the barracks, in it I have stated the facts of the case against this convict. "Shenkin will be among the first group of convicts ashore. He will be taken to the convict barracks on Macquarie Street and there placed in a solitary cell where he will await trial for the killing of Kettlewell. Note my lord, in a solitary cell with no contact with the other convicts, crew or soldiers of this ship."' Again the captain swept his eye over his busy crew. 'I think we can safely say that our little problem will be hung within the next few days.

Thus protecting our interests while also saving the reputation of my niece,' he said.

'Finally our days of reckoning are here Moxey. After all the insults I have had to endure I am grateful to you sir, well done. It's all in the bag then or in our boxes, what," said Feltsham, allowing himself a small titter. The captain squirmed inside but managed to force a smile. 'If you are free from your duties captain, I suggest we retire to your cabin to celebrate with a glass of madeira,' said his lordship, removing yet again, invisible lint from his coat.

A long boat was sent out of Port Jackson. In it was an official, a doctor, and some marines. Pulling alongside the official requested to know the reason for the yellow flag and the nature of the fever. Captain Moxey turned to Tarn standing alongside him. 'Your report I believe sir.' Tarn took the hailer. 'We had,' he said, looking at the doctor holding unsteadily on to what was obviously a medical bag. 'Vibrio cholerae which I believe is no longer active,' said Tarn.

'Dear God,' said the medical man. 'Explain this medical term, please for all my party to understand.' On hearing it was cholera he, together with the others, instantly put their hands to their mouths. After a long drawn-out moment, the doctor in the long boat called out. 'You will be in isolation for two weeks, at the end of which time a doctor will come aboard to examine everyone on the ship,' he said, his words now sounding muffled through his fingers. 'Then and only then will you be allowed to land.' Hurriedly, he gave orders to row away. The boat left at a quicker speed than it had arrived.

'This is outrageous, I am Lord Feltsham don't you know.' shouted his lordship, but the boat was already out of hearing distance. 'I insist you advise the Governor that Lord Feltsham is aboard,' shouted his lordship.

Moxey stared at him. 'They can not hear you my lord,' he said in a resigned voice. 'We must wait it out.'

Feltsham, his previous good humour gone, said, 'If you had not flown that flag we would be going a shore today, damn you.' Then added. 'Who is the Governor now that Darling is gone?'

'Sir Richard Bourke my lord,' said Moxey, knowing the effect this would have. 'The bloody man's a Whig,' said Feltsham. 'Isn't he for reform?'

Moxey nodded. 'Indeed he is, Lord Percival. He was appointed Governor in December of last year, but he will face a great deal of opposition here in the colony to any form of reform. The conservative establishment, the military and the press are all opposed to his views. It is far better to have, as we always have had, military governance rather than civil. A firm hand my lord that is what is needed, above all here in the Colony. Any Reformer will come under very robust opposition in Sydney,' said Moxey, glancing down the length of the ship once more. Satisfied he turned back to Feltsham. We know how to reject any suggestion of a Reform Bill my lord.

'As they should do at home,' said Feltsham, a firm Tory. After some moments of refection Feltsham spoke. 'So we sit it out captain?'

'We do my lord,' said Moxey, removing his cap and wiping his brow. The sun beat down on the *Runnymede* as she rose and fell on a gentle swell. Protected inside the heads of the Cove, Moxey felt he could indeed enjoy a glass of wine. It was going to be a long, and possible a difficult wait.

***

Now that they were so close to land the convicts were kept in their cells day and night. The heat was horrendous between decks. Men were stripped to the waist, sweat ran off them like streams of water. Some of the older convicts and those still recovering from the fever fainted. Water rations were kept as before regardless of Tarns demand to increase the allowance. The guards were even worse off, in full uniform they stood guard in shifts around the clock. As the days went on everyone was becoming restless and irritable.

Elizabeth complained to her uncle at the inhuman treatment, but to no avail. On the fifth day Shenkin called out to the other prisoners. 'We are losing too much fluid our bodies will not take a great deal more. I suggest we go on hunger strike. Refuse water or food until our rations are increased,' said Shenkin, looking at Regan has he spoke. Regan was aghast. 'What! we are almost dying of thirst now, so we are,' as shouts came from every cell.

Shenkin was not to be shouted down. 'Wait listen to me!' he shouted, above the roar of the other convicts. 'The captain is paid per head of convict he disembarks, I know that to be true.' Shenkin waited for this to sink in. 'He has already lost twenty-six to cholera and one to a knife.' Laughter from the convicts met this remark. 'He will not want to lose anymore. Is it a risk, yes, but so is our continued need for water. Let's try it for two days, what have we to lose, apart from our lives that is,' said Shenkin, a wry smile crossing his sweat-drenched face. For heartbeats it was silent, these men were from the gutters of the poorest places in the King's realm. They had never had full bellies in their lives. They had been brought up to expect little and receive even less.

Most had been poor from the beginning of their lives, so they remained poor in spirit for the rest of their lives. Those who were here because they believed in political change, a change that would ensure the poorest were never left thirsty or hungry. These men were committed already.

After some time one convict spoke, he was hard faced, rough shaped, not a man to meet in any dark place, like all cornered rats he was dangerous too. 'I'm for giving it a go, it's better than just melting here, let's see if the bastards can deal with it Shenkin's right what have we got to lose?'

The guards looked at one another and drank warm water from the butts that stood at their sides. With general approval all the convicts settled down and waited. A few hours later Ketch stood in the middle of the gangway, as the small amount of water and food rations were given out. All were refused. 'So, who's put you up to this then,?' said Ketch. No one answered. 'Right! Well it don't worry me. I'll see you die of thirst or starved to death, good riddance to you say I,' Ketch said, turning for the companionway ladder. Shouting over his shoulder as he pushed past the guard. 'Fuck you all, time and the sun will change your mind I'd bet my good eye on it.' Meal times came and went. Ketch threatened punishment of ten lashes a man. Still they refused so in the end Ketch was forced to report to Moxey that the prisoners were refusing to eat or drink. He had noted that they all looked to Shenkin for leadership. Ketch was beside himself with frustrated rage. 'I'll get you yet, you Welsh bastard, ashore it will just be me and the hangman's rope,' he said spitting into Shenkin's water. Shenkin smiled, as he threw the water through the bars into Ketch's face. In rage Ketch lifted his musket. He pushed the thirty-nine-inch barrel through the bars level with Shenkin's stomach. Shenkin stood unmoved. 'A lot of witnesses here Ketch, we'd be sure to dance together on the end of a hangman's noose, if you pull that hammer. With effort Ketch fought to control himself as he looked around the cells. He slowly pulled the barrel back. 'I swear we'll met somewhere dark one night, then it'll just be you and me.'

'You can depend upon it, Ketch,' said Shenkin. Ketch started to turn back towards Shenkin's cell his cosh raised but stopped halfway. Pulling down his uniform over his belly he turned back to the ladder. Laughter rang in his ears has he climbed. 'Right!' said Ketch, turning to two of his men. 'Close those hatches no light, no air and no water. Got it?' said Ketch, with a snarl.

'Sir,' said the men, rushing to his orders.

At dinner that night the tension at the captain's table was palpable. Tarn had already requested the convicts be allowed on deck and fresh water be given them.

Moxey had refused. The steward served the meal, no one spoke, when the steward was done Tarn said. 'From this date Captain Moxey I refuse to take responsibility for the wellbeing of the convicts. I will put that in writing into my official report.'

Moxey considered his answer. He was soon to be a rich man, he had a growing business in Port Jackson and about to open another in Van Diemen's Land. In nine days, they would enter the harbour and dock, he would disembark the seventy-six remaining convicts. There would be a court of inquiry as to the loss of any lives and Tarn would report the reasons.

Lord Feltsham tapped his fingers impatiently on the table. Elizabeth, anxious for Shenkin, was about to say something when Moxey spoke. 'Very well doctor I will comply with your advice. One hour on deck each morning, under full guard. I'll increase the water ration and food. However, the responsibility for each prisoner will be yours. If one convict escapes the value of that convict, to me, is to be taken from your salary. You will confirm this in writing,' said Moxey.

'You miserable piece of sh–' said Tarn, then looking at Elizabeth stopped himself. 'You will have that undertaken in writing on your table within the hour.'

'When I do Tarn, then I'll give the order.'

Tarn stood up, pushed back his chair and left, slamming the door behind him.

Tarn entered the cells area, behind him a number of the crew were carrying leather bags full of water also baskets of bread, cheese and some fruit.

At the sight of which a cheer went up from the convicts. 'Sweet Jesus, Shenkin we've done it,' said Regan.

Tarn stood at the bottom of the companionway between the two guards. 'Before I serve these, I want you to know that I had to given my word that none of you will try to escape. Do I have that promise?' All eyes were on the rations. 'Yes!' roared the men in unison.

'Very well,' said the doctor, turning to the crew. 'Give them some water first then the food, you know the amounts each man will receive. Carry on,' said Tarn, walking over to Shenkin's cell.

'Thank you doctor they'll not let you down, we'll see to that,' said Shenkin, looking at Regan who gave a nod of agreement.

'So we will,' said Regan.

As the rations were given out a chant went up from the convicts. 'SHENKIN, SHENKIN, SHENKIN.'

'Now where have I heard that before?' said Regan, with a smile. Shenkin called for quiet. 'Listen, by your determination we've got what we wanted but the doctor here has given his word that no one tries to escape. We are in sight of land but it's still a hell of a swim, also we are in leg irons. It would be suicide to try. And I'll not let anyone let the doctor down. I'll personally have words with anyone who tries.' There was general agreement as they grabbed at the water and food.

The brilliant sunshine blinded them as they came onto the open upper deck, the air never smelt so good thought Shenkin, looking at the shore line. 'Bloody close, so it is,' said Regan, shielding his eyes against the sun. The sound of a splash sounded as a crew member called out. 'Man overboard, portside.' A rattle of chains went to the rails. The captain shouted to lower a boat, but it took time as the man struggled to keep afloat. Weighed down by his chains the man sunk lower and lower into the water, his arms threshing the surface furiously in an effort to keep afloat. He had got no more than a few yards before the long boat caught up with him. Two crewmen had, after a number of attempts, that caused them to cut the man's face, finally managed to fasten the boathook onto the man's collar. A convict on board screamed and pointed. Behind the man, who was now leaving a stream of blood in the water, was a big fish. Its fin cutting through the water at an alarming speed. 'Dear God,' said a sailor at Shenkin's side. 'It's a shark.' The men pulled on the boathook to haul the convict into the boat. The man screamed as a gush of blood raised to the surface. 'The shark's got hold of him,' said the sailor. The crew in the boat struggled to free the man from the shark. Everyone aboard became mesmerised by the macabre scene. A tug-of-war took place as men and shark fought for possession of the convict's body. At the rail, men shouted their support to the boat crew who, after a great heave fell back into the boat. The convict was holding onto one of the oars as they lifted him over the side. A grisly view met the eyes of everyone as the man came over the side into the boat. His left leg was hanging from the leg chain, it had been completely severed from his body. His trousers torn ragged at the hip, as blood flooded the floor of the boat. Aboard, Tarn was already holding a burning stake of wood. The top was covered in tar which was running down the shaft onto the deck. Once they were back aboard Tarn quickly pressed the hot tar into the man's open wound to cauterise it. The smell of seared flesh mixed with the morning air. The convict had fainted, he had lost a lot of blood, but was alive and no threat to Tarn's salary. Shenkin nodded at the doctor as they lifted the convict and carried him to the sick bay. Moxey called for the ship's crew and soldiers to resume their duties. 'See to it Mr Lawson, Sergeant Ketch.'

'Sir,' came the chorus.

All the while Elizabeth had kept her eyes fixed on Shenkin, who gave a roguish smile in her direction. Elizabeth blushed while a small sigh broke from her lips.

Feltsham turned back to his cabin, finding again that invisible piece of lint on his well-cut coat. Ketch was already shouting orders to the guards. 'That's enough air and excitement for one day, get these convicts back to their cells.' Turning to one of the men he had promoted to corporal since the loss of Burke. 'Corporal Wellings, take two men with you and make sure convicts 71013 and 71014 are escorted back to their cells from the sick bay, sharply now.'

'Sir,' said Corporal Wellings. 'You, Brannon and you Hare, follow me.'

'Swill down and stow that boat, bosun,' called Lawson.

'Ay ay, sir.'

Shenkin was dismayed to find the man who had tried to escape was Dewi Davies. Regan looked at Shenkin. 'Well, we are now down to four and a half, so we are,' said Regan, tight-lipped.

Shenkin nodded. 'Can you save him doctor, better half than only four?'

'He's lost a lot of blood, but I'll do my best Shenkin.'

'That's good enough for us doctor,' said Shenkin, as the soldiers prodded them forward with their muskets.

***

For the remainder of their quarantine, the *Runnymede* lifted and swayed on the sparkling sun-kissed waves, although the nights were cold. On the final morning a long boat came alongside. In it was the official, two doctors, oarsmen and marines. All had scarves tightly tied around their mouths and noses. They looked as if they were coming to rob the *Runnymede* instead of vouching for her health.

After a full day's examination of all on board the *Runnymede* was declared safe to enter harbour.

Moxey gave out the orders to make way, by evening they were moored alongside of the harbour wall. 'Secure all convicts Sergeant Ketch, Mr Lawson make fast we disembark at first light.'

Ay ay, sir.'

That evening Tarn went down into the cargo hold with Lawson who had told him he could not account for some of the ship's cargo and was suspicious about what the boxes held. Also of Ketch's constant visits to the hold during the voyage. Pointing out the boxes to Tarn, who had his own suspicions, Lawson lifted a jemmy bar hanging from a timber strut. Tarn nodded his agreement; with a creak the lid came up. The straw-covered top spilled over the side. Tarn removed some of the straw, underneath the light from their oil lamps played on the bright gold and silver of plate, candelabras, goblets and trinkets of every description. 'So that's their game I knew something was amiss, Elizabeth told me of a meeting she witnessed back in London involving Lord Feltsham, Captain Moxey, Ketch and the late Kettlewell,' said Tarn.

Lawson whistled between his teeth. 'What do we do doctor?' said Lawson. 'Ketch is a very dangerous man.'

'I know,' said Tarn adding, 'so this is why Shenkin has been a marked man he had shared a cell with Kettlewell and must have seen something.' For a moment neither spoke. 'We do nothing yet, no one can be brought aboard the ship without the captain's permission, we wait until the captain has these cases stowed away in his warehouse,' he said.

Lawson nodded.

Ketch hidden behind a bale of garments smiled a sour smile then slipped back out of sight, thinking it was a good thing he had thought to check the boxes. He knew Lawson was on duty tonight to ensure that no unauthorised persons came aboard and that the rat-guards were fitted properly, deck lights in place, together with all the other requirements of a ship in port. That would be his chance to remove one of the witnesses, it would then just be Tarn's word against the three of them. Anyway he had never liked Lawson, he'd not tell his lordship or the captain no need to upset their sensitive nerves.

Come morning, Dewi Davies was running a fever, Tarn declared him unfit to be moved, but would live.

At first light Captain Moxey stood on the quarterdeck shouting for Lawson. Travis came up from the forecastle deck. 'We can't find the mate sir he's seems to have disappeared sir. I came up on deck to relieve him this morning but no one has seen him.

'If the bastard has jumped ship, I'll find him and have his ticket,' said Moxey. 'Beg pardon sir but that's not like Mr Lawson sir,' said Travis. Moxey knew it, they had sailed together to many times, but where was the bloody man.

'Right coxswain, take over his duties, I want gangplanks in place.'

'Ay ay, sir.'

Two gangplanks were run out, one for convicts the other for cargo. Under surveillance of the barracks' constables, an officer and twenty guards, the convicts in leg irons rattled ashore.

It was May 1832; it had taken 126 days to get them to a 'place beyond the sea' for the first time they set foot on the soil of their futures. Slowly, painfully on shaking legs they were marched up Macquarie Street to Hyde Park Barracks. Shenkin became aware that no one along the way took any notice of these pale faced, raggedly dressed, chained felons. It was, after all, a penal colony most of the bystanders were or had been convicts themselves. At the barracks they were lined up in front of the Deputy Superintendent's Office and waited in the heat of the late autumn sun.

They shuffled their feet to ease the weight of the irons, while trying to slacken the chains around the waists that the shackles were attached to. Dust raised around them in dry clouds causing some to cough. They waited.

At last his breakfast finished, Deputy Superintendent William H. Roach came out of his office to address them. He was holding a paper in his hand. Stepping forward onto a raised platform, Roach, a thin stooped back man in his late forties, cleared his throat, puffed out his narrow chest and proceeded to speak in a high-pitched shrill voice.

'You have been sentenced to varying lengths of years as befits your crimes. You will serve out these years in useful employment. That is to say chain-gangs for the building of roads, the manufacture of various tools, the hired labour of tradesmen, shop owners and farmers. Any convict who fails, or refuses to do these tasks, will be punished most severely. A Punishment List is posted up at all the cell huts. Those of you who can read, will advise those who can't, so that all are aware which transgression warrants which punishment. I strongly recommend you pay close attention to this list, and to the notice of the Rules and Regulations of the prison. All prisoners will be mustered on the courtyard daily before heading off in gangs to worksites. Each convict will be given two sets of clothes, these will be as follows.

'Two Parramatta frocks, two Parramatta trousers, three striped shirts, three pairs of shoes, and one straw hat or cap.' Roach paused, coughed, took a deep breath coughed again then spoke. 'Each convict will be issued with one blanket during summer and two blankets during the winter months. Punishment for damage to, or loss of, will be the fitting of a crank iron around the neck for twenty-four hours to be followed by twenty lashes. The clothing will not be replaced for the duration of three months. I assure you with the coming of the winter you will regret the loss of any clothes or blankets.'

Again, Roach paused for this to sink in. After a moment and another cough, he continued. 'Each convict during a twenty-four-hour period will receive bread or flour, some maize, one pound of beef, one ounce of salt, some sugar and a quarter of an ounce of soap. Any hoarding or selling of food will be dealt with harshly, the rations of that culprit will be stopped for one month,' said Roach, lifting the paper in his hand up, slowly he read the letter again. A long silence followed as the Superintendent read. The bright sun shone down while strange birds made noises like the creaking of a barn door. A light wind blew the dust around them, it settled back on the ground leaving a mantle of brown covering. The iron metal around their legs became hot. Two convicts fainted, no one moved. They tried to ease the burning red marks that formed a circle around their ankles. They waited. Superintendent Roach had moved back under the shadow of his office, has he continued to read. They waited. The Superintendent cleared his throat, brushed off some flying insects and spoke.

'Convict Daniel Shenkin 71013 step forward.' Shenkin shuffled out of the line.

Roach glanced again at the letter then slowly looked up at Shenkin. 'Convict 71013 you are charged with the unlawful killing of one Ebenezer Kettlewell aboard the convict ship the *Runnymede*. For this, the most serious of offences, you will be held in solitary confinement awaiting trial under the Lord Ellenborough's Act unless provocation can be proved. And if the violence that had been committed in such a way that the other party died, it be regarded as murder,' said Roach, folding the letter.

'Overseer Blake, assign two constables to take this man to solitary.'

'Sir,' said the overseer, pulling Shenkin shuffling towards two waiting guards.

The Deputy Superintendent turned back to the line of convicts. 'Convict Regan O'Hara 71014, step forward.' Shuffling forward, Regan stood in the rising dust around him. Clearing his throat yet again, then buffing out his concave chest Roach said. 'You are charged with damage to the property of the convict ship the *Runnymede* that is, one stove and a branding frame. You will be held with other prisoners awaiting trial. In the meantime, you will work on a road chain gang.' :He paused, then said, 'That is all fall back into line.' O'Hara shuffled backwards. Roach turned. 'Overseer Blake, escort the prisoners to the cell huts.'

'Sir.'

The Superintendent walked back into his office slamming the door behind him. Dust fell from the door frame together with some paint that had peeled from the wood. The convicts' introduction to the barracks had been completed.

'Right you heard the Sup. turn left!' A number turned right, then left. Once they were all facing the same way the overseer and his constables marched them to their new home of daily hard labour and punishment. So far, their first feel of Australian soil was the dry dust their feet kicked up has they shuffled into the thankful chill of their cells. They would get to know well the dust, dirt and the rocks it contained over the coming months and years.

CHAPTER 26

Shenkin was pushed into a small cell where light found it hard to penetrate. At first he welcomed the dark shelter from the bright sun. It was a familiar darkness, it seemed to have followed him through all the days of his short life.

The noise from the courtyard of rattling chains accompanied by barked orders were also becoming familiar. The thoughts of escape were pointless, where would he go, who did he know, apart from Elizabeth and Doctor Tarn, anyway how would he find them? No he would have to see what would develop, first there would be the trial which may end at the end of a rope. In resignation he sat down heavily on a low bed, the frame covered by a thin flat soiled straw filled mattress. His leg irons clanked over the bottom metal frame, the chain links up to the belt around his waist pulled tight.

***

Regan, his eyes adjusting to the dark was gazing at the row of hammocks that lined both sides of the hut. Overseer Blake and his constables had left them, a new man of imposing presence stood at the doorway. He spoke in a clear well-modulated voice. 'After a wash down with a water hose you will be given your government marked cloths, these are called Parramatta's. Parramatta is the place where they are made by your fellow convicts up river. I recommend you keep these clothes safe; it is now May and soon we will be into our winter, becoming very cold at night. Once these are on you will become known as Government Men, that is to say convicts who work in the Penal Colony of Sydney,' he paused for a dramatic moment then continued. 'My name is Edward Fleet I am the Convict overseer of this hut. For the last ten years I have ensured that this hut is run in accordance with the Rules and Regulations laid down by the government. You will not spoil my good record, one that will soon result in me receiving my ticket-of-leave. It is gained by good behaviour and conscientious work, it can be granted even before you complete your full sentence, so mark it well. Those of you who wish to serve their sentence the hard way should read the list of punishments notice nailed to the wall at the doorway. All of you should read the Rules and Regulations, both of these notices will be carried out to the letter. As you can see, I am a gentleman by manner and bearing, tall and slight of build. My crime was fraud, my sentence fourteen years. However, the men each side of me are not gentlemen, they are robust in build and ruthless by nature. You may think they are my bodyguards, you would be wrong, they are my enforcers,' said Fleet, looking at both men. Regan also looked, one was as tall has he was, his arms hung loose from a powerful chest, a broken nose decorated his already ugly unshaved face, his cropped hair gave evidence to many scars placed there by a number of sharp or blunt instruments. The other was shorter but just as broad, a face of swarthy skin which sat below jet black lank hair. He had a slightly closed right eyelid that went back to what appeared to be a ripped-off ear.

'As you can see, they have both been brought up in life's school of brutality,' said Fleet, turning to the man on his right. 'Stubbs is a convicted murderer sentenced to a life term. While Costantini here is a convicted highwayman, pickpocket, a heavy for a London gang and a rapist. A thoroughly bad person who has also been sentenced to a life term. Study them well, they do my bidding,' said Fleet. No one spoke, no shuffling of feet, no body movements, nothing.

'Right! Now that we are all acquainted, you will each be allotted a hammock under which you will find a long wooden box for clothes,' said Fleet, turning to his hard-faced assistants. 'Stubbs, Costantini show them to their places.' Still no one spoke. All was silent, lessons had been well learnt from the hulk onwards, this was just another set of rules to be learnt fast.

Outside the sun shone bright on red brick buildings that stood solid in the square that made up the government area of Sydney. St James Church proudly lifted its steeple to heaven in a prayer for these ungodly convicts. Church wardens passed collection boxes around the congregation of free settlers, the exclusives of the Colony, smug in their rightness in the sight of God and greedy in their avariciousness for land and money.

Lord Feltsham, in all his aristocratic finery, stood among them the lint on his coat still clinging invisibly to the sleeves. He had taken spacious lodging rooms at the Australian Hotel on George Street. This was a temporary abode while on the lookout for a grander place that befitted his standing. One of the many large farm lands perhaps that were worked by cheap convict labour. Or one of the wool mills that was becoming an expanding industry in the colony. He and Moxey would soon convert Kettlewell's goods into hard cash, Spanish dollars, copper coinage, rupees, or even rum. The spirit formed part of the Colony's method of payment and could be turned into a good profit. Lord

Feltsham felt pleased with himself as he bathed in the glory of God and the midday sun. He was surround by a group of eager mothers telling him how sad they were to hear of the death of his dear wife and all eager to introduce him to their daughters. Feltsham swept his eyes around the eye fluttering young women. Smiled his charming smile as he bowed low to every introduction. But Feltsham had set his mind upon marrying Elizabeth Moxey – he had set his mind on this while on the *Runnymede*. She had youthful beauty, brains and good breeding, a step up from his late mousy wife. It would also bind Moxey even closer to him, another possible loose end neatly tied tight. Moxey too would benefit socially from such a marriage it would prove to be a boon to his business activities and his standing in the colony. Feltsham had already sent a letter to the Governor requesting an appointment, Governor Bourke regretted that due to pressing government business he was unable to meet Lord Feltsham, however there was to be a ball in honour of his appointment as Governor at Government House in five days' time and that an invitation would be sent to him. Feltsham intended to take Elizabeth with him it would be an excellent opportunity to introduce them both into the social whirl of Sydney. Casting his eye around him he felt this would be rather limited.

***

On being told by her uncle of Feltsham's intentions, Elizabeth was furious. Captain Moxey would hear none of her protestations at nineteen years of age and his legal ward she would do has she was told.

Going to her room she lay down on her bed and wept; she was, she felt already married physically to the man she loved. A man who was about to stand trial for his life. The sobs became louder she buried her face deeper into her pillow so that her uncle could not hear her – she would not give him the satisfaction of her distress. For some time she lay still, at this ball would she not meet many who were officers of the law courts some might even be sitting in judgement at Shenkin trial. She could tell them of his unselfish service in saving many lives from cholera, she would enlist Doctor Tarn in supporting her witness to Shenkin's contribution and his good character, also that the fight with Kettlewell was in the defence of a young convict. Yes! she would go to this ball and on the arm of Lord Feltsham with her own agenda in mind.

Feltsham was pleased to hear that his invitation, in Moxey's words, had been joyously accepted. Moxey was also able to report that after some searching

Ketch had found Goldspick a small, grey-faced bespectacled man in his early thirties, but he looked to be in his late fifties. Arrangements had been made for a meeting in the backroom of a pub near the docks. Handshakes, at least from Captain Moxey, had sealed an agreed price, to be paid in mixed gold, copper coin and a large consignment of rum upon Goldspick's receipt of the boxes.

***

During this time, Tarn had also searched for Lawson but there was not a trace. He suspected foul play, but to his frustration he could not prove anything. Feltsham had waved his hand in dismissal and Moxey just said, 'Sometimes these things happen doctor, a man just has enough of the sea, in being cooped up on a ship on a long voyage, he'll turn up.' But he never did.

Five days later, dressed in a satin ballroom dress shot with silver and gold that had been her mother's, Elizabeth Moxey looked ravishing as she stepped down from one of the new hackney carriages that Sydney now boasted.

In front of them stood Government House, a long low building with a grand veranda in front on which stood sentinels in full dress uniforms their muskets smartly at rest on their shoulders. Before the veranda lay a well-manicured lawn that ran almost down to the water's edge. Other buildings, if not fine by London standards, stood nearby. Walking up the path between the lawns they were met by the sound of stringed music; it floated on the air from the open double doors of Government House as the good and the great of the colony flowed into the ballroom. Feltsham preened himself as the other men glanced with envy at Elizabeth smiling on his arm. This would indeed be an excellent match, if not made in heaven, then perfect for this backwater of English society, thought Feltsham. She was a mere child who would bear him beautiful children and leave him free to enjoy the pleasures his new found wealth would afford him. At Lord Feltsham being announced Governor Bourke turned to greet him with the formality that his lordships station commanded. Bourke's Irish charm extended itself to Elizabeth who, knees bent, head slightly bowed, curtseyed most ladylike to the delight of all around her. Feltshem almost quivered in his preening, but he recovered in time to remove that elusive piece of lint, as he too bowed his head to the Governor. Governor Bourke was already turning his attention to other guests. Most were the 'exclusive' faction from the Legislative Council. To a small fanfare the Colonial Secretary was announced and he fell into immediate conversation with the Governor. Smiling all the while, Elizabeth noted each man and his rank for she intended to seek them out later.

***

Strange how music travels on the evening air. Shenkin turned to the small barred window of his cell, pulling his bed over to the wall he climbed up to look out. 'What you looking at you ugly bastard, listening to music from the Governor House are we? Well you'll soon be hearing harps you will,' said the guard, laughing at his own sense of grim humour. 'Get down before I ram this musket butt into your face, do you hear?' Shenkin lowered himself down wondering where Elizabeth was at this time, she'd be off the ship by now he thought, perhaps she too could hear the music.

In one of the long huts, Regan swung to and fro in his hammock wondering what the morning would bring and how Shenkin was faring. His new clothes itched like hell, the bloody shoes were not left and right so it was painful to get them into any sort of comfortable position. 'To hell with them all,' he said out loud.

A small voice called out. 'Who are you talking to Paddy?' said his cockney neighbour, who had fallen out of his hammock twice already. 'Never you mind you little runt and don't call me Paddy, only my enemies calls me that, so they do. The name's Regan, and who the sweet Mary are you?' said Regan, putting out his big fist to shake the little fellows hand. With relief, the cockney put out his hand and promptly fell out of hammock again setting them both laughing. Picking himself up he put out his hand again.

'George Fewens Esquire, at you service,' said Fewens, bowing with a flourish. 'Well little man what brings you to this abode?' said O'Hara. George smiled a wicked smile. 'I'm a chimney sweep, the best dear old London ever lost. Born and bred to the sound of Bow bells or at least the bells of Newgate Prison which is where my dear mother offered me to the world. She was a pickpocket and coin maker, good too but took to the gin she did, sloppy workmanship led her to the Newgate jig,' said George, pushing his tongue out has he tilted his head to one side.

'Sorry to hear it, so I am,' said Regan.

'It was a long time ago now I was six at the time. I grew steadily downwards from there. I find myself here due to a judge giving me ten years transportations for cleaning out the contents of a house in Lambeth, as well as their smokestack. I was out of the rasher-wagon and into the fire so to speak.'

Regan looked at him confused. 'Rasher-wagon?'

'Frying pan, blimey don't you speak the King's English? Anyway, what's up with the crabshells then, the shoes mate, the shoes, what's the matter with them?' Not waiting for a reply he went on. 'First new bleeding shoes I've ever had,' he said, lifting his foot. 'Flash ain't they?'

Regan smiled. 'You'll have to teach me the words or we'll never understand each other.' 'Well, we got plenty of time, for we are all lags now,' said George climbing with difficulty back into his hammock setting it swinging violently. 'I need to be careful of this or I'll bleeding top myself. It's like being in a Mary Blaine, a railway train,' he said, looking at Regan by way of explanation.

***

To Feltsham's annoyance, Elizabeth's dance card was soon full. While she danced the evening away, he had the impression that she was always talking to her dance partner in a most earnest manner. However, he contented himself in speaking to one of the Supreme Court judges. The only court that could pass the death sentence and the one that he expected Shenkin to come before. The judge was standing in as an assistant to Chief Justice, Sir Francis Forbes, who was ill at the time. The assistant judge, a man easily flattered by, and in awe of any aristocrat, especially one fresh from England. Feltsham took every advantage of the situation. Explaining to Judge Perkins that Shenkin was a dangerous fellow capable of the most heinous crimes. Had he not led a revolt against the Crown leaving many soldiers and ordinary hard working men dead in the streets of a small mining town in Old South Wales. Who could say what harm he might do to the fledgling colony of Sydney? The trial for murder against Shenkin should be brought forward without delay. He himself would stand as witness for the Crown, as would Captain Moxey of the convict ship the *Runnymede*. Indeed, his own dear wife may now be alive if the ship had not been unfortunate enough to count Shenkin within the ranks of their convict cargo.

Perkins, lifting his third glass, agreed that the man should be dealt with swiftly. He would write a letter to the office of the Deputy Superintendent of the barracks first thing on the morrow. It would read that this convict be made aware that he was to be tried for murder within three days. The trial to be held at the Supreme Court House of New South Wales, who had the powers to sentence to death, under Lord Allenborough's Act; any man found guilty of murder if, without provocation, the other party died.

Feltsham praised the man's prompt action in pursuing justice, he would pass this praise on to his powerful friends in London.

The man actually blushed. Feltsham caught Elizabeth's eye. 'Time we left my dear, your uncle would not be pleased with me keeping you away from him at such a late hour.' Elizabeth too had spoken to many people in particular their wives, she was content with her evening's work. She would let Tarn know of the contacts she had made and also get a letter somehow to Shenkin. If she had known that she only had three days she would not have felt so encouraged. As the hackney rattled down Macquarie Street his lordship placed his hand on hers, which she quickly removed. Feltsham smiled. 'There is time my dear to adjust to the realities, there is time.'

The following morning the barrack yard was full of chained convicts as the work details were being called out. To witness the start of the day, the Superintendent stood clearing his throat in front of his office, then addressed them. 'Those of you who arrived over the last month are now Government Men. Your convict number will be noted then followed by your name. You are now clothed in government-issue clothing and are to be placed in the assignment system, that is to say, you are lent out as labourers, by the government to free settlers or to work on government public works, roads, digging ditches, tunnels, building constructions. Your work day will be from sunrise to sunset, those who have skills will be assigned, to blacksmiths, carpenters and stonemasons. You will carry out your work assignments to the best of your abilities, failing to do so will result in punishment of the most severe kind,' said Roach, pausing for this to register, satisfied, he again cleared his throat. 'When doing work for private settlers you will obey their orders to the letter. I will receive reports of any men who fail to carry out their work duties. These men will be placed in solitary confinement after a minimum of fifty lashes. Mark this well as you are assigned your day's work,' said Roach, turning to the overseer. 'Carry on with the work details Mr Blake.'

'Sir.'

The overseer called out for those in the batch who had arrived yesterday to step forward if they had any skills.

No one moved. 'We have your records, so once more step forward if you have a skill. Five men came forward. 'Good! but I don't see Thomson, a graveyard stonemason from London who used his tools to break into a shop in Camden Town,' said Blake, running his eye along the line. Thomson stepped forward.

'Constable take this man to the punishment block for hiding his talents under a bush.' Thomson screamed out. 'I didn't hear you I swear.'

'I guarantee you will hear me in future,' said Blake. Another lesson firmly in place thought Regan., 'You will all stand silently while we wait for Thomson to return.'

A scream cut through the chill early morning air then again and again. Superintendent Roach cleared his throat, impatient to get to his breakfast. Thomson was dragged back into the line his Parramatta frock over his shoulders. The whip had cut into the flesh of his back, blood ran freely down his spine. 'Now Thomson do you, a stonemason, have a skill.' 'Yes sir,' said Thomson, in a shaky voice.

'Good! I knew you would remember. Get on with it, Overseer Blake,' said Roach.

'Sir.'

For the next hour work details were called out. Gangs were formed, men were chained together. The skilled men escorted to business premises around the town. Regan, fettered to George Fewens, was detailed to a chain gang to work on a new bridge construction. George whispered to Regan. 'We are working on the Argyle Cut mate, bloody hard work it is to, the word is it isn't possible due to the hardness of the bloody rocks. But they are going to try, using us as the blunt tools to cut into the rock. The bridge is to span across from Sydney Cove to Millers Point. To save the good citizens of Sydney having to go down steps then up again to cross over,' said Fewens, adding, 'God help us.'

'Shut up, the next bastard that talks will stay behind to answer to the lash,' said Blake. Silence prevailed as they stood outside of the gates as Blake and an officer of the 73rd Highlanders stood talking. 'So a new batch for us to break in Blake, is that so?'

'They are sir, after a few weeks in their cells to settle them in, so to speak and a motley lot they are too, so make sure they come quickly into line,' said Blake, with a snarl.

'I'm a soldier, Overseer Blake, not a bloody prison guard,' said the officer.

'I know but that's the way of it so take it out on them not me.' It was an old conversation. With bad temper the officer ordered his men to flank the convicts to begin the march to Sydney Cove. Regan's ankle hurt, his new cloths rubbed his skin, and his shoes pinched. His cockney friend smiled. 'You'll get used to it Regan, I promise.'

Shenkin had watched from his cell window as the chain gang slowly moved out of sight. Bolts slipped to one side as the door opened. 'Right out you come Shenkin, the Superintendent wants to see you.' Shenkin walked blinking into the chilly morning sun.

'Come.' called Roach.

'Convict 71013 Shenkin, sir.'

'Thank you, constable.'

Shenkin stood in front of the Superintendent's desk as Roach studied a sheet of paper in front of him. Looking up he cleared his throat. 'You are to be tried for murder by the Supreme Court of New South Wales. Judge Perkins presiding with two magistrates, witnesses for the crown will be Lord Feltsham and Captain Moxey of the convict ship *Runnymede*. The date of the trial to be as early as the court calendar permits. If found guilty you will be hung within two days of the sentence.' Roach had not taken his eyes off Shenkin as he spoke. 'Do you understand?'

'Does it matter if I do or don't?' said Shenkin, pulling himself up straight.

'No, it does not, it's simple, my duty to advise you. Take him back to solitary constable.'

'Yes, sir.'

William H. Roach placed the paperwork and Judge Perkins letter back into Shenkin's file. He had no doubt that a verdict of guilty was written all over it.

***

Mortimer Thistlewaite, manager of the Bank of New South Wales, jumped to his feet as Lord Feltsham came through the door. He was a bespectacled bald man of about forty-five, a pen permanently lodged behind his left ear, ink stains marked his devotion to the many ledgers that covered his desk..

'Your lordship this a great honour sir, how can we be of service?'

'I wish to open an account here without delay,' said Feltsham.

'Of course sir, we will be privileged to count you has one of our most esteemed clients,' said Thistlewaite, with a deferential bow.

Feltsham stood waiting his eyes fixed on a chair.

'Forgive me your lordship please take a chair,' said Thistlewaite, adding hurriedly, 'Can I offer you a glass of wine or, a cigar perhaps?'

'Not unless you have a Bolivar or a Cuban to accompany a glass of good claret, then no.'

Thistlewaite gave a sickly smile. 'I regret your lordship that we do not stretch to that.'

A hurt look upon his face as his lordship shrugged. 'I'll send a case over when the rest of my goods arrive.'

The bank manager's face lit up. 'Your lordship is most kind.'

Seating himself Feltsham crossed his well-heeled legs and was ready for business.

Brushing the elusive lint, he began. 'Firstly, I need a line of credit to be accessible from today, say £2000. I am waiting for transfers of money from England within the next month or so. In the meantime, I need funds made available. I will instruct you as to the dispersal of capital once all monies are in place. Is that understood?'

'Indeed it is sir, the colony needs respectable personage of wealth to invest in its many opportunities to turn a profit. The bank at a very advantageous interest would be pleased to extend any capital or property purchase his lordship requires,' said Thistlewaite, mentally rubbing his hands together.

'Good then arrange for a withdrawal of £200 now,' said Feltsham.

'It will be in mixed coinage my lord, we have very little silver here in the colony.'

'Very well as long as it pays its way, what!'

'It will, indeed I guarantee it my lord. Perhaps your lordship would join me in an excellent glass of rum which we do have, while the money is being arranged,' said Thistlewaite, ringing a bell.

'Indeed I would, while doing so I'll tell you all the news from London.' Thistlewaite beamed has he poured two generous glasses of rum.

His lordship noted it was raw rum but he took a glass.

Sipping his drink Feltsham gazed over the rim. 'Is it a fact that the Government will offer free land and free labour to sound investors in the colony?'

'It is Lord Feltsham, also further parcels of land can be purchased at only two shillings an acre. We would be only to pleased to act on your behalf my lord.'

Feltsham beamed. 'Excellent, excellent, start a land search without delay,' he said, smiling.

Feltsham left the bank an hour later. A money bag was being carried by one of the bank's men. 'Tell me young man is there any place one can indulge in a little gambling, nothing too extravagant just an evening of amusement?'

'Yes sir, the Rocks is the place to go. Cards, cockfighting and bare-knuckle fighting, most of the pubs on George Street and Market Street holds one or the other most evenings. Near King's Wharf is the best, but it's pretty rough around there you needs someone who can protect you sir.'

'What about you, would you take me there?' said Feltsham.

'Not me sir I'd be no good, I fight figures on a page not in the taverns,' he said, with a rather anxious grin. By now they were outside the Australian Hotel, Feltsham looked up and down the street. There were drinking establishments indeed, the Commercial, the Union, the Keep within Compass and all just a short distance away. Feltsham took the bag of coin, thanked the bank man, and stepped into his hotel. He'd get a message to Moxey at his business premises, asking him to find Ketch.

The following day Feltsham opened the doors to Moxey's warehouse, the aroma of rope, rum, resin and all manner of ships rigging wafted towards him. It was a large building on the King's Wharf. Ketch had enlisted some of his men to stack Kettlewell's goods in one of the corners well hidden behind sails and tackle. After the men had finished he took Lord Feltsham and Moxey to the pub where he'd arranged to meet Goldspick. Ketch ordered drinks while Feltsham dusted off a chair to sit upon Moxey stood at the long bar. Slipping into a backroom Ketch found Goldspick drinking a rum and smoking a clay pipe at a round, rather battered wooden table.

Looking up he said. 'All ready then, Ketch?' in a rasping smoke-caked voice.

'They're all yours once we see the coin, and don't think we don't know the going rates either, because if we do see any short changing it will go bad for you,' said Ketch, his hand on his pistol that was tucked just inside the band of his wide belt.

'Now why would I do that and you bringing more stuff over in the next few months. It's true I was a little concerned when Kettlewell didn't turn up but everything seems kosher, your associates have solid backgrounds don't they. They wouldn't want us all to end up in the old salt box would they?' Ketch looked at Goldspick hard, he was not completely happy with this Jew. Once the money or rum was safe in their hands, he may have to deal with Goldspick on a more permanent basis. He knew Feltsham would rather just the three of them knew the full story, a great one for tying off loose ends his lordship. Shenkin first then Goldspick all neat like. He smiled at Goldspick. 'Of course we all serve the same end my friend, namely ourselves,' said Ketch. Goldspick forced a grin. 'You are so right my dear, so right,' he too was going to be very careful of his new business partners, very careful.

***

Moxey, a ledger in his hand to record their deal with Goldspick, joined Feltsham, so as not to be overheard. 'Bank accounts opened my lord?'

'Indeed,' said Feltsham, in a low voice. 'Also I have spoken to one of the judges regarding Shenkin, he'll be up for trail in a few days.'

Moxey nodded. 'Good work, who's the judge?'

'Perkins a man of great ambition, but little or no integrity, he'll probably go far.' They both laughed. 'We need now to make sure everything goes according to plan with this Goldspick,' said Feltsham

'I agree,' said Moxey, closing the ledger with a thud, as Ketch beckoned into the small back room. Before standing Feltsham turned to Moxey.

'Also, this evening you and I must speak of Elizabeth's forthcoming marriage,' said Feltsham, with some excitement, for he had seen her in the outer room, a beauty if ever there was one.

'She's not taking it well my lord, thinks she is being forced into it.'

Feltsham shrugged. 'Give her time to get accustomed to the idea, there are many social and financial advantages in it for us all.'

'I agree, do not worry she will see sense. As her guardian she will obey my advice, or find herself penniless in Sydney.'

'Right let us met this Goldspick and get the measure of him Moxey we will tie up any loose ends at the end,' Moxey nodded. 'After you, my lord.'

Ketch called out to the landlord. 'No one will enter and no one will leave, understood?'

The red-drink-flushed face of the landlord looked up. 'The door and these lips are sealed Ketch, as agreed.' 'Good,' said Ketch, slamming the door behind him. Goldspick stood and offered his hand to Feltham who ignored it and sat down. 'Let us get to the inventory.'

CHAPTER 27

In the end it was three weeks before Shenkin was taken to the courtrooms. Feltsham had badgered Perkins but he could not move it forward any sooner. By this time Feltsham and Moxey had converted all the current boxes into some form of payment. In the warehouse at King's Wharf there now stood a number of barrels of rum. The spirit was now selling at three times its usual price; Feltsham's bank account was swelling to a small fortune. A grateful Thistlewaite had secured for Feltsham some government land in the form of a farm, about thirty miles north of Sydney, together with free convict labour. Plans for a grand house to be built there were also being drawn up by a former associate of the convict architect Francis Greenway, who had designed, and built many of the public buildings in Sydney. Moxey was busy preparing to open his Van Diemen's business. With his share Ketch had bought himself out of the army and was planning to purchase a pub in Sussex Lane with a publican's license to sell spirits and beer, which Feltsham had used his influence to secure. However, Feltsham was aware that the more they had the more necessary it was to ensure nothing threatened it. The sooner Shenkin was hanged and Goldspick removed the easier he would feel. Then early on the day before the trial Tarn came to see Feltsham. At the door to his rooms Feltsham greeted Tarn with a limp handshake. 'Well doctor I understand you are to open a practice here in Sydney, be assured that any of my paid house servants who become ill will be sent to you.'

'Thank you Lord Feltsham, but I am here to talk about the trial of the convict Shenkin.'

'I see, but what does this have to do with me?'

'I understand my lord that you, together with Captain Moxey, are to be witnesses for the crown is that correct?'

Feltsham paused for a few moments. 'I feel it is my duty, don't you know.'

'I too am a witness my lord. A witness to the provocation of Kettlewell that led to the knife fight. I will also bear witness as to Shenkin's character and his contribution during the cholera outbreak, without which many more would have died,' said Tarn.

'I see, then we must let the court decide doctor, as to the truth of the matter.'

'Lord Feltsham let us not banter with each other. I know, as did Lawson, what was in the boxes in the hold. I also know that Shenkin was suspicious of Kettlewell having seen what he was carrying on his person when they shared a cell on the hulk.'

'Ah, yes, the necklace a fine piece, complete it would have brought a handsome sum,' said Feltsham. 'The fool should have left it in one of the boxes as he was told. But like all thieves he did not trust us.' For a long drawn-out moment neither spoke. Then Feltsham removed some lint from his apparel. 'Doctor let me be just as frank with you. Ketch told us he saw you and Lawson open the boxes,' said Feltsham, throwing up his arms in mock despair. 'But alas! What a pity for you that Lawson has disappeared therefore, he is unable to corroborate your story. Also Moxey tells me you did not mention it in your report, which of course, he read and countersigned,' said Feltsham, a smug smile on his face. 'Do I take it then that this is blackmail my good doctor. To finance your new practice perhaps?'

'It is indeed blackmail, my lord, but not for financial gain, but for the truth. Unless you both confirm that the fight was one of provocation and that were it not for Shenkin we may well have all died of cholera.'

Feltsham considered this for a moment. 'Your word against ours I believe doctor. A nobleman of the King's realm and a respectable sea captain of unimpeachable reputation. Both of which have brought desperately needed wealth to the colony. Against that of an Irish papist scraping a living as a Surgeon-Superintendent on convict ships. Forgive me for being so blunt, but there it is.' Feltsham paused for effect. 'Judge Perkins will see it our way, no Tarn your convict will hang and your report will seal your lips,' said Feltsham, ruffling a crimson handkerchief that shyly showed itself from the end of his left sleeve.

'You should not judge others by your own actions Lord Feltsham. Firstly Shenkin even though he is a convict can give his side of the story, secondly O'Hara can confirm his story.' Feltsham put his hand up again. 'Come, come Tarn, a pair of convicts up against an ambitious judge who I have let know of to my friends in London.'

'I have not finished my lord, thirdly Elizabeth Moxey who witnessed your meeting with Moxey, Ketch, and Kettlewell at the George Inn in London,' said Tarn, pausing for this to sink in. For the first time Feltsham looked ill at ease.

'A damn interfering snip of a girl, her guardian will forbid her to be a witness,' said Feltsham, in a hurry of words.

'Maybe, but let us not forget Bosun Travis in whom Lawson confided. They had been sea mates for many years, these past weeks Travis has been searching for Lawson, for he did not believe he had jumped ship. Given what he knew he became suspicious and came to me.' Feltsham shifted in his chair. You may well look alarmed my lord, we may add aiding and abetting a murder to the list.'

The room became very still, the coach clock on his lordship's dressing table thundered out the seconds. Lord Percival Hugo Feltsham knew the feeling of holding a poor hand of cards, but still felt Perkins was his man, he needed time.

'I see Tarn. I need to consider this matter, speak to Moxey to get his views you understand. I'd also need to be assured of how you intend to proceed, can you give me until tomorrow, say here in my rooms before the court convenes at midday?'

'Very well, nine of the morning clock on the morrow,' said Tarn, leaving for the door. 'Remember my lord, Travis will testify if needed. My concern is Shenkin, if he is exonerated then it will go no further but if not, then whatever you had in mind for your future here in the colony, will come to nothing.'

'Understood doctor. We are indeed, playing for high stakes. Something that you too should remember,' said Feltsham, meaningfully. Tarn nodded. 'Till tomorrow then,' he said, firmly closing the door behind him.

Feltsham sat down heavily in a chair by the bow window of his room. He watched as Tarn walked across the red dirt road of George Street, hoping a hackney carriage would run him down. The whole thing was getting out of hand he needed Ketch's special talents in removing these impediments. But first he would send a message to Judge Perkins inviting him to dinner this evening as a matter of urgency. Then speak to Moxey to contact Ketch, the three would meet late tonight in a private back room of the Fortune of War pub near the King's Wharf. If he could make sure Perkins would cut the trial to their evidence only then all was saved. Deep in thought he finally came to a resolution. He'd prepare a letter to his government friends in London telling them of Perkins admirable work on the bench of the Supreme Court here in the colony, that he believed him to be a Chief Justice of the future. To fully win him over he would then show the letter to Perkins, explaining that Shenkin was also having an undesirable effect upon Miss Elizabeth Moxey by paying her unwanted attention during the voyage while the ship was in the grip of cholera. He would confide in Perkins his intension to marry Elizabeth. After all, had he not seen at the ball how attached Elizabeth was to him? Once the trial had the outcome he wanted, he would of course, never send the letter. Ketch would deal with Travis has he had with Lawson. There was now far too much at stake, he would do, whatever it took to remove any threat to his future once and for all.

***

The overseer opened Shenkin's cell door. 'Tomorrows the day of reckoning my lad, you'll be for the high jump and no mistake. We even have new gallows, you'll be the first to try it you will,' said Blake, a bundle of clothes in his arms. 'First we'll shave your head, then hose you down in cold water so your neck is nice and clean to stretch. After that you can put on your fresh government suit all ready for the courtroom,' he said, turning to two constables at his side. 'Right lads let's get on with it.'

They went to remove Shenkin's scarf and all hell broke loose. Hitting the nearest man with a solid punch to the man's chin Shenkin headbutted the other, splitting open the man's right eyebrow. Shocked by the sudden turn of events, for heartbeats, Blake stood frozen to the spot, then screamed out for help. Four men rushed into the cell one swinging a cosh. The cosh caught Shenkin a glancing blow on the shoulder; before the man could use it again Shenkin kicked him in the crotch, the man folded up in agony. Three were down while in the huts opposite convicts were rattling their metal mugs against the bars of the windows. Blake swung the bunch of heavy keys across Shenkin's head sending him to his knees. Semi-conscious, Shenkin held on tightly to his only link with home, his scarf. As he was being hit and kicked, he tied the scarf around his neck as he began to lose consciousness.

In the dark he slowly came around the blood had dried on the side of his, light from the window of the cell told him it was morning. His back, stomach and head hurt. His hand shot to his neck, the scarf was still there, bringing a smile to his face as the door swung open. 'On your feet convict Shenkin 71013,' said overseer Blake, a number of guards stood ready with heavy sticks and clubs. 'Any trouble and we'll save the hangman from tying the knot. Now get up.'

Shenkin not wanting to give them the pleasure of seeing the pain he was in got up quickly, the leg irons almost tipping him over.

'Right escort the bastard into the yard.' At the gates the military took over, the officer detailed two soldiers of the 73rd to march each side of Shenkin, who fought back the pain from across his back his whole kidneys seem to be on fire, while blood stained his Parramatta top. Through the gates they proceeded to cross the square and into the courthouse. There Shenkin was placed into another cell to await the day's proceedings. The door slammed shut, the key turned and Shenkin collapsed onto a low bunk that stood in one corner. Sweat poured down his face as he tried to control the pain. He placed his right hand on the scarf holding it tightly as he ran his left hand over his shaved head.

At his hotel Feltsham allowed himself a smile the previous evening had gone well, he lit himself a cigar has he waited for Tarn. Perkins could hardly contain his excitement has Lord Feltsham handed him the letter to read. He assured his lordship the sentencing of this scoundrel would be swift he saw no need for any other witness the good word of his lordship would be sufficient. Moxey was in total accord with the plans, Ketch was delighted to hear of Shenkin's early departure at the end of a rope, he would indeed deal with Travis.

'Come in,' said Feltsham in response to a knock at his door.

'Good morning doctor, please sit down.'

'I prefer to stand, Feltsham.' His lordship noted the absence of title and smirked. 'Come now Tarn a little respect if you please.'

'Respect is earned Feltsham, the more I know of you the less respect I have.'

'Well then let us proceed to the matter in hand shall we?'

'By all means.'

'Very apt doctor, by all means at my disposal I have proceeded. We will let the court decided the outcome of the trial in true English fashion. Which neither an Irishman nor a Welsh convict would appreciate,' said Feltsham, drawing deeply on his cigar.

Tarn knew instinctively that something was afoot, but was unsure what it was, perhaps Feltsham was trying to pull his bluff.

'Very well we will indeed see what comes out in the trial, I wish you a good morning but a poor afternoon,' said Tarn, making for the door.

'High stakes Tarn,' called Feltsham, after him. 'High stakes.'

Moving across to the window Feltsham pulled the curtain to one side. 'Very high stakes,' he said, out loud.

Tarn was joined in the lobby of the Supreme Court by Elizabeth and William Travis. 'Well?' said Elizabeth.

'He is going through with it. I believe he has friends in the court.'

'The bastard, sorry Miss, but if Shenkin had been found not guilty then it would have made the loss of a good seaman and friend more bearable, for we can not prove foul play,' said Travis

'No we cannot but I urge you William to take good care of yourself, for by coming forward you have put yourself at risk,' said Tarn, placing a hand on Travis's shoulder.

'Never fear doctor I'll be watchful, Ketch will not find me off guard.'

Elizabeth gave a small sob. 'It's all so terrible, if he is found guilty and hung Doctor Tarn, I don't know what I'll do,' said Elizabeth, the sobs coming a little faster.

'Come now we are not going into top court tearfully are we?'

Travis nodded. 'It's not over yet Miss, even if it goes bad, we can appeal. Is that not so doctor?' said Travis, lifting his eyebrow to Tarn.

'Yes! Let us see what transpires,' said Tarn, tight-lipped.

The big clock on the wall of the courthouse struck eleven. At that moment Captain Moxey strode into the lobby followed by Feltsham and Ketch. Seeing his niece, he turned to speak to her. 'Madam you do me a disservice, have I not cared for you since your parents died. Is this the way to repay me by preparing to speak against me in a court of law? I assure you I have no intention of allowing that to happen. The clerk has a warrant issued by me has your legal guardian restraining you from giving evidence in this or any other court until your age of consent, some two years from now.

Elizabeth looked dumbfounded as the paper was handed to her. Feltsham turned to Tarn. 'High stakes sir, high stakes.'

Ketch came close to Travis. 'Early dark nights here in the colony, bosun, especially in the Rocks around where your lodgings are, why anything could happen to a man,' said Ketch, lifting his patch from his empty eye. 'You'd better see where you are going along the lanes of the Rocks.' Travis did not move but his face took on a fearful look.

'They'll be bringing up our convict soon so we had better take our places in the courtroom, should we not?' said Feltsham, inspecting his sleeves for lint. Satisfied none rested upon them, he nonetheless brushed his hand over the material of his fine London tailored coat. The three began their way up the convict built stairs of the Supreme Court. Feltsham voice echoed down. 'Ketch I feel sure you should be in the lower row of seats, please be good enough to do so.'

Ketch nodded, he knew his place. Anyway, it was costing his lordship a few barrels of Bengal Rum to have him do his bidding.

While in the lobby Shenkin's hopes of justice ebbed and flowed, has he sat on a long wooden bench watching the clock opposite tick away the minutes to midday.

CHAPTER 28

Shenkin, with chains rattling, shuffled into the courtroom, his convict clothes covering him like a cloak of shame. His head shaved, blood staining his top shirt, his scarf now tied around his neck. He swayed slightly as he was ushered into the dock. Once there he straightened his painful back with the same pride that Tarn had seen when he first met Shenkin all those months ago on the *Runnymede*.

At the sight of Shenkin, Elizabeth gave out a cry of anguish. Tarn placed his hand on her arm. 'Courage my dear he is strong and will not bend to tyranny, he has already faced that once back in his black valley.'

On the right of the courtroom sat a jury of free settlers and one or two ex-convicts now emancipated under the law.

'Court rise,' called the clerk of the court.

Through the side wing of the courtroom came a man of presence and authority. Flanked by two magistrates, he sat in the middle on a high-backed chair, the emblem of the crown emblazoned on the top.

Feltsham turn ashen white. 'Who is that?' he asked.

'That my lord is Sir Francis Forbes, Chief Justice of the Supreme Court of New South Wales, a man of total integrity determined to hear all, I repeat all, the facts of a case before passing judgement,' said Moxey, whose face mirrored Feltsham.

'But, but…' stammered Feltsham. 'Where is Perkins?' As if on cue, Perkins slid along the bench towards him. 'Sir Francis returned this morning, so I have been briefing him on the case all morning, so have been unable to speak to you my lord. Sir Francis asked if anyone would bear witness for Shenkin. I had to tell him that there was.' Perkins was breathing hard, beads of sweat stood out on the top of his bald head, as he wrung his hands in a state of anxiety. All the while the proceedings were being read out.

Feltsham, deep in thought, slowly turned to Moxey. 'We support Tarn as to the provocation from Kettlewell that led to the fight and the valiant work Shenkin performed during the outbreak of cholera, understand?' said Feltsham, in a rush of words. Seeing there was now no alternative Moxey nodded. 'Of course.'

Feltsham pointed to Ketch in the lower seating. 'Get word to him while I give my evidence.'

Judge Perkins began to say something. 'Shut up you damn fool, I am trying to think,' said Feltsham.

'But the letter my lord, the letter to London?' Feltsham ignored him. Finally Perkins sat beside them close to tears, as Sir Francis Forbes called for witnesses for the Crown.

'The court calls Lord Percival Hugo Feltsham to bear witness.' Feltham stood up, adjusted the silk handkerchief at his sleeve and walked purposefully, if slowly forward, at a pace and bearing that befitted his station. If the jury was impressed by the sight Sir Francis was not. 'We are a busy court sir I would appreciate a little more alacrity.' Unruffled, Feltsham finally arrived at the front to deliver his testimony. Having sworn to tell the truth the court heard about the threat to young Collins who regrettably, died later of cholera. Of Kettlewell's provocation that led to Shenkin having to defend himself against Kettlewell's assault. That he also wished publicly to commend Shenkin for his actions during the outbreak of cholera, that undoubtedly saved lives on board the convict ship the *Runnymede*, even though it failed to save his dear wife – at this Lord Feltsham lowered his head in sorrow.

A general mutter of understanding and sympathy rolled over the courtroom.

'Thank you Lord Feltsham, you may stand down,' said Sir Francis Forbes with a raising of his hand.

If this evidence and that of Captain Moxey and Ketch, was a surprise to Surgeon-Superintendent Tarn, Elizabeth Moxey and Bosun Travis, it was nothing compared to the shock it gave Shenkin. Given the pain he was in it was difficult for him to hold back the surge of emotion that coursed through his battered body.

Elizabeth was sobbing with relief and joy. Tarn had kept his eyes on Feltsham during his evidence and could only assume that something had gone wrong with his plans. Finally, late in the day when all had given their evidence, Sir Francis Forbes summed up. He cautioned the jury not be prejudiced in their assessment because the man in the dock was a convict. He had already been tried for that crime. They must judge the case on the merits or otherwise of the prisoner's behaviour since his incarceration on the London hulk and then aboard the convict ship the *Runnymede*. They must consider very carefully, in the light of provocation, his defence of himself and that of the convict Collins. Running his stern authoritarian eye over the jurors, Judge Forbes paused for this to register. Satisfied they were all attentive to his remarks he called for a recess while they considered their verdict.

In the lobby, both parties were deep in conversation into how and why the trial had gone the way it had. On their return to the courtroom Lord Feltsham walked close to Tarn has they climbed the stairs. 'What this court may fail to do Tarn I will take steps to correct, Shenkin is a threat to my future both financial and personal, do I make myself clear sir?'

'You do indeed Feltsham, thank you for the warning,' said Tarn, with a nod of his head.

In the courtroom they were brought to their feet again as Sir Francis Forbes came back into court. 'Please be seated, this court is now in session,' said the Clerk of the Court.

For some while silence held the floor as Judge Forbes read the verdict of the jury. Shifting through his paperwork, he caused small particles of dust to swirl visibly in a shaft of light from the window behind him. A few coughs broke the tension of the moment then Sir Francis looked up. 'We have considered the testimony of the case before us, and have come to a verdict. Will the prisoner Daniel Shenkin stand?' Shenkin with effort got to his feet to the loud accompaniment of rattling chains.

'On the charge of murder Daniel Shenkin is found not guilty due to provocation.' A cheer came up from a part of the courtroom. 'Silence please,' called the Clerk.

Judge Forbes waited. 'The court is conscious of the fact that the prisoner is a convicted convict sentenced to 20 years hard labour for rioting against the Crown. However, this court is committed to the reformation of convicts who will bring about their entrance into the colony as worthy citizens. Consequently, in view of the prisoner's good character references, together with his commendable behaviour on the *Runnymede* resulting in the saving of lives, we feel some recognition by this court should be put on record. Therefore, you Daniel Shenkin will serve two years hard labour in the service of the government to pay back your due to the Crown. You will not be allowed to sell any part of your labour during this period. If, after the term of two years you demonstrate good behaviour and are not implicated in any riotous or disorderly doings, this court recommends, as an inducement for reform, that you be granted a ticket-of-leave that will allow you to work as a free man here in the colony. Any misdemeanour will annul the ticket and you will be sent to Port Arthur Penal Settlement on Van Diemen's Land to serve the balance of your twenty-year term.' Judge Forbes addressed Shenkin directly. 'This is an opportunity to change the course of your life, I strongly advise that you take every advantage of it.' Sir Francis paused for a moment, then returning the paperwork to his case file he turned to the court. 'Constable take the prisoner down, this court is adjourned.'

Shenkin looked towards Elizabeth, a shadow of a smile broke across his pain-wracked face. She mouthed back at him, 'I love you, I love you, I love you.' Then as Shenkin was taken away she turned to Tarn and wrapped her arms around him. 'We've won doctor, we've won.'

Tarn disengaged himself from her embrace. 'I fear we have a long way to go yet my dear. The safe environs of a court of law are one thing, but the outside world is fraught with danger. Feltsham will not let it go at this, something has gone wrong with his plans. He is now playing for time, for opportunity. Shenkin must be vigilant, you too Travis, we must all be.'

William Travis nodded. 'I'll find a berth on the next ship leaving Sydney, my home is at sea. I'll be safe there, I wish you good fortune doctor and you too miss in your guard against Feltsham,' said Travis, heading for the stairs.

'Well Elizabeth we must now fight for Regan O'Hara at the Quarter Sessions which sits next week. Hopefully they will take the outcome of this trial into account.' At that moment Captain Moxey called for Elizabeth to join him. At the same time Feltsham walked over to Tarn. 'Two weeks on a chain gang is a very long time, two years and the possibilities are overwhelming,' said Feltsham, delighted to find a piece of dust to flick from his sleeve. Then turning to Ketch, he said. 'Join me in a glass of wine sergeant I have a number of things to discuss with you,' said Feltsham, inclining his head to Tarn. 'Another time doctor, another place, good day sir.'

No thought Tarn, they had a long way to go yet as he followed them into the bright afternoon sun. Ahead of him he saw Shenkin being frogmarched back to the barracks.

Shenkin winced as the leg irons cut into his ankles. 'So you cheated the hangman did you, well you'll pay for the crime you are here for convict, make no mistake about that,' said the guard pushing him forward.

At the gates, Overseer Blake snarled. 'I hear you're not to hang Shenkin, believe me there will be times you'd wish you had been by the time we are finished with you. Now get your ass over to the big hut,' he said. The two guards dragged Shenkin forward. One of them had a closed eye from the night before in Shenkin's cell. He kicked Shenkin's feet from under him, sending him painfully onto his back. Shenkin gritted his teeth and stood up. 'Is that your best effort, you miserable bastard?' said Shenkin. The guard turned back to Blake. 'This convict just swore at me sir.' Blake came up beside them quickly. 'Punishment List states "For using foul language to a guard, ten lashes. Get him over to the triangle."

'Right away sir.'

The guard pulled harshly at Shenkin's clothing, finally removing the top he pushed him forward. Shenkin was secured to the flogging triangle, his hands tied to the top his legs to the base. As Shenkin's arms were spread-eagled onto the wooden frame the dried blood on his back tore at the wounds from the night before. Blake stood watching as behind him the chain gangs were being returned to the barracks. Seeing Shenkin hanging from the post Regan started to go towards it. 'Get back in line that man or you'll join the Punishment List,' said one of the guards, laying a vicious blow across Regan's back with his stick. The first lash made a mark similar to a white line of frost, the second split the swollen skin open, the third tore the flesh to ribbons. To Overseer Blake's disappointment Shenkin did not cry out. 'Put some effort into it, you're too light, harder man harder,' said Blake. The constable was sweating, as lash after lash ran across Shenkin's back, which was now no more than a bloody mess. Regan clenched his fists as he was marched with the others into the huts.

Shenkin forced his mind to concentrate on other times, better times. His father holding forth on the rights of man, his sister saving for her marriage. Her bridal dress being bought in small pieces of silk, which hung like a jigsaw at the back of her bedroom door. His young brother Owain wearing his father's miner's hat to be all grown up. Most of all his mother scrubbing, polishing, pouring hot water for baths at the end of their shifts.

'Nine, ten,' said the guard. Thankful to stop the constable stood back to admire his work. He was covered in sweat and blood, his right arm hung loose at his side, the cat-o'-nine-tails glisten wet and bloody in the late day sunlight. Taking Shenkin down they spread salt over the wounds then dragged him over to the hut. Convict overseer Fleet pointed to a corner. 'Drop him over there lads, we'll see to him now. Stubbs get a hammock unfurled, two men to lift him.' Regan ran forward, Fewens joined him together they placed him belly down on the hammock. Gingerly Regan rubbed the salt into the wounds. Shenkin groaned. 'Just can't keep out of trouble can you?' said Regan.

'Stop talking there leave him, get to your own places,' said Fleet. Windows were closed, doors were bolted, lights were out. Another day is over, thought Shenkin, gritting his teeth against the pain, only 730 to go. Then he passed out.

The morning came soon enough. Regan had been at Shenkin's side since early dawn. 'Some more water Shenkin, or a drop of rum given to me by my cockney friend George, don't know how he got it but he knows his way around. A born scrounger is George. Your neighbour is Dewi still recovering from his fight with the shark.' Shenkin turned his head. Dewi Davies had lost not only his leg but was as thin as a blade of grass. 'How are you Dewi?' His pale face looked at across at Shenkin. 'Lighter,' said Dewi, with a forced grin. 'They are going to make me a crutch, so I can work. Good news is I won't need leg irons.' 'Remember how well Billy one-leg got around?' said Shenkin, smiling 'Quick on his foot was Billy and always in the thick of everything. You'll be fine Dewi, just fine.'

The bell in the Yard rang out to announce the start of the day. It was 5:30 am –after washing they'd have some bread and sweet tea, Regan told him, then nothing till midday. With a wince Shenkin pulled on his Parramatta top. 'Perhaps they'll let you off the chain gang for today,' said Regan. His cockney friend started to laugh. 'Don't make me laugh, if he don't move they'll use a Neddy on him. Cosh Regan cosh, why he'll be into the rasher-wagon and no mistake.' Before George Fewens could say more, Regan said frying pan. 'Right you are mate,' said George, gulping down his tea. Shenkin looked confused. 'You'll catch on,' said Regan. At that moment Tarn came through the door with the doctor of the barracks. Walking by Shenkin he dropped his hat, bending to pick it up he passed Shenkin a note. 'Well Dewi how are you this morning, I asked the prison doctor if I may see you,' said Tarn. 'Still a bit shaky doctor, but I'll be up on my feet, I mean foot, soon,' said Dewi Davies, with as much vigour as he could muster.

'Good,' said Tarn – looking over at Shenkin he gave a nod. Shenkin returned it as he clasped the note.

Fleet called out. This is not visitor's day, let's have you Government Men into the yard, quick now. Check their leg irons Stubbs.'

The Superintendent stood in the doorway of his office, a look of boredom on his thin face, as Blake shouted out names and assignments of work. 'Argyle Cut chain gang, mark convict 71013 Shenkin down for this detail. It will free your back off Shenkin,' whispered Blake, as Shenkin marched past him.

Shenkin felt as if each step would be his last, his back was on fire. He felt Regan's arm giving him support. 'I'm alright Regan thanks, it will pass better to keep moving or it will stiffen up just like after a fight,' said Shenkin, lifting his head a little higher.

'What's this Argyle Cut then?'

'It's to join Sydney Cove with Millers Point, we are cutting through the stone to build a bridge so that people can go straight across instead of down and up steps on each side. The rubble we cut and dig is used to pack the mouth of what they call the Tank Stream. It's hard labour alright, damn hard. Guards watch over us, there is no slacking, it can be dangerous too, the stone ledges are unstable, there have been a number of rock falls, so be careful.'

'Shut that chatter, the flogging post will be waiting for the next man that talks,' said a guard. From then on only the rattle of their chains broke the sound of their shuffling feet. In the cold air of the morning the dust came up from the road like drifting clouds as they passed the courthouse where only yesterday Shenkin was found not guilty of murder. The note Tarn had passed to him was from Elizabeth.

My Dear Darling,

I was so pleased that you were found not guilty of killing Kettlewell. Two years will pass dearest, and I will be waiting for you. In the meantime I will send messages to you with some small gifts and watch out for you while you are assigned to government work. Do not give up hope I will always be nearby, loving you, thinking of you. We will be reunited my love.

Elizabeth x

Shenkin held the note tightly in his hand, hoping she was right. His hand went to the scarf around his neck, his talisman. Regan looked at him. 'Thinking are we?' he whispered. Shenkin let the scarf go. The day went slowly and painfully for Shenkin, his back burnt beneath his thin top. The bright hard sun adding further heat to the open wounds. At midday, a small man, a water bag over his shoulder gave water to each convict. Shenkin never knew how good water could taste until that moment. Regan turned to him, sweat running down his face as if someone was pouring water over his head. 'And to think I only used it to wash in before.'

By evening they were all exhausted, and now cold. Two had collapsed and this was nearly winter. Dear god, thought Shenkin what would it be like in the heat of summer?

'Collect tools and place them in the tool shed at the low end of the Cut. All allocated tools to be counted,' shouted the overseer. Overlooking them at the top were soldiers of the 73rd regiment. With muskets at the ready they watched every move the men below them made. Finally, they began the march back to the barracks. The sun thankfully dipped into the horizon and it became surprisingly chilly. Grateful for the cooler air Shenkin braced himself for the return, his first day on the Cut was over.

George Fewens shuffled along beside him as they came towards the barracks. 'Did you know they call it Hyde Park Barracks, blimey it don't look like Hyde Park to me, as I used to wear my whistle and flute up in Hyde Park.' Seeing Shenkin's confusion he said. 'Best suit mate, best my thieving could afford.'

'I'll have that bastard whose talking if he keeps it up,' said the guard. George smiled lifting his eyes up to heaven. At the gate they began the count and search. Blake run his eye down the call sheet. 'Right into the wash rooms the lot of you, be quick about.'

Turning to Shenkin he said, 'Anything to say rioter, any swear words you want to share with me?'

'No,' said Shenkin

'No what! you Welsh bastard.'

'No Mr Blake.'

'Learning are we, but I'll be watching you Shenkin now move your bloody self.'

Shenkin gritted his teeth as he shuffled into the wash room. Regan was stripped to the waist, his body covered in dust and sweat. The paleness of his skin was turning a bright red. The top of his cropped head was burnt, his broad shoulders bent slightly to scoop up the cold water. It seemed to hiss on his skin. 'You look a bloody mess Regan,' said Shenkin.

'I look a mess! I wish we had a mirror, so I do,' said Regan through chapped lips.

'It'll get easier as you brown up,' said George. His small thin body the colour of dark china tea.

The guard at the main door shouted out. 'Come on let's have you, last one out gets no oatmeal soup.' They rushed pushing and stumbling to the doors.

***

Tarn smiled at Elizabeth and for the third time told her he had given Shenkin her note and, not wanting to tell her the truth, said yes he looked fine. No, he had not given him a message for her, how could he? 'I know doctor it's just I need to hear something,' she said.

'He'll get a message to you when he can my dear,' said Tarn, with little conviction.

'Have you found premises yet for your practice doctor?'

'I have, it's not that far from the barracks, would you believe it's called Elizabeth Street? It must be fate.' They both laughed.

Then Elizabeth became very serious, her beautiful face took on a grim look. 'Do you really think Lord Feltsham will still do Shenkin harm?'

Tarn considered his reply, he did not want to over alarm her. 'He sees Shenkin as a threat to his future Elizabeth, so yes I think he will if he can. Remember he wants your hand in marriage. Your uncle is in too deep to refuse him.' Sadness spread across Elizabeth's face. 'It seems both Shenkin and I have a two-year sentence. He as a convict and myself till I am of age, will we survive it?'

Tarn turned to this girl who in every way was already a woman, and a strong one at that. 'If its true love then it will survive, perhaps it is a test of that love,' he said.

'Then my good doctor I have no fear, for it will survive, I know it will,' said Elizabeth walking Tarn to the door. 'Goodnight doctor and thank you again for delivering my missive.'

'Goodnight, sleep well, pray for us all.'

Outside Tarn stood for a moment in the shadow of the old warehouse. He lit his clay pipe while musing on the future of them all. Feltsham would try to get to someone inside the barracks if he could. One of the guards or overseers, perhaps even the Superintendent. He may enlist the help of Ketch. Now that Ketch had a pub he'd meet all the riff-raff of Sydney Town. Those convicts who had free labour to sell or someone assigned to the pub. A puff of smoke circled his head, for a moment it seemed like a halo, around the only Irishman in Sydney who didn't believe in God. It broke, swirling into the night air as Michael Patrick Tarn stepped into the dirt road of King's Wharf. Drunken laughter, loud shouts, and the high-pitched voices of women came up from the waterfront. He shook his head, thinking to himself, it's really one big prison with walls 12,000 miles thick.

CHAPTER 29

For the first months Shenkin managed to stay out of harm's way. Blake had grown used to his silent acceptance of convict life, but still taunted him whenever he had the chance. With Tarn acting has a go-between, Shenkin and Elizabeth had been able to exchange messages.

Slowly Shenkin and Regan began to settle into the harsh routine of the chain gang. The work at the Argyle Cut was brutal, their hands were cut and painful where the sandstone had torn into the skin. By now they had been burnt brown by the sun. Like the tough work in the mines the chain gang had hardened Shenkin's muscles, his body was again toned. Every night for the first few weeks Regan had cleaned the wounds on Shenkin's back until they too settled down and finally healed. But Dewi Davies was not improving, each night that passed he seem to sink further, his body was becoming so thin that even the weight of his blankets seemed too heavy for him to bear. Night after night Shenkin listen to Dewi's shallow breathing. Then into their third month Dewi called out to him. Shenkin turned in his sleep. 'What is it Dewi, what can I do. Shall I call the doctor?' Dewi looked at him, he seemed to Shenkin to be all eyes. 'I want to go home Shenkin, will you take me home?' said Dewi, his voice a mere whisper in the still night air. Shenkin got out of his hammock. 'One day we may Dewi but only God knows when and he hasn't spoken to us since we left chapel.' If he understood the humour in the remark he did not smile. Although the night was cold his face was drenched in sweat. Shenkin came closer, he instinctively held Dewi's clammy hand. A croak left Dewi's throat as if to say a hoarse farewell, then his hand went limp. They were down to four, just four out of so many who had marched beside him down that mountain to their dark black mining town. How long ago was it, a year? No thought Shenkin with bitterness, it was two summers and a thousand years ago.

Shenkin called a guard. Stubbs bleary eyed from sleep, stamped down the centre of the hut.

'What the hell is it now?' said Stubbs.

Shenkin had been joined by Regan then George Fewens. They all stood around Dewi's hammock as if in silent prayer. 'You'll have the whole bloody hut awake in a moment. This had better be good 71013 or so help me I'll have you on the Punishment List,' said Stubbs.

'It's Dewi Davies I think his number was 71018,' said Shenkin, with a sigh.
'What about him?'

'He's dead,' said Shenkin

'Jesus! You didn't call me down here for that did you?' Not waiting for a reply Stubbs took a look at the skin and bones that had been Dewi Davies. 'Dead is he, then it saves us having to see to him all the time. Water, food, he never stopped calling out. Good bloody riddance I says,' said Stubbs, beginning to pull the body violently off the hammock. Shenkin spun him around. The first blow sent him across the hut in a heap in the corner. By now most of the hut were awake and began shouting them on. Stubbs got to his feet pulling a cosh from his belt as he rushed back at Shenkin. He had to pass Regan to get to Shenkin, he never made it, Regan drove his head into Stubbs' stomach, then up under his jaw. Stubbs lay out cold on the floor as Fleet and Consantini ran into the hut. They were followed by a number of guards all partly dressed in night clothes. Shenkin and Regan turned as one to greet them. Not to be left out, George Fewens stood beside them, his small fists raised in the defence of his friends. 'Now if this was London's East End we'd have a couple of iron bars mates, to even things up a bit. I'll take the big one on the left,' he said, rushing forward. It lasted over an hour by which time the hut was in chaos. Stubbs never got to feet, his jaw was broken. Consantini had blood pouring down his face, a guard was draped over a hammock. Little George had what looked like a broken arm, but was still swinging his good fist. Shenkin's old mining scar had split open from the blow of a cosh, but he was still on his feet. Regan was singing an Irish fighting song has he sent one guard through a window. Then the room was full of soldiers an officer fired a pistol into the air. All went silent the swirling smoke of the officer's pistol drifted gentle upwards. 'Fix bayonets!' he ordered, drawing his sword. At his side, his feet standing on broken glass, was Superintendent Roach. Convict overseer Fleet had been forced to call for the Superintendent, knowing this could cost him his ticket-of-leave, for by now the fighting had spread to other huts.

'Well Fleet what started it?' said Roach

'Stubbs was on night duty sir. Stubbs?'

Stubbs painfully explained what had started the fighting. That the sick man Davies had died. He had tried to put the dead man into more secure position but while he was doing this convict 71013 Shenkin had hit him from behind.

'As the convict overseer of this hut Fleet, where were you?'

'Sleeping sir,' said Fleet, through clenched teeth

'I see,' said Roach, turning to the room.

He cleared his throat. 'All those who were involved will be severely punished. I want their names, or everyone in this hut will be punished. Do I make myself clear?' Shenkin stepped forward. 'I started it Superintendent no one else is to blame.'

'With a little help from me mind, sure he couldn't have done it all on his own,' said Regan

'And I'd like to know which one of these bastard guards broke my arm, when I was mostly fighting fair,' said their cockney friend.

'Constables take these men into solitary I'll deal with them in the morning. Convict overseer Fleet I'll see you in my office, now.'

They were frogmarched into three solitary cells. Once the guards were gone, Fewens called out to Shenkin through the connecting iron door. 'Can you hear me Shenkin?'

'Yes I can,' Shenkin said, trying the door which was of course locked.

'Good,' Fewens said. 'You can bet your last penny that we'll be put on the shin scraper,' he said.

'The shin scraper?'

'The Treadmill mate, they have one that can take up to ten men at a time. It's a big bloody wooden wheel with steps, that go round and round, a never bloody ending staircase.'

'And me wearing my Sunday-best shoes,' Shenkin said.

Further along Regan joined in. 'Solitary is it, but we can talk to each other, so we can, so that's not too bad.'

'They're not normally all occupied at the same time mate.'

'It's all my fault, none of it helped Dewi, dead is dead. I just could not take seeing that bastard Stubbs dragging poor Dewi's body off the hammock,' said Shenkin.

'Sure I'd have done the same, so there's an end to it. And haven't I been wanting to have a good brawl these past long months, sure it was a great evening lads, so it was.'

'Hope they splint up this arm, it's bloody painful now.'

'Shut up talking,' said the guard, who had just taken up his post.

Come morning, a doctor saw to Fewens arm, but they were given no water or food. Stumbling out of their cells they were marched over to a tall wooden structure. Running the length of the timber frame was a large elongated mill wheel, the horizontal blades of which were just wide enough for a man to stand on. In all it looked as if it was long enough to take a number of convicts at a time.

'What did I tell you, it's the bloody Treadmill,' said George Fewens

'Quiet!' shouted Blake. As Roach clearing his throat he walked slowly up to the Treadmill. 'You are going to learn that violence to a guard and fighting will not be tolerated. This Treadmill has broken many men who thought otherwise. Your punishment is simple; it requires you to walk up stairs. The stairs are in a circle, you will, I assure you never get to the top. You will be stripped to the waist, your leg irons will be left on. After a number of hours they will became very heavy,' said Roach, pausing. 'Each of you step on to the blade in front of you,' ordered Roach. It was difficult with the leg irons but finally they were all on. Clearing his throat, yet again, Roach spoke. 'In front of you, you will see a round wooden crossbar, which is separate from the wheel and attached at chin height to each end of the main frame. You will hold on to this with your hands, the guards will then release the wheel to start it turning freely. You will then step from one blade to another to keep it going. The wheel is heavy, very heavy. Do not miss the wooden blade, if you do your legs will be mutilated by the next blade. It will certainly, in a few hours, skin your shins as you fail to fully lift your legs up to the next blade. However, your manual efforts will not be wasted for at the end of the wheel is a grinder which will grind the flour to be used for your fellow convicts' breakfasts,' said Roach, with satisfaction. Then stepping back Roach turned to the guards. 'Start the wheel turning, report to Overseer Blake any problems.' Roach cleared his throat, puffed out his puny chest then looked at the three men as they stepped on to the next bladed platform. 'The Treadmill is yours for the rest of the day and every day for the next three days. A doctor will be standing by, he will attend to anyone that requires medical attention. When that convict is fit again, he will resume climbing. You will rest every forty minutes for a period of twenty minutes. Pausing Roach looked directly at Shenkin. 'This may seem to you to be no great chastisement, but I can promise you the stop-start will stiffen your muscles, it will also break your concentration, making it difficult to time each blade.' Roach took one final look at them before walking back to his office for his breakfast.

It was not long before they were all sweating and panting but so far they had kept their legs clear of each descending wooden blade. After two hours Fewens caught his ankle on the edge of one of the blades, blood trickled down from the skinned flesh. Five hours later all their lower legs were scraped raw.

The doctor looked on dispassionately, he came out of the hospital every hour to spend a few moments checking the state of each man, then returned to his duties.

In one of their twenty-minute rests, Shenkin asked for water. The guard sitting at a table with a covered shade over it said nothing. But lifted a tin mug of water to his lips, drunk then poured the remainder on the ground and smiled.

At midday the bell rang for change of guards at their various duties, including the Treadmill guards. The new guards conferred with each other for a moment, then the new guards sat in the shade. On the next rest period Regan asked for water. The taller guard on hearing Regan's Irish accent turned to the water butt. He dipped a ladle into the water butt then gave it to Regan, who drunk a small amount then passed it on to the others. 'Sure it takes a good Catholic to ignore the rules, so it does,' Regan said, through gasps of breath.

'No talking,' said the guard.

As the sun went down the bell rang again as the chain gangs began returning to the barracks. Fewens was in a bad way, as they were taken off the wheel he collapsed.

Back in solitary no one spoke, the doors slammed close and the bolts were driven into place. On the low bunks they found some bread and water. Shenkin took a few sips of water his hands shaking. He found he could not stop his legs from trembling, nor did he feel like eating, finally he simply collapsed onto the bunk. Regan called out. 'Are we all alright, are we?'

'I'm fine,' said Shenkin. They waited for George Fewens to call out, nothing came.

Regan pressed against the iron dividing door. 'George where is that cockney chit-chat of yours?'

For heartbeats they waited. 'I'm just doing some exercises mates it's been such a slow moving boring old day,' said Fewens, but his strained voice said much more. 'Now let a reasonably honest London sweep have some feather and flip. Not hearing any reply, he said. 'Sleep Regan, some bloody kip, feather and flip.'

'I'm with you on that, so I am, what say you Shenkin.'

'Yes it's been fun but let's call it a day,' Shenkin said, with a deep sigh.

***

If, in the convict barracks Shenkin had had a brutal day, Lord Feltsham was experiencing very heady days, his house was slowly taking shape. It was a fine imposing colonial designed house, that was being built with free convict labour. He had ordered furniture from London and some pieces were even from Paris, these were due to arrive within the next month on the *Isabella*. Moxey's other two ships, the *Norfolk* and the *Lady Anderson* had brought more of Kettlewells 'acquired goods' in their holds with their main cargo of convicts. The goods were now safe and sound in Moxey's King's Wharf warehouse, the cargo being stored for inspection and valuation.

Goldspick was slowly converting their horde into considerable amounts of coinage and rum. Ketch's shares had set him up nicely in a pub, while Moxey's Van Diemen's business was open and already turning a profit. When all the boxes were emptied and their value in the bank, Feltsham felt Ketch was coming to the end of his usefulness. If, when in his cups one night, he might, blabber it would be most unfortunate. He was a loose end he would have to go. Also, a word in the right ear would find Goldspick having to answer certain difficult questions regarding his collection of expensive items. As a former convict it would mean he would face a term in Port Arthur Penal Colony – it would be easy for an accident to happen to him while there. For the moment, Shenkin was safe in prison but he too must be dealt with. Indeed the two year sentence would be up soon enough, he must give that some thought. And then there was his marriage to Elizabeth to be arranged. Feltsham gave a smile, sighed an agreeable sigh, and lit a Bolivar cigar. He really must remember to order some more. Lifting a glass of claret to his lips it caught the light of the fading evening sun. Heady days indeed, all his plans were falling neatly into place he thought. The glow from the fire lit the room with soft flickering lights, it made him wonder how his poor mother was doing in England, if indeed, she was still alive. After all a debtors' prison is a hard place to spend one's old age. Loose ends indeed.

***

By the last few hours of their punishment all three had lost weight. Fewens was particularly in a poor way, over the last two days the doctor had taken him off the wheel half a dozen times. Each time Roach had insisted he be returned to the Treadmill to complete his sentence. In the end the doctor refused to be responsible for Fewens' health. With only short time to go, George Fewens died. His legs had collapsed beneath him they went into the turning blades of the heavy wheel jamming the machinery, bringing it to a shuddering stop.

Roach was brought from his office, the doctor from the hospital. Fewens was declared dead. Shenkin and Regan were taken down and returned to solitary. Roach turned to the doctor. 'After you have seen to the body doctor, please come to my office.'

'Very well Superintendent I'll be about an hour or so.'

Back in his office Roach went over the doctor's personal record. Doctor Rufus Jameson was from a family who were either private or military doctors going back three generations. He had been in Sydney for eight years and had, over the last year, repeatedly requested, on medical grounds, to be relieved of his duties so that he may return to England. Since he still had two years to go on his contract Roach had refused his request. Explaining to Jameson that the medical profession was not well represented in the colony. At many of their meetings on this subject Jameson had pleaded his case. Apart from his poor health his wife was not at ease in the colony. She did not like the climate, the convicts, or the lack of social graces among the free settlers.

At the knock on his door Roach looked up at Doctor Jameson as he entered. 'Take a chair doctor.'

'Thank you but before you say anything, I did advise against the continued punishment of the convict Fewens. Also that I could not be held responsible for his health if he continued on the Treadmill.'

'You did indeed doctor, you did,' said Roach, reading again the paperwork in front of him.

'I take it you are still of a mind to return to England at the earliest opportunity?' said Roach, leaving a moments silence hanging between them.

Jameson eyes narrowed. 'Have you been able to find a replacement?'

'Let us say I am determined to find one. You appreciate it may take me a month or two but I feel confident enough that among the next ships to dock I can find a willing replacement. I assume you have not yet written your report on the convict 8743 George Fewens.' Not waiting for a reply Roach went on. 'A hardened criminal by the way, I hope there will not be a lengthy investigation that may well delay your leaving.' For heartbeats neither spoke.

Jameson gave a slight cough. 'He was of course a poor specimen of manhood. Due I am sure to his background and up bringing, in I believe, the slums of London. I feel my report should cover this point and its bearing on his most unfortunate death.'

'We understand each other then?' said Roach, closing the document case of the doctor's file.

'Yes we do. However, perhaps you would put your recommendations as to my replacement due to poor health in writing Superintendent. I am sure you understand my need for reassurance before I submit my report to the authorities on the death of convict 8743.'

'Of course. I'll have it sent to your surgery first thing in the morning,' said Roach. After another long heavy silence Roach spoke. 'Well I think that is all doctor, goodnight and do give my good wishes to Mrs Jameson,' he said, walking the doctor to the door. 'I am sure you will have much to talk about this evening, many plans to make. Goodnight again doctor.'

'Goodnight to you too Superintendent, I trust you are able to sleep well,' said Jameson, unable to resist the barbed comment.

Roach simply nodded. 'Do call into the solitary block doctor, I don't want to lose any more Government Men today.'

The doctor turned. 'With only a little time to go for the end of their punishment and the Treadmill damaged I will treat their legs, if satisfactory I suggest come morning they are both returned to their work assignments. I agree let us not take further risks.'

'Indeed so, perhaps you would inform them.'

'I will,' said Jameson, closing the door.

Shenkin stood up as the doctor entered. 'He should not have been made to continue doctor.'

'Not your decision Shenkin. I just want to check you over, you are to be returned to your work gang tomorrow.'

'But Fewens, what about him?'

Jameson looked at Shenkin. 'A most unfortunate affair, I will be preparing a full report. Of course these things take time you understand, but I am sure everyone will be satisfied as to the outcome. Now let me examine you for I have yet to see the other convict.'

'His name is Regan O'Hara doctor,' said Shenkin, trying to hold his temper.

'O'Hara, quite so. You have lost weight but are fit to return to work goodnight,' said the doctor, leaving hastily without treating Shenkin's bleeding ankles.

The following day found them back at the Argyle Cut the grit from the sandstone caused their raw ankles to burn even more. But finally the day passed. On their return Shenkin saw Elizabeth standing on the steps of St

James's Church. She waved to him mouthing the words I love you. He could not respond but nodded his head. He was sure this meant a letter would soon be passed to him by Doctor Tarn over the next day or two. Sure enough, the next evening Tarn came into the prison barracks for a meeting with the Superintendent. It was at a time when the work chain gangs were returning, walking alongside the gangs Tarn dropped his walking cane, stooping to pick it up he pressed a letter into Shenkin hand.

***

'Doctor Tarn it's always good to see you, please take a seat,' said Roach. 'How can I help you?'

'I understand you are seeking a replacement for Doctor Jameson, is that so?'

Roach smiled. 'News travels quickly in the colony doctor, yes it is true, poor man is in ill health and wishes to return to England. One tries to be understanding in these matters, don't you know.'

'Indeed,' said Tarn. 'My rooms are close by I thought I may be able to meet the medical needs of the barracks, while still free to attended to my own private patients. I put it to you that it may well meet both our requirements.'

Roach was delighted to hear it. Jameson would be out of the way, and the facts of the death of convict 8743 would also be officially closed.

'Delighted to have you Tarn but I fear the remuneration is not great however the duties are not too demanding, we have, as you know, military medical orderlies who see to most cases.'

Tarn smiled. 'My very thinking Superintendent, also all income is grist to the mill.'

Roach winced at the word mill but nodded his head. 'Quite so doctor, shall we agree terms over a glass of rum?' said Roach , rising from his desk.

'Music to the ears of any Irishman sir, pour away.'

Dear Daniel the letter began.

How I miss you. Each night draws out it's long black hours like a knife. During the day I am kept busy at my uncle's premises but the nights, oh the nights my dear they are so long and empty. My uncle is pressing me to name a date to marry Lord Feltsham if I refuse he says he will arrange for my return to England. I could not bear that my dearest, to be away from you to never see you again. I have, my darling, continually told him

*of my love for you, but this enrages him. But I will not deny my love for
you. As he is my guardian for still another year I find it more difficult to
find reasons to delay. Feltsham is building a grand house outside Sydney.
Until it is ready I have used this to put his lordship off. Please take care
that you complete this next year safely, for I am sure Lord Feltsham is still
intending to do you harm. You know too much and he also knows my
feelings for you. I am waiting for you my darling with an eager heart.
I have scented this letter which I trust brings something of me to you.*

Love Elizabeth x PS, Are we not fortunate to have Doctor Tarn?

Shenkin lifted the paper to his noise and breathed in the fragrant aroma
that he had come to know so well during the voyage. He read and reread the
letter until the light was to dim. His passion aroused he too found the night
a torment to his mind and to his body. Come what may he would survive this
last year. But the days and months passed slowly and painfully.

***

Ketch bought Fleet another glass of gin. 'So you know Shenkin do you?'
he said.

'Is he a friend of yours, for he isn't of mine. Cost me my ticket-of-leave
he did,' said Fleet, drinking the gin in one mouthful. Fleet as a trusty was
allowed out of the barracks twice a week, he was now able to sell his services,
that of a bank clerk, to any of the colony's businesses.

'He's no bleeding friend of mine mate. Caused me problems he did and the
loss of a good mate too. The bastard's been nothing but a source of difficulties
ever since I met him. How come you know him?'

Fleet looked at his empty glass. 'Rest easy mate I'll get that filled,' said
Ketch. Placing another glass in front of Fleet he sat down opposite him.
Fleet's hand grasped the glass, but Ketch restrained him. 'How come you
know him then?'

'I'm his hut overseer I am, have to look at him every bloody day.' Having
already made enquiries Ketch knew this well enough.

'Is that so? Cost you your ticket you say?'

Fleet started to drink then placed the glass back on the table. 'With just three
weeks to go for my ticket Shenkin caused a fight in the hut didn't he. Almost

wreaked the bloody hut, him and that big Irish friend of his. After it was all over the Superintendent withdrew the ticket. I'll get even with him somehow but it's the ticket-of-leave I want, so it's difficult,' Fleet said, downing the gin.

Ketch came up closer to Fleet. 'What if I told you I know someone who also wants to put an end to Shenkin and is in a position to do you some good with your ticket-of-leave?' Fleet turned to Ketch his eyes wide. 'Who'd you know who could do that?'

'Only a judge, that's all,' Ketch said.

Fleet was beside himself. 'If he can get me my ticket I'll have Shenkin dead within a month.'

Ketch leaned over. 'Done! I'll have a word with his nibs. Why it's as good as in your hand already. Now what about a glass for the road?'

'That would be most kind,' Fleet said, as Ketch walked back to the pub's long bar. Fleet smiled he'd get even for Stubbs and Consantini at the same time.

Back in the barracks Fleet came into the hut a little unsteady on his feet he staggered over to Shenkin's hammock where Shenkin was asleep.

'Sleeping are we, well enjoy it for you are in for a long sleep soon. Turning to Consantini who was on night duty he said. 'We have plans to make, so wake up Stubbs.'

'Right, I hope it means something real nasty for Shenkin.'

Fleet beamed. 'Oh yes something very nasty and final.' They talked on through the best part of the night as they laid their plans.

The bell rang out for the start of yet another day. In the yard Blake began his usual ritual of assigning first the convicts to their skilled jobs then calling out the chain gangs. The doors swung open, the military detachment stood to attention, awaiting their officers order.

'Fix bayonets! Escort positions at the double,' barked the officer.

Dust climbed into the morning air as the soldiers marched to their positions. With the slow coming of summer, it was going to be another hot day – the sun was already lighting up government square. Shadows were being chased away across the road to the courthouse. Cockatoos screamed out their unearthly sound that Shenkin could still not get used to. At the Cut they were, as usual, issued with their tools. 'Convict 71013 Shenkin, one pick, one spade, next,' called the guard.

A convict that Shenkin did not know managed to get beside him. He smiled up at Shenkin. 'New spot for me, makes a change mind,' he said. Then putting out his hand he said. 'Names Henry Hare, 6174, and you?' Shenkin told him.

They were on the high part of the Cut, the Miller's Point side, as Shenkin began chipping into the face of the sandstone. The other side of him was 3163 John Welling; he had been Shenkin's working partner for the last three months. Welling was a small wiry man of about sixty, whose clothes hang on him like a scarecrow in a field. The heavy work was beginning to take its toll on him, for the last few weeks he had developed a cough. Shenkin had began to carry Welling's tools from where they were working back to the collection point each day. 'How do you feel today John?'

'Bloody awful Shenkin I can't take much more of this.' Welling had been sentenced to fourteen years for safe cracking. To pass the time in the barracks he had shown Shenkin how to crack a lock. Shenkin had got so good at opening the food locker in the hut that Regan and he never went hungry.

'Let me give you a hand with that big stone John.'

'Thanks Shenkin,' Welling said, spitting up blood.

'I'll speak to the guard for you to be sent back to the hospital,' said Shenkin.

Swinging his pick down into the sandstone, Hare said, 'He'll not be with us much longer mate I wouldn't bother.'

'I'll be the judge of that,' Shenkin said, lifting the stone.

'Thanks Shenkin,' said Welling, with a cough.

Shenkin turned to look down at Regan who was working just below him. He was stripped to the waist and swinging his pick as if all Ireland depended upon it. Shenkin smiled. 'The crazy bloody Irishman,' he said out loud.

'What's that mate?' said Hare, leaning on his pick handle.

'Just talking out loud.'

'You'd better not let the guard see you friend or you'll be on punishment.' But the guard was looking straight at them. Now that's strange thought Shenkin, it's just as if he knows this Hare. Shenkin caught sight of the raised pick swinging towards him just in time. Moving quickly to the side he caught hold of Hare's hands around the handle. Gripping the handle Shenkin pulled Hare towards him. Caught off balance, Hare fell forward, the guard began running over to them. But the ledge was narrow and began to break up under their combined weight so he made slow progress. He managed to hold Hare by his top as he tottered on the edge. Then all of a sudden, the whole ledge gave way. Shenkin just managed to scramble up to the top land of Miller's Point, pulling Welling with him, as the ledge fell into the Cut taking Hare and the guard with it.

That evening on their return to the barracks Roach addressed them. 'Today we had a terrible incident that resulted in the death of one inmate and a prison guard. Did anyone witness what happened?' No one spoke.

'I see, you were all busy working I take it. Mr Blake have your constables reported anything that they saw?'

'No sir.'

Take them to their huts, Overseer Blake.'

'Sir.'

From the door to Shenkin's hut Fleet swore under his breath. There would be another time he'd make sure of that.

Regan sat down on his hammock. 'That was no accident Shenkin, Feltsham is still trying to get to you, so be damn careful. We have only ten more months to go then if they don't hold that fight against us, we've got our tickets.' Holding his scarf in his hand Shenkin smiled a weary smile his black hair had grown again and was now long enough to tie back. Regan grinned at the ritual that he had seen so many times, as Shenkin proceeded to pull the hair back into a ponytail. 'It's my hair and my bloody scarf which I've kept all this time, it's home, it's that black valley, its Cathy, Sean all of them and much more,' said Shenkin, tempering his remarks with a grin.

Regan nodded. 'It is so.'

Shenkin pulled the knot tight has he sat down on his hammock. 'Like you Regan, all my life I have needed to be careful. The coalmines, the iron works, labouring for the riches of others. No say in our future, unable to plan our lives for they are fashioned by the rich and powerful. But as fate would have it this maybe is our chance to change what we failed to change in the Rising. We just have to stay alive until we get our tickets-of-leave.'

Regan lay back setting the hammock swinging. 'Sure you may be right with the help of the Sweet Virgin Mary in Heaven we'll do it,' he said, closing his eyes.

Shenkin turned to look at him. 'Let's make sure of it by helping ourselves, we were born free Regan, yet everywhere I see chains. Where has your Sweet Mary been?' But all that came from Regan was a snore.

Welling walked unsteadily over to Shenkin's hammock. 'I owe you my life Shenkin,' Welling said, between coughs.

'Remember what I said John you pulled a muscle in your back during the fall, so you can't work for a while.' 'Right! I'll ask to see the doctor in the morning. 'Now for god's sake let's get some sleep,' said Shenkin.

CHAPTER 30

The months that followed stretched their nerves to the limit as they watched every move their fellow convicts and guards made. As always, Overseer Fleet seemed to take a particular close interest in them, with both Stubbs and Consantini constantly close by. In the final weeks Shenkin again had a letter from Elizabeth. She was excited that only seven weeks of his sentence remained. But told him that Feltsham was now pressing hard for a wedding date, as the house on his farm was now built and furnished. This weighed heavily on Shenkin's mind but he was helpless to do anything. By good fortune Tarn had now taken up his duties at the prison, so it was easier to exchange messages with her.

Stubbs shook his head. 'The bastard is never alone; he and O'Hara make sure they are always in a group. We must plan something for the night, a smothering or a shiv, nice and quiet like,' Stubbs said, with almost relish on his face.

Fleet knew time was running out, Ketch was pressing him for results if he wanted to get his ticket. It was all taking longer than they thought. Shenkin had just been too vigilant these past months, but he knew he must act soon. Fleet nodded his head. 'Quite so, when he is asleep, but he'll be in the hut that's the problem.'

'Solitary,' Constantini said.

Fleet turned to Constantini. 'Of course, solitary. Who can we trust to do it?' 'It'll have to be one of the constables on night duty – if he'd open the door you could be in and out in seconds, Stubbs. I'd make it worth your whiles, both of you once I have my ticket that's my word on it. A steady supply of rum and tobacco,' said Fleet, putting out his hand to seal the deal.

Rubbing his chin he said, 'First we got to get him into solitary. It would be better coming from the superintendent.'

'But he's careful not do anything wrong he wants his ticket too don't he?' said Stubbs.

Edward Fleet bank clerk, fraudster, cheat, clever. 'We'll put him in solitary for his own protection from unknown assailants. We'll tell Roach that we believe there is a threat against his life, which after all there is.' said Fleet, with a smile. 'The superintendent won't want to risk another death, not one that has been promised his ticket at the end of his sentence, by the Chief Justice too. One that saved lives on the Runnymede, including that Lord Feltsham who is spending a fortune in the colony.'

Constantini looked at Fleet with awe. 'Why it's perfect, the sup. will have Shenkin inside quicker than you can say knife,' he said looking at Stubbs.

Stubbs thought for a moment. 'Charlie Pitts our man easy to bribe and scared of us two.'

'Good, this week then will see the end of Shenkin, or maim the bastard for life,' Fleet said, offering them both a drink from a flask of rum.

At the Australia Hotel, Feltsham turned the glass around in his gloved hand. He was just back from his new mansion a ten-mile horse ride away. 'We seem to be getting nowhere Moxey. I am determined to wed the wench so there's the top and bottom of it,' he said, taking a delicate sip of his wine.

'She's stubborn your lordship just like my brother her father. I have threatened to have her shipped back to London, but so far she will not name a day. It's that convict Shenkin that she pines after, a convicted revolutionary with no money or future.'

Feltsham brushed his sleeves and pulled at the silk handkerchief. Removing his fine leather gloves, he turned to Moxey. 'Indeed, the bloody man, but arrangements have been made to resolve that problem, I expect news of his demise at any moment.'

Moxey looked alarmed. 'I don't wish to hear anything about your plans your lordship.'

'But you'd be glad to know that Shenkin could no longer bear witness to our profitable activities, would you not sir?' Moxey said nothing, which said everything.

Lord Percival smiled. 'Of course you would and once he is removed from the board of play Elizabeth will bend to both your and my wishes. Time is on our side my dear captain. Now to our future plans,' Feltsham said, pouring another glass for them both.

***

Fleet knocked on the superintendent's door.

'Come.'

Looking up Roach saw it was the Convict Overseer Fleet. 'What is it man? I have a mountain of paperwork to get through.'

'It's convict 71013 Daniel Shenkin sir.'

Roach put down his pen with a thump, some ink splattered up landing on a sheet of paper at his side. Roach closed his eyes in exasperation. 'Well out with it, why have you not spoken to Overseer Blake about whatever it is?'

'He felt I should see you sir, its rather difficult.'

'Right, out with it man, don't waste my time.' Roach said, getting more and more irritated.

Fleet took a deep breath. 'There's talk among the convicts sir of a threat to Shenkin's life; he's rubbed someone up the wrong way or something. You know how touchy they can become.'

'No I don't, also I have no wish to. But go on.'

The talk is that he's a marked man, something is going to happen to him, something possibly terminal.'

Silence held the moment, only the light tick of Roach's timepiece made a sound. Roach was deep in thought. It was the last thing Roach wanted, having to explain the death of Shenkin to the court would be very embarrassing. Especially as Sir Francis Forbes commended Shenkin for his endeavours on the Runnymede. No, it would be most unfortunate should anything happen to this convict. Then after a moment Roach said, 'What do you suggest Fleet?'

'Somewhere safe sir for I feel a responsibility to the Government Men in my hut sir.'

'Very commendable Fleet.'

Roach thought for a moment; perhaps he had been injudicious in denying Fleet his ticket-of-leave. Still it was done now, but he'd bear it in mind. Roach looked up. 'Somewhere safe you say, but where, this is a communal prison apart from solitary they are always together.'

Fleet said nothing, then said, 'Apart from solitary sir, you are right sir.'

For a moment Roach still did not grasp the point, then a smile crossed his pinched face. 'Solitary, Fleet, that's the answer.'

'Of course sir.' Fleet smiled conspiratorially 'But for what reason sir?'

'I don't need to have a reason man I'm the superintendent; it's for the man's own safety, he only has weeks to go.'

Fleet straightened up. 'Brilliant sir, I don't mind telling you it's a great worry off my mind.'

Roach nodded. 'Good work Fleet thank you for bringing it to my attention, send Overseer Blake into me.'

'Yes sir, very good sir.' It was as well that Roach did not see the look of achievement on Fleet's face has he turned for the door; he may have wondered what he had just been talked into.

'Shenkin! Come down here, bring your tools with you,' called the duty guard at the Cut. Sweating and covered in stone chippings, Shenkin made his way to the guard. 'What is it?'

'These soldiers are taking you back to the barracks you are going into solitary.'

Shenkin looked incredulously at the guard. 'But for what offence?'

The guard shrugged his shoulders. 'I don't bleeding know do I, just get moving.'

Back at the barracks Shenkin was taken to the superintendent's office.

'Come.'

'Its 71013 sir, you asked to see him.'

'Ah! Yes, send him in constable.'

Shenkin shuffled in and stood in front of the superintendent's desk. 'I've brought you back from the Cut early Shenkin, because there is a rumour of a threat against your life, are you aware of this?'

'It seems someone outside the prison maybe arranging to upset my prospects of a long happy life.'

Roach tapped his fingers on his snuffbox. 'Do you know who?'

'It's between him and me.'

Roach moved in his seat. 'Convict 71013 Daniel Shenkin, you will address me as superintendent or sir.'

'Very well, superintendent.'

'While you are in my care it becomes my business, do you hear?'

'Yes,' Shenkin said, then added, 'sir.'

I can see why this man has made enemies thought Roach, he has no regard for his superiors. 'Since you only have days to go before your release I am placing you in solitary for the duration of that time. When leaving here you will be taken to your hut to collect your clothes, bedding, cleaning and eating utensils. When done you will call out for the hut guard who will take you to solitary.'

'Yes,' Shenkin said.

Noting the absence of respectful address Roach glared up at Shenkin. 'Get out.'

In the hut Shenkin began to pack his belongings that over these two years seem to have mounted up. From the bottom end of the hut Welling coughed.

'How do you feel John?'

'Better since I've had this rest thanks. But that bleeding Stubbs has been giving me a bad time, making me get up every time I've rung this bleeding bell for attention. I just can't do it any more Shenkin. I shouted at him that I'd kill him next time, a few of the cleaning convicts told me to be careful, of what I said to him, you know how dangerous Stubbs is. Anyway, how come you are back from the Cut so early.' Shenkin told him what the superintendent had said. 'He's right because that fall was no accident, Hare had swung a pick at me. I've been in one danger or another ever since the Woolwich hulk,' Shenkin said, continuing to collect his things.

Welling was quiet for a moment. 'Come down here Shenkin I want to talk to you, shouting to you hurts my throat.'

Shenkin went down to his hammock. 'What is it is there anything I can get you?' As he said it he thought of Dewi, it was the last thing he had said to him too. 'I'll get the doctor now.'

'I'm alright I just wanted to say something. Most of us have been in solitary from time to time. As you know there are dividing doors between each cell, bloody heavy iron ones. I should know for I've cleaned out the solitary block a few times. You are all on your own in solitary, right?' continued Welling. Shenkin nodded.

'So if someone bribed a guard to open the outside door at night while you were asleep, well anything could bleeding happen couldn't it?'

Shenkin's face took on the full meaning. 'The bastards! You're right I'd be a sitting duck.'

Welling took from his shirt, what he called his little lock persuader. It was a thin piece of steel about four inches long with a series of bends in it. Shenkin had used it to unlock the food locker.

'Those dividing doors are locked, but if you could spring the lock with our friend here, then you could move into the next cell locking the door behind you.'

'You always said you would never let that out of your sight'

'You've been good to me son saved my life, for what it is worth any more. And anyway if something happened to you who'd carry my bleeding pick and spade.' he said, with half a cough and half a laugh. 'Also if they intend to do it, it'll be tonight, they won't wait.'

'Thanks Jonathan,' Shenkin said, touching the old man's shoulder. He put the wire into his washing bowl and covering it over with a drying cloth.

Welling nodded. 'Now, as soon as you are in there start to practise on that lock, you can do it, I taught you how to feel with it and you have strong hands.'

A guard came into the hut. 'What the hell's keeping you.'

'I'm coming, just saying goodbye to Welling.'

At the solitary block the guard slammed the heavy door shut causing some rust to fluttered down from the iron door. Dropping his belongings on to the bunk Shenkin took a look at the dividing door lock. It took him until the bell rang at the end of the day to finally know how to spring the lock quickly.

At midnight the guard Charlie Pitts went on his rounds passing the solitary block he looked into Shenkin's cell through the spy hole. He could see Shenkin's form in the bed fast asleep. Turning the key in the lock he left the door slightly ajar and continued on his rounds.

A figure came out of the shadows near the hut. It crossed the yard muffling a cough as it crept into the cell bringing the door back to the ajar position.

As St James's clock struck three o'clock another figure moved across the yard and into the cell.

'Bastard!' screamed a voice. A bell began to ring furiously, bringing Overseer Blake running into the yard. Crossing over to the solitary block he called out for the guards. Rushing into the cell they found Stubbs, knife in hand over the body in the bed. A hand was holding him tight as he struggled to free himself but the hand would not let go. Two constables finally managed to yank Stubbs away from the bed. Blake pulled the bedcovers back. John Welling was bleeding from several knife wounds to the chest and stomach. Shenkin shouted from the cell next door. 'What's happening?'

'Shut up Shenkin, there's been a murder. Welling is bleeding to death in here. one of you call the doctor I'll get the superintendent.'

In the superintendent's office, Stubbs stood before Roach a bewildered look on his face. 'But, but, but I....' began Stubbs

'Be silent,' said Roach, sleep still blurring his eyes. The doctor has just advised me that convict Welling has died. I'll see you hang for this Stubbs, Blake, take the man down to the solitary block and put two guards on it.'

'Very good sir, let's go Stubbs. 'But, but...' muttered Stubbs.

Shenkin sat on the edge of his bunk. He slowly turned the lock pick over and over in his hand. So, you had it all worked out John boy, you fixed Stubbs as you said you would, and saved me at the same time. A sigh left Shenkin as he wondered at the inconsistencies of mankind. Debts are paid in the strangest ways.

Back at the Superintendent's Office, Roach was advising Convict Overseer Fleet that Stubbs had confessed everything and that he and Constantini were to go back to the chain gangs. He told Fleet that this was with immediate effect and that he doubted very much if he would ever receive his ticket-of-leave.

At the end of his time in solitary Shenkin was brought to the superintendent. There he found Regan waiting just outside the door of the office, flanked by two soldiers and Overseer Blake. Regan grinned his broad Irish grin. 'Top of the morning to you, you've had an interesting time it seems,' whispered Regan.

'You could say a great sacrifice was made that I'll never forget,' replied Shenkin.'

'Quiet.' Blake said, knocking on the door.

'Come.'

'Convicts 71013 and 71014, sir.'

'Leave us Blake, I'll call when I need you.'

'Sir,' Blake said, closing the door firmly.

Roach sat back in his chair. 'I'd ask you to sit but you have not got your conditional tickets-of-leave yet.' Roach paused for a moment. 'Early at the start of your sentence or a few months into them you were both on the Treadmill for causing a riot. Therefore, I must advise you that this may now jeopardise you from receiving your tickets.' Both Shenkin and Regan began to talk at once. 'Wait! I have not finished.' Roach said. 'During this punishment convict 8743 George Fewens died.'

For heartbeats only the rattle of Regan's leg chains was heard, has he impatiently moved his feet from side to side.

Roach cleared his throat. Shenkin hoped it would the last time he would hear the sound.

'Before I sign your good behaviour reports, can I take it that this is forgotten? That you have no wish, at this important time of your sentence, to challenge the findings in the report, as to the nature and cause of Fewens' death?'

Shenkin looked at Regan. Roach smiled. 'Take your time in deciding, after all if it's the wrong decision it maybe that you have more time then you think.'

Roach glanced down at his files. 'Yes indeed, your terms were twenty years, were they not? And if your behaviour was less than perfect you would serve out these terms at Port Arthur.'

Shenkin studied Roach's face he wanted a clean sheet on his term of office as Deputy Superintendent of the Hyde Park Barracks. Fewens was dead nothing could change that. With a heavy heart he turned to Regan whose fists were clenched at his side.

'Let it go, we have some living to do. George is never coming back. If he was here, what would he say?'

'He'd say no point in us being lags all our lives.' Regan said, but there was a lump in the big man's throat has he said it.

'Agreed, we'll honour him by living reasonable free men, for we all have scars from our time here and things we would rather forget.'

'Good we are agreed, if you both just sign this, I'll put it with the report on Fewens' death.'

They did but with heavy hearts, somehow thought Shenkin they'd redress the balance one day. Regan signed, then added Long Live Ireland in large letters after his name.

Placing the paperwork back in his cabinet Roach returned to his seat. 'Please sit down both of you. Today you will receive your tickets, let me explain what that means. Roach cleared his throat, Shenkin winced. 'As ticket-of-leave holders you are permitted to work for yourselves and can acquire property on condition you live within the district of Sydney. You must also report regularly to a magistrate of the district. The tickets can be withdrawn for any misbehaviour.' Roach waited for a moment. 'Right I think that is all, the magistrates will explain any other points to you. For myself on behalf of the barracks I trust we do not see either of you again.

Blake?'

'Sir?' Blake said, opening the door.

'Take these men down to the blacksmith to have their leg-irons removed. Then take them over to the courthouse under guard,' Roach said, handing their Good Conduct Reports, in a waxed sealed envelopes to Blake.

'Very well sir.'

Roach did not look up he was already turning his attention to other matters.

Their march across government square was both slow and emotional. Dust rose up around from their shuffling feet even though their leg-irons were now gone they found it hard to break the habit. More dust flew into their faces as hackney carriages drove passed them. As the clouds of dust began to settle Shenkin saw Elizabeth standing on the steps of the courthouse, she was near tears as they approached. 'I will be waiting here for you,' she said as Shenkin passed her. He nodded.

Inside they were taken to a side office where a clerk went through their Conduct Reports.

'Wait here,' he said, going into another office.

After a moment he returned. The magistrates will see you in a while. Overseer Blake talked to the soldiers, who in turn stood at ease, their officer lit a long clay pipe. Shenkin felt as if the irons were still on him; he kept rubbing his ankles to reassure himself that they were indeed gone. After what seem like hours, yet the clock only said it was thirty minutes. The door to the inner office finally opened, there a man holding bits of paper held the door open. A voice from inside called. 'Convicts Shenkin 71013 and O'Hara 71014 please enter.'

Still under guard they were taken in. At a long table sat three magistrates. The middle one looked up. 'We have read your Good Conduct Reports and together with the recommendations from your trials we find you fit for tickets-of-leave. These are subject to your continued good behaviour any breach therefore, will result in the tickets withdrawal. Is that understood, Daniel Shenkin?'

'Yes sir.'

'Regan O'Hara?'

'Yes sir.' Both noted the absence of their numbers.

'Very well, Clerk of the Court pass me the tickets-of-leave.'

These were filled in with their names, ticket numbers, issued at the office of the Principal Superintendent of Convicts in Sydney. Then the Senior Magistrate signed them, this was countered sign by the Chief Clerk. The Clerk handed one to Shenkin then one to O'Hara. They were conditionally free.

'Call in the next convict,' said the magistrate.

Outside, the officer ordered his men into single file then marched them off. Overseer Blake turned to Shenkin. 'You'll be back, your type always are, when you do I'll be waiting,' he said pushing past Elizabeth on the steps.

Shenkin started for Blake but Elizabeth stopped him. 'Forget him my dear you have your ticket, leave it.'

'Elizabeth is right Shenkin, to hell – sorry Elizabeth – to the devil with him we're out, so we are. Now, tell us all the news Elizabeth, and don't you look a pretty sight in your fine dress, does she not Shenkin?'

Shenkin smiled. 'She does and if I am not mistaken that's the same perfume that's been wafting into the barracks on letters these last two years.'

'It is,' she blushed.

'I'd kiss you cariad, if this lump of an Irishman was not standing by my side.' Regan walked quickly away with a smile on his broad Irish face.

Catching up with him Shenkin said, 'We are on our first social call Regan, to Doctor Tarn's rooms where he and Elizabeth will tell us all that's gone on.'

'Come in, come in,' Tarn said, shaking them by the hand.

'What would you say to a tot of rum.'

'I think I could just about manage that, so I could,' Regan said.

Filling their glasses to the brims, with a sherry for Elizabeth he raised his own glass. 'Congratulations on your tickets, and your safe return to us.'

'Thanks to you doctor, and to Elizabeth, we certainly had a few close moments and a few scars to prove it.'

'Oh no! Did they mark you my love?' Elizabeth said.

They all began to laugh. 'I'm fine cariad, don't fret,' Shenkin said, embarrassed. Which raised even more laughter from Regan and Tarn.

Once they were seated with refilled glasses, Tarn told them about Feltsham.

'He's now a powerful landowner, has his fingers into a number of businesses he and Captain Moxey now own, two other ships trading between Sydney Cove and Van Diemen's. He's a force in the colony Shenkin, you'll need to be very careful of him, he knows you are aware of his past activities. Also he is still pursuing Elizabeth for her hand in marriage. Is that not so my dear?'

Elizabeth nodded. 'In another three months I will reach my age of consent but in the meantime my uncle is being pressured by Feltsham to force me into this marriage.'

Shenkin's face took on a dark look. 'I'll not let it happen.'

Tarn rested his hand upon Shenkin's shoulder. 'Be very careful Shenkin he has already made attempts on your life. I am sure his efforts will now be doubled, now that you are out of the barracks. Also Ketch is still on Feltsham's payroll he knows many lowlifes that he can call upon to get the job done.'

'Yes please, please be careful Shenkin both you and Regan must act cautiously,' Elizabeth said.

'I will not live under his shadow, continually having to look over my shoulder. No, I'll confront him, in his own house if necessary.'

Regan nodded. 'Nor will I bend my knee or tip my hat to the bloody man, if it's a fight they want then let's take it to them. For we have a number of scores to settle with Lord Feltsham and Ketch.'

Tarn shook his head in exasperation. 'Damn it Shenkin that's why I asked Elizabeth to bring you here to see me, I knew this would be your attitude. We all have scores to settle with his lordship but we must plan thoroughly, bide our time. He now has powerful friends in the government whom he entertains at his country house. A word in the right ear could see you both losing your tickets and back in prison, even sent to Port Arthur where you'd both serve out the balance of your sentences. it's a brutal place that few return from.'

'Oh! Shenkin I could not bear that, if you love me, please listen to the doctor,' Elizabeth said, with a sob.

'Now don't fret yourself cariad,' Shenkin said, turning to Tarn. 'Tell me what you have in mind doctor.'

Tarn recharged their glasses. 'You must both keep a low profile by finding work on one of the remote farms, it would be much better and safer if you get out of the town completely. After a while, say a year or two with a little money behind you perhaps start an enterprise, stone cutting, a pub, or some other small business.' Tarn paused, waiting for a response.

Shenkin looked at Regan. 'Well Regan what do you think?'

Regan pulled himself up to his full six foot four. 'I'm sorry but in all that we have gone through Shenkin we have never hidden from anything. I'll not start now,' said the big man. Shenkin smiled knowing this would be Regan's response. 'I agree, sorry doctor but that's the way of it, also there's Elizabeth what if during this time she is forced to marry Feltsham?'

'I considered that but she could go with you, I have already discussed it with Elizabeth,' Tarn said, turning to her.

'I would go with you Shenkin. To the ends of the earth if necessary, my love.'

'Forever being on our guard, taking anything that was offered to us for yet another two years. Is that what you want?'

'Yes. If it means you would be safe dearest. Feltsham is now a very wealthy man, Ketch has introduced him and my uncle to a man called Abe Goldspick who comes regularly to the warehouse. He hands over coinage and rum in exchange for Kettlwell's and other London stolen goods. This money has enabled them to purchase two more ships, the *Norfolk* and the *Lady Anderson*. There is no stopping them Shenkin, with his title and money Feltsham is now at the centre of society in the colony. By just dropping one of his silk handkerchiefs, he could send you back to serve out your sentences. Above all he is a man who would prefer a neat ending to your knowledge. He wants you dead.' For heartbeats no one spoke, only the pouring of another glass disturbed the silence.

'Elizabeth, Doctor Tarn, my father always said every man should grow from his own seed not someone else's. So I think I speak for Regan as well when I say come what may we will meet it on our terms in our own way.'

Tarn smiled. 'I expected as much so I wish you well, if in the future you need my help you have only to ask. In the meantime, may your god go with you Shenkin.'

'I carry him in a clenched fist doctor, always.'

Elizabeth sighed. 'I am still with you Shenkin for I have never met a man so much a man as you, so let's all three of us face it together.' Arm in arm, they walked out of the doctor's rooms.

On the steps Regan looked over Elizabeth's head at Shenkin. 'Well it was a pretty speech, so it was. We have our freedom, as limited as it is, but we have no job, no money, and nowhere to sleep. What now my poetic friend?'

Shenkin began to undo his scarf from around his ponytail. Regan gave a grunt. 'Not again. Elizabeth you'll have to get used this whenever he wants to think what to do next.' Elizabeth gave an indulgent smile. 'If it helps Regan then its fine by me, for I have also seen him do it many times,' she said, with a smile.

A look of surprise came over Regan's face as Shenkin threw the scarf to the ground. Then standing in the road his black hair loose about his shoulders Shenkin tossed something into the air. For a moment it hung in the air, then dazzlingly, it twisted and turned. Its polished facets caught the rays of the antipodean sun, they gave off a virtual rainbow of colours. Slowly, almost grudgingly, it returned to earth. Regan caught it in his hand. Then opening his huge fist, he gazed upon the largest, most beautiful cut diamond in the shape of a teardrop he had ever seen.

Shenkin smiled. 'Right! First lodgings, then we find a man named Goldspick.'

Regan began to laugh first nervously, then incredulously. Slowly it turned to howls of laughter from them all, has arm in arm they walked down the middle of Macquarie Street.

'Well I'm damned, I'm damned,' said Regan in a roar of continued laughter.

'I hope not Regan for there is much to live for,' said Shenkin. Then turning to Elizabeth he said, 'Is that not right my cariad?'

'If you say so Shenkin, so it will be,' she said holding his hand close and tight.

Shenkin did say so, and it would be for they would carve out a life for themselves in this land beyond the seas. But that was for tomorrow, today they would enjoy their moment of freedom, tomorrow was another time yet to happen. Shenkin a smile on his scar mapped face was looking forward to it. He squeezed Elizabeth's hand, bent down and kissed her lightly on the cheek.

Shenkin would indeed have further ventures in this 'place beyond the seas' for the worst and best was yet to come.

Historical Note

The first Reform Bill of 1831 saw a great upheaval in the valleys of South Wales. Thousands of working men, and many of their women, gathered on the hills above the town of Merthyr Tydfil on the morning of Monday 30th May 1831. Ironstone miners, skilled iron workers from William Crawshay's Ironworks, together with coal miners were led by men determined to create for the first time a voice and vote for the ordinary working man.

On the 2nd June, for the first time the red flag (a white sheet dipped in goats blood) was raised. The flag would come to symbolise the future of Trade Unions. It fluttered that day at the head of a demonstration that marched on the town.

They were demonstrating against rising food prices, wage cuts, credit crisis, redundancies and bad working conditions. They wanted fair pay, better housing, shorter working weeks, payment in wages not tokens and above all the vote.

Since this did nothing for the profits of the Iron and Coalmasters they were met by strong resistance against any reform. The civil authorities called out the military to put down the uprising. The Riot Act was read to the mass of workers who were assembled in front of the Castle Inn where the leaders of the rally intended to present their demands.

Failing to disperse the mass, a detachment of the Argyll and Sutherland Highlanders matched in to restore law and order; in the struggle that followed, twenty-four workers died and many more were injured. The so called 'Rioters' drove the military out of the town, they held the district for four days, they defeated regular soldiers twice with nothing more then pick handles, shovels, iron bars, muscle, blood and heart. They stood against trained muskets and sabres and were only finally defeated when the Government sent in over eight hundred troops to surround and retake the town by force of arms. The leaders were placed in detention to await trail.

Within two weeks of the rising the first trade union lodges began to spring up in many parts of the country. Most of the leaders of the Merthyr rising

317

would not see these results. One, a miner named Richard Lewis known as Dic Penderyn was hanged at Cardiff County Goal. The charge read 'for rioting with others at Merthyr Tydil and feloniously attacking and wounding one Donald Black, a soldier of the 93rd Regiment with the soldier's own bayonet.'

The sentence handed down by Justice Bosanquet at the Glamorgan Summer Assizes on 9th July was 'Death by Hanging' and that his body would not be returned to Merthyr Tydfil for burial. Thereby, insuring that he would not be the focus of martyrdom or a rallying point. He was hanged at 5am on the morning of Saturday 13th August. He protested his innocence until the end, he was twenty-three years of age and has become a martyr and folk hero in the memory of South Wales. The other leaders were given long jail sentences or transportation to a penal colony.

The Runnymede is based on an actual convict ship, the Mangles, she was built in India in 1802 and was in continuous use during the 19th century. In 1833 with two hundred and thirty-six convicts on board she sailed the direct route London to Sydney in one hundred and twenty-six days. My admiration for the masters and crews of these vessels knows no bounds, it was of course a commercial enterprise but their seamanship was extraordinary. However the conditions for the convicts were brutal; the branding frames and flogging posts were only too real.

Once in Sydney they found themselves in Hyde Park Barracks which was used for the secure holding of convicts during the night. The central building served as a dormitory for up to six hundred men. The surrounding buildings consisted of a bake-house, kitchen, mess-rooms solitary confinement cells and that dreaded Treadmill. The chain-gangs were harsh work assignments, the Argyle Cut was a punishing hard labour project that was indeed began in 1832 but due to difficulties was abandoned until 1843. It took its toll and the lives of many convicts. Today the rocks from the excavation of the Cut form the sea-wall of Circular Quay.

Any convict being tried at the Supreme Court would have indeed been fortunate to have had Chief Justice Francis Forbes sit in judgement on his case. He was a man of whom Governor Bourke said. 'It would be difficult, in the whole range of colonial courts to point out a person on the Bench who, from integrity and ability, is better entitled to the honour of a knighthood.' The knighthood was conferred in April 1837. He did a great deal in removing the abuses of convicts, and in opening the way to a better course of government in the Colony.

Daniel Shenkin and Regan O'Hara, unfortunately are fictitious, but they represent the background, courage, determination and sacrifices made by these men to change the world to a more egalitarian society. I hope today's Irish, Scottish, English and Welsh would be proud of them, be they convicts of whatever crime or political dissidents of whatever persuasion. For all suffered the indignity of transportation, in over crowded, often brutal convict ships. Collectively they contributed to the building of a great nation - Australia.

I hope I have done them justice. If there are any errors they are entirely mine.

Davey Davies
January 2022